Praise for #1 *New York Times* bestselling author Susan Mallery

"Susan Mallery is one of my favorites."
—#1 *New York Times* bestselling author
Debbie Macomber

"The wildly popular and prolific Mallery can always be counted on to tell an engaging story of modern romance."
—*Booklist*

"Holidays and marriages can be a wonderful and crazy mix, as exemplified by mega-star Mallery's newest tale!"
—*RT Book Reviews* on *Marry Me at Christmas*

Praise for *New York Times* bestselling author Maisey Yates

"[F]ull of double entendres, sexy sarcasm and enough passion to melt the mountain snow!"
—*RT Book Reviews* (Top Pick!) on
Hold Me, Cowboy

"Fans of Robyn Carr and RaeAnne Thayne will enjoy [Yates's] small-town romance."
—*Booklist* on *Part Time Cowboy*

#1 *New York Times* bestselling author **Susan Mallery** writes heartwarming and humorous novels about the relationships that define women's lives—family, friendship and romance. She's best known for putting nuanced characters into emotionally complex, real-life situations with twists that surprise and delight readers. Because Susan is passionate about animal welfare, pets play a big role in her books. Beloved by millions of readers worldwide, her books have been translated into twenty-eight languages. Susan lives in Washington State with her husband and two Ragdoll cats. Visit her online at susanmallery.com.

Maisey Yates is a *New York Times* bestselling author of more than thirty romance novels. She has a coffee habit she has no interest in kicking and a slight Pinterest addiction. She lives with her husband and children in the Pacific Northwest. When Maisey isn't writing, she can be found singing in the grocery store, shopping for shoes online and probably not doing dishes. Check out her website, maiseyyates.com.

#1 *New York Times* Bestselling Author

SUSAN MALLERY

BABY, IT'S CHRISTMAS

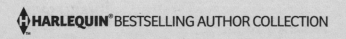

HARLEQUIN® BESTSELLING AUTHOR COLLECTION

ISBN-13: 978-1-335-90512-3

Baby, It's Christmas

Copyright © 2017 by Harlequin Books S.A.

The publisher acknowledges the copyright holders of the individual works as follows:

Baby, It's Christmas
Revised text edition © 2017 by Susan Mallery, Inc.
First published as Their Little Princess by Silhouette Books in 2000

Hold Me, Cowboy
Copyright © 2016 by Maisey Yates

Recycling programs for this product may not exist in your area.

Printed in U.S.A.

www.Harlequin.com

CONTENTS

For a complete list of titles available from
Susan Mallery, please visit www.SusanMallery.com.

BABY, IT'S CHRISTMAS

Susan Mallery

Chapter 1

"You're going to tell me that I'm crazy," Tanner Malone said as he paced the length of his brother's office. "Maybe I am. Maybe I've been working too hard, or maybe it's because I'm going to be forty in three years. I don't know why I have to do this—I just know that I do."

He paused in the center of the office and stared at his brother, Ryan, who sat behind his large wooden desk. "You're not saying anything," Tanner told him. "Don't you want to talk me out of this?"

Ryan gave an easy, familiar smile. "I've got three kids already. Who am I to advise anyone against fatherhood? You might find that you like it."

Tanner nodded once, then collapsed into the leather chair opposite Ryan's. "Fatherhood," he muttered under his breath. "I *am* crazy. What do I know about being a father?"

"You're a really great uncle, if that helps. My kids adore you. All kids adore you. For that matter, women seem to find you irresistible. I'll bet that puppies and kittens follow you around, too."

Tanner didn't have to glance at his older brother's face to know that Ryan was kidding him. "This is serious," he said. "I have to make a decision."

"I know you do, and I'll give you whatever information you want. It's just…" Ryan shrugged. "I can't help it, Tanner. For years you made fun of my boring married life, all the while being the carefree bachelor. You've gone through girlfriends like most guys go through a six pack of beer over Super Bowl weekend. You gave it a good race, but someone finally caught you."

"So what you're saying is I'm due." Tanner didn't like the sound of that, but he wasn't sure his brother was wrong. He'd avoided paying for his lifestyle for a long time. But in the next twenty-four hours, that was all going to change.

"I'm pointing out that it's taken you a long time to come to the place where you have to make some difficult choices," Ryan said. "Most men have already gone through this by the time they're your age."

Tanner leaned back in his chair. He knew Ryan was right—about a lot of things. What his older brother *wasn't* saying was that Tanner had occasionally needed to fall on his butt before life or circumstances or whatever got his attention. Well, he was paying attention now. The problem was what to do.

"I don't know how to be a good father," Tanner said as the knot in his stomach went from the size of a baseball to that of a basketball. He felt as if he'd taken a tumble from one of his high-rises, and, while the fall hadn't killed him, it had sure shaken him up some.

"No one knows anything at the beginning," Ryan said. "You learn by doing."

"What if I mess him up? I don't want my son suffering just because his old man couldn't get the hang of parenting."

"He or *she* needs you to love them and be there. Everything else is negotiable."

Ryan continued talking, but Tanner wasn't listening. His brain had frozen at the sound of a single word. *She.* Dear God, the baby could be a girl! That would be worse. As a result of his messed-up personal life, the amount he knew about women wouldn't fill a teaspoon.

"She can't have a girl," Tanner said, interrupting Ryan. "I can't have a daughter."

Ryan chuckled. "There's logic. I hate to remind you about this, Tanner, but that decision was made a long time ago. About nine months, to be exact, and the decision was made by you."

Tanner swore under his breath. He glanced at the clock. Lucy had called him two hours before to say she was on her way to the hospital. The mother of his unborn child had long since signed the papers giving the baby up for adoption. Lucy expected him to do the same. It was what they'd agreed to do. It was the smart thing to do. It was what nearly everyone had told him to do. But he hadn't been able to do it. All the logic in the world couldn't make Tanner sign away a life that was a part of him.

He pushed to his feet and headed for the door.

"Where are you going?" Ryan asked.

"To the hospital."

"What are you going to do?"

Tanner gripped the door handle and glanced back at the only family he'd ever known. His big brother had always been there for him. This time, Tanner was on his own.

"Hell if I know," he said and slammed the door shut behind him.

"Pretty girl," Kelly Hall murmured as she stared down at the squirming newborn she held. "You look so worried, but I promise that we grown-ups know how to take care of you."

Sandy, one of the obstetrics nurses, stroked the infant's cheek. "You tell her, Dr. Hall. But I don't think it's going to help. I've been watching babies being born for over twenty years, and every one of them has had that same worried look."

"It's our job to reassure them." Kelly gave Baby Ames a last smile, then reluctantly handed her over to Sandy. The competent nurse would take her to the nursery, where, for the next couple of days, she would receive excellent care. As for what would happen after that, who could say? The child was being given up for adoption.

Kelly had long since learned that it wasn't her place to judge her patients or question their nonmedical decisions. Even so she couldn't help glancing at the weary woman about to be wheeled to her room.

"Are you sure you don't want to see your daughter?" she asked one last time.

Lucy Ames, a platinum blonde who managed to look stunning, even after giving birth, rolled her eyes. "Get over it, Doc. I know you were hoping that I would get bitten by the maternal bug when the kid popped out, but it's not gonna happen. I signed the papers a long time ago, and I haven't changed my mind. I'm heading to LA, and I'm not coming back. With luck, I'll be there by Thanksgiving. I plan to live in the land of sun and movie stars. The last thing I want in my life is some kid messing everything up."

"I understand," Kelly said politely, even though she didn't. Lucy was a grown woman with options. How could she turn her back on her own child?

"I appreciate everything you did," Lucy told her. "You're good at this."

"It's my job," Kelly said lightly, then slipped off her gloves. "I'll be in to check on you in a few hours. Just to make sure everything is fine. But based on the delivery, you're going to heal quickly."

Lucy gave a little wave as the nurse wheeled her out of the delivery room. Kelly followed more slowly. She thought about the patients she still had to see that day and about those who would soon be giving birth. Most of her patients were thrilled to be pregnant and anxiously awaited the births of their new babies. The holidays added their own special magic to the moment in a family's life. With Thanksgiving next week and Christmas soon after, new moms, dads and grandparents had even more of a tendency than normal to go overboard on gifts for the baby. But occasionally she had one like Lucy—a woman to whom giving birth was an inconvenience.

It wasn't that she didn't understand Lucy. In some ways she understood too well. Maybe that was what got to her. Maybe Lucy's situation reminded her too much of her own shortcomings.

Knowing that she should head back to her office, Kelly walked toward the elevator. Hospital volunteers had decorated the hallways in an autumn theme that would soon give way to Christmas. Instead of pushing the button for the ground floor, she found herself heading over to the nursery. She told herself she just wanted to quickly check on Baby Ames. A complete lie because the pediatrician on duty wouldn't have finished examining her yet.

Regardless of her reasons, twenty minutes later Kelly stood in front of the glass-enclosed nursery. Nearly a dozen babies slept or squirmed in their soft blankets. Pink and blue caps clearly defined gender.

She could see through to the opposite wall, where a man stood with his arm around a young woman in a bathrobe. They were both pointing and smiling at a tiny child. The woman wasn't Kelly's patient, but she recognized the slightly stunned glow. Their child had been the couple's first, she thought. As new parents, they were equal parts thrilled and terrified. She knew that over time, love and joy would replace the terror, right up until their baby became a teenager, at which point they would want to pull their hair out.

The thought made her smile. She pressed her hand against the glass and studied the tiny infants. She found three that she'd delivered in the past twenty-four hours, then watched as one of the nurses put Baby Ames into her isolette.

"Let it go," she murmured to herself, knowing there was no point in getting upset or attached. Lucy Ames had made her decision, as was her right. The beautiful baby girl would be given up for adoption. It wasn't as if she, Kelly, had done any better.

But I was only seventeen, a voice in her head whispered. Didn't that make a difference? Kelly wasn't sure anymore. Maybe she'd never be sure.

"Dr. Hall?"

The low male voice broke through her musings, and she turned to face the man who came up to stand beside her.

The overhead lights were bright in the hallway. Even so Kelly blinked several times to make sure she was really seeing who she thought she saw. Tanner Malone.

She thought about cursing him, or simply walking away. She thought about giving him a piece of her mind, then reminded herself it wasn't her business. She was Lucy's doctor, nothing else. Still, for once, she was grateful for her five feet ten inches and the fact that she'd changed out of scrubs and back into a skirt, blouse and heels. With them she could look Mr. Malone in the eye… or almost. His work boots gave him an inch or so on her.

She wondered how he knew her name, then figured it wouldn't have been difficult to track her down. From what Lucy had told her, she and Tanner weren't an item anymore, but that didn't mean the couple didn't talk. After all, they'd just brought a child into the world.

Kelly fought against the anger rising inside her. So what if Tanner Malone was an irresponsible bastard? She could be courteous for a few minutes.

"I'm Dr. Hall," she said.

"Tanner Malone."

She was afraid he was going to hold out his hand for her to shake, but he didn't. Instead he shoved them both into his jeans pockets and blew out a deep breath.

"I've been looking all over for you," he admitted. "Now that you're here, I don't know what to say."

"I see." She glanced at her watch. It was nearly noon.

Her morning patients would have been rescheduled, but she still had afternoon appointments. "Perhaps when you think of it you can call my office and we'll—"

"No." He grabbed her arm before she could step away. Even through her temper she felt a quick jolt of...something...as his fingers closed around her. Was it heat? Was it—

Don't even think about that, she told herself angrily. How dare her body react in a favorable way toward this man? He was slime. He was lower than slime. He was the single-cell creature fifteen million years away from evolving into slime.

"I need to talk to you about the baby." He gestured to the nursery behind them. "I..." He released her. "I want to know what Lucy had. I asked at the desk, but because she already signed the adoption papers they're not giving out information."

He looked tired, Kelly thought irrelevantly. Shadows pooled under impossibly blue eyes. Malone blue, she'd heard a couple of nurses saying a while back. Yeah, he was good-looking. So what? He was still slime.

"I don't understand why anything about the baby is important to you, Mr. Malone," Kelly said crisply. "Once you sign the release forms, the child ceases to be your responsibility."

"That's the thing," he said. "I haven't signed them. I'm not sure I can."

Kelly didn't know if she would have been more surprised if he'd started yapping like a poodle. She felt her mouth drop open, and she couldn't seem to pull her jaw back into place. "What?"

Tanner glanced over his shoulder, then waved toward the corridor. "Is there somewhere we can go to talk for a minute? I'm sorry if I seem out of it, but I haven't had much sleep in the past few weeks. Between the hours I've been working and thinking about the baby, I've been pacing more than I've been sleeping."

She pressed her lips together. Tanner Malone had to be playing some kind of game. A man in his position would never consent to raise a child alone. He was the head of a busy commercial construction team, and he had something of a playboy reputation. Still, he'd captured her attention, so she decided to hear him out.

"There are a couple of consultation rooms just down here," she said, leading the way.

They turned left at the nurses' station and paused as Kelly checked the first room. It was unoccupied. She entered, then waited for Tanner to follow her before closing the door.

The room was small, maybe eight by eight, with a desk and three chairs. She moved around Tanner and settled into the single chair behind the desk, then motioned for him to take one of the remaining seats. He glanced at it, then shook his head and paced from the door to the wall. It took him all of three steps.

"The thing is, I know it's crazy," he began, not looking at her and instead staring at the floor. "The hospital is adding a new wing."

The comment seemed irrelevant until Kelly remembered that Tanner Malone owned the company building the wing. Construction had been going on for months. "Actually, I've noticed that."

"Really?"

He glanced at her, and she was again caught up in the realization that his eyes were really a very deep blue.

Forget it, she told herself firmly. *Ignore the man—listen to the words.*

"Then you probably know that my company is in charge of the construction. It's a huge project, involving thousands of man-hours, not to mention dozens of subcontractors. I've been working twelve-, fourteen-hour days."

Kelly nodded.

"We had a couple of delays, and now we're playing catch-up," Tanner continued. "I rarely see my house. We're going to make the March deadline for the dedication, but it's going to be tight. So I don't have time for a child in my life. Certainly not a baby."

Kelly leaned back against the chair and worked hard to keep her face impassive. So he hadn't been asking about the child at all, she thought grimly. He only wanted to talk to her so that he could explain his case to someone— anyone. He wanted to make excuses. She waited for the anger to return, but it was gone—transformed into a sadness she wasn't sure she could explain.

There were so many hopeful couples wanting to adopt infants. Baby Ames would be placed with a loving family. She might grow up with every advantage. It was probably best for everyone. Kelly drew in a breath. If only she could let this go. Why was this one child getting to her?

"I can't do it," Tanner said.

"Mr. Malone, you don't have to explain this to me, and frankly I'm not interested in your reasons for giving up your child for adoption."

"But that's my point," he said. "I can't do it. I can't give him up." He pulled a thick sheath of papers from his back pocket and dropped them on the desk. "Lucy and I talked about this, and we both agreed it was the best thing. She's got a job waiting for her in LA, and I've got a busy life here. Adoption made sense."

Kelly picked up the sheets and flipped through them. Lucy had carefully signed away all her rights to the child, but the space for Tanner's signature was blank.

"What do you think?" he asked.

She glanced up and saw that Tanner had braced his hands on the back of one of the chairs and leaned toward her. His thick, dark hair fell over his forehead. He wasn't the kind of man who usually populated her day. Most of them were other doctors or husbands of patients. She saw more suits than jeans and work shirts. Tanner might own Malone Construction, but he obviously didn't mind getting his hands dirty. She could see scars on his fingers, and there were thick muscles bulging in his upper arms and chest. She nearly matched him in height, but he had to outweigh her by forty pounds, all of them muscle.

"What do I think about what?" she asked.

"What should I do? Should I sign the papers?"

"I can't answer that for you. We're talking about a child, Mr. Malone. This isn't a decision to be made lightly. Your daughter's future is at stake."

His eyes widened, and a grin split his face. If she'd thought he was good-looking before, he was amazingly handsome now. *That smile could cause a woman to stumble at fifty paces*, she thought, refusing to soften toward him.

"A girl!" He sank into the chair, then rubbed his eyes. "Damn. Like I know anything about women."

"You know enough to get one of them pregnant." Kelly regretted the words as soon as they passed her lips. She sighed. "Sorry. I didn't mean to say that."

"Don't apologize. You've got a point." He leaned forward. "Is she okay? Ten fingers and toes?"

Kelly smiled. "She's perfect. A real beauty. Her Apgar score was a nine at one minute and a ten at five minutes." When Tanner looked blank, Kelly explained. "We check newborns for several characteristics right after birth. Their heart rate, whether they are crying, moving around, that sort of thing. Your daughter scored very high. There's every indication that she's healthy and normal."

"A girl," he said, his voice filled with awe. "Jeez. I feel like that changes everything, but I'm not sure it does." He looked at her. "Tell me that the adoption is the best thing. Tell me that I have no business trying to raise a kid on my own. When would I find the time? Tell me I don't know the first thing about babies or children."

"No one can make that decision but you, Mr. Malone."

Tanner had been hoping for a little guidance from Lucy's doctor, but Kelly Hall wasn't going to be much help there. Based on the look she'd given him when he'd first approached her, she wasn't very pleased with him at all. He wondered if her anger was at him specifically or men in general. Or maybe she didn't like men who avoided their commitments and responsibilities. Could he blame her for that?

"I want to see her," he said. "My daughter, I mean, not Lucy. If I haven't signed the papers, can I do that?"

Some of the tension left Kelly's face. Her full lips curved up in a sweet smile. "I can do better than that, Mr. Malone. I can let you hold her."

"This isn't a good idea," Tanner said ten minutes later as Kelly started to put a tiny wrapped bundle into his arms. "I don't do the baby thing. I sort of ignored my nieces and nephew until they got past the breakable stage."

"She's tougher than she looks," Kelly promised, even though he knew she was lying. "Just relax. Bend your arm so she's completely supported and her head can rest in the crook of your elbow."

The baby was red and kind of squished-looking. He couldn't see any part of her except for her face. Even her head was covered with a little pink cap. She was too tiny not to scare the pants off him. And when Kelly placed her in his arms, she seemed to weigh nothing at all.

"Oh, God." He placed his free hand against her side to keep her from slipping and stayed completely still. "She's about the size of a football."

"I'll have to take your word on that."

He glanced up and saw that Kelly was still smiling at him. No doubt she was amused by his stiffness, but he'd never held a newborn before.

"Now what?" he asked.

"Say hello or anything else that comes to mind. She's your child, Mr. Malone. What would you like to do?"

Give her back, he thought, but he didn't say that. "Call me Tanner."

Kelly chuckled. "Most fathers prefer Daddy."

He glanced at her. "I was talking to you. You keep saying Mr. Malone. I'm Tanner. I'd shake hands, but they're tied up at the moment."

"I understand." She pointed to the baby. "It's okay to move around if you'd like."

He shook his head, too scared to do anything but stand there holding his daughter. Feelings swelled up inside of him, emotions that he could barely identify. There was pride and fear but so much more. A sense of having been part of a miracle. Was this creature really flesh of his flesh? Had he had some small part in creating her?

Kelly seemed to understand his confusion. She patted his arm, then stepped back to give him time alone.

Tanner took a tentative step, then another. His daughter didn't wake up. He risked a tiny rocking motion. When she stirred, he froze.

Against his arm he felt small movements. His daughter puckered her mouth, then opened her eyes and stared up at him.

She had blue eyes... Malone blue. He remembered reading somewhere that newborns couldn't see all that well, but at that moment it seemed to him that his baby could see into his soul.

Tanner Malone had never been a believer in love at first sight, nor had he ever experienced anything even remotely close to it. But as he stared down at the infant who was his child, he felt himself falling faster and harder than he ever had before in his life.

Chapter 2

Kelly watched the play of emotions across Tanner's face and knew he was a goner. Deep inside, she felt the first flicker of guilt. Maybe it had been wrong to let him hold his daughter. There was something special about holding a newborn. A friend of hers had once described it as one of life's few perfect moments. She'd allowed Tanner to experience the magic, but what about the reality?

Kelly told herself that if he hadn't been open to wanting his child, he wouldn't have felt anything while the baby was in his arms, but she wasn't sure she believed that. Was she doing the right thing? Could Tanner Malone handle having a baby in his life? Unfortunately, based on his stunned expression, he no longer had a choice in the matter.

He looked at Kelly, his eyes dark with panic. "I want to keep her. Is that wrong?"

"She's your daughter, Tanner. How can wanting to raise her be wrong?"

"I can give you about three dozen reasons, starting with the fact that I know less than zero about babies. Then there's the issue of my twenty-hour days."

"You'll make it work. Millions of single parents do every day."

He didn't look convinced. "Maybe. So what happens now?"

"Now I notify the hospital that Baby Ames won't be given up for adoption and that her name should be changed to Baby Malone."

Tanner smiled that devastating smile again. Fortunately for Kelly's equilibrium, it was focused on his daughter, not at her. "Did you hear that? You're my little girl, and everyone is going to know it. You're Baby Malone."

"You might want to think about getting her a first name," Kelly said drily. "She's going to find Baby Malone a little difficult when she gets to school."

He nodded. "You're right. So what happens after you tell the hospital?"

"You're going to have to talk to the adoption agency and tell them you've changed your mind. Legally it's not a problem. If you haven't signed the papers, they can't make you give up your daughter. However, you're still going to need a good lawyer. You'll have to make custody arrangements with Lucy. I'm guessing that if she was willing to give the baby up for adoption, she won't want visitation rights, but you'll have to check. There's also the issue of support." She frowned. "There might be more, but a good family lawyer can answer those questions better than I can."

"Too much to think about," he said quietly, still looking at his daughter. "I don't want anything from Lucy. If she wants to walk away from her daughter, then that's fine with me. I don't need her money."

"You'll have to work that out with her. She's still in the hospital if you want to talk with her."

He glanced up. "She can have visitors?"

"Of course. It was giving birth, not brain surgery. She probably feels like she was run over by a truck, but she's healthy and in great shape. She'll recover quickly. Both she and the baby will be released tomorrow." She hesitated and wondered if Tanner had any clue what he was getting into. "I can ask that your daughter be kept here until the afternoon. That should give you time to arrange things."

"What kind of things?"

Kelly drew in a deep breath. It was worse than she thought. "Tanner, have you ever been around a newborn before?"

"No. Like I said, I avoided my brother's kids until they were past the fragile stage."

"I see." She wasn't sure how to break the news to him. "Your life is about to change in a big way. You'll need baby furniture, clothes, formula, diapers, not to mention a couple of good books on dealing with an infant. You're going to have to arrange for child care at home for at least the first couple of weeks. While most day care places will take a newborn at six weeks, you don't want her exposed to a lot of children right now. Young kids have frequent colds, and that's not good news for an infant."

He took a step back, then another. She saw his muscles tighten, although his hold on the baby stayed relaxed and supportive. "You're saying I don't have a prayer of making this work."

She stared at him, at the too-handsome face and the worry in his eyes. She could practically hear the thoughts racing through his mind at light speed.

"Not at all. I'm not trying to scare you, but I do want to point out that this is a little more complicated than making a home for a puppy."

He swore under his breath, then paced to the glass wall in the alcove of the nursery. Kelly ached for his pain and confusion. He had to be scared to death, but she sensed he wasn't going to change his mind about his daughter. Despite her initial dislike of him, she had to respect that. Fifteen years ago, she'd had to make the same choice. In the end, she'd given her daughter away. It had been the hardest thing she'd ever done.

She respected Tanner for wanting to try. Unfortunately, he had several strikes against him. The most significant were a complete lack of knowledge and preparation and his impossible work schedule. If he had an office job, it might not be too hard to schedule at least a couple of weeks off. But Tanner was the general contractor for the hospital's hundred-million-dollar renovation. For reasons that had nothing to do with him, the project was behind schedule. When was he supposed to find the time to take care of his daughter?

"I can help," she blurted out impulsively, then wondered where on earth that thought had come from.

He turned and looked at her. "What do you mean?"

"Just what I said." She glanced at her watch. "Meet me back here at six tonight. I'll take you to a baby store, then help you set everything up for her. I'm on call this weekend, but assuming no one gives birth, I can even be around to give you pointers those first few terrifying hours when you bring her home."

His thick black hair fell across his forehead in a way designed to make women desperate to push the lock back in place. Kelly was no exception. She found she had to clutch her hands together to keep from doing just that.

"Why are you doing this?" he asked.

She understood the real question. Why was she going out of her way to help a stranger—someone of whom she didn't much approve? Except by being willing to take his daughter, Tanner had forced her to look at him in a new way.

"Because I think you'll be a great dad, and I want her to have that."

Relief settled over him, easing away his tension. "Thanks, Doc. I really appreciate it. I know that she's going to need a ton of stuff, but I don't have a clue where to start."

"Please, call me Kelly. And as for the baby—figuring out what to do with her can't be harder than building a hospital wing."

He grinned. "Want to bet?"

"Why don't we just wait three weeks, and you can tell me yourself."

Tanner paused outside the hospital room and thought about what he wanted to say. He knew that Lucy wasn't going to be happy with his change of heart, but there was nothing he could do about that. He had as much right to their baby as she did. A quick call to the family lawyer his business lawyer had recommended had confirmed that.

He squared his shoulders and stepped into the room. "Hi," he said when he saw Lucy sitting up in bed.

She glanced at him for a second, gave a quick, insincere smile, then pushed the mute button on the remote and silenced the television she'd been watching.

"Tanner. I didn't expect to see you," she said, her voice flat. "If you're here to check up on me, I promise I'm fine. The delivery wasn't much fun, but my doctor is great. She said everything went as expected. I'll be leaving first thing in the morning. In a few weeks, I'll be good as new."

"I'm glad you're all right."

He shifted uneasily and pushed his hands into his jeans pockets. He stood about five feet from the bed. The blinds were open, allowing afternoon light to spill into the room, and he could see her clearly. The ordeal of giving birth had left her pale but still beautiful. Her long, silky platinum-blond hair had been pulled back into a simple braid. The high cheekbones, perfect mouth and wide green eyes were as lovely as when he'd first met her. But during their brief time together, he'd learned that she had no heart.

He couldn't help wondering what he'd seen in her all those months ago. They'd met at a cocktail party, and too many drinks had caused them to end up in bed together. He'd thought he was old enough to ignore the appeal of a pretty face, but he'd been wrong. Or maybe he'd just been lonely. None of that mattered now. Whatever had first drawn them together had faded, and by the end of that weekend they were both content to part company. Until Lucy had called a couple of months later to say she was pregnant.

She pursed her lips. "Tanner, you're just staring at me. You're not going to get all weird because of the baby—are you?"

"Yes, but not in the way you mean."

Her gaze narrowed. Suddenly features that had been beautiful were now pinched. "We've been over this before. What exactly do you want from me? I told you I was pregnant because I thought it was the right thing to do. If I'd known you were going to talk me out of having an abortion, I wouldn't have said a word. I did as you requested—I had the kid. Now I'm giving it up for adoption. The papers are signed. I'm not going to change my mind."

"I am," he said quietly.

She blinked at him. "What?"

"I haven't signed the papers, and I'm not going to. I want to keep the baby."

"Dammit, Tanner. What the hell are you thinking? If you have some fantasy about a cozy family with me playing mommy, you can just forget it."

"I don't," he told her. "This isn't about you. As far as you're concerned, nothing has to change. I'm going to have a lawyer draw up some papers. Basically you walk away from the kid, and I keep her. You don't ask to see her, and I don't ask for support. It's just like the adoption, only I'm going to be the one taking her."

She brushed at her smooth bangs. Her nails were long and painted a dark shade of pink. "Why don't I believe you?"

"I don't know. I'm telling the truth."

She stared at him for a long time. Tanner held his breath. He knew that Lucy couldn't stop him from keeping his daughter, but she could make things more complicated. Adoption, from her point of view, was much tidier than the father of her child wanting to muscle in on the action.

"This isn't about you," he said. "It's about me. I don't want anything from you, except for you to sign the papers."

She continued to study him. "And if I don't, you'll haul me into court," she said, her voice resigned. "After all, I've already agreed to adoption, so I've indicated that I have no interest in my child."

"I don't know," he said honestly. "I didn't discuss that with my lawyer."

The bed had been raised so that she could sit upright but still lean against the pillows. Now she lowered the bed a few inches and closed her eyes.

"I have a great job waiting for me in LA. I'm going to work for an agency that handles really high-powered actors, directors and producers. I'm going to be meeting these clients and entertaining them. This is my chance to move in those kinds of circles." She opened her eyes and stared at him. "It's what I've always wanted. I'm beautiful enough that I'll attract the eye of some mogul type, and we'll get married. I don't care if it lasts—I just want to get my foot in the door. Once I'm there, I'll make a place for myself." She sighed. "Children have never been a part of my plan. I don't want them. I don't want ours."

Her flat statement shouldn't have surprised him, but it did. He wanted to rage at her, to tell her that he'd just held the most beautiful, perfect creature in the world. How could she walk away from their baby? But he didn't say a word. For one thing, Lucy wasn't going to change her mind. For another, selfishly, he wanted her gone. Lucy was many things, but maternal wasn't one of them. In this case, their daughter would be better off without her mother around to mess with her head.

"None of your plans are going to change," he said.

"All I'm asking is that you sign the papers allowing me sole custody of the baby."

"Do you really think you can do this? Raise a kid on your own? What do you know about babies?"

"Less than nothing," he admitted. "But I'm willing to learn. I can't let her go, Lucy. I know that doesn't make sense to you, but I've never been more sure of anything in my life."

Her expression turned wistful. "You're a fool, Tanner Malone, but you've got a big heart. I guess that's a start."

"I can't regret her."

Lucy turned away. "I can. I guess that's the difference." She waved her left hand toward the door. "You know where I live. Have your lawyer draw up the papers and get them to me before Monday. I want to be in Los Angeles by Thanksgiving." She looked back at him. "I don't want this kid showing up in my life in twenty years. Tell him that."

"It's a her."

"Whatever."

He nodded once. There were so many things he could have said, but why bother? He'd gotten what he was after. Maybe one day he would understand how someone who was so beautiful and perfect on the outside could be so incredibly ugly on the inside.

"Thanks, Lucy. My lawyer will be in touch." He turned to leave.

"Tanner?"

He paused and glanced back at her.

She flashed him her best smile, the one that had first made him saunter across the room to engage her in conversation. This time all he could think of was that he couldn't wait for her to be out of his life forever.

"Thanks for the flowers."

He'd sent her a dozen roses when he'd found out she'd had the baby. He stared at the bright yellow buds, still tightly curled as if afraid to open and show themselves to the world. They were as coldly beautiful as she.

"You're welcome," he said and walked out of her room. If all went well, he would never see her again. He prayed that was what would happen.

He walked down the hallway, not really aware of his surroundings. While their relationship had been a short-lived mistake, the ramifications were about to change his life forever. Because of his incredibly poor taste in women, he was about to become a father. A smile tugged at his lips. Not a bad trade.

He stopped and glanced around, then realized that he'd instinctively made his way back to the nursery. His gaze drifted over the sleeping babies before stopping on one in particular. He already recognized that precious face. His daughter.

Panic flared in him again, along with apprehension and about fifteen other forms of "Oh, God, can I really do this?" But none of them were as strong as the sense of rightness in his heart. Maybe he was making a big mistake. Maybe he couldn't do it, but he was determined to give it all he had. They would just have to learn this whole parent-kid thing together. She was his daughter, and he would die to protect her.

"Boss?"

He looked up and saw a bulldog of a man standing next to him. An unlit cigar poked out from puffy lips, while eyebrows drew together in a permanently worried frown.

"What is it, Artie?" he asked.

Artie was one of three foremen in charge of the new

wing. Artie's particular responsibility was coordinating the materials needed for construction.

"Toilets," Artie said glumly. He wasn't a real happy guy at the best of times. "They're wrong. We ordered fifty-six toilets, and what did they send? Bidets. You know, those weird-shaped things to wash your butt after—"

Tanner choked back a laugh. "I know what a bidet is. Did you call the supplier?"

"Sure, but they're squawking about how long it's gonna take to get new ones. I told 'em we don't got time. In a few months, the wing opens, and those toilets better dang well be in place."

Tanner started walking toward the elevator. They had to go down to the ground floor to find their way into the construction area. Artie moved with him.

"You'd think these bozos had never heard of a light-bulb before. And you won't believe what they sent me instead."

Tanner's brain quickly focused on the problems at hand. After he'd dealt with Artie, he needed to get an update from his other foremen, then make a quick tour of the work completed in the past couple of days. After that, he had reports and a meeting with his bookkeeper about who had been paid what. Then he was meeting Kelly Hall at six. Hell, it was never going to get done.

But instead of being discouraged, he found himself continuing to smile. Because it wasn't every day that a man became a father.

Kelly tapped her pen impatiently against her desk. *Be there*, she willed silently, waiting for her friend to pick up the phone. While she waited, she glanced up at the clock.

Her afternoon appointments started in ten minutes, which meant if Patricia didn't pick up soon, they weren't going to be able to talk until that evening. Kelly figured she'd disrupted her patients' lives enough by having to cancel without warning if there was a baby to deliver—the least she could do was be on time when she was in the office.

"Dr. Malone," a familiar voice said crisply.

Kelly sighed in relief. "It's Kelly, and I did a really stupid thing." She paused and tried to figure out the best way to ask her question. "I need you to tell me if your brother-in-law is a good man."

"Tanner is your stupid thing?" Patricia, a pediatrician and close friend for the past three years, laughed.

"Sort of. Did you know about his baby?"

"Sure," Patricia said. "Ryan told me. Tanner was involved with some woman last spring. The relationship didn't work out, but she ended up pregnant. She's due anytime now, isn't she?"

"She had the baby today," Kelly said.

"I didn't know that. Well, as I understand it, both she and Tanner agreed to give up the child for adoption. Is there a problem?"

"That depends on whether or not Tanner is a decent guy. He changed his mind. He's keeping his daughter."

This time Patricia was the one who got quiet. Kelly pictured her green eyes widening with shock as her mouth dropped open.

"Tanner's keeping the baby?"

"That's the plan. As far as I know Lucy will still be giving her up, so Tanner's going to have sole custody. Do you think he can manage?" Kelly rubbed her temple. "I feel a little responsible. I'm the one who dragged him to the nursery so he could hold her. You know what it's like to cradle a newborn."

"Pretty amazing," Patricia agreed. "I'm stunned by the news. Fortunately, Tanner is a great guy. He's wonderful with our kids, but honestly, he kind of avoided them until they started developing a personality. I don't remember him being around all that much when they were newborns. Besides, being an uncle is very different from being a father."

"That's what I think," Kelly agreed. "I know that there are a lot of single parents, but most of them have some kind of warning. Tanner made his decision today, and the baby goes home tomorrow. Not much time to prepare."

"You're right," Patricia said. "He can't even take a couple of weeks off because of the construction project at the hospital. He's been working too many hours as it is, just to get things caught up. What was he thinking?"

"So you think I was wrong to encourage him?"

"Not for a minute," Patricia told her. "All this stuff is just logistics, Kelly. How can it be wrong for a man to love his child? And don't give me any lines about mothers being more nurturing. I don't believe that, and I don't think you do, either."

"No, I don't." How could she? Her mother had died shortly after she'd been born, and her father had raised her on his own. In her opinion, he'd done a wonderful job. She couldn't imagine a parent being more supportive or caring.

"So it's just a matter of getting Tanner up to speed," Patricia said. "I'm free tomorrow. I'll check with Ryan and see if we can go over and help him. Maybe a couple of lessons with a doll will prepare him for that first diaper change."

The thought of Tanner Malone bent over, staring at the contents of a newborn's diaper, made Kelly smile. "He's not going to like that part at all."

"Few people do."

Kelly cleared her throat. "Yes, well, I'm going to help out, too. I figure it's the least I could do after getting him in this mess."

"You're not the one who had the baby."

Kelly could feel her cheeks getting hot, which was silly. She pressed the back of her free hand against her skin. "I know, but, well, anyway, I'm meeting him tonight. We're going to a baby store, and I'm going to help him pick out furniture. I also thought I'd take him one of those books on what happens during the first year."

"Dr. Hall, do you sound flustered?"

"Of course not. I'm just watching the clock. I have patients in a couple of minutes."

"I think not. I think you are, in fact, interested in Tanner."

"You're crazy. I'm helping out a friend."

"Oh. When did you two become friends?"

Kelly glared at the phone. "Fine. I'm helping a fellow human being in need."

"You're hiding the truth, maybe even from yourself. I think *you* think he's hot."

"I'm concerned about a new father taking care of a child when he's had no preparation or experience. My thoughts are for the baby, not Tanner."

Patricia sighed. "All right. Have it your way, but you're missing out. I have to tell you—there's something pretty wonderful about those Malone brothers."

Kelly smiled. Patricia and Ryan would be celebrating

their tenth anniversary next month. "I think you've been influenced by your relationship with Ryan."

"Maybe, but only in the best way possible. Besides, would it kill you to be interested in a man? You've been living like a nun for the past three years."

"Say goodbye, Patricia."

Patricia laughed. "Bye."

Kelly was still smiling when she hung up the phone. She collected her charts and made her way out of her office, all the while ignoring the little voice that whispered Patricia might be onto something after all.

Chapter 3

Kelly glanced at her watch. Four minutes after six. Not bad, considering she'd stopped at a local bookstore to pick up something for Tanner. She pushed through the swinging doors that separated the hospital from the new wing still under construction. From there, she passed through an alcove and hanging sheets of plastic, then found herself in the middle of a beehive.

Despite the fact that for much of the city the workday had ended, dozens of construction personnel labored on. The unpainted walls were up in what in time would be the new pediatric floor. To her right was the lab setup, nearly complete but devoid of equipment. The only remotely finished section of the first floor was the new day care center, probably because it would be opening first.

She turned right. Tanner had left her a voice mail that afternoon telling her that she could find him in his office, which was in what would eventually be the new lab. As she crossed the floor, she saw a big sign warning that this was a hard hat area, then saw a stack of the yellow construction headgear on a table below the banner.

Kelly picked one up and plopped it on her head, all the while trying not to think about the last dozen or so people who had done the same. Then she made her way in the general direction of Tanner's office.

It wasn't hard to find. Signs spray-painted directly onto the unfinished walls pointed the way to various locations on the construction site. "Boss Man's Office" was marked in red with a ten-foot-long arrow. She followed it to the end and found herself entering a medium-size room with a desk, several chairs and building plans covering most of the walls.

Tanner sat behind the desk, staring at lists and making notes. The overhead lighting was harsh, but he still looked as handsome as she remembered. His brother, Ryan, was also a good-looking guy. Talk about a great gene pool. Between her father's roguish appeal and her mother's model-perfect beauty, Baby Ames—make that Baby Malone—was going to be a looker herself.

Kelly leaned against the door frame and studied Tanner. He was lost in his work and hadn't noticed her presence. She thought about all he was going to have to deal with over the next few weeks as he adjusted to life with a newborn. If nothing else, it would be a great test of his character. She just hoped he was up to it.

"Ready to go shopping?" she asked.

He raised his head, then smiled when he saw her. That same smile that made her feel sixteen and awkward. It also did funny things to her stomach and her knees, something she didn't remember from high school. Oh,

Tanner Malone was a deadly combination of male beauty and charm, but she was fairly immune. At thirty-two, no man had really captured her attention, and there was no reason to think anyone was going to do that now.

"Kelly," he said, his voice pleased. "Thanks for meeting me here. I had some paperwork to finish up."

"It wasn't a problem. I had something I wanted to get before we went shopping anyway."

His gaze dropped to the bag she carried. "Generally I like unexpected presents, but this time I'm not so sure."

"Don't be scared. It's not going to bite you." She set the package on his desk, then waited while he pulled out the book.

"*What to Expect the First Year*," he read. "It's really thick."

"Yes, but there are a lot of pictures and a ton of valuable information. Everything you'll need to know to survive those first twelve months." She pointed to a slip of paper sticking out the top of the book. "I've marked the pages that talk about buying for a baby."

Tanner opened the book. His expression shifted quickly from stunned surprise to amazement to shock. "This list is longer than all the material requisitions for the entire hospital wing."

She grinned. "Not quite. But babies need a lot of stuff. How's the balance on your credit card?"

He flipped the pages, shaking his head slowly. "They're all fine. I pay them off each month, and they have big limits."

"Oh, good. You're going to be needing that."

"I can tell."

He rose to his feet and grabbed his jacket and a hard

hat, then took the book. "I guess we'd better get started." He looked shell-shocked.

"Are you all right?"

"Yeah. I'm just trying not to think about it too much. If I let myself dwell on the fact that this time tomorrow I'm going to have a baby in my house, I might be tempted to head for the hills."

"You'll be fine. Just take things one step at a time."

"Easy for you to say. You're a doctor." He followed her back to the entrance, where they both dropped off their hats. "I guess we should take my car," he said as they walked through the hospital. "I drive an Explorer, so there will be plenty of space for furniture."

"Good idea." She didn't dare tell him that she doubted they would fit everything in his sports utility vehicle in just one trip.

Tanner shrugged into his jacket, then held the door open for her. He was parked in the main parking lot, which had been recently enlarged as part of the new project.

"I appreciate you helping me with this," he said, leading the way to a black Explorer. "I'm sure you're very busy, and it's nice of you to give up your time."

"I'm glad to help," she said sincerely. "Most parents have several months to get used to the idea of having a baby around. They take classes, talk to other parents, buy slowly. You're going from zero to sixty in less than twenty-four hours. It's a daunting concept."

He flashed her a grin. "So you're trying to tell me that it's okay to be terrified?"

"You wouldn't be normal if you weren't. But I have every confidence in you." Which she did, she thought with some surprise as he unlocked the passenger door and held it open for her.

She stepped up into the well-used but clean vehicle. Her skirt rode up slightly on her leg, and she had to resist the urge to cover her thighs with her hands. Like Tanner was even looking, she thought.

As she tried to casually glance at him, he closed the door and headed to the driver's side. So much for bowling him over with her feminine charms, she thought humorously. So what if the man made her body react in ways it hadn't before? All that meant was that she wasn't dead. She should enjoy the occasional flickers and sparks. Feeling them didn't mean she had to do anything about them.

He backed out of the space, then drove toward the exit. "Which way?"

"Do you know the big electronics store on the corner of Green's Way and Carson?"

"Sure."

"There's a place called Baby Town in the same shopping center."

He glanced at her and frowned. "Are you sure? I've never noticed it."

"I'm not surprised. We only see what's important to us at the time. You probably never noticed the designer outlet beside the electronics store, while I didn't know there was a sporting goods store there until I called for directions and they told me the baby store was next to it."

"Gotcha," he said, then concentrated on his driving.

Honeygrove, Oregon, was a charming place that hovered on the cusp between town and city. Large enough to have all the amenities, but with the cozy feel of a small town. Next week, on the day after Thanksgiving, the annual tree-lighting ceremony would take place. Already wreaths had been hung from streetlights downtown.

Kelly leaned back in the seat and tried not to stare at her companion. Why was he so intriguing? Was it because he was about to take on a daunting task? Or was it more simple—had she just gotten tired of being on her own? She couldn't remember her last date. Certainly she hadn't been out with a man since she'd moved to Honeygrove, and that was three years ago. Talk about pathetic.

"I talked to Patricia today," Tanner said, interrupting her thoughts. "She said you'd called her."

Kelly pressed her lips together, not sure if she should apologize for that. Before she could decide, Tanner continued.

"I appreciate that you wanted to check me out. I'm an unknown to you, some construction worker who suddenly wants to keep his kid. You're concerned about the baby's welfare. Thanks for that."

"You're welcome. I'm glad you understand why I did it."

"Sure. You wanted to make sure I'm decent father material." His mouth twisted down. "I don't know what the hell I'm doing, but I'll give it my best shot. Of course, Patricia didn't help things."

"What do you mean?" She couldn't imagine her friend being difficult.

"The good news is that she said she would be happy to be the baby's pediatrician. That's a relief. What with her being family and everything, I'll even know how to get her at home." He grinned; then the smile faded. "It was the rest of what she said that scared me. She says she knows a couple of great baby nurses. Aren't babies too small to need their own nurse?"

"It's because they are small they have a nurse."

"Yeah, well, that's what Patricia said. She pointed out what we already talked about—that I can't put her in day care for a while and that I have to be at work, so a baby nurse is a good solution. In a few weeks I can look into home day care until she's old enough for a regular place. I've even been thinking of getting a college kid or some-one like that to look after her at my office. Not the one at the hospital," he said. "I meant after the project's done. There's room, and I'd see her more."

Kelly impulsively touched Tanner's arm. "I know it seems overwhelming right now, but you're taking things one step at a time. That's what's important. The baby nurse is a great idea. It will give you some space to make other decisions. As for bringing your child to work—I think it's terrific that you want to."

"Yeah?" He looked at her briefly before returning his attention to the road. "I guess. Ryan told me that Lily said she'd be available in a pinch. Lily is Patricia's mom." He frowned. "After Patricia went back to work, Lily moved in to help with the kids. She's still there and plans to stay. Anyway, she said she's happy to help out, but I figure she's got her hands full with Ryan and Patricia's three."

He pulled into the parking lot. "I wish I could take time off work, but with the hospital wing still behind schedule, it's not possible." He stomped on the brakes and swore under his breath. "I've never seen that before. And it's huge."

Kelly glanced out the window and saw the Baby Town store. A gigantic wreath decorated with pastel blocks hung above the entrance. Teddy bears and snowmen rode sleds down hills painted across the windows.

After parking the car, he stopped the engine but didn't

get out right away. "I spoke to Lucy," he said. "She's going to sign off on the kid. She doesn't want to be involved. I know the relationship was a mistake, but I'm kind of surprised she's just going to walk away. It's not that she *can* do it so much as it seems like it's going to be easy for her."

Kelly didn't know what to say to that. After all, she'd given up a child, too. But for her, it had been anything but easy. In fact the pain continued to haunt her, fifteen years after the fact. "Not every woman finds it easy to walk away."

"Probably," he agreed. He looked at her. "Listen to me. This is the most I've talked in a month. I'm sorry for dumping it all on you."

"Tanner, don't apologize," she told him. "Really. I'm happy to listen. You're working through a lot, and, in my opinion, you're incredibly calm."

"That's on the outside."

"In time you'll be calm on the inside, too. You and your daughter will get used to each other. You'll develop a relationship with rituals that will be so meaningful, you won't be able to imagine what life was like without her. I'm happy to be a part of this."

"I have this bad feeling that the only reason I'm going forward with this is that I don't have a clue how hard it's going to be."

Kelly couldn't help laughing. "Unfortunately, you're exactly right."

This was hell, Tanner thought grimly from his place in the center of the store. Hell with miniature furniture, too many cutesy, fuzzy things and Christmas carols sung in high-pitched cartoon voices coming from speakers all around the store. He looked around and spotted Kelly talking to one of the salespeople. The older woman was nodding and typing information into a computer.

Not knowing what else to do, he glanced at a display of quilts. They were small, about four feet by three feet. He turned over the price tag and took a step back. *Six hundred dollars?* He peered at the quilt again, trying to figure out why on earth it cost so much. *Jeez. Six hundred dollars.* He thought about the list in the book and swallowed hard. Kelly hadn't been kidding about his credit limit. He wondered if it was going to be enough.

"Okay, here's the plan," Kelly said, coming to stand next to him. "I had the store—what's wrong? You're practically green."

He pointed to the quilt. "It's six hundred dollars. If a scrap of cloth costs that, how much is a crib?"

She looked from him to the quilt, then fingered the cream-colored lace and read the tag. When she returned her attention to him, humor danced in her hazel-brown eyes. "Don't panic, big boy. That's a handmade quilt, covered with imported lace. They're a one-of-a-kind item, and not for the likes of us."

He breathed a sigh of relief.

"Besides," she added casually, "babies spit up on just about everything, so it's better to have bedding you can just throw in the washer."

Her words planted an image in Tanner's brain that made him uncomfortable. "How much do they spit up?"

"Don't worry about that now," Kelly said. She waved a long computer printout in front of him. "This is a basic baby registry. It lists every possible item a baby could use. Between that and the list in the book, we'll be sure to remember the important stuff. This second list tells us what's in stock. There's no point in falling in love with a crib or dresser only to find out it's not available."

"I don't generally fall for furniture," Tanner muttered, but Kelly wasn't listening.

"Let's start with the big stuff," she said. "Crib, stroller, car seat, changing table, dresser, maybe a couple of mobiles. Then we'll move on to linens, bath stuff and clothes." She tapped the list. "You'll want some kind of portable crib, as well, so you can take her to a babysitter, or even to work. They have some that turn into playpens for when they're older."

Tanner could only nod as he tried to take in what she was saying. He felt as if he'd entered a strange and frightening new world, and he wondered if it was too late to go back.

"Furniture," Kelly said, pointing to the large display on the far side of the store.

He followed her down an aisle crammed with car seats and wondered how on earth he was going to pick one. Maybe he should have asked Ryan to come along. He knew about this kind of stuff. But it hadn't occurred to Tanner that buying a kid a bed or a car seat was going to be complicated.

"How big is the room?" Kelly asked. "And is there furniture in there now? Do we have to work around anything?"

Tanner shook his head. "I have a guest room, but it's not furnished. It's about twelve by fourteen, with a big closet."

"Okay, so size isn't an issue. Basically all cribs serve the same function. These are all new and look well made. The important factors are the height of the mattress when it's all the way up, and the spacing of the rails. So pick what you like, and then we'll check for the safety features. I'm guessing all of them are going to comply with safety recommendations."

Pick what he liked? He looked at the various displays. Many were set up to look like individual rooms. There were dividers covered with wallpaper and border prints, cribs filled with ruffled comforters and too many stuffed animals for any man to be comfortable. He found himself stepping around fuzzy bears and pink elephants. There were tigers and lions, fluffy kittens, puppies and some creatures of undetermined species.

He glanced from the displays to Kelly and back. The cribs all looked the same to him. Too-small beds with guardrails. The dressers were almost normal-looking.

"What kind of wood do you like?" Kelly asked, coming to his rescue. "Light or dark. Or would you prefer something painted?"

She stood next to him, looking patient and completely comfortable. Was this a chick thing? Did all women have the baby gene, or was she relaxed because part of her job was bringing infants into the world?

He allowed himself a moment to appreciate the way the overhead lights played on her medium-blond hair. It fell to about the middle of her back, and she'd pulled it into a neat but fancy braid. Bangs hung down to her eyebrows, but in a soft, sexy way that made him think about wanting—

Down boy, he told himself. He didn't have time to get distracted. His life was one big crisis right now, and he didn't have room to add attraction to a female doctor to his list.

"I don't know what she'd like," he said. "You used to be a little girl. What would have made you happy?"

"I'm not sure babies have strong opinions on furniture, but I'll give it a try." Kelly turned in a circle, then pointed to a display of white furniture.

They moved to that aisle. While Kelly read the tag and made sure the rails were the right distance apart—or whatever—he checked the construction, the quality of wood used and made sure there were no sharp edges.

"I like it," she said. "What do you think?"

He shrugged. He wouldn't have picked white as his first choice, but he didn't have strong opinions about any of the other colors, either. "It's fine."

But she wasn't listening. Instead her face had taken on an expression of such tenderness, Tanner felt his blood heat up about ten degrees. Then he noticed that her longing gaze wasn't directed at him but focused on a comforter in the next display. He stared at it, blinked twice and bit back a groan.

If he'd given a second's thought to decorating a child's room, he would have pictured primary colors, or building blocks, or maybe even a train. But that wasn't what had caught Kelly's eye. She'd been transfixed by a pink-and-white comforter decorated with a teddy bear in a ballerina getup.

"It's darling," she said, taking his sleeve and tugging. "Don't you love it?" She pulled him toward the display. "They have the comforter and linens and bumper pads. Oh, look, there's a diaper stacker. I'll bet there's a border print for the walls and even a valance for the window. You could…"

Her voice trailed off. She released his sleeve and sighed. "You hate it."

Hate implied an emotional energy he wasn't willing to commit to ballerina teddy bears. Kelly was a woman.

She'd once been a little girl; therefore, her taste had to be better than his. With any luck, the pattern would fade in the wash.

"It's fine," he said. "Let's get it. What's next on the list?"

"But, Tanner, you don't think it's cute. We can pick something else."

He looked at her and found himself intrigued by her height. In her heels, she was only about an inch shorter than him. He'd generally gone in for the petite types, but there was something to be said for looking a woman dead in the eye without having to tilt his head.

"Kelly, this is fine. I'm sure she'll adore it."

By this time, the sales clerk had joined them. She was a middle-aged woman with a cheerful smile—and she was dressed like an honest-to-goodness elf. Pointy ears, bells on her toes and all. By the way she kept out of the discussion, Tanner suspected she'd heard more than her share of arguments over baby accessories.

"If you're sure," Kelly said and turned to her. "All right. The white crib, the four-drawer dresser and the three-drawer changing table. Then this bedding set with the diaper stacker." She paused. "We can worry about the wallpaper another time."

Like never, he thought, trying *not* to picture a wall covered with ballerina teddy bears. The three of them moved on.

They spent nearly thirty minutes in a discussion about car seats before they all agreed on one. Then they chose a mattress, crib pads, receiving blankets—although he didn't know what they were going to receive—towels with hoods, a stroller and dozens of things he couldn't recognize. Tanner surprised them and himself by insisting on a mobile of fuzzy animals, of which his favorite was the lion, and a matching wall hanging.

When they moved onto baby clothing, he told himself not to watch as Kelly chose tiny shirts and nighties and wraps, plus sleeper things with and without feet. The store clerk carried armloads over to the cash register, toes jingling with every step, then returned for more. They even bought a diaper bag, which Tanner could not imagine having to carry through the construction site. When they reached the stage of discussing bottles for feeding and the best brand of diapers, he couldn't stand it anymore. He touched Kelly's arm.

"Could I talk to you for a minute?" he asked.

"Sure." She excused them from the clerk and led him to a corner of the store. "What's wrong?"

"I can't do this," he said. "You're buying bottles, and I don't know how to physically feed her. Or how much. Or how warm it's supposed to be." He could hear the sharp edge to his voice, but he didn't think he could control it.

Kelly looked at him for a long time, then reached in her purse for her cell phone. Tanner panicked. Was she calling the hospital to tell them he couldn't be trusted with his own child?

"Patricia, hi, it's me. I'm with Tanner at the baby store." She paused, then smiled. "Oh, he's definitely having a dose of reality, and he's looking longingly at the door. But he'll be fine. Tomorrow when you drop by Tanner's to give him the diaper-changing lesson, could you also teach him about feeding and anything else he might need? You know, the first-time-parent baby lesson." She paused again. "*Clueless* is a strong term, but in this case appropriate. I'll let him know. Thanks. Bye."

She hung up. "That was your sister-in-law."

"I guessed that." He was going to complain that he wasn't clueless, but unfortunately he was. It was pretty sad.

"Patricia's going to phone the hospital and arrange for them to keep Baby Malone until early afternoon. Patricia and Ryan will come over to your place in the morning. Ryan will help with whatever furniture isn't finished and Patricia will take you through the basics."

Some of the tension in his chest eased. "That's great."

"And as I already promised, I'm available this weekend." She pointed to the impressive pile by the cash register. "All that isn't going to fit in your car. I suggest we take home as much as we can, starting with the biggest things. I'll swing by tomorrow and get the rest of it."

He didn't know what to say to her. Part of him wanted to explain that while her offer was really nice, he didn't want to put her out. But that was a very small part of his brain. The rest was doing a cheer in relief.

"Thanks," he said. "I don't want to think about spending that first afternoon with her by myself."

"You won't."

He studied her face. She was pretty enough but not a beauty. Not at all the kind of woman who normally caught his eye. "Why are you doing this?" he asked.

"Because I want to," she said easily. "I think you and your daughter deserve a fighting chance, and I want to give you that."

"Thanks," he told her, and he had the sudden urge to give her a hug.

That would be dumb, he reminded himself. Dr. Kelly Hall wasn't interested in him—she was concerned about the baby. As long as he remembered that, they would both be fine.

Chapter 4

It was a few minutes after eight the next morning when Kelly knocked on Tanner's front door. A light snow had started to fall half an hour ago, dusting the world in whispery white. She juggled to keep the two large coffees from spilling as she balanced the bag of bagels and cream cheese. She figured Tanner wouldn't have thought to eat much in the past twenty-four hours. Certainly neither of them had eaten dinner the night before.

She heard footsteps from inside the two-story house; then he opened the door.

"Morning," he said.

Kelly could barely manage a squeak in response. He'd obviously been up most of the night. There were dark shadows under his eyes, and his expression was slightly dazed. But he'd showered that morning. His strong jaw was freshly shaved, and the dampness in his hair only added sheen where the light reflected on the thick, dark layers.

His clothing wasn't all that much different than it had been the day before. A soft-looking, worn sweatshirt replaced the long-sleeved shirt he'd had on the previous day, but he still wore jeans and boots. Today they were cowboy instead of reinforced work boots.

"Morning," she managed on her second attempt to speak. "You look tired. Did you sleep at all?"

He shrugged. Big, muscled shoulders made a casual male movement. It shouldn't have affected her heart rate, but it did. Her palms got a little damp, too, and she had to worry about the coffee slipping and falling.

"A couple of hours. Mostly I just worked and worried." He motioned for her to come into the house.

"You'll be fine," she said, handing him a cup of coffee as she entered. "It's not as if you're going to be on your own. Patricia is going to come by and give you that lesson in basic baby care, and I'll be right here." She smiled. "Although I do have to warn you I have a couple of patients ready to go into labor. I'm caught in one of those cycles. Currently over two-thirds of my practice is in various stages of pregnancy. I have twelve due before Christmas, if you can believe it."

He helped her remove her light winter jacket. "When I have an emergency at work, it's just a building crisis. Not one about giving birth."

"Such are the differences in our professions." She handed him the bag. "Bagels. Did you eat last night?"

He shook his head.

"I figured you wouldn't. Men get upset, and they stop eating. Most women go in the other direction. I know during finals there were semesters when I felt like I was chowing my way through the entire candy aisle of the student union."

His gaze brushed over her body before returning to her face. "You'd never know it."

"That's because I'm tall." After a moment of relaxing, she found herself getting nervous again. It was all this body talk. She didn't know how to handle it. For as long as she could remember, her body had been merely functional. She didn't think of herself as especially feminine and certainly not sexy. But around Tanner, she remembered she was a woman. And she enjoyed the fact.

"I spoke to the hospital this morning," she said briskly, to change the subject. "Your daughter had a great night. She's sleeping well, taking formula with no problem and she'll be released anytime after noon. You just have to go pick her up."

"Okay," he said cautiously.

"Don't worry. Patricia will be here in about an hour, and she'll take you over all you need to know. At the hospital, one of the nurses will give you the same lesson, so you'll have reinforcement. Besides, I'll be here through the weekend."

"Yeah, okay," he muttered, but he didn't sound convinced. He shifted awkwardly. "I put together most of the baby furniture and some of the clothes."

"I'd love to see what you've done," she said. "And when we're finished, we can empty my car. It's packed."

The previous evening she and Tanner had loaded as much as possible into his Explorer; then he'd taken Kelly back to the hospital. She'd collected her own car, returned to the store and picked up the rest of their purchases, which she was delivering this morning. Tanner had looked stunned by the amount they had bought, so she hadn't had the heart to tell him there was a lot more yet to buy. She figured she would make the grocery-drugstore run later that afternoon to stock up on lotions, shampoo, baby wipes, a thermometer and the like.

Tanner took a couple of steps into the house, then paused. "Want the nickel tour of the place?" he asked.

"I'd love it." She glanced around at the spacious living room. There wasn't any furniture yet, but the walls had been stripped of wallpaper and she could see that he was in the middle of refinishing the wood around the bay windows. Underneath the drop cloths on the floor, she spotted scarred but still beautiful hardwood.

This beautiful old home was made for the holidays, she thought. The banisters cried out for garland with red velvet bows and twinkle lights winding through. She could picture a Christmas tree in the bay window, sharing a message of joy with passersby. She felt a pang of regret. Or was it longing? She hadn't decorated for Christmas in years. Not since she was seventeen. The reasons were many—she was too busy; she didn't have children. But the truth boiled down to one thing: she didn't feel she was worthy.

"I'm working on this room now," he said. "I've been doing a room at a time, mostly because that's all I have time for. Sometimes I think I should just get a crew in here and finish it, but I like doing the work myself. It's relaxing."

He led the way down a short hall. To her left she saw a dining room. The walls were still covered with a flocked print in burgundy and gold. Heavy furniture made the large space seem small and dark.

"I bought that set from the former owners of the house. It's about a hundred years old. It's in great shape. When

I finish a few more rooms, I'm going to start moving pieces around. The table and buffet can stay in the dining room, but I'll move the old armoire into the guest room."

"But you're keeping the wallpaper, right? I mean it's so you."

He opened his mouth, then closed it. A grin tugged at the corners. "You had me going there for a second. I thought you really liked it."

"Scary, huh? Someone must have liked it. Not only is it in this dining room, but I'm willing to bet it wasn't ordered custom, which means hundreds of people chose it."

"You wouldn't believe some of the ugly stuff I've seen in houses I've remodeled." He continued down the short hall, which ended in a bright, open kitchen. "Before I bought the company, they were split about fifty-fifty between residential and commercial contracting. I changed that, making the business one hundred percent commercial. I'd rather work on one big job for four or five months than have sixteen small ones."

He set the bagels on the counter and took a sip of his coffee. "The kitchen turned out pretty good."

She turned in a slow circle, taking in the beautifully fitted and finished cabinets, the granite countertops and double ovens that were perfect for baking Christmas cookies. "Did you do the cabinets yourself?"

"Yeah. I made them up because it was more fun than ordering them. It took about a year, but I didn't mind."

To the right of the kitchen was an oversize family room. There were two sofas and a couple of recliners, along with a movie-theater-size television and more remote controls than she'd ever seen outside an electronics store. He caught her studying the coffee table and smiled sheepishly.

"Okay, I know. I'm a guy. What can I say? I like my toys."

"I guess."

Sliding doors on the far side of the room led to a huge backyard complete with room for a play area. Patches of green peeked through the thin layer of snow.

"This is very nice," she told him. "You have a beautiful home."

"Thanks. The baby's room is upstairs. I'm converting the guest room because that's where I started remodeling. I needed a small project to make sure I remembered everything," he said as he led the way up the stairs. "Owning the company has meant spending more time in the office and less time working on the projects."

At the top of the stairs, around to the left, were a pair of double doors leading to the master suite. Kelly caught a quick glimpse of a king-size bed, a sitting area complete with fireplace and, beyond that, a bathroom to die for. Then Tanner was motioning her across the hall.

The new baby's room was large with cream-colored walls and a bay seat window. Tanner had put together the four-drawer dresser and the crib. The three-drawer changing table was still in pieces, but he'd put the rocking chair into the alcove by the closet and moved in a floor lamp. A couple of bags of bedding and clothes reminded her that she still had a car full of stuff downstairs, but before she could mention that, her gaze fell on the mobile hanging over the crib.

She crossed the thickly carpeted floor and turned the key, activating the mobile. Instantly music filled the room, and the collection of fuzzy animals began to turn in a slow circle. Of all the items in the room, this was the one that made her realize that Tanner Malone was really going to have a baby in his life. Waiting in the hospital was his own precious child.

So many years had gone by since she'd given up her daughter for adoption. For the most part, the pain of loss had dulled. While she frequently thought about her daughter, she didn't ache for her very much anymore. Unless something happened—something like seeing someone else have the very thing she'd given away.

"What are you thinking?" he asked.

"That you're very lucky. You have a lovely daughter." She gave him a quick smile. "Sorry. I don't mean to get emotional. It's just that I always wanted a large family, and it doesn't look like that's going to happen."

He leaned against the door frame and folded his arms over his chest. "Why hasn't it? You could have an even dozen by now."

That made her laugh. "I wasn't looking for *that* many." She paused. "I'm not sure of the reason. Some of it is being a doctor. Medical school, then my residency didn't leave much time for a personal life."

"So what's your excuse now?"

What *was* her excuse? She couldn't tell him the truth… that her past made her feel guilty and small. That if any man knew about the flaws in her character, he would never want her. She knew that her sense of lacking worthiness was something she should work on, but she'd never found the time. Somehow it was always easier to get lost in her job.

"I'm not sure I have an excuse," she told him. "It takes time to get established in a new town. I haven't met anyone who interests me. You know, the usual stuff."

He grimaced. "That makes sense. I, on the other

hand, have had too many relationships, but that's going to change now."

She couldn't hold back her smile. "Don't be so fast to think so. Many women will find you even more attractive now that you have a child."

"It's not about them," he said. "It's about me. For the past few months, I've been looking at my life, and I'm not sure I like what I see. It was one thing to fool around while I was on my own, but now I have a child to think about. She deserves a father who makes good relationship choices. I want her to be proud of me."

Kelly couldn't help thinking that Tanner was much deeper than she'd given him credit for. Between the muscles, the incredibly blue eyes and the smile that screamed seduction, she'd thought he was a player, with no interest in anything of value. And she had been wrong.

The doorbell rang.

"I bet that's Patricia. She probably brought Ryan along," he said as he headed for the stairs.

Kelly followed him. Patricia and Ryan stood in the family room. Ryan held up a container holding three cups of coffee and a pink box from a bakery. "I see we both thought to bring breakfast," he said with a smile. "Great minds think alike."

"Good to see you both," Kelly said. "I brought bagels."

Patricia set down the brightly wrapped gift box she'd been holding and reached for the bag of bagels. "Thank you, Kelly. I'm dying for a Danish, but I can't eat all that sugar on an empty stomach. So I'll have a bagel first. Then a Danish. Maybe even two."

She glanced up and saw everyone staring at her. "What?" she asked, sounding indignant. "Don't judge me."

Kelly shook her head. "Fine. But don't be screaming to me next time you step on the scale."

Patricia pressed her lips together. "Fine. I'll have half a bagel and then half a Danish." She sighed. "Spoilsport."

Ryan hugged Patricia and brushed his cheek against her red hair. "You eat whatever you want, angel. I'll help you work it off later."

Patricia shoved the box toward Tanner, then reached for the bag of bagels. "Open this, Dad."

Tanner stared at the box. "It's for me?"

"No, it's for your daughter."

"Oh. Thanks." He sounded more confused than sincere; then he reached for the box and studied the paper.

It showed pink angels and curly mauve hearts. Tied on top was a small pink rattle. Looking more uncomfortable by the second, he ripped into the paper, then lifted the lid off the square box.

First he pulled out a frilly dress in pale peach. The tiny sleeves had little bows, and there was lace on the hem.

"It's beautiful," Kelly said. "Patricia, that's so adorable."

"I know. I fell in love with it the second I saw it. I adore Drew and Griffin," she said, naming her two boys, "but shopping for them is not as much fun as shopping for Lisbeth. All those lacy, frilly whatevers. It's great."

"It's a dress," Tanner said doubtfully. "Does she need a dress?"

"All girls do," Patricia said as she cut a bagel in half and smoothed on cream cheese. "For when you take her out."

"Take her out where?"

"Anywhere. Don't you want her to look good?"

Tanner stared at the dress as if it were a subversive

plot to overthrow the government. Kelly was worried he might bolt at any moment.

"What else is in there?" she asked to distract him.

"There's more?" Tanner sounded more alarmed than pleased.

Kelly noticed that Ryan wasn't saying much, but he appeared to be highly amused by his brother's apprehension. She studied the two Malones, noting the similarities in their dark hair and blue eyes. Ryan was a little taller and more slender, while Tanner was solid muscle.

"Well, this is okay, I guess," Tanner said, holding up a stuffed bear. Then he glanced at a book touting the joys of having a daughter. "I'll need this for sure. I've finally figured out I don't know diddly about women."

"Fortunately she's not going to be a woman for a long time," Kelly said. "You will have learned a lot by then."

"Which reminds me," Patricia said as she licked cream cheese off her fingers. "I brought my practice baby. She's in the car, along with diapers and bath stuff."

"I'll get it," Ryan said.

"I'll come with you," Kelly told him. "My car is filled with the things Tanner couldn't bring home last night."

"Then we'll all make the trip outside," Tanner said as he set the gifts on the kitchen counter.

Patricia waved. "You go ahead. I just want to eat more."

Kelly was still laughing when her phone beeped. She glanced at the text message from the hospital. She had a patient in labor.

"I'll be right with you," she said as she started to make a call. Two minutes later she'd confirmed that one of her pregnant patients would be ready to give birth later that morning.

"I have to run," she told Tanner as she walked out toward her car. He'd unloaded most of the bags she'd picked up from the store and was holding an overnight bag. "You might as well take that inside."

"So you'll be back?"

She tried not to smile at the panic in his voice. "I promised I'd stay, and I will. I don't expect this to take too long, so look for me later this afternoon. When are you picking up the baby?"

"Around eleven," he said. He swallowed. "So you'll really be back?"

She touched his arm. Through the soft, worn sweatshirt, she felt the firmness of his muscles. She squeezed. "Don't worry. You'll be fine. Ryan and Patricia are here. She'll give you your baby lesson, and that will give you the confidence you need to handle this. Remember when you first started working for the construction company? Didn't you have a lot of things to learn?"

He nodded. "But if I screwed up I wasn't messing up a kid."

"You're not going to mess her up. In fact, I'm willing to bet you're really going to like being a father."

"Yeah?"

She released him. "I promise. See you later."

With that she got in her car and started the engine. As she backed down the driveway, she couldn't suppress a faint thrill of excitement that she was going to be coming back later. She wanted to spend more time with Tanner. She told herself it was because of the baby and nothing else, but she wasn't sure that she really believed that. In her heart of hearts, she knew that somehow it had become something more.

* * *

"Okay, I know you're worried," Tanner said as he carefully steered his Explorer onto the main road. He had to force himself to merge with traffic when all he wanted to do was drive twenty in the slow lane so he could be sure they got home safely.

At the stoplight, he quickly glanced over his shoulder and saw his daughter sleeping soundly in her car seat. Hope and love and terror battled it out in his chest. He felt like he'd been sucker punched and handed his heart's desire, all in the same moment. Nothing was ever going to be the same again.

"We'll get through this," he told her, then returned his attention to the road. "I've screwed up more than once in my life, but I swear I'll do my damnedest not to screw up with you." He paused and cleared his throat. "I should probably start by not swearing in front of you, huh? Sorry about that. See, I don't have any practice at being a father. Fortunately you don't have any practice at being a kid, either. So we'll learn together. I'll be here for you, no matter what. I learned that from my brother. Ryan was always there for me. He did a good job, and he was only a year older than me. I've got thirty-seven years on you, kid."

He looked at her again. "Thirty-seven. Does that sound old to you?" Not surprisingly, she didn't answer.

He drew in a breath. He couldn't remember ever being this unsure of himself. He didn't want to break her or hurt her in some way. How did people become parents more than once? The task seemed so daunting. Maybe it got easier with practice. He could only hope.

He turned right at the next signal and entered his neighborhood. Ryan had wanted to come along while he picked up his daughter, but Patricia had said he had to do this by himself. The sooner he got used to being alone with her, the better for the both of them.

Tanner frowned. "We can't keep calling you 'her' or 'the baby.' We're going to have to come up with a name. I wish you could tell me what you'd like...or at least what you'd hate."

He pulled into his driveway, which circled in front of the large, two-story house.

"This is it," he said as he switched off the engine. "You're home."

His daughter wasn't overly impressed. She continued to sleep as he unstrapped her car seat. He slung the bag of supplies the hospital had sent home with him over one shoulder, then picked up the seat and carried it, and his daughter, inside.

Ryan and Patricia were waiting in the foyer. "How did it go?" his brother asked.

"Okay." He let the bag slip to the floor and held out the carrier. "Here she is." He stared down doubtfully. "She's sleeping."

"Don't complain. She'll be up soon enough. Come see what we did."

He followed them upstairs and into his daughter's room. While he was gone, Ryan had finished putting together the three-drawer changing table, and Patricia had put all the clothes and linens away.

"Newborn-size clothes are in the top drawer," she said, pulling it open to show him. "Everything else is in the lower drawers. Oh, and I hung the dress in the closet."

He glanced over his shoulder and saw the tiny dress hanging alone on the rack. It looked impossibly small and foreign. He sucked in his breath.

"I, ah, guess I'd better get her in bed," he said.

"Absolutely. I washed the sheets and the comforter. They've only been out of the dryer a few minutes, so they're probably even still warm," she said helpfully.

Tanner glanced at Ryan, but his brother shook his head. "You're going to have to learn how to do this sometime. Might as well be now."

Tanner grunted because the alternative was to say something unpleasant, and he'd already promised his daughter he wasn't going to do that.

First he unfastened the straps holding her in place. Carefully, supporting his baby's head the way Patricia and the nurse at the hospital had shown him, he lifted her from the car seat and cradled her against the crook of his arm. Then he crossed the room and gently put her in the crib.

She barely stirred. Then her big blue eyes opened, she wiggled once, yawned and drifted back off to sleep.

"I guess you're really a dad now," Ryan said and slapped him on the back. "Congratulations."

"Thanks. I've got to do something about a name." He glanced at his brother. "I was thinking about Cecilia after our mother. I like it, but it sounds stuffy for such a little girl, so I was thinking that would be her real name, but we'd call her Lia."

Ryan nodded. "I like it."

"Me, too," said Patricia, then sniffed. "Let's go downstairs. If I stay here much longer, she's going to make me want another baby."

Both men hustled her out of the room. They went downstairs into the family room. Tanner remembered the baby monitor and had to run back up to get it. He turned on the unit on the dresser, clicked on the one in his hand, pausing by the crib.

"Hi, Lia," he murmured. "I'm glad you're sleeping. You should think about sleeping a lot. That would give your old man a break. Want to give it a try?"

Because he couldn't help himself, he stroked the back of his index finger against her cheek. The warm skin was so incredibly soft. She barely stirred.

"I don't usually fall this fast, kid, but you seem to have a firm grip on my heart. I guess we're stuck with each other."

Despite the fear, he knew then that there was nowhere else he would rather be.

Chapter 5

Tanner glanced at his watch as he walked down the stairs. It had been all of twenty minutes, and so far, so good. If the next twenty years would go as smoothly, he might just get the hang of this whole parenting thing.

As he stepped into the family room, he saw Patricia leaning against Ryan. His brother had his arms around his wife, and they were talking quietly. Nothing about their posture was sexual, yet Tanner sensed the intimacy between them. Ryan had been lucky enough, or smart enough, to find an extraordinary woman to share his life. They'd been married almost ten years, and if anything, they were more affectionate today than they'd been in the beginning. Patricia was a model wife and mother, very loving.

Tanner pushed down the unexpected surge of envy. He reminded himself that he'd never been one for commitments. Of course, he'd never gotten the point of kids either and now he had one. Everything changed.

Ryan glanced up and saw him. "Patricia and I are going to let you off the hook about babysitting the kids," he said.

Tanner stared blankly. "What are you talking about?"

Ryan grinned. "See, that's what happens. You get a child in the house, and the parents start losing their minds. The first thing to go is short-term memory. Trust me on this. It's only going to get worse."

Patricia shook her head. "What your big brother is trying to say is that we have that second honeymoon planned for December. With a newborn in the house, you're not really in a position to take care of three more children."

Tanner set the baby monitor on the counter closest to the family room and ran his fingers through his hair. "You're right. I did forget." When Ryan and Patricia had decided to go away, he'd offered to take their kids for the long weekend. Lily, Patricia's mom and their usual source for live-in help, was going to be taking a cruise with her sister.

"Look, this is your anniversary," Tanner said. "I still want to take the kids. Drew's a big help with his younger brother and sister, and I don't want you two worrying. You're barely going to get away for more than a weekend as it is."

Ryan and Patricia exchanged a look. "We'll find someone else," Patricia said firmly. "It's sweet of you to offer, but you have no idea what you're getting into. Having a baby in the house changes everything. We'll arrange child care for our little monsters." She glanced at her watch, then at Ryan. "We need to be going," she said.

Ryan nodded. "She's right." He tapped his shirt pocket.

"I've got my cell phone with me—call if you need anything."

They were leaving? Tanner fought down a sudden surge of panic. "You guys can stay a little longer, can't you?"

"Sorry." Patricia picked up her purse and slung it over one shoulder. "I'll be in touch later this afternoon with a couple of numbers for baby nurses. I have two in mind, and I think one of them is available."

He watched helplessly as they headed for the front door. "What do I do if she wakes up?"

"Take care of her," Patricia said. "Check her diaper. Then feed her."

"I don't know how."

"Yes, you do. We went over it this morning."

Yeah, right. Like practicing on a doll was the same as feeding a baby. "But…"

"Be sure to check the temperature of the formula and burp her when you're done," Patricia said, giving him a reassuring smile. "If you get into trouble, call. Ryan and I can be back here in less than twenty minutes."

He would prefer they didn't leave at all, but he couldn't bring himself to insist that they stay.

"Sure," he said with a confidence he didn't feel. "We'll be fine."

They waved as they walked out the front door. Tanner wanted to go running after them and beg them to move in with him for the next two or three years. Maybe he should ask Patricia to find a baby nurse who could start today, in the next fifteen minutes.

He paced the length of the family room, then turned and stared at the baby monitor. It was just a matter of time until Lia woke up and started crying. Dear God, what was he going to do?

* * *

"Hush, Lia," Tanner pleaded as he rocked his daughter in his arms.

When she'd awakened a little more than an hour before, he'd rushed upstairs at the first whisper of her cry. He'd checked her diaper, which had been dry. He'd carefully fed her. After double-checking the temperature of the formula, he'd positioned her as both Patricia and the nurse in the hospital had shown him. Lia had taken to the bottle with no trouble at all. When she'd finished her meal, he'd held her against his shoulder and patted her back until she'd let out an impressive burp. But since then, all she'd done was cry.

The harsh, hiccuping sound made him frantic. Did she have a temperature? Was she sick? Had he given her too much formula or not enough?

She drew in her breath and let out another sob. Her face was all scrunched up, with her eyes squeezed tightly closed and her tiny fists waving in the air.

"No one should be this unhappy," he murmured to her as he rocked her back and forth. In the past twenty minutes it felt as if her weight had doubled. He paced the length of the downstairs and wondered if he should just give up and call Patricia.

Before he could decide, the doorbell rang. He rushed to the foyer and pulled it open.

Kelly stood on the porch, holding several plastic grocery bags. "I brought supplies," she said over the sound of Lia's crying. "From the drugstore. Baby wash, diaper wipes, that sort of thing." She stepped into the entrance and glanced at Lia. "What's wrong?"

He resisted the urge to hold out the screaming child to her to fix. "I don't know. When she woke up, she was fine. I fed her and burped her. I thought she'd go back to sleep."

Kelly crossed to the kitchen, where she set down her bags. "What about her diaper?"

"I checked it first thing."

Kelly began unpacking the bags. He clamped down on his frustration. How could she be so calm about this? Something could be seriously wrong with Lia. Didn't she want to recommend that he rush her to the emergency room?

"Did you check her diaper after you fed her?"

He blinked at the question. "After?"

She gave him a quick smile. "Sometimes babies go after they eat, rather than before. Sometimes they go both times. Have you checked recently?"

Just then he caught the odor of something...not pleasant. He swallowed. "Do I have to?"

"Oh yes. And before you think of passing that job off on me, I'll just go ahead and mention I have a lot more stuff in my car. I'll bring it in right now."

With that, she disappeared.

Tanner stared at his daughter. "About this poop thing," he said. "I'm not up to it. Maybe you should just dispose of everything in liquid form. What do you think?"

She gave another cry, so he headed up the stairs. Two minutes later he had her on the changing table and was staring at something that looked like a prop out of an alien horror movie.

"What is it?" he asked when he heard Kelly's footsteps in the hall. "It's disgusting."

"It's something you're going to have to get used to." She poked her head into the bedroom and grinned. "It could be worse."

He looked up. "How?"

"She could be a boy. They are notorious for sending up a little shower while they're having their diapers changed."

"Great," he muttered, returning his attention to his daughter. "There are too many firsts for me, sweet Lia. Bringing you home, your first bottle, now this first diaper. Things are moving too fast. Let's all just relax for a bit and catch up, okay?"

She'd stopped crying. He gently wiped her bottom, collected a new diaper and set it into place. Her gaze seemed to look at his face, and, as usual, her expression was faintly worried.

"I think she knows I'm clueless," he told Kelly. "She's got this look on her face as if she's sure I'm going to drop her or something."

"All babies do that," Kelly said, walking over and smiling down at Lia. "I heard your daddy call you by a name. Lia. Do you like it?"

Lia responded by fluttering her eyelids a couple of times, then dozing off.

"I'll take that as a yes," Kelly said.

He glanced at her and saw she carried an armful of supplies. He saw baby wash, baby shampoo, cotton balls and swabs, tiny washcloths and a host of other boxes and jars he didn't want to even think about. Babies required way too much stuff as it was. How was he supposed to keep it all straight? What if he used the wrong product on the wrong part?

"Don't go there," she warned as he buttoned Lia back into her sleeper.

"Go where?"

"You're getting nervous. I can see it in your eyes."

Her eyes were a hazel brown, and this close he could see flecks of gold in the irises. They were wide and pretty, and perfectly set off by the fringe of bangs falling almost to her eyebrows. She didn't wear any makeup that he could see. Even so, her lashes were long and thick, and her skin smooth.

He picked up Lia. "I don't want to get it wrong."

Kelly nodded at the sleeping infant. "So far, so good. Why don't you set her down, and I'll go put this stuff in her bathroom?"

He watched as Kelly crossed the room and disappeared through the doorway; then he carefully set his daughter into her crib. She barely moved as he pulled the comforter up to her chest. Kelly met him in the hall.

"I've put the bath supplies on the counter. For the next few months, you'll be using a small baby tub. I wasn't sure if you'd do that in her room or downstairs in the kitchen sink."

"The kitchen sink? She's not a piece of zucchini."

Kelly grinned. "I know, but the sink is at least at a decent height. With the bathtub, you'll be all bent over."

"Oh. I hadn't thought of that." But then there were dozens of things he hadn't thought of yet. Like the baby monitor. He checked it to make sure it was turned on, then led Kelly down to the family room.

There were more shopping bags waiting there. He stared at the pile. "Please tell me that everything comes with instructions," he said.

"Pretty much. And if it doesn't, you'll find out about it in the baby book I gave you. Or you can ask me while I'm here."

"Patricia's getting me a baby nurse," he said, hoping

the nurse would arrive soon with about fifteen years of experience. "So I can ask her, as well."

"You'rc all covered."

He still felt like he was a nonswimmer who'd been thrown into the ocean, but he didn't tell her that. "Want something to drink?" he asked, walking into the kitchen and pulling open the refrigerator door. "I have different sodas."

"Anything diet?" she asked.

He glanced at her, at her long legs in tailored slacks and the casual shirt she'd tucked into the waistband. She was tall, athletic-looking and very appealing.

"Sure," he said. "But tell me why?"

She glanced down at herself and laughed. "I'm not on a diet, if that's what you mean. But one of the reasons is I'm cautious about what I eat. I choose my calories carefully, and, to me, soda is a waste. So I prefer the low-cal version."

He made a face but pulled out a can for her. When he reached for a glass, she snagged the container from him. "I never bother," she said. "It just means something more to put in the dishwasher and something more to return to the cupboard."

"A woman after my own heart," he said, collecting a regular cola drink for himself and following her back into the family room.

Kelly settled on one end of the sofa, while he took the other. Afternoon sunlight spilled into the room, making her medium-blond hair seem a little lighter. He'd only ever seen her with it pulled back into a braid or fastened up on her head. He wondered how long it was when it was loose and how it would look tumbling around her face.

The image produced instant heat inside of him. He

realized then how distracted he'd been with Lia. He'd been alone with Kelly several times in the past couple of days and hadn't been able to appreciate that she was funny, intelligent and easy on the eye. Not that he was interested in her that way. She was helping out, and he was grateful. They were friends, nothing more. They had to be. For one thing, Kelly wasn't his type. For another, he had a child to think of now. He couldn't keep practicing his own version of serial monogamy. Lia would get confused.

He popped the top on his soda. "I almost forgot to ask," he said. "How was the delivery?"

Kelly sighed as her face took on a look of radiance. "It was great. Everything went perfectly." She paused. "The mother might take issue with that. After all, she spent several hours in labor. But the birth was smooth and easy on the baby. They had a healthy little boy, and both the parents are thrilled." She looked at him. "Usually when I deliver a child, I rarely get to see him or her again, so it's nice to be able to follow up with one of my babies. Lia is doing very well."

"I hope so. She seems okay. I'm glad that Patricia's going to be her pediatrician."

"Nothing like having a doctor in the family?" Kelly asked.

"Exactly."

She leaned back against the sofa. "So how did you pick Lia for her name?"

"Actually, her real name is Cecilia, after my mom, but I thought we could call her Lia. It's a little more contemporary, not to mention easier for her to spell."

"That's so nice. Your mom must be thrilled."

Tanner set his soda on the coffee table. "My parents

are both dead. They died when Ryan and I were really young."

Kelly frowned. "I didn't know that. I'm so sorry."

The phone rang. He reached for it and spoke into the receiver. "Hello?"

He listened as a man on the other end talked for a couple of minutes. Tanner started laughing. "Yeah. I wish I could tell you otherwise, but they're mine." He paused and listened. "No, I appreciate you following up on them. Thanks." He hung up. "You're not going to believe who that was," he said.

"Tell me."

"My credit card company. They wanted to confirm a very large charge to a baby store. Apparently that purchase didn't match my normal charging pattern, and the computer flagged my account."

She laughed. "They'd better get used to that kind of thing with you. There's going to be lots more for you to buy."

"I don't want to think about it."

She picked up the teddy bear that Patricia and Ryan had brought for Lia. "Isn't he a charmer," she said, smoothing the soft fur around the stuffed animal's face. "Bears have always been my favorite."

Her expression turned wistful as she rubbed the animal's head.

"Tell me again why you don't have a dozen kids of your own," he said impulsively.

Something dark and painful slipped across her eyes. Then she blinked, and it was gone. "Interesting question for which I don't have an equally interesting answer," she said lightly. "But you're the important one right now.

I want to know how you're feeling. Is the panic under control?"

"Seems to be," he said, recognizing that she was deliberately changing the subject but not sure he should let her. Then he remembered that she was being kind enough to give up one of her weekends to help him with his daughter. He owed her. More important, her personal life was none of his business.

He glanced at his watch. "Hour four of having her home and all is well."

"I'm glad." She stood up. "I thought I could go to the grocery store. I'm guessing you don't have a lot of food in the house, and it's not as if you can go out easily. Then I'm available to assist with the baby care. That is, if you still want me to stay over."

"Are you kidding? I won't make it without you."

She smiled. "Then what about making a list?"

But even as he went through his cupboards and figured out what he had and what he needed, he couldn't get those words out of his head. *I won't make it without you.* They'd both known what he meant when he said it. He was talking about Lia and his lack of parental experience. Nothing more. But for a moment he wondered how his life would be different if he could for once allow himself to really need someone.

Chapter 6

Kelly stirred and rolled over. She opened her eyes and saw that it was a little after two in the morning. She blinked as she looked at the unfamiliar room. This wasn't her apartment and it wasn't the hospital. *Where...*

Then her memory returned. She was at Tanner's house, in one of the spare bedrooms. Unlike Lia's room, this one hadn't been remodeled. Old-fashioned wallpaper still covered the walls, contrasting with the heavy drapes on the window.

Kelly stretched and tried to figure out what had awakened her. Was it Lia? She looked at the clock again. She'd expected to be up before now to help Tanner, or even take over one of the feedings. Oh well, now that she was awake, she might as well check on the baby.

Kelly threw back the covers and stood up. She'd deliberately worn sweats and a T-shirt to bed so all she had

to do was fumble for her slippers and slide them on. She
tucked a loose strand of hair behind her ear and made
her way into the hall.

The house was all shadows. Lia's door stood open, and
she could see the faint light from a Disney night-light il-
luminating a patch of hardwood flooring. As she stepped
into the room, a slight movement caught her attention.
She looked up and saw Tanner standing by the window.

Kelly froze in place, staring. Tanner wore jeans and
nothing else. He held his tiny daughter in his arms, cra-
dling her against his bare chest and rocking her gently.
Moonlight filtered through the half-open blinds, high-
lighting, then shading, the shape of his shoulders, the
muscles in his arms, the warm color of his skin.

Deep in her stomach, something stirred to life. Some
small producer of female hormones, some long-dormant
cells secreted a forgotten bit of magic that made a woman
want a man. She felt the first flickering of desire, but it
was more than that. Her attraction wasn't just to the perfectly muscled body but also to the tenderness inherent
in those incredibly strong hands. A woman could trust a
man who held a baby with such tenderness.

She knew she hadn't made a sound, but Tanner turned
toward her. "Did I wake you?" he asked softly. "I tried
to be quiet."

"It wasn't noise that got my attention," she admitted,
"but the absence of it. I came to check on Lia."

"Great minds," he said. "That's what I was doing.
She was awake and looked hungry, so I got her a bottle,
then changed her diaper. She ate great and is already
back to sleep." He smiled. "I couldn't figure out why
she was sleeping so much, but then I got a look at her

diaper. It must take a lot of energy to produce all that waste product."

Kelly laughed. "Waste product, huh? Interesting way to describe it."

He was the kind of man women dreamed about meeting—handsome, charming, successful. So why was he awake at two in the morning holding a child?

"Who are you, Tanner Malone?" she asked before she could stop herself.

"You mean why me, why her?" he asked, nodding at Lia. "I guess I'm just one man who wants to do the right thing. I'm terrified but trying."

"That's all anyone can ask of you."

"Oh, I think Lia is going to have more expectations than that, but I have some time before I have to worry about them."

She'd been wrong about him. She realized that now. All those months she'd been Lucy's doctor, listening to her patient grumble about the guy who'd knocked her up and had then insisted she have the baby, but who didn't want responsibility for it. Kelly had been furious with both of them for being careless during sex, but she'd been angrier with Tanner. It was easy for men, because they didn't get pregnant. They just walked away from the problem. Except Tanner hadn't.

She leaned against the door frame and crossed her arms over her chest. "I was wrong about you," she said, her voice low. "I've been angry at you for most of Lucy's pregnancy. I thought you were an irresponsible bastard who'd gotten caught and wanted out. But I was wrong about all of it. I'm sorry, Tanner."

He was quiet for a long time, just staring at her in the darkness and rocking Lia. "Thank you for apologizing," he said at last. "That means a lot to me. But you were also right about me. Not about me being irresponsible. We used a condom. As an obstetrician, I'm sure you're very aware that they sometimes fail. But about the rest of it. When Lucy told me she was pregnant, I didn't know what to think."

He turned back to the window. Kelly didn't feel that he was shutting her out as much as protecting himself. As if he was embarrassed or ashamed of what he was saying. She wanted to go to him and touch him, tell him that she understood. But they didn't know each other that well. Instead she stood her ground and waited.

"The entire relationship was a mistake. In fact, calling it a relationship gives it more credit than it deserves. It was in early February. We met at a party. I hadn't had a woman in my life for a long time. It was crowded—we were both in the mood. And then I took her home and one thing led to another. I knew it was dumb even then, but what the hell, right?" He glanced down at his daughter. "Sorry, sweetie, I know I'm not supposed to swear."

"You don't have to tell me this," Kelly said, more because she thought she should than because she didn't want to know.

"Probably not, but I think it's important information." He walked over to the crib and set Lia down on her back. "We said goodbye, and I never expected to see her again. About two months later she called to tell me she was pregnant. Apparently she'd been debating whether or not to inform me. I think her plan had been to go get an abortion and get on with her life."

Kelly thought about Lucy and realized Tanner had summed up the other woman fairly accurately. Lucy had not been thrilled to be pregnant.

"I didn't want her to do that," he said. "I didn't want the kid, either, but I wanted her to carry it to term." He leaned over and stroked his daughter's cheek. "Thank God. Lucy fought me, but eventually I convinced her. I promised to cover all the out-of-pocket medical expenses her policy didn't. We both agreed to give the baby up for adoption."

He glanced at Kelly. In the dimly lit room, it was impossible to see what he was thinking. "I swear that's what I planned to do. Right up until the day she was born. Then something happened. I guess she went from being an abstraction to something real. And I couldn't walk away from that...or her."

Kelly dropped her arms to her sides. "I feel responsible for a part of that," she said. "If I hadn't let you hold her, you wouldn't have bonded."

His teeth flashed white. "I don't think so. While it would be really nice to be able to blame you, it's not your fault. If I hadn't wanted Lia, all the holding in the world wouldn't have changed my mind."

Kelly wasn't so sure. "Something happens when a parent holds his or her newborn for the first time."

"Do you think holding her would have changed Lucy's mind?"

His quiet question made her pause. She'd checked her patient before Lucy had been released. The younger woman had expressed only relief at having her pregnancy behind her. She hadn't mentioned anything about the baby or what was happening to her.

"No, I don't," she admitted.

"So that proves my point." He straightened. "Tell you what, Doc, you can be guilty about any number of things in your life, but you're going to have to let this one go.

You're not responsible for Lia." He motioned to the room. "But I do owe you. You've been a great help, and I want to return the favor. I can fix the plumbing, remodel a bathroom, hang wallpaper—you name it."

"I'll have to let you know," Kelly said, thinking of her small, spare apartment. The management company handled any maintenance problems she had. She'd never done much of anything to make her three-room place a home, not even for the holidays. Especially then. For her the apartment was utilitarian, nothing more. She hadn't had a true home since she was seventeen.

"You do that," he said. "Because I'm not going to forget what I owe you."

Somewhere in the house a clock chimed.

"It's late," Tanner told her. "We'd better get to bed and get some sleep while we can. I have a feeling this little girl is going to be up a couple more times before sunrise."

"You're right."

She turned to leave. At least that was her intent, but somehow her gaze got locked with his. She told herself to look away, to start walking back to her room, but she couldn't move. Her legs were too heavy, and those suddenly awake hormones were busy swaying through her body, leaving her weak and wanting.

As she watched, his attention seemed to drift downward…toward her mouth. She told herself it was her imagination. That he wasn't thinking about kissing her any more than she was thinking about being in his arms. That she didn't wonder about how strong he would feel, or the warmth of his bare skin under her fingers. And that she'd never even once fantasized about the firmness of his lips or how his tongue would taste.

Then, because her thoughts both frightened and excited her, she turned on her heel and escaped.

"So when can I buy one of the backpack baby carriers?" Tanner asked. He sat on one of the stools and leaned his forearms on the counter that divided the kitchen from the family room.

Kelly stood at the stove, stirring spaghetti sauce. She inhaled the spicy-sweet fragrance. In another hour or so, it would be finished. They would have some tonight, and she would freeze the rest for Tanner to heat up. If he'd thought he'd eaten on the run before, he was in for a shock. There was nothing like having a baby around to interfere with regularly scheduled meals.

"She has to be able to hold up her head," Kelly told him. "You can get the front kind of baby pack fairly soon. They protect the infant's neck more."

"Right." He made a note on the pad of paper in front of him.

"How's the list coming?" she asked.

"Not bad. I can't believe I have to go to that baby store again. I didn't think there was anything we *hadn't* bought."

Kelly laughed. "Babies are like that. But you're getting the hang of it."

He looked at the baby monitor, then at his watch. "I'm starting to. I figure we've got another half hour before we hear the first stirrings from Lia. At least she's sleeping a bunch. I like that. Now if only she'd stop leaving that junk in her diaper."

"You'll get used to it."

"Maybe. The thing is, I don't want to."

Tanner's grin was boyish and contagious. Kelly had

to turn her attention back to her sauce before she said or did something stupid. She'd been in Tanner's house barely forty-eight hours and already the man was getting to her. Knowing why didn't make him easier to resist.

It was just situational, she thought. Being around a man bonding with a baby was fairly irresistible. Then there was the additional problem of her life. She'd spent most of it living like a nun. She didn't encourage men, and she wasn't beautiful enough that they came on to her regardless of the signals she sent. Add to that her impossible schedule throughout her years in medical school and during her residency. All together, it made perfect sense for her to respond to the first good-looking single guy to do more than say hi to her.

The trick would be keeping him from figuring it out. She liked being friends with Tanner, and she did not want him feeling sorry for her. She didn't know what his type was, but she was reasonably confident it wasn't her. He would prefer flashier women. Those who had time to develop a sense of style and adventure. She was cotton sensible and not the least bit romantic. He would want Miss July with a brain.

"We need to get some toys," Tanner said, continuing to work on his list. "Lia has the mobile above her bed and the bear that Patricia and Ryan brought. I definitely want another mobile for above the changing table, but that's not enough." He tapped his pen against the counter. "She's too young for dolls, right?"

"Just a little." Kelly shook her head. "She's a newborn. Toys are not a big priority right now."

"But they will be. And Christmas is coming."

"It's still a month away."

"Right. Only a month. I'm a dad now. Christmas is

my responsibility. What about all that educational stuff? So she can learn to recognize shapes and colors. When does that start?"

"Not this week. In fact, the most exciting event you can look forward to in the next month is her lifting up her head while she's on her stomach."

"Okay. So she won't be reading anytime soon, but I still want to buy her some toys."

She glanced at him over her shoulder. "You know that Lia shouldn't go out into crowded places for a few more days. You don't want her exposed to a lot of germs."

Tanner looked insulted. "I'm hardly going to take her to the toy store with me. Then she'll know they're not from Santa."

Kelly didn't know whether to laugh at him or throw the spoon she was holding. "Santa? You think she'll notice?"

"Of course. She's an incredibly bright baby. I would have thought as a doctor you would have recognized that already." He jotted down a couple more items. "I'll either go at lunch, or ask Mrs. Dawson to stay an extra half hour while I stop at the toy store on my way home."

Mrs. Dawson was the baby nurse Patricia had recommended. The lovely older woman had stopped by that morning to meet both Tanner and Lia. She was gentle, experienced and had enough credentials and recommendations to get a job with a visiting head of state.

"Are you sure you don't want Mrs. Dawson to stay at night?" she asked. Tanner had surprised her by requesting the baby nurse take care of Lia only during the day.

"No, but I want to try it that way first. If I can't get any sleep, I'll have to have her stay longer. But I want to get used to taking care of my daughter myself. As soon as she's old enough, I'll bring her to the office with me.

I've got several recommendations for day care for times when bringing her to work is impossible." He shrugged. "It's not a perfect solution, but I'm willing to be flexible until I find what works best for both of us."

"Very impressive," Kelly told him. "Less than a week ago you had no plans to keep her, and now you're pulling it all together."

"I don't have a choice."

"That's true. Once you decided to keep her, you were stuck. But you're still handling it well." She knew that if she'd met him at a party, she would have dismissed him as too good-looking to be anything but self-centered and shallow. But Kelly would have been the shallow one by making that judgment without getting to know him. She also would have been wrong.

She turned down the heat on her spaghetti sauce, picked up her glass of wine and walked over to the counter where Tanner worked. It was surprisingly easy to spend time with him. She'd been worried that the weekend might be awkward, but she'd enjoyed herself very much.

"All right, Mr. Malone, it's time for you to spill the beans. Why don't you have a wife and half a dozen kids, or at least three, like your brother?"

He set down his pen and looked at her. "Not my style."

She motioned to the kitchen. "Confirmed bachelors don't remodel. At least they don't remodel a perfect home for a family. You told me you don't cook very much, but look at this kitchen. You did a terrific job."

"For resale."

"Liar," she said softly. His blue eyes were the most amazing shade, she thought, wishing she could get lost inside them. "I don't get a chance to cook all that often, but even I'm dying to make Thanksgiving dinner in there."

"I wouldn't stop you," he said.

"I've heard about your reputation with women. You can't be lacking in offers for permanent roommates."

He shrugged, then took a drink of his wine. "It never worked out that way. I've always had long-term relationships that just ended."

"Did you know they would end when you started?"

"What?"

She leaned against the counter. "I have this theory about people who practice serial monogamy. Most of the time they aren't interested in a permanent commitment, but they don't want to admit that. So they find someone who appears to have all the qualities they could want in a mate. They go out for a few months or even a few years, then something happens. There's a fatal flaw and they break up. Later, when they talk about the relationship, they always mention knowing from the beginning that something was wrong. Instead of looking for Mr. or Ms. Right, they are secretly searching for the almost-right person who has a fatal flaw. That way they look like they're trying to get involved, but they're really not."

He frowned. "That's pretty twisted."

"Does it sound right?"

"I'm not sure. Ryan did the wife and family thing, but it was never anything I wanted."

"Has that changed? You have a daughter now."

"Tell me about it." He took another sip of wine. "Things have to be different. I know I'm going to have to be more careful about who I let into our lives now that it's not just me. If I want a relationship, I'll need to find someone who will be accepting of Lia, too."

"That won't be a problem," Kelly said.

He leaned toward her. "I have to ask you a question. As a woman, I mean."

"All right."

He took a deep breath. "What am I supposed to tell Lia about her mother? I'm not upset about Lucy's decision. In fact, I'm glad she's gone. She never wanted to have children and I don't think she would have been very patient with a baby. But I don't want to say that to Lia. I don't want to tell her that her mother didn't want her. I never want her to know that Lucy thought about having an abortion and that I had to talk her out of it. How is a kid supposed to survive knowing that?"

Kelly felt as if all the blood had rushed out of her. She felt cold and lightheaded. She'd had this exact conversation with herself a thousand times in the past. Maybe more.

"Some mothers don't give up their children so easily," she said, working hard to keep her voice steady. "Some spend the rest of their lives wondering if they did the right thing."

"Maybe." Tanner sounded doubtful. "That still doesn't answer my question. How do I tell Lia that her mother didn't want her?"

Kelly took a step back. "I can't help you with this," she said. "Maybe you should talk to Ryan or Patricia. Maybe a child psychologist could help. It's not something you have to deal with for a while."

"I guess not." He stared at her. "Are you all right?"

She wanted to leave, to run away and hide. Except she'd done that before and the problem always followed her. So instead she straightened her spine and squared her shoulders.

"I'm fine. Your question caught me off guard because it's something I've thought a lot about."

"Because you deliver babies who are going to be given up for adoption," he said. "I understand."

"No, you don't. I've thought about this because I once gave up a child."

Chapter 7

Kelly figured she'd already started down the road of telling the truth, so she might as well continue. "It was a long time ago," she said. "I was all of seventeen when I got pregnant. It was difficult for me then and to be honest, it's still a little tough to talk about."

She risked a glance at Tanner, then wished she hadn't. He was staring at her wide-eyed, his face a mask of stunned surprise. She folded her arms over her chest. This was why she didn't share the details of her past with many people. So few of them understood.

He continued to stare at her. She had to dig down deep to find enough anger to combat her hurt. So he was going to judge her. She shouldn't have expected anything else... except she had. She'd thought Tanner might understand.

"You weren't there," she said crisply. "You can't know what it's like."

"I never said I could," he told her. "I don't think less of you, I'm just…"

"Surprised, shocked, disapproving?"

"None of those." He placed his hands flat on the counter and stared at her. "Never anything like that. I have great respect for you, Kelly. If I'm feeling anything it's that I'm relieved to find out you're human, just like the rest of us. Until five minutes ago, I'd assumed you were one of those annoying, perfect people. You know the kind—always showing everyone up with their neatly planned lives. You're everything I could never be. I can't believe you made a mistake."

"I'm just a regular person." She bit her lower lip, not sure she could believe him. Was he really not judging her?

"You're not like the rest of us," he said. "Look at you. You're a gifted doctor. You've saved dozens of lives, maybe more. You committed yourself to years of schooling when most people just want to get on with their lives. I'm just some guy who builds hospital wings. No special talent required there."

She moved closer to the counter. "You're wrong. It does take talent to coordinate a project that size. We're talking about adding on a hospital wing that's going to cost a hundred million dollars. I can't even comprehend that much money, but you're going to make it happen." Kelly felt the corners of her mouth turn up in a slight smile. "I have trouble keeping my checkbook balanced."

He grinned. "Me, too. I give it to my bookkeeper, and he does it for me." He patted the stool next to him. "Have a seat."

She hesitated, then took her glass of wine with her

as she circled the counter. When she'd settled in place, he faced her.

"I'd like to hear about what happened to you. If you were just seventeen, you were probably still in high school when you got pregnant, right?"

Kelly drew in a deep breath. Something about Tanner made her want to share her past. Maybe it was the way he studied her face so intently, or the kindness in his eyes. Maybe it was nothing more than the desire to unburden herself to someone willing to listen. Whatever the reason, she found herself needing to talk.

"I grew up in a small town in Kansas," she began. "My mom died when I was born, and my dad raised me by himself." Pictures from her past appeared in her brain and made her smile. "He's a good man and a great father. I always felt as if I were the center of his universe."

"I hope I can do that for Lia," Tanner said.

Kelly studied him. "I think you will. The fact that you're worried about it means it's all the more likely to happen." She paused. "My dad's a Baptist minister. He has a huge church and the members keep him busy, but he always made time for me."

She touched the base of her wineglass but didn't lift it to drink. "I was a normal kid. I did well in school, and I'd always wanted to be a doctor. There wasn't a lot of extra money, so I'd planned on getting a scholarship. I did the usual things in high school. There were ups and downs, but whatever happened, however badly I was feeling, I knew I could always go to my dad and tell him. All I had to do was look into his eyes and see the light of his love shining out. That light—his love really—gave me the strength I needed to do the right thing."

Tanner's warm hand settled over hers. The heat of him

and the pressure of his strong fingers nearly distracted her from her story. She had to force herself to remember what she'd been saying.

"In my senior year of high school I fell in love for the first time."

"I'll bet you were the prettiest girl in school and all the boys wanted you desperately."

His compliment made her smile. "Not exactly. I'm five-ten, and I achieved my full height by the time I was thirteen. It took them a while to catch up. But they finally did. Anyway, the night of the homecoming dance, one thing led to another and in the front of Bobby's car, I lost my virginity and got pregnant. It was a full evening."

This time she did take a sip of her wine, but she used her right hand to hold the glass. She didn't want to pull her left one away from Tanner's touch. Contact with him gave her strength and a feeling of support, which was silly because they were just friends.

She squeezed her eyes shut for a second because nothing made sense anymore. Why did it seem like things had just changed between them?

"You don't have to finish the story if you don't want to," he told her.

"Thanks, but there's not much more to tell. I ignored the truth for as long as I could. I think I figured if I ignored it, it would go away. Of course life and pregnancies don't work that way. Then I received word that I'd earned a full scholarship to college. All I had to do was keep my grades up my last semester."

"No pressure there," Tanner said.

Kelly nodded. "I didn't know what to do or where to turn. Finally I knew I'd have to tell my dad. Somewhere between breakfast and presents on Christmas morning,

I confessed all and broke my father's heart." She withdrew her hand from Tanner's grasp and laced her fingers together on her lap.

"He was the best," she said softly, not looking at him, barely allowing herself to remember that time. But it was so hard not to get lost in the past, in the pain of that day and the days that followed.

"He went to the school district and made arrangements for me to finish my classes, even though there was an unwritten policy against pregnant teenagers attending regular classes. He dealt with the parishioners who thought I should be punished. He took me to the doctor, made sure I ate right. And when the time came, he helped me pick out the parents who adopted my child."

"But?" Tanner probed gently.

"But the light in his eyes had died," she whispered. She drew in a deep breath and risked glancing at him. "I never saw it again. The one thing that told me I was perfect and loved unconditionally was gone. And no matter what I've done since, it's never come back."

She rose to her feet because it had suddenly become impossible to stay seated. After crossing to the sink, she pressed her hands against the cool porcelain and bowed her head. That had been the day Christmas had become more about sadness than joy.

"That was the hardest seven months of my life. At school no one would talk to me. My boyfriend disappeared the second I told him I was pregnant, and my friends were too embarrassed or too angry to have anything to do with me. Going to church was a nightmare. Most of the congregation understood, but the ones who judged me were also the most vocal. And I wondered. Was I doing the right thing? After all, I was smart and motivated. Maybe I should forget the idea of being a doctor and get a job instead."

"But you didn't."

"No. We found a nice couple who desperately wanted a child. So I gave her up."

She heard Tanner swear under his breath. "You had a girl?"

She nodded. "Annie Jane. She was born in the middle of the summer. I had an easy delivery, but they wouldn't let me hold her. Instead they took her away. All I could do was wonder if I'd done the right thing or the easy thing."

Feelings welled up inside of her. Pain at the past, regrets for what she'd done and what she'd not done. It was too late, she reminded herself. Choices had been made, and they couldn't be unmade.

"I've never had any contact with her or her parents, but her grandparents on her adoptive mother's side have stayed in touch with me. They keep me updated on her progress, send pictures. Their daughter couldn't have children, so they're very grateful to me for giving them Annie."

"Does she know she's adopted?" he asked.

"Oh yes. It hasn't been a secret. But she's not interested in meeting me. Maybe in time, but for now she's happy with her family the way it is." She straightened. "I know she's fine. I know that her life is a good one and that she has loving parents. But I can't help wondering how it all would have been if I hadn't chosen to be selfish. If I'd just—"

She hadn't heard Tanner move, but suddenly he was standing behind her, turning her to face him. "Don't," he commanded. "Don't say it, and don't you dare even think it. You were seventeen years old, Kelly. You had a hell of a choice to make, and you did the best you could. Sure you could have kept her, and then what? Gotten a job right out of high school? What about your dream of being a doctor?"

"What about my daughter?"

"What about her? Are you saying you could have done better?"

"I don't know."

His blue eyes darkened as he gripped her shoulders. "Don't do this to yourself. Don't second-guess the past. You have a wonderful life, and so does she. If the situation were to happen today, you would have chosen differently. But it wasn't today. You were a kid. Give yourself a break."

"I want to," she said. And she did. She'd spent so much of her life beating herself up for her choices back then. Was it wrong to let the past go? She wanted to believe she was allowed, but she wasn't sure. "As for my life being wonderful, sometimes it is, but sometimes it's very lonely."

Especially during the holidays, she thought but didn't say.

Tanner's mouth tightened. "Why did I know you were going to say that?" he asked, but he didn't seem to be expecting an answer. Instead of holding her shoulders, his hands were moving up and down her arms. "I wish you hadn't told me this," he said, then shook his head when he saw the look on her face. "Don't get all weird on me. I don't mean because I think less of you. If anything, I admire you even more. But knowing about your past makes you…"

"What?"

"Approachable."

He was standing so close, she thought. She could feel his heat warming her. His hands were firm on her arms. He was a strong, solid man—the kind of man who made women feel safe and protected.

"It's as if you're just like everyone else," he murmured.

"I always have been."

"Not to me, and I think I preferred it that way."

"Why?"

"Because it would have kept me from doing this."

She knew what he was going to do before he did it. Even so, his kiss startled her. Not the fact that his lips pressed against hers, but because they felt so right. There was a sense of coming home—which was crazy but true. The scent of his body filled her, and it was as though she already knew that scent. He kissed slowly, as if they had all the time in the world. As if taking that time would only increase their passion. Desire flickered low in her belly as heat poured through her body.

He drew his arms around her and pulled her close. She went willingly—practically melting into him—as her arms encircled his neck.

They were nearly the same height, but he was so powerfully built that she felt small by comparison. Her breasts nestled easily against his chest, and her hips seemed to surge against him with a will of their own. But all that faded when compared to the perfection that was their kiss.

He brushed her mouth gently with his, moving back and forth so slowly that she could have escaped at any time—if she'd wanted to. But what woman would want to move away from the wonder that was Tanner Malone?

She felt the faintest rub of stubble against her chin. The friction delighted her, making her want to feel that slight scratchiness all over her body. Delicious images filled her mind, of them together like this, only more. Pressed hard and naked, in the most intimate dance of all. She was overheated and breathless, and all they'd done was kiss. Good grief, what would happen to her if they actually did make love? She would never survive.

But it would be a glorious way to go.

He drew his tongue along the seam of her mouth. The sensual movement pulled her back to the present. She slipped one hand up so that her fingers could bury themselves in his thick, dark hair. Her other hand moved down his back, feeling the movement of muscles against her palm. Then she parted her lips and invited him inside.

The jolt when his tongue touched hers nearly made her scream. There was a flash of heat and energy, but that wasn't what aroused her the most. It was Tanner's reaction to their shared intimacy. She felt the muscles of his back tense. Strength turned to rock. At the same time, he took a step closer and pressed himself against her fully. She felt the length and breadth of his arousal… and it was as impressive as the rest of him.

Kelly found herself getting lost in the experience of kissing him. She clung to him, wanting to be closer. His tongue moved against hers, then explored her mouth. Each caress brought with it new and exciting sensations. She found herself needing more, kissing him back, wanting more. She was thirty-two years old, and she couldn't remember the last time a man had *really* kissed her. It was a sad statement on her life.

But it wasn't just being with a man that reduced her legs to jelly. It was specifically this man. Because she'd been on the occasional date, and those men had sometimes given her a chaste good-night kiss. Not once had she ever reacted so strongly.

She wanted him, and it felt so good to want a man. She wanted to tell him that it was okay with her if he pushed her up against the counter, pulled down her jeans and panties and did it with her right there in the kitchen. She, who had never been daring enough to even leave the lights on.

His hands moved from her back to her face. He cupped her cheeks as if he was afraid she would try to run away. Had she been able to speak, she would have told him there was nowhere else she would rather be.

He nipped at her lower lip, then soothed the erotic ache with his tongue. He drew her lip into his mouth, sucking her and creating tiny pulls that tugged all the way to her breasts. Her nipples were hard and as hungry as the rest of her.

"Kelly," he breathed against her mouth, then slipped one hand under her braid.

He kissed her again, deeply, and she welcomed him. They circled each other, stroking, learning, breathing heavily. She was so incredibly aroused. Shudders rippled through her as if they'd been kissing for hours. Maybe they had. Maybe the rest of the world had disappeared, and only they were left to live in the magic of this moment.

Boldly, she let her hands trail down his back to the high, tight curve of his rear. As if reading her intent, he pressed against her, rubbing his arousal against her belly, making her gasp. One of his hands dropped to her waist, then moved up her side toward her breasts.

In the back of her mind, a voice whispered that things were getting out of hand and wouldn't that be nice. She caught her breath as his fingers moved higher and higher, reaching for her aching curves. Then her side vibrated.

Tanner wrapped his arms around her and rested his forehead against hers. "I would like to take credit for that, but I'm not good enough."

She smiled faintly, still caught up in what had, until this second, been going on between them. "Too bad," she murmured as she removed her phone from her pocket and stared at the display. "It's the hospital. I'm guessing it's one of my patients."

She tapped the screen to call work. Her head was still thick with passion, and she was afraid her voice would sound funny. She cleared her throat a couple of times before the nurses' station picked up.

"This is Dr. Hall. I received a text. How's Wendy?"

"Yes, Doctor. She came in half an hour ago..."

The nurse continued talking, and Kelly carefully wrote everything down, but it was incredibly hard to concentrate because Tanner had come up behind her and was trailing damp kisses down the nape of her neck. It was all she could do to keep taking notes. Finally she hung up the phone.

"You have a patient in labor," he said, still standing behind her. He wrapped his arms around her waist and pulled her against his chest. "You have to go."

"Yes," she said as she placed her hands on top of his. Had they really just shared the most extraordinary kiss?

She pulled out of his arms and turned to look at him. Passion darkened his eyes to the color of sapphires. His expression was equal parts aroused and self-satisfied.

"You're something of a kisser, Dr. Hall," he said.

"I could say the same about you."

"Go ahead."

She laughed. "You're a great kisser, Mr. Malone. Thank you."

They were standing close together but not touching. Then Tanner cupped her face. "I'm not sorry. The timing is probably poor, but I can't regret kissing you."

Kelly drew in a deep breath. With his words, reality crashed in around her. Who they were—why they were together. This wasn't a date, and they weren't a couple. She was helping out a friend, nothing more. She didn't do relationships. And Tanner—well, she didn't know all that much about him except that he was in the middle of a $100-million construction job and had just brought an infant into his life.

She took a step back. "I agree with both sentiments," she said. "The timing is less than perfect. Everything about your life is changing, and the last thing you need right now is a woman getting in the way."

"That's my excuse. What's yours?"

Kelly didn't really have one except she'd fallen in the habit of being alone. Right now she couldn't think why.

"I would like to help you with Lia, but it will get complicated if we're more than friends," she said.

She held her breath, then relaxed when he seemed to accept her explanation.

"So now what?" he asked, shoving his hands into his rear pockets. She tried not to notice how the action pulled the material of his jeans tight. Thank goodness she'd been called to work. If not, they might have acted out her fantasy of doing it in the kitchen.

"Now we agree to keep it simple. Friends. Good friends."

"I get the message. No more kissing." His mouth tightened. "But I'll be thinking about it, Kelly. Probably for longer than I should."

She swallowed. "Yeah. Me, too. I've got to go."

She collected her purse and walked out of the house. When she got in her car, she found her gaze drawn to the front door. What would it be like to know that after she'd safely delivered her patient's baby she would be returning here? Not just as Tanner's friend, but as someone important to him?

She didn't have any answers, she told herself as she backed out of the driveway. Nor were they necessary. For now she and Tanner would keep things simple—they would be friends. In time...

Here Kelly wasn't so sure. In time, what? Maybe she would have to figure out why she'd spent all her adult life running from relationships. Maybe she could figure out what was wrong with her. As a child and a teenager, she'd always planned on getting married and having a family. What had happened to that dream? Was it too late to get it back, or was she destined to spend the rest of her life alone?

"Tell me good news, Artie," Tanner said as his foreman slumped into the opposite chair.

"It's all good, boss," the short, stocky man said with a grin. He gestured with his unlit cigar. "We're sticking to your revised schedule, so we're catching up a little each week. I've been calling suppliers, and for once they're getting it right. If this keeps up, we'll coast right up to our deadline. Oh, and the toilet problem is fixed."

Tanner let out the breath he'd been holding. For a while he hadn't been sure they were going to come in on time, let alone on budget. Having the funding pulled when he was more than a third of the way through the project had about done him in. Between having to pay for labor and delivered supplies while trying to stall other orders, he'd been within days of going under.

He leaned back in his chair. The situation had been unavoidable, he reminded himself. He always paid for many of his materials up front. Suppliers gave him a discount that way, and that discount had been figured into his bid on the project. Labor costs were paid as incurred. Most large projects required loans to float the costs of building until the general contractor was paid, but this time Tanner had decided to use his own money. He had enough, as long as the regular funding came through. Who could have predicted that one of the executives would embezzle the foundation's money?

"It's November 21 now," Artie was saying. "The exterior painting was finished before the first snowfall, just like we planned. The inside work is going faster than expected." He held up a hand before Tanner could interrupt. "Every department is making sure there are inspections and quality checks every step of the way. No one is going to shortcut on this project."

"Good, because you know the rule." Tanner made a practice of firing any individual or company who cut corners. Everything was built to code, with the finest materials available.

Artie grabbed his clipboard and stood up. "That's it, boss. Now I'm gonna go explain to the electrical contractor that hospitals need a lot of plugs. They're saying we made a mistake in the design. No one needs that many plugs in each room. Not to worry. I know the design's right, and by the time I'm done with them, they're gonna know it, too. Gotta burn some calories with a little whoop-ass before Thanksgiving."

He gave a wave and stomped out of the room. Tanner grinned. Artie might not be the most refined guy in the world, but he got the job done.

Maybe he should get a turkey for Thanksgiving, Tanner thought. Lia was too little to eat it this year, of course, but the rest of her childhood was on him. If he didn't provide turkey and all the fixings, she would miss out on a special tradition. During his childhood in foster care, it had been hit or miss, and he didn't want Lia to go a single year without that special day. Ryan and Patricia were taking the kids to a resort in northern California for the weekend, so Lia was the only family he'd have around on Thanksgiving. And he was hers.

He was about to turn on his computer and start checking scheduling, when someone else walked into his office. He glanced up and saw his brother.

"How's life?" Ryan asked as he settled into the chair Artie had vacated. "Did you get much sleep this weekend?"

"More than I thought. Lia wakes up every few hours, but then she goes right back to sleep. The baby nurse Patricia recommended is great. She calls me every couple of hours just to let me know that things are going well at home."

"Sounds like you have it under control."

Tanner nodded. "Here, too, Ryan. I know you've been worried, but the project is on schedule."

Some of the tension in his brother's face eased. "I knew I could count on you."

"You can also count on me to take the kids when you and Patricia head off on your second honeymoon next month. I can handle them and Lia, too."

Ryan laughed. "Yeah, right. In your dreams. Your daughter is sleeping her life away right now, but that changes. Besides, we've already made other arrangements. My three are going to be well looked after."

"If you're sure," Tanner said. "I'll be happy to take them."

"Worry about your own right now." Ryan rose and shook his brother's hand. "Congratulations again. Both on the project and on Lia."

"Thanks. Have a good time in Maine."

Tanner watched his brother leave, but instead of returning his attention to his computer, he rose and crossed to the window. His temporary office was going to eventually be the lab. Right now scaffolding obscured most of the view, but he could see out. It was a sunny autumn day, with temperatures near fifty. The dusting of snow had melted. But he didn't see the leaves blanketing the hospital grounds. Instead he pictured his daughter sleeping peacefully in her crib.

He was flying by the seat of his pants with her— which was what he'd done with most of his life. When he'd bought the business, he'd been afraid he would fail completely and publicly, but he hadn't—despite his history of screwing up.

Maybe he was maturing. It was bound to happen eventually. His business was successful, and so far fatherhood was even better than he'd thought it would be. He loved Lia, and he was willing to do whatever he had to so that he could give her a decent life.

Thinking of Lia made him think of Kelly because for some reason they were linked together in his brain. And thinking of Kelly made him remember the kiss they'd shared on Sunday. The kiss he hadn't been able to forget.

He was done screwing up, he reminded himself. Which meant no more weekend flings with women like Lucy Ames. He had to go for someone right or not bother. When he'd first decided to take Lia, he'd told himself he wasn't going to do the relationship thing at all. That would be easier. But now he wasn't so sure. He might be willing to give it a try if it meant being with someone special…someone like Kelly.

Chapter 8

"So how's my favorite girl in the world?"

Kelly leaned back in her chair and smiled. "I'm great, Dad. How are you?"

"Not bad for an old man."

Kelly shifted the phone so it nestled between her shoulder and her ear as she slipped off her pumps. She'd spent most of the on her feet. For once she hadn't been interrupted by one of her patients giving birth, so she'd actually gotten through her regular appointments. Now it was nearly six on Wednesday evening, and the office was quiet.

"You're not old. You're just getting started."

"I like to think so," Daniel Hall answered. "But some mornings it's tough to pull on my sweats and go jogging. The boys are starting to beat me."

"I don't believe that."

Her father was as fit today as he had been when she was a little girl. He ran every morning with the high school athletes. Some of them were members of his church, but most weren't. Daniel had been a fixture on the morning exercise scene through hundreds of students' lives. He was always available to listen, or give advice if asked. More than one crisis had been averted because the kids involved had gone to Daniel. Somehow a man out jogging and sweating wasn't nearly as scary as approaching a minister of a church.

"Tell me what's going on in your life," her father said. "I know you're keeping busy."

"Of course. It comes with the job." She told him a little about work, then brought him up-to-date on the situation with Tanner and Lia.

Daniel chuckled. "A newborn in the house and a girl at that. I can relate to his shock. You weren't at all what I expected. You were pretty enough, but those diapers. I always wondered how something so small and sweet could produce something so nasty."

"Oh, Dad. You need to let the diaper thing go."

"I can't. I'm scarred for life."

She grinned. "I think Tanner is going to be, as well. He's still getting used to the challenges and the responsibility. Lia is a sweet baby, but it's changed everything for him. He's involved with a huge construction project at the hospital, and now he's got a daughter."

"He's going to find that she's the greatest joy of his life," he said. "Just like you're mine."

"Thanks." As always, his loving support made her feel safe inside. Even if her father had stopped being proud of her when she'd gotten pregnant, she never doubted that he loved her.

"So," Daniel said. "Tell me about this Tanner Malone. He sounds like a decent guy. Is he cute?"

"Oh, Dad."

"That's two 'oh, Da-ads' me in one conversation. What am I doing wrong?"

"Nothing. It's just that you're matchmaking, and it's not like that between Tanner and me." She forced herself *not* to think of the kiss they'd shared. Despite the fact that memories of it haunted the past two nights...not to mention her days.

"So there's no spark between you two? Is *spark* the right word, or am I dating myself?"

"No one says spark much anymore," she said, then tried to figure out how to answer the question without actually lying. "As for Tanner and me, we're just friends. Neither of us are in a place where we'd be comfortable having a relationship. He has a new baby and his work, and I'm always swamped with my practice."

There was a long pause; then her father sighed. Kelly's hand tightened on the receiver. She hated that sigh—she knew it meant she'd disappointed him in some way.

"Dad?"

"I don't understand why you're still hiding," he said at last. "When you were younger and medical school kept you busy, I thought things would change in time. You've done so well. How can I not be proud of you? But you've been in practice for three years. Other doctors manage to find time to have a life. Why not you? Why are you making excuses?"

"It's not like that," Kelly said, stumbling over the words. Hiding? Is that what her father thought?

"Maybe it's not surprising," Daniel went on. "After all, you grew up without a mother, but more important, you grew up without being able to see a loving marriage firsthand. I worried about that, and many times I thought it would be better if I remarried. Except I could never find someone I loved as much as I had loved your mother."

"Daddy, you did a great job," she told him. "No daughter could have asked for a better father. I never missed having a mother because you were always there for me." It was true. When there were awkward "girl" things to discuss, her father had always sensed her needs and had one of their family friends take her out to lunch so she could talk.

"I hope that's true," he said. "But I wish you could have seen the two of us together. Loving her changed my life. It changed me. I was a better person when I was with her. She was the light of my life—my other half—and I still miss her."

"I know you do."

"Do you? You've heard me talk, but you have no memories of your mother. I want so much for you, Kelly. I want you to be happy in your work, but I also want you to be happy in your personal life. You don't have to sacrifice everything all the time. Sometimes it's okay just to be."

"I'm fine," she insisted, trying not to think about her sterile apartment or the fact that she hadn't been on a date in several years.

"If you're sure, then I won't interfere. I love you, Kelly. I hope you know that. I just want what's best for you."

"I know, Dad. I love you, too."

"Call me in a few days?"

"I promise. Bye."

She hung up the phone. But it was a long time before she collected her purse and left the office. All the way to her car and even as she drove out of the empty parking lot, she thought about what her father had said to her. That she was hiding.

Was he right? Was that what she'd been doing all these years? Thinking about it, she could see that it was a hard habit to break. She'd been determined to maintain her grades when she'd started college. As a premed, biochemistry major, there hadn't been much time for anything except studying. That first year of school, when everyone else had been making friends and joining clubs, Kelly had buried herself in her books. When she did surface, it was to deal with the guilt of having given up her daughter.

The past returned and with it the moment on Christmas morning when she'd told her father that she was pregnant and then had watched the light go out of his eyes. No matter how hard she'd studied or what she'd achieved later, she'd never been able to make the light come back. When she'd finally realized it never would, it had been the only time in her life when she'd wanted to die.

The other kids in college had decorated their dorm rooms for Christmas, but not Kelly. She told herself it was out of respect for her Jewish roommate, but when she managed to get a single room a couple of years later, she still couldn't bring herself to do it. "Too busy" was the mantra in her head whenever she walked past Christmas displays in stores. After college, medical school, then residency. Now this would be her third Christmas in Honeygrove, and she had continued to be "too busy" to make her apartment feel like a home.

Kelly drew in a deep breath. Part of the reason she'd worked so hard had been because of her father, but the rest of it had been because of her daughter. It was as if she had to keep proving that her decision to give up Annie

Jane was the right one. If she turned out to be a good doctor, then her daughter would understand why she'd made the choice she had. Except deep in her heart Kelly still believed she'd taken the easy way out.

Despite what her father had said all those years ago and despite what Tanner had told her over the weekend, she knew they could have made it. Oh, their lives might not have been full of material things. She would have had a baby and been working while going to school part time. But they would have survived. At least then she wouldn't always wonder how it could have been.

As she wondered now. Except all the wondering in the world didn't change the past. She'd made her choice and there was no going back.

So why was she still hiding?

Her father's question returned to her. She knew there was truth in his words. Was it because she hadn't paid her debt? Was it fear or simply habit? And if she accepted that she was hiding, how much of life had already passed her by? It was too late to change the past, but could she still change her future?

"Now I'm happy to stay a little longer," Gabby Dawson told Tanner as she slipped on her coat. "Your Lia is about the best baby I've ever seen. So sweet and those pretty eyes. Just like yours. She's going to be a beauty when she grows up."

"Tell me about it. I'm going to have to get a really big stick to scare off all the boys in the neighborhood." Tanner glanced down at the sleeping infant. "We'll just start calling you 'Trouble' as soon as you hit fourteen. How does that sound, little girl?"

Lia slept on, oblivious of being the subject of conversation.

"We'll be fine," he told Gabby.

"All right then. I'll be off. You're sure you won't need me over the weekend?"

"Absolutely. Go enjoy Thanksgiving with your husband."

The doorbell rang. "I'll get that on my way out," Gabby called as she headed for the stairs. "You have a nice evening, Tanner."

"I will," he said as he followed her into the living room. Despite her fiftysomething years, she moved with quick grace. She was a whiz with Lia, and Tanner was grateful Patricia had recommended her. Until his daughter was old enough to come to the office with him, or attend regular day care, he could rest easy with Nurse Gabby in charge.

"It's Dr. Hall," Gabby said as she pulled open the front door. "I was just leaving," she told Kelly. "Lia has been an angel. I doubt she'll give you a minute's trouble. Now you two have a happy Thanksgiving."

She gave a quick wave and was gone.

Kelly stared after her. "She reminds me of Robin Williams in that movie *Mrs. Doubtfire*, although she's a lot prettier."

"And she doesn't have the accent. So you think my baby nurse is a cross-dresser?"

Kelly laughed. "No, that's not what I meant. She's just a warm, caring person, like that character." She set her purse on the small table by the front door. "How was your day?"

"Good." But not as good as she looked, he thought.

Tanner had to shove his hands into his pockets to keep

from walking over to her and pulling her into his arms. She wore a navy suit with a silky pink blouse. High heels made her legs look even longer than usual. She'd pulled her hair back into a fancy twist. From head to toe, she was a class act.

He, on the other hand, had barely walked in the door fifteen minutes ago. He hadn't even had a chance to shower.

"What?" she asked. "You're staring at me. Do I have ink on my nose or something?"

"Not at all. I was just noticing that you look terrific, while I had a close encounter with a paint machine." He turned slowly to show her his paint-splattered back. "We come from two different worlds—that's for sure."

"Is that bad?"

"No. But I've been thinking." He rocked back on his heels. He didn't want to talk about this with her, but he didn't have a choice. "You've got a life of your own, and I've sort of taken it over. You've been here every night, except when you had to deliver a baby. You've been a great friend, but I don't want to take advantage of that."

"You're not. I've been happy to help." She folded her arms over her chest. "You're throwing me out, aren't you?"

Tanner didn't know how to answer. Despite the fact that he was dirty and tired, he still wanted her. He'd wanted her before they'd ever kissed, but now that he'd experienced the passion possible between them, his desire had only increased. She was an incredible woman—everything a man could want. Smart, successful, caring, warm, sexy as hell and completely out of his league.

He'd played the game enough times to know when it was going to work and when it wasn't. Between their differences in career and his status as a new father, he didn't stand a chance with her. Under different circumstances, he might have given it a run anyway, figuring something short term would be better than nothing at all. Except he wasn't comfortable with that. Not only because of Lia, but because Kelly was someone he cared about and he didn't want to play games with her.

"I'm not throwing you out," he said at last. "You're welcome to stay as long as you'd like. However, I don't want to take advantage of you or cramp your style."

She stared at him. Her hazel-brown eyes were wide and clear as she studied him, obviously assessing the truth of his words. "And if I told you I didn't have enough of a personal life to warrant a style?"

"Then I'd ask you if you'd like to join me and Lia tomorrow for Thanksgiving dinner. But I have to warn you, I'm making it, and I have no idea what I'm doing."

"You're making it?"

He led her to the kitchen and opened the fridge. "I stopped at the store on the way home. I thought this would be a good year to practice, before Lia's old enough to realize her dad's an idiot. I won't have time to cook every day, but I figure I can make an effort for the big holidays."

Kelly reached inside the fridge and knocked on the turkey. "It's still frozen solid. If you're going to cook that tomorrow, you'll need to thaw it in a cold-water bath overnight. It takes a few days to thaw in the refrigerator."

"I told you I have no idea what I'm doing. How do you know these things?"

She laughed. "I grew up without a mother, with a dad who was busy with his congregation. I did our cooking from the time I was about twelve. Except when kindly parishioners cooked for us. Let's get this turkey in water—I'll come over early tomorrow to help."

Ten minutes later, he dried his hands and said, "Now, how about a glass of wine?"

"Red or white?"

"Whichever you'd prefer."

She smiled. "We could mix them together and make our own special blend."

He shuddered. "No, thank you."

She laughed. "I think red tonight," she told him as she slid onto one of the stools by the counter.

"Red it is."

He pulled a cabernet from the built-in wine rack, then put it back and drew out a merlot. He held up the bottle, and when she nodded, he started to open it.

"So was that really about me, when you tried to send me away?" she asked. "Are you genuinely concerned about my personal life, or were you thinking of your own? While I don't have a style, I'm guessing yours had been refined by years of practice."

He set the open wine in front of her and collected two glasses. "I had one once. I don't anymore."

"So you've pulled yourself out of the dating game. Are hearts breaking all over Honeygrove?"

"Maybe one or two."

"Let me guess. Young, stunning women with aspirations to be models or actresses?"

He wasn't sure if she was teasing or insulting him. "Attractiveness helps, but it's not the only requirement."

"And none of them ever convinced you to walk down the aisle?"

"A few tried," he admitted as he poured them each a

glass of wine. "But I never wanted that. I'm more the se-rial monogamy type. It's all I know."

Her expression turned serious. "What do you mean?"

"Ryan and I grew up in foster homes. We were con-sidered too old to adopt. Some of the time we were in the same family, but just as often we were split up. It was tough."

She frowned. "I can't even imagine. I lived in the same house and slept in the same room until I left for college. In fact, it's still there now. My dad didn't even turn it into a guest room. Not that he's keeping it as a shrine or anything, but there are already enough spare rooms. I know it's waiting for me whenever I go back to visit."

"That would have been nice," he said as he touched his glass to hers, then took a sip of the wine. "But Ryan and I moved around a lot. When we were in the same house, we often talked about what it would have been like if our parents hadn't been killed. Ryan could remember more than I could. He wanted to re-create what he'd lost, which is one of the reasons he married Patricia. She wanted to make a home, and he needed that."

She looked at him. "But you went in a different di-rection. Because you didn't know what a normal family life looked like?"

"Maybe."

"I understand that completely. I mean my father loved me and was always there for me, but it was just the two of us. I never had a mother—she died giving birth to me."

"Is that why you became an obstetrician? So you could save other women?"

Kelly blinked several times. "I don't think so. I never thought about it that way." She shrugged. "It's funny. I talked to my father earlier, and he was discussing this very topic. He said he felt badly that I'd never had the experience of watching a loving marriage at work. He thinks that's one of the reasons I'm not married myself."

"Is it?"

"I don't know that answer, either."

"I'm not sure watching would have helped," he said. "I saw plenty of married couples. Some got along great, but others—" He shook his head. "They were a disaster."

"Ryan and Patricia have always seemed very happy to me."

He leaned against the counter. "He thinks the world of her."

She leaned forward and rested her elbows on the counter. "Ryan's a lucky man—he's married to a wonderful woman."

Tanner couldn't help wondering why some man hadn't gotten lucky enough to snag Kelly. She was incredible. It had to be by choice that she was single.

She took another sip of wine. "You said that your style was serial monogamy, but what do you like in a woman? Aside from her being incredibly beautiful."

"I'm going to ignore that last comment. I already said that beauty isn't all that important to me."

"Uh-huh." She didn't sound the least bit convinced.

Tanner was intrigued by the question. He liked that Kelly wanted to know about his favorite "type." While it wasn't a guarantee that she was interested, it did indicate that she'd given him a little thought.

"What do I like in a woman?" He grinned. "You want the absolute truth or the politically correct version?"

"Oh, absolute truth."

"Can you handle it?"

The corners of her mouth turned up. "Mr. Malone, if

you're attempting to challenge me, do not for a moment underestimate my abilities."

He leaned forward, resting his forearms on the counter. Their faces were only inches apart. He could see the flecks of gold in her eyes and several tiny freckles on her nose. Her lips were a temptation he warned himself to avoid.

"I like an equal combination of intelligence, humor and trashy lingerie. Leather isn't a requirement, but black or red lace is."

Her well-shaped mouth fell open as her eyes widened in shock. "Oh my."

"You asked."

"So I did." She licked her lips. "And how successful are you at achieving your ideal?"

"The trashy underwear is pretty easy. It's the intelligence and humor that I have trouble with. I'm not in the right profession for women like that to come calling."

"I don't understand."

He straightened. "I'm a contractor," he said bluntly. "I make enough money, but I wear jeans, not suits. Yeah, I have a degree, but I got it going to school at night. Actually I had a scholarship, but I screwed up partying too much my freshman year and got kicked out. I didn't have any skills, so I got a grunt job working for a contractor. Ten years later I had a degree and was a partner. Two years after that, I bought him out and changed the name."

"Impressive."

"Is it?" He shrugged. "I'm just some guy from the wrong side of the tracks. I prefer movies and sports to ballet and opera, although I do like the theater. I like good wine, but I'm not a snob about it. In my opinion beer and potato chips are a perfectly acceptable food group."

"None of that sounds bad to me," she said.

He wanted to believe her. He wanted to think they were doing more than just playing, but he knew that wasn't the case. When Kelly made up her mind to get involved, it would be with another doctor or a lawyer, or maybe some upper-level corporate executive.

"So tell me about your Mr. Right. He's rich and successful, with a bunch of degrees."

She straightened. "You seem to have more answers than I do. I haven't thought much about Mr. Right, or Mr. Anybody. I don't really date much. Work keeps me busy."

"Not that busy. You're way too pretty and successful not to have a bunch of men hanging around you."

She surprised him by blushing. Color climbed up her cheeks, and she looked away. "Yet I remain surprisingly unfettered by men. It's one of life's great mysteries."

I want to change that. But he only thought the words, he didn't say them.

Nor did he move closer, even though he wanted to.

The kitchen seemed to shrink in size, and all he could think about was taking her in his arms and kissing her. He wanted to feel her next to him again. He wanted her tall, lean body pressed against him, her breasts flattening against his chest. He wanted to get hard and rub his arousal against her belly, then—

"I have to warn you that I'm only yours for the next two weeks," she said. "After that, my time has been committed to someone else."

"I see." He tried to ignore the flare of jealousy burning inside of him. An old boyfriend returning?

"Yes, I'm going to be involved in a rather complex relationship. There will be four of us all together."

He caught the light of laughter in her eyes. "Four of you, huh? Sounds kinky."

"Actually, it's going to be a lot of fun. I'm taking care of your niece and nephews while Ryan and Patricia run off on their second honeymoon."

"You are?" They'd asked Kelly?

"Don't sound so surprised. I'll remind you that I've been the one helping you out with Lia. I do know something about children."

"It's not that. I told them I could still do it."

She laughed. "You're incredibly optimistic. Lia isn't going to be sleeping this much forever. In the next couple of weeks, she's going to be awake more and more. You'll have your hands full. You don't need three other kids tossed into the mix."

"We could join our forces together," he said impulsively. "You're staying at Ryan's, right? I could bring Lia and stay with you. I know my niece and nephews pretty well, and they can be challenging."

As he waited for Kelly to answer, he told himself he was being crazy. Even if she wanted him along, they were already spending too much time together. Did he really want to head into this dangerous territory?

"I'd like that," she said.

As she spoke the words, something clicked into place inside of him. He had a bad feeling he was already in too deep and it was too late to think about getting out now. The only course of action left to him was to follow this road to the end. Maybe, for once in his life, he was going to get it right.

"Let me," Kelly said the following evening when Lia began to fuss in her carrier on the kitchen counter. They were cleaning up after a surprisingly delicious Thanksgiving dinner, and Kelly could use some space between her and Tanner. Doing dishes side by side was entirely too domestic. Every time she reached toward the dish rack, she brushed his broad shoulder, and warmth suffused her body from the point of contact.

She dried her hands and reached for the crying infant. "What's the matter, little princess? Are you hungry?"

"Go sit down," Tanner said. "I'll bring you her bottle."

Fifteen minutes later, Lia had been fed and changed. Kelly settled with the baby in the rocking chair, which Tanner had moved to the living room early that afternoon. She couldn't bring herself to put Lia to bed just yet. Her slight weight and small movements filled Kelly with equal parts contentment and yearning. Was there anything more heartwarming than holding a baby? Anything more heartbreaking than letting her go?

Snow had begun to fall outside, but inside the house was cozy, warm and quiet.

She heard a movement in the doorway and looked up to see Tanner watching her. Their gazes met and held for one long moment before he cleared his throat and shifted away.

"I picked up a few other things when I was at the store yesterday." He opened the door to the closet under the stairs, disappeared inside, then reappeared carrying a long, narrow box and a plastic bag.

"You bought a Christmas tree?" she asked.

"An artificial one. I didn't know if Lia could be around a real tree yet."

"They're not toxic, but there are a lot of choking hazards. Next year you'll really have to worry. She'll be crawling for sure, maybe even walking, and those shiny lights and ornaments will be irresistible."

A lot could happen in a year, she thought. Would they

still be friends? Would she be around when Lia took her first steps? Tanner might even be married. Lia could have a new mom. To hide the sudden tears in her eyes, Kelly leaned down to place a kiss on the baby's head.

"Before my parents died, we used to decorate for Christmas on Thanksgiving night. I thought it would be a nice to carry on the tradition for Lia." He efficiently snapped together the small tree. "I'll take a picture of her every year in front of the tree. Do you think she'll like that?"

"Until she's a teenager. Then she'll hate it, but then she'll love it again when she's an adult. Such is the circle of life."

She watched him decorate, aware that she was allowing herself to be entirely too charmed by this man. He placed an ornament, stepped back, then adjusted it by an inch to the right or left before reaching for the next.

He had turned his life upside down for the baby in her arms. And once he'd made the commitment, he had thrown himself into being a father with enthusiasm. She never would have imagined that he would be thoughtful enough to consider the importance of traditions in a child's life.

She wouldn't have imagined a lot of things. Especially not how quickly her feelings could grow.

Chapter 9

The Women's Center Clinic took up half the second floor of a small, older office building in downtown Honeygrove. Kelly spent every other Thursday afternoon and evening at the clinic, donating her time. Her office here, with its scarred wooden desk and a cracked window, was a far cry from her spacious suite back at her regular practice, but Kelly didn't mind. Her purpose was to provide quality health care for those who wouldn't otherwise be able to receive it.

"All right, Granny Bea," Kelly said as she patted the older woman's arm. "Those supplements are working. According to the latest test, you have the bones of a seventeen-year-old runner."

The white-haired grandmother grinned at her. "You're exaggerating, Dr. Kelly, and we both know it."

"Maybe a little, but you're doing better. Keep taking

those pills. Tell Sharon, the nurse up front, to give you another refill. Be faithful, all right?"

The tiny woman, a little bent but still in good physical condition, rose to her feet. She used a cane to help her balance. "You're a good girl," Granny Bea said. "I appreciate that you worry about me."

"Of course I do. You have my number, right?" Kelly made sure all her clinic patients had her number. If there was an emergency, most of them wouldn't bother going to a hospital. Large institutions hadn't been kind to the women in this neighborhood.

Granny Bea patted her purse. "Right behind my driver's license." She chuckled. "Not that I drive anymore, but I figure if I win the lottery one day, I want to be current so I can go right out and buy a big Mercedes. A black one."

"I can't wait to see you behind the wheel."

Granny Bea was still laughing as she walked to the door. "See you in six months, Dr. Kelly. You take care of yourself."

"Granny Bea," Kelly called. "You know the rule."

The elderly lady shook her head. "Silly child. You really think I'm doing anything like that, with my husband gone to his reward nearly ten years ago."

"You never know, Granny Bea. If you win the lottery, you're going to find yourself chasing away young men with your cane. I want you to be prepared."

"I think it's foolish. I only use them for water balloons with my grandson. Of course he thinks I'm incredibly hip for such an old lady."

She reached into the large jar of condoms Kelly kept by the door. One of the rules of both her clinic and her private practice was that every patient had to take a handful home. She didn't want anyone telling her she'd gotten pregnant or caught a sexually transmitted disease because she didn't have any handy protection.

"Bye, Granny Bea."

"Bye, child. You take care and find yourself a man one of these days."

Kelly grinned. "Yes, ma'am."

She was still smiling when she walked into the first examining room.

"Hi, Dr. Kelly," Corina said from her seat on the table.

"How are you feeling?"

"Fat." Corina wrinkled her nose. "I can't believe how huge I am."

"Hey, you're eight months pregnant. What did you expect?"

"I'm the size of the space shuttle."

Kelly studied the seventeen-year-old's round belly. "Generally women don't make space shuttle size until their ninth month. You're more like the nose cone."

"Very funny."

"I am," Kelly agreed cheerfully. "How are you feeling otherwise?"

While Corina told of swelling and the occasional aches and pains of a basically textbook pregnancy, Kelly examined her. Unfortunately Corina hadn't become a patient until after she was pregnant, so the free condoms hadn't been available in time. Now this pretty, intelligent young woman faced motherhood a few months before she was supposed to be graduating from high school.

"Tell me what you're eating," Kelly said.

Corina rolled her eyes. "Three servings of protein, one with each meal. Milk with every meal. Fresh vegetables, four servings, and at least two fruits. No sodas, only one candy bar every couple of days."

"You're still getting the food stamps?"

Corina nodded. Her long black braids swayed with the movement. She had beautiful wide, brown eyes and skin the color of café au lait.

"I keep them at a friend's house," Corina said. "And I only shop for a couple of days at a time. My mom doesn't know about them."

"Good."

The teenager's mother had a drug problem, not to mention a fondness for alcohol. There wasn't much money left for things like food and heat. Until Kelly had stepped in, Corina had often gone without a decent meal for days at a time.

"How's school?" Kelly asked.

"Okay. I'm studying hard. I've been talking to my teachers about maybe taking my midterms early, so that I don't miss them. The baby's due that week."

"I'm glad you're planning ahead, but you do know that the baby might be late, right? This is your first, and they like to take their time."

"I know. I just want to be prepared." Corina's chin dropped. "I'm thinking of getting a job when I graduate."

"For the summer, you mean?"

"Not exactly."

Kelly's heart froze. As the teenager continued to avoid looking at her, her concern grew. "I thought you were going to college in the fall. You have that scholarship to Stanford. Corina, that's an incredible opportunity. You're one of the smartest young women I've ever met. You have a chance to be anything you want. Why would you turn your back on that?"

The girl shrugged. "I wouldn't, exactly."

"Then what's going on?"

Corina shrugged again.

Kelly struggled for patience. "If you stay here, you'll always be trapped by your past. Look around you. Is this what you want for yourself? Your mother has been on drugs since she was twelve. You don't know who your father is. You have half brothers and sisters scattered who knows where. When you leave this town, you can be anyone you want. Your past stops here, and you only have to worry about your future. You have dreams—I know you do. We've talked about them. Why don't you want the chance to make them come true?"

Corina blinked back tears. "I want that so much," she whispered. "But it's not like you think. All my friends… they keep their babies. They stay here and find a life. They've been telling me that I'm a bad person for wanting to give up my baby. Half of them won't even speak to me anymore. They're saying if I was a real woman, I couldn't give up my child, and that I'm selfish and wrong."

Tears flowed in earnest now. Corina brushed them away. "Dr. Kelly, I want to be just like you. I want to go to medical school and make something of myself. Then I want to come back to a place like this and save people's lives. I can't do that with a baby. I can't. I want to go to college, but now I'm afraid that it's wrong to want so much. Maybe they're right. Maybe I should stay here and just get a job. Maybe learn to do hair or something."

For Kelly, listening to Corina was like staring into the mirror of her own past. She wasn't sure what to think, let alone say.

"Dr. Kelly? You have to tell me what to do."

Kelly pressed her lips together. Who was she to give

answers? She'd messed up her own life so much she hadn't been on a date in years. She was afraid to allow herself any joy because she felt she didn't deserve it. According to her father, she was hiding behind a busy schedule. And she suspected he was right.

She knew the past had a way of catching up with a person, but she hadn't expected it to come in the form of a lost, frightened seventeen-year-old.

Kelly opened her mouth to speak, but she couldn't find any words. Just then she heard a text message notification. Grateful for the interruption, she glanced down at the display.

"It's the hospital," she said, trying to keep the relief out of her voice. "I have to call them."

When she made the call, she was told about an emergency with one of her patients. She hurried back into the examining room.

"I have to go," she said, telling herself there was no need to feel guilty. "Make an appointment for two weeks and we'll talk then, all right?"

Corina was still crying.

"I'm sorry," Kelly said. "It's an emergency. Remind Sharon to give you your vitamins. You're doing great. Hang in there."

What pitiful advice, Kelly thought as she ran down the stairs and raced toward her car. The worst thing Corina could do was to be like her.

As she drove toward the hospital, Kelly vowed she would make it up to the girl. Just as soon as she figured out how.

Tanner felt as if he'd stumbled into an old master's painting. Kelly sat in the rocking chair in the corner, holding Lia in her arms. Subtle light brought out the gold in Kelly's hair and made her skin glow. Lia was awake and staring up into Kelly's eyes.

Mother and child, he thought as he continued to study them. The same thought had crossed his mind on Thanksgiving. A few weeks ago he couldn't have imagined having either of them in his life. Now he didn't know what his world would be like without them.

Kelly looked up at him. "You're not working," she said. "The wallpaper isn't going to hang itself. Or are you waiting for me to offer?"

"No, I'll do it."

She smiled, and some of his tension eased. When Kelly had first arrived a couple of hours before, she'd been quiet and withdrawn. Normally she enjoyed talking about her day, but this time all she'd said was that she'd had an emergency at the hospital and that it had cut into her time at the clinic. She'd gone back to see as many patients as possible, but some hadn't been able to wait for her.

Tanner knew there was something else bothering her, but he wasn't going to pry. When she wanted to talk, he would listen. Until then, he was content to enjoy her company.

He checked the back of the border print he held. It was tacky but not too wet, so he climbed the short ladder and carefully smoothed it into place.

"It's crooked," Kelly said helpfully. "And there are about a dozen air pockets."

"Thanks," he muttered, reaching up to adjust the paper. But he'd waited too long and it didn't slide against the wall anymore. He gave a hard shove. Instead of moving, the border print tore. A short piece separated from the rest and fluttered to the floor.

"Don't say anything," he commanded as he ripped off the rest of the strip and flung it down. "I hate hanging wallpaper."

Kelly cleared her throat. "Wow, so when you offered to pay me back by wallpapering my house, you were lying. Even I can do better than you."

"Yeah, well, I hate hanging wallpaper. Why can't people just use paint?" He hunched his shoulder and turned to glare at her. "I wasn't lying. I would have done it. I was just hoping you'd let me do something else. Maybe something simple like rewiring your house."

"Or you could have one of your men do it."

He shook his head. "That wouldn't work. It's my debt, so I have to pay you back."

"No debt," she said softly. "We're friends, Tanner. I'm happy to help."

She was tall and athletic, not at all petite or dainty, yet she was the most feminine woman he'd ever known. The hands holding his daughter were strong and capable. She was someone he could depend on, and there hadn't been many types like that in his life.

"I can't believe I'm doing this," he said, snagging one of the fallen strips of border print.

"Hanging paper?"

"No, hanging a print that's ballerina teddy bears. It's so girly."

Kelly laughed. "You have a daughter. Get used to the girl thing."

"I guess. I even ordered curtains and the matching lamp. The good news is that when I told Lia about it, she was really happy."

"Oh? How did you know this?"

"She smiled at me." He made the statement faintly defensively, but he knew that she'd been smiling at him. Her lips had curved and everything.

"Tanner, she's two weeks old. She can't smile. It was gas."

"It was not."

"Right." Her look and her tone were indulgent.

He shifted his attention to his daughter. Two weeks. Was that all the time it had been? It felt longer.

"She still doesn't have any toys," he said. "I have to find time to get some before Christmas."

Kelly shifted Lia and crossed her legs. "Speaking of buying things for your daughter, I've been thinking about throwing you a baby shower."

"Why?"

She grinned. "Don't look so panicked. It won't hurt… much. Actually the shower isn't for you—it's for Lia. So many people want to see her, and probably see her with you. It would be a lot of fun. We can make it a combination Christmas party/baby shower. We could register you at the baby store and at a toy store. What do you think?"

"Why?"

"You keep asking that. It's a girl thing. Trust me. I'll take care of everything. Just say yes."

He had a bad feeling he was going to regret it, but he muttered, "Yes," then asked if anything strange happened at baby showers.

"Define *strange*," she told him.

"Never mind."

"We'll need to pick a date so that I can mail out invitations. We can't do it this coming weekend because I can't plan that fast. Next weekend is booked. I'll have Ryan's kids until Sunday evening. What about three weeks from today, on the Friday evening before Christmas?"

"Whatever." He began measuring out a length of the border print. At least he'd remembered to buy double the amount so that he would have enough, despite the occasional mishap. "I can't believe you're taking Ryan and Patricia's three kids for the weekend."

"I tried to take just a couple of them, but they got pretty insistent that I take all or none. What perfectionists."

He glanced at her. Laughter glittered in her eyes. "You're nothing like I thought you'd be," he told her.

"Meaning?"

"You have a sense of humor. You're human. I thought doctors were stuffy by nature."

"They try to teach us that, but I never had time to fit that particular class into my schedule."

"It's not just that," he said. "You don't act like you're God. You treat people with respect. I thought you'd disapprove of what I do for a living."

She straightened in the rocking chair and stared at him. "How could you think that? Tanner, you're brilliant at what you do. How many people do you know who could coordinate a project of this magnitude? We're not talking about recarpeting a living room. This is a one-hundred-million-dollar project."

"It's just a building. You save lives."

"And without buildings, people would die from exposure. Everyone contributes in a different way. I would never judge someone based on their work."

"Like I said, you're not how I imagined."

"Doctors are real people, too," she said. "If we seem

a little crabby at times, it's just because we had to spend so much time in school."

He looked around the room; then his gaze settled on his daughter, now dozing in Kelly's arms. "I never thought I would see anything like this. You sitting there, holding my daughter. Of course, I never thought I'd have a child."

"How do you like it?"

"She's the best thing that ever happened to me."

Kelly's smile turned tender. "I'm glad. I'm glad you kept her, and I'm glad you two are so happy together."

"Me, too."

He was also glad that Kelly was in his life, but he didn't tell her that. This wasn't the time. Then he wondered if that would ever change. Kelly wasn't for him— even if he was the kind of man who did long-term commitments. Which he didn't. So they would just stay friends, and he would make sure that was enough.

Tanner clutched the handle of the baby carrier so hard, he was afraid he might crack the plastic. This was fine, he told himself. There was nothing to worry about. Except he *was* worried.

He stared around the brightly colored waiting area of the medical office. A parade of animals danced across the walls. There were child-size chairs, as well as those designed for adults, and a collection of toys in the corner. Nothing to fear. So why was there a knot the size of a basketball sitting in the bottom of his stomach?

The office door opened, and Kelly walked in. She wore tailored dark slacks and a red, soft-looking sweater that hugged her curves. The swell of her breasts was

nearly enough to take his mind off his panic. Nearly...
but not completely.

"Sorry I'm late," she said. "I was running behind with
my patients and..." She took one look at him and laughed.
"Relax, Tanner. Lia's the one getting the examination,
not you."

"I wish it was me," he said glumly. "What if there's
something wrong? What if she's sick? What if—"

"Stop!" Kelly said. She took the baby carrier from
him and glanced down. As usual, Lia was sound asleep,
apparently unaware of her father's concern. Kelly took
a seat and patted the cushion next to her.

"You could take a lesson from your daughter," she
said. "Now sit down and take a deep breath."

He glared at her, then perched on the edge of the sofa.
"You're not taking this seriously."

"Of course I am. Lia is here to see her doctor. She's
three weeks old, and Patricia is going out of town tomorrow, so she just wanted to check Lia over. There is every
indication that she's a normal, healthy, thriving infant.
If there is a problem, better to catch it early. Patricia's a
great doctor. You know that."

"I know." He shifted on the sofa. "Sorry. I know I'm
acting crazy."

"You're acting like a worried parent, but in this case,
there's no reason to be."

"You're right." He studied her. "Thanks for being here
with me. I hadn't really intended for you to take time off
work to hold my hand."

She smiled. "Oh, please. That was exactly your intention. No way you would have survived this on your own."

The office door opened again, and a mother with a
young boy walked in. While the woman went to the glass

partition at the reception desk to sign them in, the boy walked over and stared at Lia.

"What's her name?" he asked.

"Lia," Tanner told him.

"I'm John." He held out his hand. There were several tiny stitches along the side of his index finger and across his palm. "Billy and me were playing with a broken bottle and we got cut. I'm better now, but playing with a broken bottle is bad. But Mommy said Santa Claus will forgive me if I clean my room and promise never to do it again."

Kelly smiled at the boy. He couldn't be more than five or six. She scooted forward and stared at the stitches, then pointed to a thin, pale line on her own hand.

"That exact thing happened to me," she said. "I was about your age."

John's brown eyes widened. "Did you have to get stitches, too?"

"I sure did. I cried and cried. I was very sorry I'd ever picked up that piece of glass and I never did it again."

"I didn't cry," John said. Then he glanced at his mom and shrugged. "Well, I did a little."

Tanner found himself caught up in the conversation. Kelly was so easy and natural with the little boy. It was as if she'd known him for years instead of just a few minutes. When John's mother came over to collect him, she smiled an apology.

"Sorry. He's a talker."

"He's very sweet," Kelly told the woman.

It made no sense, Tanner thought. Why on earth hadn't some guy snatched Kelly up before now? She was a prize. Not only was she bright and successful but she had the most giving heart he'd ever seen.

She was different from the kind of woman he usually found himself attracted to. He would bet a month's paycheck that she didn't go for trashy lingerie, nor did she wear much makeup. But he was starting to see the appeal of the natural look, not to mention the fact that thoughts of Kelly in plain cotton had kept him up more than one night.

"What a cutie," Kelly said when John's mother had led him to the other side of the waiting room, where they started on a puzzle.

"You're great with kids. Why didn't you become a pediatrician?"

She didn't say anything, nor did her body language change, but Tanner could tell she'd shut him out as surely as if she'd started building a brick wall between them.

"What?" he asked. "What's wrong? What did I say?"

"Nothing."

"Kelly, don't. Why are you upset?"

"I'm not."

But her gaze avoided his. Then, before he could pursue the matter, a nurse opened the door leading to the examining rooms. "Lia Malone?"

"That's us," Tanner said. He took the carrier from Kelly and stood up.

"It's just through here," the nurse said. She led them into another brightly colored room, this one with a small examining table and too much medical equipment for Tanner to ever be comfortable. The knot in his stomach doubled in size.

"Hi," Patricia said as she entered. She wore a white coat over scrubs. "Don't say it. I'm a mess. My first appointment of the day threw up on me, and I haven't had time to go home and get a change of clothes. I normally keep a spare set here, but they got thrown up on last week and I haven't brought them back. How's my little niece?"

"Great," Tanner said. "I'm sure there's nothing wrong."

"I'm sure, too," Patricia said, her voice reassuring. "I know the first couple of baby visits are nerve-racking on you new parents, but it will get better."

Kelly leaned against the closed door. "Speaking of nerves, how are you holding up?"

Patricia wrinkled her nose. "You mean given the fact that Ryan and I are leaving tomorrow for our second honeymoon, and I still have a million things to do?" She held up her hand to show it was steady. "I'm nervous but only on the inside. I can't believe we're doing this. I'm incredibly happy and a little sad to be leaving the kids. But more happy than sad. I know kids are better off in the long run when their parents take time for themselves as a couple."

"That's what you have to focus on," Kelly said. "I'm going to keep the kids too busy to miss you."

"I, on the other hand, will miss them like crazy," Patricia said. "But I'll get over it."

The two women laughed, but Tanner didn't join in. He was too busy thinking, once again, that his brother had gotten lucky with the woman he'd chosen. Patricia and Ryan had a great life together. They made it look so easy. How did Ryan do that? How had he known when it was right? How had he known that it was okay to commit himself to a particular woman?

Not that it mattered, Tanner told himself. He wasn't the marrying kind. And even if he was, there weren't any likely candidates around.

His gaze settled on Kelly. He already knew that she was

a prize. He also knew that she was out of his league. So there was no point in wishing for what he couldn't have.

Words to live by, he told himself. Words he'd repeated more than once. Words that suddenly didn't seem to ring so true.

Chapter 10

Patricia carefully placed the last of her clothes into her luggage. "I think that's it." She glanced around her and Ryan's bedroom. Her husband was meeting her at the airport. "Okay, so all that's left is the kids. Are you going to be all right with them, Kelly?"

Kelly grinned. "I swear we'll be fine." She began ticking off points on her fingers. "Drew and Lisbeth are still in school. The babysitter will pick them up when they get out, then swing by and get Griffin from day care. She'll stay with them until I get back here. My last appointment is at four." Kelly paused to glance at her watch. It was about twelve thirty now. She had used her lunch break to stop by and wish Patricia bon voyage.

"The sitter can stay late tonight if you get hung up with an emergency," Patricia told her.

"I don't think that's going to happen. This isn't my

weekend on call." Kelly smiled. "One of the reasons I wanted to go into a larger practice was to have the occasional weekend off. So once I leave the office, I'll be with the children until you and Ryan return, all blissful."

"I appreciate you helping out like this," Patricia said. "I don't know what Ryan and I would have done without you. Tanner thinks he could handle Lia and our three, but we all know that's wishful thinking on his part."

Kelly waved aside her thanks. "I'm happy to do it." If anything, the weekend was going to be a lot of fun. She enjoyed being around children, and Tanner had promised to stay at the house, as well. She didn't want to admit to anyone, least of all herself, how her heart beat faster when he was around.

She should have known she couldn't hide the truth from her best friend.

"Something's different, Kelly, and I'm not sure what. Is it being around Tanner's daughter? I know you're spending a lot of time at his house. Are you having thoughts about children of your own?"

Kelly drew in a deep breath. "My thoughts aren't that organized. I'm just... I don't know. Restless maybe." She played with the strap of her purse, which was lying on the bed. "I'm just rambling. Am I keeping my life so full because then there isn't room for a man?"

"I've wondered the same thing about you," Patricia admitted. "I think it's a very good step that you're asking yourself that question."

"Maybe," Kelly said. She couldn't help thinking that at times her life was a cold and empty place. Sometimes she wanted someone else to share things with. Someone she could depend on. Someone she could love who would love her back.

A loud honk sounded from outside. Patricia froze. "Oh no. It's the cab. I have to go. I'm not ready."

Kelly stood up and patted her shoulder. "Don't panic. You're completely prepared. You have your clothes, your shoes and your makeup. Oh, and this." She fingered the lacy strap of Patricia's nightgown. "Nothing else matters."

"I know, but I think I want to scream anyway."

Kelly picked up her purse and Patricia's overnight bag while Patricia closed the larger suitcase. After a quick once-over of the room, they headed for the front door.

On the small porch, they hugged. "Have a wonderful time," Kelly said. "I have the phone numbers if anything happens, but remember that no news is good news. Just enjoy yourselves."

"We will." Patricia waited while the cabdriver loaded her luggage into the trunk, then she slid into the backseat.

Kelly stood watching her until the cab rounded a corner and Patricia was lost from sight, then got into her car. As she pulled out onto the street, she couldn't help thinking about what she and Patricia had talked about. Since high school, she'd gone out of her way to shut men out of her life. During college and medical school, she'd had lots of male friends but no emotionally significant relationships. The question was why?

No one had really hurt her, not unless she counted her father's disappointment. Her high school boyfriend had dumped her when he'd found out she was pregnant, but while she'd been disappointed, she hadn't been devastated. She liked men. She thought many were attractive. There were times when she thought about making love with a certain man, and she found herself feeling desire. So why turn her back on that part of her life?

She didn't have any answers, and then she found herself suddenly thinking about Tanner. She was attracted to the man—no question about that. She wanted to dismiss those feelings by saying he wasn't her type, except she didn't have a type. He was good-looking, and while that was a nice plus, it wasn't the reason she found him appealing. Most of it was the man himself. How was she supposed to resist him when he was so devoted to his daughter? And easy to be with. And funny. And caring.

She sighed. So if Tanner Malone was so all-fired perfect, why wasn't he married? Or why wasn't there a line of women camped outside his house? Was it them, or was it him? Or was it something in his past…something she didn't know about?

So many secrets, Kelly thought. Even though the past was long over, it had a way of hanging around and influencing the present. She knew she was dealing with some issues of her own. When she and Tanner had been in Patricia's waiting room and he'd made a comment about her being so good with kids, she'd felt as if he'd ripped her heart out. It hadn't been his fault, of course. He had no way of knowing how much she'd wanted to be a pediatrician. It had been all she'd wanted when she was a young girl. Except it hadn't worked out that way.

Kelly turned the corner and headed toward her office. As she drove, she tried to figure out what had gone wrong. From the first day she'd entered medical school, every time she'd stepped into a hospital and had seen a young girl, she'd thought about her daughter…the child she'd given up for adoption. She wondered about the girl, about her parents. Eventually the guilt and pain grew to be too much. She decided that she didn't deserve to work with children, so she'd chosen something else. Something that allowed her to be around babies.

"It's not second best," she murmured to herself as she pulled into her parking space. Except she wasn't sure she believed the words. Not that it mattered. It was too late to change now. Sometimes it was important to stand by one's choices, and she knew in her heart that this was one of those times.

"Can we make purple for some of the ornament-shaped cookies?" Tanner asked Saturday afternoon as he scanned the bowls of icing lined up on the kitchen table. "What is that, blue and red, right?" He looked to Kelly for confirmation.

She set down the sheet of cookies she'd just pulled out of the oven and laughed. "Tanner, you already have just about every color that ever existed. Yes, purple is a combination of red and blue, but you don't need to make it. Besides, I don't think there are any more bowls."

"I know where they are," six-year-old Lisbeth said helpfully. "Grandma keeps extra bowls in here." She dragged her chair over to a cupboard and climbed up, then pointed to the top shelf. "Up there."

"What a bright little girl you are," Tanner said as he reached above her head and snagged two more bowls. "Just in case the mixing process runs into trouble." He set the bowls on the table and dumped in a couple of spoonfuls of white icing. "Want to help me with this, Lisbeth?"

"Sure." The young girl returned to her uncle's side and grinned. "Don't add too much color. Remember what happened when you tried to make orange."

"I remember."

Kelly glanced at the sink, which was filled with bowls glowing with rejected colors. It was going to take a week to get everything cleaned up. She smiled. Not that she wanted to be anywhere but here. She was having the best time.

"Aunt Kelly?" Drew, Ryan's oldest, moved up next to her.

"Yes, Drew. Did you want to ice some of the Christmas cookies?" She pointed to the dozens already cooling on the rack. Somehow tripling the recipe for sugar cookies had produced more than she'd expected. They were going to have to freeze a bunch.

"You know they sell cookies at the store," he said, his voice low as if he didn't want his brother and sister to hear. "That would have been easier for you and Uncle Tanner than making them."

Drew was only nine, but he was plenty responsible. His big blue eyes were filled with concern. "I don't want to be rude, but you're not really used to kids, and the three of us are a real handful."

Kelly set the cookie sheet on the counter, then dropped to her knees and pulled Drew close. "You know what? I think I can handle it. But you're a sweetie for being concerned."

"Okay. If you're sure." He didn't look the least bit convinced. "I guess this is practice for when you have your own children."

"I hadn't thought of it that way, but you're right."

He glanced over his shoulder, then leaned close and whispered in her ear. "Uncle Tanner is really good with Lia. I didn't think he'd like having a baby, but he does."

Kelly touched his face. "You're not really nine, are you? You're actually a thirty-year-old disguised as a nine-year-old."

Drew shook his head. "I'm nine."

"I don't know."

"He's just responsible, like Ryan was," Tanner said from his seat at the table. "It comes from being the oldest."

"So if I'm the oldest, like my dad, were you the youngest?"

"Yup."

Drew's gaze narrowed. "So you were like Griffin?"

Together the three of them looked at Ryan's youngest son, who was all of four. He sat pulled up close to the table, with six cookies spread out in front of him. His intense expression never wavered as he focused on getting just the exact amount of icing on each of his cookies. Of course there was also icing on the front of his shirt, coating his hands and all over his face. Not to mention several globs in his hair.

Kelly covered her mouth to hold in a giggle. Tanner looked a little indignant. "I wasn't exactly like him," he said.

"I'd hope not," Kelly said. She turned to Drew. "I have to tell you that your uncle is a little too big and grown-up for me to imagine him like Griffin."

"Maybe," Drew agreed, glancing from his brother to his uncle.

"But I still like to ice cookies," Tanner said, holding out a bowl for them to inspect.

Kelly pursed her lips. "All right. I've got to hand it to you. That's a great shade of purple."

He'd created a dark, vibrant color that would look perfect on the cookies but probably would be difficult to get out of clothes. She held back a sigh. If the kids ended up with stains on their shirts, Patricia and Ryan weren't going to be so thrilled by her offer to babysit.

A faint snuffling sound caught her attention. She glanced up and saw that Tanner had heard the noise, too.

He was already pushing back his chair. "I'll go check on Lia," he said as he walked past the baby monitor.

Kelly surveyed the mess that used to be a very nice kitchen. Somehow she and Tanner would get it all cleaned up. The clothes would come clean, and regardless of the hours spent to make things right again, it would be worth it. She couldn't remember the last time she'd had this much fun.

"My dad says that Lia is good for Uncle Tanner," Drew said as he settled back in his chair and reached for a cookie. He studied the bowls, then picked up the yellow one and reached for a popsicle stick, which he used to smooth on the rapidly hardening icing. "Dad says it will settle him down." Drew looked up at her and frowned. "Not that Uncle Tanner is, you know, wild."

"Of course not," she agreed, wondering where this conversation was heading. She had a feeling that Drew had been listening to talk that might not have been meant for his nine-year-old ears, as it was unlikely that Ryan would discuss his brother with his young son.

"He's very nice and caring. He's a great uncle." Drew painted wings on the angel-shaped cookie, then started making eyes and a big smile. "It's just that Lia gives him a family of his own. Dad says he'll be getting married soon. Do *you* think Uncle Tanner is a good dad?"

He asked his question with the studied casualness of someone pretending not to care about the answer when in fact he was deeply interested. Suddenly all the odd statements and comments made sense. She stood facing a nine-year-old matchmaker. And perhaps his matchmaking father, as well. For all she knew, Patricia was in on it.

Kelly waited for a couple of seconds, but she decided that she wasn't angry. Ryan and Drew and everyone else were just trying to make sure that Tanner was happy. If they thought Kelly was a likely candidate, of course they would encourage any relationship. Too bad she and Tanner were just friends. Everyone was destined to be disappointed when they found out.

Tanner walked back into the kitchen. He held Lia in his arms. She stared at all the activity, and her big eyes got bigger. Pink fists flailed about, and her rosebud mouth puckered into a pretty decent facsimile of a smile.

"How's the cookie detail coming?" he asked.

Kelly glanced at the mess on the table. Less than half the cookies were iced, but she sensed that the kids were getting tired of helping. "I think they're pretty close to done. I thought I'd finish up frosting while they watch a movie."

Lisbeth glanced up, a smudge of blue icing on her cheek. "What are we going to watch?"

Drew and Griffin offered opinions at the same time. Lisbeth protested. The volume in the room increased. Kelly met Tanner's gaze and smiled. Yes, it was chaos, but she had to admit it was also everything she'd ever wanted. All her life, she'd longed for a big family. While her father had loved her deeply, and had always been there for her, his ministry had kept him busy. Besides, he wasn't another kid she could play with.

She'd started babysitting as soon as she was old enough. She'd adored infants, toddlers, little kids, even teenagers. Every stage had its ups and downs, and she'd wanted to experience them all. Somewhere along the way, her dream had gotten lost. Was there a way to get it back or was it too late?

"Actually," Tanner said loudly into the din, "Lia was

telling me that she would like to watch *Elf*, and as she's the guest here, I think it's her choice."

All three children stared at him. "Lia can't talk," Lisbeth said.

"Not very well," he admitted, "but I know what she's thinking."

"Is that so?" Kelly asked.

"Sure." Tanner's blue eyes danced with laughter. "Besides, the girl in the movie is pretty cute."

"I thought this was Lia's choice."

"It is, but I happen to agree with her."

"Uncle Tanner, you don't get to pick," Lisbeth insisted. "You're not a kid."

Drew shook his head. "You'd better let him. Otherwise, he'll be cranky all night."

"I'm not cranky," Tanner said, even as he headed for the family room. "Why would you say I'm cranky? We can arm wrestle to see who picks. Griffin, want to arm wrestle with Uncle Tanner?"

Kelly watched the three children trail after their uncle. She couldn't help smiling. Life around Tanner was certainly interesting. When he didn't need her anymore and she returned to her old ways, things were going to seem very quiet. But for now she was living in the center of chaos, and it felt wonderful.

"How do you know they live happily ever after?" Lisbeth asked with a yawn as she burrowed her head deeper into her pillow. Kelly had just finished reading her a book.

"Because it's a fairy tale and that's always how they end. It's the point."

"Will I live happily ever after?"

"Of course," Kelly said, kissing her cheek. "We always have challenges to keep us growing as people, but on the whole life is generally happy."

Lisbeth rolled onto her side. She didn't take up much room in the single bed, but she was surrounded by an army of stuffed animals. They crowded her feet and legs, leaned on her pillow and pressed up against her back.

"Go to sleep," Kelly said as she stood.

Tanner pushed off from the wall where he'd been leaning and approached his niece. "'Night, Lisbeth. You have sweet dreams."

"I will." She held out her arms to hug him.

He'd always thought she was so small, but she wasn't when compared with Lia. Funny, but he couldn't picture his own daughter ever being so big. Or worse, talking. Kelly had handled Lisbeth's question about living happily ever after with an ease that he couldn't imagine. If it had been him, he would have hemmed and hawed before coming up with some philosophical reply that would have only confused her. Parenting was harder than it looked.

"I love you, Uncle Tanner," she murmured.

He kissed her forehead. "I love you, too, kiddo. Now go to sleep."

But instead of resting her head back on the pillow, she grinned slyly. "I think you should kiss Kelly good-night."

Tanner didn't dare turn around to glance at Kelly. He wasn't sure he wanted to know what she was thinking. "Do you now?"

"Uh-huh. A nice, big kiss, like the way Daddy kisses Mommy when he thinks we're not watching."

"I'll have to tell your father that you *are* watching. What do you think of that, you minx?"

She giggled.

He kissed her forehead again. "Go to sleep."

"What about Kelly?"

He stood up and clicked off the bedside lamp. "That's none of your business. We'll see you in the morning."

"Okay. 'Night."

He followed Kelly out of her room and into the hallway. Griffin was already asleep and Drew was tucked in his bed, reading. Tanner tried not to notice the quiet of the house, or the dim lighting in the hall. Had it looked this intimate before? He couldn't remember.

"Sorry about that," he said quietly as he shut the door behind him. "I can't figure out why the kids are behaving like this."

"They're matchmaking," Kelly said lightly. "What I can't figure is who put them up to it."

"The list of suspects is long. I'd guess everyone from Ryan to Patricia. Maybe even the kids' grandmother." He shrugged. "I hope it doesn't make you uncomfortable."

"Not at all. I think it's pretty funny. Are you okay with it?"

Maybe it was the silence of the night, he thought as he resisted the need to step closer to her. Maybe it was the fact that he could inhale the sweet scent of her body. Or maybe it was just plain stupidity on his part. Regardless, he found himself wanting to pull her hard against him and kiss her, just like Lisbeth had requested. He wanted to kiss her the way a man kissed a woman he was attracted to.

Instead he swallowed. "Yeah, I'm fine. You're right. The situation is pretty funny." He cleared his throat. "So, ah, do you want to watch some television?"

"Sure. It's a little early to go to bed."

"Great."

But neither of them moved. He motioned toward the stairs. "The family room is down there."

"I know."

Damn. Had it gotten hot in here, or was it just him? He tugged at the collar of his shirt. "Kelly, I…"

"Yes?"

Had her eyes always been dark, bottomless pools? And was it his imagination, or did her body seem to be swaying toward him? Lord help him; he wanted her.

"Either we go downstairs right now or I'm going to have to kiss you," he told her.

"Are those my two choices?"

"Yeah."

She smiled. "Hmm, I'm going to have to think about them for a while."

"Are you?"

She nodded.

He took a step closer, then placed one hand on her waist. "Here. Let me help you decide." Then he lowered his mouth to hers.

Chapter 11

They had kissed only once before, yet Kelly had a sense of coming home as she stepped into Tanner's embrace. His arms were as strong as she remembered, his chest as broad, his taste as sweet. When his lips pressed against hers, it was easy to surrender to the passion flaring between them, to simply rest her belly against his arousal, and it was the most natural thing in the world to touch her tongue to his.

They both wore casual clothes and athletic shoes, so he was only a couple of inches taller than her. She raised her arms until they rested on his broad shoulders and leaned against him. His big hands stretched across her back, holding her…perhaps in place…perhaps just touching. Either was fine with her. She had no plans to disappear. Being close to Tanner, feeling his strength, his heat and his desire, was the best part of her day. She couldn't imagine anyone else feeling so right in her embrace.

He tilted his head slightly, then plunged his tongue into her mouth. She welcomed him, touching him, circling around, teasing him. He let her play her game, then returned the sensual torture, exploring her mouth, stroking against her in a way designed to make her whimper.

Their closeness ignited a fire inside of her. The flames didn't just flicker gently with a sensual warmth. Instead she found herself consumed by a conflagration that left her breathless and weak. The muscles of her legs trembled. Her breasts swelled and ached, and between her thighs she felt the swelling and dampness that foretold her body's readiness for this man's very male invasion.

Tanner broke the kiss, but before she could protest, he licked her lower lip, then nibbled at the corner of her mouth. She found it difficult to continue to hold her head upright. When he kissed a damp trail down to her neck, it was easy to tilt her head to the side and allow him to have his way with her.

Light, teasing, tickling kisses made her shiver. He bit her earlobe, then sucked it lightly to ease the sting. He breathed her name against the hollow of her throat, he kissed his way to the other side of her neck and back up to her mouth. Every action stirred her more deeply and left her wanting in a way she'd never wanted a man before in her life.

His hardness pressed against her belly. She flexed her hips and rubbed up and down, wanting *him* to want with the same fierceness. He groaned low in his throat.

"You're killing me," he murmured against her mouth.

"Me, too."

"Don't stop."

He licked at the seam of her lips, but when they parted, he didn't invade. Instead he touched the tip of her tongue with his and retreated. When she didn't respond, he repeated the action. Kelly finally realized that he wanted her to follow, to play a very grown-up version of tag.

The next time he tagged her as "it" she went after him, delving into his mouth, exploring him as he had explored her. She learned the tastes and textures of him, felt the smoothness of his teeth, the faint roughness of his tongue. Unexpectedly his lips clamped around her, and he sucked gently.

The incredible sensation sent lightning flaring through her core and down her legs. She shuddered and pressed harder against him, needing him, desperate for more contact.

He pulled back slightly and rained kisses on her face.

"No," she gasped, reaching up to hold him in place, then kissing him again, practically attacking him. He chuckled, then plunged into her mouth, stroking her, exciting her, making her want to rip off her clothes and beg him to take her right there.

Thank goodness he could read her mind. He pulled her into an alcove that would hide them from view if any of the children came out to the hall. His hands settled on her waist, then moved up under the loose sweatshirt she'd pulled on that morning. Strong, warm fingers traced her ribs, making her shiver, before he cupped her breasts against his palms.

Kelly considered herself fairly average on top. Not small but not huge, either. Tanner held her breasts in a way that made her think they'd been designed specifically with his hands in mind. Or maybe it was the other way around. Regardless, as he gently explored her curves, lightly rubbing his palms against her puckered nipples, she felt herself grow hotter.

One of his hands moved behind her for a second. She felt a faint tug, then her bra loosened. Tanner pulled up her sweatshirt, lowered his head and took her nipple in his mouth.

The feel of his damp lips and tongue nearly made her scream. She had to hold on to him to keep from collapsing. Heat and need built inside of her until she thought she couldn't stand it. Muscles quivered. If she hadn't known better she would have thought that she might climax right then…just because he was touching her breasts. But that wasn't possible. They were standing in a hallway, both fully dressed. It was crazy to think that—

Tanner swore, then stood up. He clutched her shoulders and pressed his forehead to hers. "I'm about to lose it, and we know this is neither the time nor the place. Right?"

"Right."

They both sounded hoarse, their voices thick with passion.

"You're amazing," he told her. "I want you so much."

"And I want you."

But he was right. There were four children in the house. They were supposed to be babysitting. Regardless of how turned on she felt now, Kelly knew that she wouldn't be comfortable if they took things any further. She was glad they'd stopped. Really. Except every part of her ached for Tanner. How had things gotten so hot so fast? The man could set her aflame with a look.

She reached behind her and refastened her bra, then straightened her sweatshirt. "Thanks," she whispered.

"Oh, it was my pleasure. And I mean that." Tanner studied her.

"What?" she asked. "Why are you staring?"

"I'm trying to learn your secrets."

She frowned. As far as she knew, she didn't have many. "What secrets?"

"I want to know why you aren't married." He reached up and touched her face. "Don't even think about giving me the 'I've been so busy' line. We both know it's more than that."

What was she supposed to say? Kelly didn't have an answer. She opened her mouth, then closed it and shrugged.

"Not good enough, Dr. Hall. You're an amazing woman. Bright, beautiful, sexy as hell. If you'd kept rubbing against me like that, I would have embarrassed us both."

She smiled. "I wouldn't have been embarrassed."

"It would have done me in." He paused.

She knew he was waiting for an answer. "I'm not hiding anything, Tanner. I'm as confused as you are. I think it's a combination of things. I've been thinking about this a lot lately, and I think it's my past and fear and maybe circumstances. I'm not sure. What's your excuse?"

She expected him to make some flippant response. Instead he said, "I'm a screwup. Look at what happened when I went to college."

She took his hand and led him to the top of the stairs, where they both sat. Their shoulders brushed against each other. "I don't believe that," she said. "It took you a little while to get it all together. So what? Some people aren't ready for college at eighteen. They need to figure a few things out first."

"Maybe. I guess I'm something of a late bloomer. It takes me a while to get it together."

"Now you have Lia."

"Yeah. A child."

But no wife.

Neither of them spoke the phrase, but Kelly suspected they were both thinking the same thing. Was he ready now? If so, where did that leave her? Did she care? Did she want to care?

"I think we're both in a transition stage in our lives," she said carefully. "That's not a healthy time to get involved in anything…" She paused. "You know, personal."

He turned toward her. "Is that your professional opinion?"

"I'm not a psychiatrist. But it is my opinion, professional or otherwise."

"I see." He tucked a loose strand of her hair behind her ear. "And if I were to kiss you again right now?"

Instantly her body went up in flames. It took every ounce of strength she had to keep from swaying toward him. "I'm not sure I could resist."

He smiled. "Thanks for telling me that." He leaned close and brushed a kiss across her mouth. "Go to bed, Dr. Kelly Hall. Go right now or I won't be responsible for my actions."

She hesitated. What did she want? Was it Tanner? Or did she want the safety of her boring, impersonal life? Then she glanced around at the unfamiliar house and realized that regardless of what she wanted, she couldn't forget where they were.

"Good night," she said regretfully as she rose to her feet.

He didn't say anything. He just watched her walk toward the guest room. She had a feeling it was going to be a long time before either of them slept.

* * *

The cacophony of the shopping mall blended perfectly with the sound of shrieking, screaming children. Kelly glanced around at the madness that was the line to visit Santa Claus at the Honeygrove Central Mall and was incredibly grateful she wasn't prone to headaches. She looked at the child in her arms, but Lia slept on, apparently unaware of the frenzy around her.

Lia's young cousins, on the other hand, were taking it all in with wide eyes and lots of fidgeting. Nine-year-old Drew spoke with the voice of experience as he advised his younger siblings about appropriate behavior.

"Don't tell Santa a whole big list of things. Just pick one thing that you really, really, really want."

"I want a magic wand," Lisbeth said. "So then I can make anything else I want. And do good deeds," she quickly added.

"You're not supposed to tell!" Griffin shouted. "Now your wish won't come true."

Before Lisbeth could begin to cry, Tanner stepped in to assure her that the no-tell policy applied only to birthday wishes and not to Santa Claus. His gaze met Kelly's over Lisbeth's head, and they shared a smile.

It was Sunday. They'd impulsively decided to surprise the kids with a trip to visit Santa, followed by lunch at Pizza Pete's. She was pretty sure the real reason behind the outing was that Tanner wanted to get a picture of his daughter with Santa Claus. He had dressed her in a red-and-white-striped onesie that he'd brought with him to Ryan and Patricia's.

They were surrounded by children, and Kelly loved it.

A familiar ache filled her. So many questions. Had she made the right choice with her daughter and had she made the right choice with her career? Not that it mattered. It was too late to change either decision.

Wasn't it?

The line progressed, and soon it was their turn. Drew, Lisbeth and Griffin played an adorable game of rock, paper, scissors to decide the order in which they'd sit on Santa's lap. Tanner made sure each kid got a picture alone; then they did a group shot with Ryan and Patricia's three.

Then Santa reached toward Kelly to take the sleeping baby.

Tanner stepped forward. "You have to support her head and neck."

"I will, Papa. Don't worry." Santa ably took Lia into his arms. "Aren't you a little angel?"

Lia looked tiny against the big man's chest. He was a good Santa, one of the best Kelly had ever seen. His beard looked real and was as white as new-fallen snow. Instead of leaning against the back of the chair, Santa turned sideways, propped his legs over one arm of the chair and reclined against the other. With Lia's head nestled against his chest, he pretended to be asleep.

All around them, people pulled phones out of purses and pockets to take a picture of the baby and Santa, dreaming sweet dreams together. The mall photographer knelt to get a close-up.

"I'm getting that one framed," Tanner said softly into Kelly's ear.

"I want a copy, too," she replied.

"That's my baby cousin," Griffin called out to no one in particular.

* * *

"You hit me fifteen times," Lisbeth complained as she studied her score sheet from laser tag at Pizza Pete's.

Tanner looked sheepish. "You're an easy target, kid. What can I say? I hit Drew a bunch, too."

"Yeah, but I didn't hit either of you once," Lisbeth said. "Santa's going to put you on the naughty list."

"You didn't hit anyone," Drew pointed out. "But don't worry. You'll do better next time."

"He's right," Tanner said, pulling the little girl close. "Besides, you're prettier than both of us."

"And smarter," she insisted.

Tanner laughed. "Maybe."

As Kelly watched him, she couldn't help remembering her own past. Her father had been wonderful with her. He'd expected a high standard of behavior, but no matter what, she'd always felt he loved her. As she cradled Lia close, she knew that Tanner was going to be the same kind of father. Gentle, kind, yet always teaching and showing by example.

"How are you holding up?" Tanner asked.

"Fine." She motioned to Lia. "She's wet, so I thought I'd go change her. I'd make you do it, but I doubt there's a changing station in the men's restroom."

"Saved by inequality," Tanner teased. "Thanks for taking care of her while I was with the other kids."

"It's hardly difficult. I adore her."

"Me, too."

Their gazes locked, and she knew they were both thinking about what had happened last night. And what had *not* happened. The kiss had come close to leading to something else. Something neither of them was ready for. But had it become inevitable? A shiver rippled through her.

She turned and made her way toward the restrooms at the rear of the restaurant. As she moved through the crowd, she heard a man yelling at his daughter. Kelly held Lia close, grateful this little girl wasn't going to have to deal with a difficult parent. She would always be loved, as Kelly had been loved…right up until she got pregnant. That was the one thing her father couldn't forgive. Was that why she couldn't forgive herself?

She reached the restroom. The door pushed open, and three teenage girls stepped out. They were talking and laughing and didn't even notice her. But she studied them, wondering if any of the three looked like her daughter. Annie Jane was a teenager. Practically a young woman.

Then, as she'd done a thousand times in the past, she pushed away the aching inside of her and focused on the task at hand. She'd lost the right to worry about her daughter the day she'd made the decision to give her away.

Two open boxes of pizza covered the wooden picnic table. "But I wanted soda," Drew said.

"Thanks for the info, but we agreed on milk," Kelly told him mildly.

"You agreed. I wanted soda."

Kelly stared at the nine-year-old. "Drew, if you're going to be difficult, I want to take this discussion outside."

Tanner waited, breath held; then his nephew nodded once. "Sorry, Kelly. Milk is fine."

"Good." She set a glass in front of him.

The mini-drama was like a dozen others that had been played out today. Pizza Pete's was a lot of fun, but it also stressed out the kids and the adults. Still, as Tanner glanced around the crowded table, he knew there wasn't anywhere else he would rather be. He had his daughter in his arms, his family nearby, good company, halfway decent food. Life didn't get much better than this.

"Do you like my hair, Uncle Tanner?" Lisbeth asked. She spun her head back and forth to show off the ribbons she'd won earlier. Kelly had braided them into her hair.

"You look lovely," he said. "I think you're the prettiest little girl here."

Lisbeth giggled and blushed. Then Griffin knocked over his milk.

Kelly started to stand up, but Tanner motioned her to stay seated. "My turn," he said. He shifted Lia to his left arm, then climbed out from the picnic table and headed for the counter. There he ordered another milk and grabbed a fistful of napkins.

"Isn't she a beauty," a woman said.

Tanner saw a petite blonde smiling at Lia. She turned her attention to Tanner. "Yours?"

"Yup."

He took the milk and pocketed his change. Unfortunately the woman didn't seem inclined to let him slip by. She stood firmly in his way.

"Does she look like your wife?" the woman asked.

"I'm not married."

"Oh."

There was a wealth of meaning in that single word. At one time in his life, Tanner might have been willing to take the woman up on her offer. After all, she was around his age, pretty enough and willing. For a while, that had been all he'd needed. But not anymore.

The woman sighed. "So you're a single dad. You're doing a great job." She pointed to a collection of boys by a martial arts video game. "Two of those are mine. It's their dad's weekend, but the jerk flakes out on a regular basis."

"That's too bad." Tanner inched past her. "If you'll excuse me, I have to get back to my family."

He pointed toward the picnic table, and she glanced in that direction. Her welcoming expression faded. "Oh. Is she yours?"

He assumed she was speaking about Kelly, not Lisbeth. "Yes."

"I see. Fine." She spun on her heel and left.

Tanner made his way to the table and took his seat. He dropped the extra napkins onto the puddle of milk and handed Griffin a new carton.

As Griffin took it, he wrinkled his nose. "Sorry, Uncle Tanner. I'll be more careful now."

"I'm sure you will be."

"I knew I was right," Kelly said as he settled next to her. "But I never thought to have it proven to me."

"What?" he asked, even though he knew exactly what she was talking about.

She pointed to the sleeping baby in his arms. "Lia *is* a chick magnet."

He frowned. "Do you really think I care about that?"

"I'm not sure. Now that you have a child, the next most obvious step is to get involved with a woman."

Tanner didn't understand. Was Kelly suggesting that he ask that woman out? How could he? She might be perfectly nice, but last night Kelly had been the one he'd been holding and the one he'd wanted to make love with.

He glanced at the woman sitting across from him. He had a thing for Kelly. At one time the information might have bothered him but not anymore.

"No," he said simply.

A wash of red colored Kelly's cheeks. She busied herself by consolidating the leftover pizza slices into one box. "Lisbeth, want to hear something exciting? I'm going to give Tanner a baby shower. Actually the shower is for Lia, but you know what I mean. We're going to make it a Christmas party, too. Won't that be fun?"

"Can I come?" Lisbeth asked, then smiled wide-eyed at Tanner when Kelly said yes.

He had to smile back. As change of subjects went, it wasn't very subtle on Kelly's part. So she was a little flustered, was she? *Good.* Let her stay that way.

Kelly and Lisbeth continued to talk about the shower. Drew asked to be excused to go play with his friends. Griffin ate with enough energy to smear pizza sauce past his elbows and ears. It was loud and messy, and for the first time in his life, Tanner felt as if he'd found a place to belong.

Chapter 12

Late Sunday night Tanner paced through his house. Patricia and Ryan had arrived home a few hours before, looking in love and blissfully happy. He and Kelly had left together, but they'd parted ways. Now he wished he'd taken her up on her offer to come over to help him with Lia. Not that he needed help with his daughter—she was currently sleeping peacefully in her crib—but because he wanted to spend time with Kelly.

He couldn't stop thinking about her. About how she'd looked all weekend with the kids. She'd been fun, funny, patient and infinitely beautiful…even with icing smudged on her cheek. He also couldn't stop thinking about that incredible kiss they'd shared. It had been passionate and intense and dangerous. Dangerous because he knew better than to get involved.

He didn't want or need the complication. He didn't

want to risk caring and losing again. At one time he'd lost everything important in his life. His parents, his brother when they were put into different foster homes and his scholarship, although that was more his fault than anyone else's. But the point was that he didn't have a lot of good luck when it came to things lasting. A long time ago he'd learned that if he didn't care, he couldn't get hurt.

Unfortunately…or maybe fortunately…he found himself on the verge of getting involved. With Kelly.

The smart thing would be to walk way, he told himself. He didn't need her or the complications a relationship would bring. They were both busy people moving in different directions. They didn't want the same things. So it was better to stay friends, nothing more. He would start pulling back right away.

But first he was going to call her.

Telling himself he was ten kinds of fool, Tanner walked down the stairs and picked up his phone. He tapped Kelly's name in his favorites, then listened to the phone ring.

"Hello?"

"Hi. It's Tanner." He paused. *Now what?* "I don't have an excuse for calling," he said. "I just want to see you. Naked." That last bit had dropped out of his mouth without warning, but it was too late to take it back. Besides, it was the truth.

He heard her breath catch, then a long silence. "Talk about coming right to the point," she murmured, sounding slightly stunned.

Disappointment overwhelmed him. He could practically see her frantically trying to come up with a way to let him down gently. *Keep it light*, he told himself. *Don't let 'em see you sweat.* "Hey, don't worry about it," he told her. "You can say no and we'll still be friends."

"Thanks for telling me that. I'm just not sure I want to, um, say no." She cleared her throat. "The thing is I'm not the trashy-lingerie type."

Desire, need, elation, all of it slammed into his gut. Was she really saying yes? "I can honestly say that I wouldn't care if you wore a snowmobile suit. I'm a lot more concerned with what's underneath."

"Yes, well, okay. Tanner?"

He gripped the phone more tightly. "Yeah?"

"What are we doing?"

"Hell if I know. And before you scold me, Lia's upstairs. She didn't hear me swear."

She laughed softly, then sighed. "You know this is crazy. I mean, it's a bad time for us, emotionally. You're dealing with Lia and all the changes she represents. I'm just barely beginning to understand that there are some issues from my past that I'm going to have to come to terms with."

"I know that."

"What I'm saying is that we have to be mature about this. I won't deny that I want you, but I'm not sure becoming lovers is wise. We're going to have to remember that this is about friends becoming intimate and nothing more. I don't want either of us to misrepresent or misunderstand the situation."

"Kelly?"

"Yes?"

"Are you going to talk all night or do you plan to get your perky butt over here?"

There was a moment of silence. "Do you have condoms or do you want me to bring them?"

He sucked in his breath. *Talk about getting right to the point times two.* "I can scrounge up a few."

"A few?"

"Hey, it's been a long time."

"I'd say no more than ten months."

"Ouch. Okay, ten months. But there hasn't been anyone since Lucy."

"It's been a while for me, too." She swallowed. "I'll be right over."

"I'll be waiting."

"Are you going to answer the door naked?"

He laughed. "Do you want me to?"

"I don't think so. I'm nervous already. That would probably send me screaming into the night."

"Then I'll keep my clothes on. But not for long."

"I can't wait." She hung up the phone.

Kelly stood on the front porch of Tanner's house staring at the wreath on his door and trying not to hyperventilate. She couldn't believe she was going to do this...or that *they* were going to be doing this. What had she been thinking? Or maybe she hadn't been thinking. How could she be expected to maintain rational thought when someone like Tanner Malone called her on the phone and told her he wanted to see her naked?

She sucked in a deep breath. This was dangerous territory; she knew that. It had been years since she'd been involved with anyone, and she knew with certainty that she'd spent her entire adult life avoiding anything like a real relationship. She wanted to tell herself that this was just about sex...nothing more. Except she didn't believe it.

Which meant, if she was smart, she would turn on

her heel and head right back to her car. Only a brain-
less woman eager for trouble or heartache would push
that doorbell.

She knocked on the door. *Oh God, oh God, oh God I
can't do this*, she told herself and took a single step back.
Just then Tanner opened the door.

He stood in front of her, backlit by the Christmas
tree in the living room. He was big and strong and about
the sexiest man she'd ever seen. It didn't matter that he
was casually dressed in jeans and a sweatshirt. The soft,
baggy shirt merely emphasized the breadth of his shoulders, while his jeans had worn white in interesting places.

"Kelly?"

"Huh?" She blinked.

"Hi," he said and motioned for her to enter the house.

She did, stumbling over the threshold and then having to take three quick steps to regain her balance. She
groaned under her breath. This was going to be worse
than she'd thought.

"Look, Tanner," she began, backing away from him.
"It's not that I'm having second thoughts. It's just that I'm
nervous. I don't do this sort of thing every day."

"Really?" He sounded surprised as he closed the door,
locked it, then flipped off the overhead light.

She glanced around and realized that something other
than the lights on the tree flickered in the empty room.
Then she saw the logs burning brightly in the oversize
fireplace. In front of the stone hearth was a thick blanket,
a couple of pillows and an ice bucket with champagne.

Her throat tightened. "You do seduction right, don't
you?" she said, then winced when her voice quivered a
little. "It's okay. Really. I'm fine with this. But maybe

we could, you know, talk some before getting right down to doing it."

Tanner chuckled. "It? What exactly is 'it'?"

"It's, well, it. Sex."

"Sex? Is that what you're here for?" He took a step toward her. "I'm not interested in sex."

She glanced nervously from the blanket to fire and back to him. "We're going to play cards instead?"

"No. We're going to make love. I've done both, and, to be honest, I'm not much interested in sex anymore. That was something I did when I was young and foolish. Now I prefer to make love with someone I care about." He took another step toward her. "Someone I respect." Another step. He was getting very, very close. "Someone I find incredibly sexy."

She made a little squeaking sound. "Me?"

"Yes, you."

In the dim light of the flickering fire his eyes were more black than blue. Despite the fact that he was only a couple of inches taller, he seemed to loom above her like a giant. She felt small and fragile and incredibly aroused. Unfortunately, she was more nervous than anything else, and it was all she could do to stand her ground. It would be so easy to turn and run.

"But we can talk first, if that would help you relax," he said, moving forward again. He stopped directly in front of her.

He was close enough that she could inhale the familiar scent of his body and feel his heat. He reached toward her and slipped her large tote off her shoulder. Not sure if she was spending the night, Kelly had thrown a couple of things into a bag so she wouldn't be caught without a toothbrush in the morning.

"So how long do you want me to stay?" she asked as he set her tote on the floor. "I mean are you a do-it-and-leave kind of guy, or do you like to cuddle after?"

He cupped her face. "Is there somewhere you have to be in the morning?"

"Yes. Work. We both have to be there."

"Good point. Okay, stay as long as you're comfortable. I'd like you to spend the night, but you don't have to."

She nodded. "I think I'll play it by ear."

"Good idea. Speaking of which..."

He leaned in close and kissed the sensitive skin just behind her ear. Then he drew the lobe into his mouth and sucked. She stiffened as fire shot through her, and her breath caught in her already tight throat. How was she supposed to think when he was doing that?

"I thought we were going to talk," she whispered. "To help me relax."

"You can talk," he told her. "I'll listen."

But he was already trailing kisses down her throat. Her sweater had a modest V-neck. Tanner nibbled his way to the bottom of the V, then licked the skin not quite exposed by the soft knit. Her thighs shook, then began to smolder as her blood heated to near boiling. Already her breasts were uncomfortably swollen.

"You're not talking," he said as his hands settled on her waist. He tugged at the hem of her sweater. Before she could figure out what he was doing, he'd pulled it over her head.

So much for conversation. But oddly enough, Kelly found she didn't mind. She knew that the only way to get over her case of nerves was to do the one thing she was afraid of. Which meant making love with Tanner.

She noticed he was staring at her bra. "You lied," he said.

Now it was her turn to feel in control. "I said I didn't have trashy lingerie. This isn't trashy."

He fingered the strap of the peach silk-and-lace bra. "It's beautiful. Not as beautiful as what it covers, but still very nice."

She raised her arms until they rested on his shoulders; then she pressed herself against him. "You're not the only one who gets lingerie catalogues in the mail. The difference is I order from them. Now do you want to talk all night, or do you want to make love?"

Instead of answering in words, he wrapped his arms around her, hauled her hard against him and plundered her mouth.

She was ready for his assault and more than met him halfway. As his lips pressed against hers, she parted, welcoming his tongue with eager strokes and thrusts. His taste was sweet and intoxicating. She adored how she could remember his flavor. She knew that if she licked his arm or his belly that he would taste similar there, as well. Variations on a theme—the essences of this wonderful man.

She clutched his head, burying her fingers into his thick hair. With her free hand she caressed his shoulders. His muscles bunched under her touch, coiling and uncoiling in a demonstration of his strength. His hands moved up and down her bare back. He was warm and smooth. She shivered when one hand reached down to stroke her bottom. He slipped his hand down the back of her thigh, then pulled gently, urging her to lift her leg up to his hip.

The position brought her hot, ready center into contact with his rock-hard thigh. Involuntarily her hips flexed forward as she sought some release from the building tension. At the same time his arousal pressed into her.

Without thinking, she slipped a hand between them and cupped him.

Instantly Tanner stiffened, sucked in a breath and exhaled her name. "You can't do that," he told her, releasing her leg and taking a step back. "Jeez, Kelly, I want to make this good for you, but it's been a hell of a long time for me and I really want you." His tense expression turned rueful. "Just think of me as a teenager facing his first time. The slightest touch will make me finish in about a tenth of a second."

"Really?" His confession surprised her. She'd thought that he'd been with enough women that one more wasn't all that special. "How much of this is time, and how much of it is me?"

As soon as she asked the question, she wanted to take it back. She accepted the fact that she was okay-looking. Not gorgeous but not hideous, either. However, she was not in Tanner's league. If Lucy had been average for him, then Kelly didn't have a prayer.

"It's about ninety-ten," he said.

"Oh." Ninety percent time. Well, at least she had her 10 percent. That was something. She tried to ignore the disappointment filling her. She'd hoped his answer would be slightly different. Their kisses had been spectacular, but maybe that had just been for her. Maybe he hadn't felt the same way. Maybe—

"Wherever you're going, get off the train right now," Tanner said, taking her face in his hands and staring into her eyes. Passion flared in his eyes. "Ninety-ten, Kelly. Ninety percent you. Ninety percent me spending many sleepless nights thinking about how much I like you, how lovely you are. Nights I've dreamed about kissing you and touching you, seeing you naked and hearing you cry out my name as I enter you. You've done more to me with just a couple of kisses than other women have done with a three month affair. I don't know what it is between us, but I do know that it's very special. I want you." He pressed his mouth to hers.

Kelly didn't know what to think. If it was a line, it was a darn good one, and frankly she didn't care.

"I want you, too."

"Good. Now follow me."

He led her over to the blanket. Once there he urged her to sit on the soft fabric. He squatted next to her and opened the bottle of what turned out to be champagne, then poured it into two glasses.

"To us," he said, handing her one.

"To us."

She took a sip. The cool, bubbling liquid teased her tongue and her throat. She took another sip, then noticed that Tanner hadn't touched his.

"What's wrong?" she asked.

"Nothing. Take another drink."

She did as he asked, but before she could swallow, he kissed her.

She didn't remember setting her glass down, but suddenly her arms were around him and his tongue was in her mouth. The tingling bubbles tickled her mouth, while his smooth warmth provided a counterpoint. The combination of champagne and Tanner was the most erotic mixture she'd ever experienced.

He urged her onto her back. She went without protest, wanting him to be close, to touch her everywhere. One hand slipped behind her to unfasten her bra; then the scraps of silk and lace were tossed aside.

"So beautiful," he breathed as he stared at her breasts. He cupped them gently in his hands.

His touch was as wonderful as it had been the previous night, only this time they didn't have to worry about being interrupted by Ryan's children. She let herself relax and savor the sweetness of his gentle caresses as he explored her curves.

He cupped her fullness, then ran his fingers along the underside. He explored the valley between her breasts, all the while kissing her deeply. Her mind split, not sure what to concentrate on more. The sweetness of his mouth on hers, or the magic of his fingers on her breasts? Then there was the whole issue of her hard, aching nipples. Why wouldn't he touch them? The need increased until it was almost pain. Heat, moisture and desire flooded her feminine place making her writhe with longing.

"Tanner," she breathed against his mouth.

"What?"

She opened her eyes and stared at him. Beneath the fire, she saw gentle teasing. "You're tormenting me on purpose."

"Maybe. Do you like it?"

"More than I thought possible."

"But you want me to touch you somewhere else, perhaps?"

"Perhaps."

"What will happen if I do?"

She couldn't help smiling. "It will be very nice."

His face was close to hers. He smiled. "Just nice? I was hoping for more."

"It will be very, very nice."

"Not exactly what I had in mind." He moved his fingers closer but still didn't touch her nipples.

"Have you thought about what it's going to be like when we're together?" he asked.

She was so lost in the sensations he created that it was difficult to concentrate on his question. "What? You mean while we're making love?"

"Yes." He licked her lower lip. "I have. I've thought about what it's going to be like to be inside you. I want you. All of you. I want you ready and gasping for me. I want you to welcome me inside you, then convulse around me. I want you begging and demanding, and I want it to be better than anything you've ever experienced before."

He kissed her then, a long, deep, passionate kiss that fuddled her already-whirling brain. The images he'd created filled her mind until she felt herself living through the experiences as he'd described them. Combined with the wonder of his kiss and the way his hands felt on her breasts, she found her arousal growing to the point of pain. She needed him desperately. More than she'd needed anyone ever. She'd never been this ready before. Every part of her trembled.

Then his finger moved slightly. She felt the first touch on her tight, aching nipples. He brushed lightly, circled, then squeezed ever so gently. At the same time he slipped between her legs, shifting so he pressed against her. Electricity rocketed through her. Her hips thrust forward, pulsing, pushing her center against his arousal. It didn't matter that they were both wearing jeans. She needed pressure there. Something, anything.

His kiss deepened. She clutched at him, panting, needing. It was too much. It was never going to be enough. She sucked his tongue, held his head in place, then moved one hand lower to his rear and urged him to move faster.

Pressure built between her legs. Pressure and something else. Something almost unfamiliar. Then, before she
knew what was happening, before she could do more than
catch her breath, she felt a hot jolt of pleasure against that
tiny spot of sensitivity. She rubbed against him harder
and faster, wanting to feel him. It happened again. His
fingers continued to dance on her nipples, and the jolt
grew and lengthened until it collected itself into an intense release. She shuddered against him. She gasped
his name and lost herself in the wonder of the moment.

Tanner continued to kiss her and touch her. With each
continued caress, she found her level of need growing
instead of easing. The release had only made her want
more. She opened her eyes and stared at him.

"I don't understand," she whispered. "What's happening to me?"

"You're very responsive. I can't believe I can make you
do that just by touching your breasts and rubbing against
you." He looked two parts proud and one part stunned.

She couldn't believe it, either. Nothing like this had
ever happened to her. But she wasn't about to complain.
Not when she was still aching to feel him inside of her.

"Tanner, please. I want you."

His eyes darkened to the color of midnight. Without
saying a word, he sat up and reached for the snap of her
jeans. In less than a minute, he'd pulled off the rest of
her clothes, and she was lying naked beneath him. The
lights on the tree dotted her skin with spots of reflected
color. Then he tugged off his own sweatshirt.

She stared at his broad chest. In the dim light of the
fire, smooth skin glowed. Each muscle defined itself,
flexing and relaxing with his movements. When he stood
up to pull off his jeans, she found herself trembling in

anticipation. She could see the outline of him straining against the zipper. Then he pushed down his clothes, and he sprang free.

He was hard and male and very ready. As he knelt beside her and pulled a condom out of his pocket, she reached over and stroked him. He caught his breath with an audible gasp. His fingers closed on top of her.

"You can't," he told her. "*I* can't. You're too much what I want, and I've been thinking about this too long." He drew her hand away.

"Later?"

He flashed her a grin. "Absolutely. I'll even beg you to touch me if you'd like."

She stretched out on her back. "I think I would like that."

He put on a condom, but instead of moving over her, he bent low to kiss her. As his tongue teased her mouth, his hand moved between her legs. She parted for him, welcoming his touch. He explored her slowly, gently, thoroughly, learning the secrets of her body. He slipped through the curls. He searched out that one tiny spot and circled it until her hips pulsed and she gasped and the moment of release was within reach. Then he drew back and moved achingly slowly, around and around, not touching that one spot but agonizingly close. Circling, teasing, making her plead, finally rubbing it so lightly, so perfectly, she thought she would weep.

The peak crept up on her. It began so slowly, she barely noticed. Then it grew and became so inevitable, the world could have ended and still she would have reached her place of perfection. Then it filled her, reaching deep into every cell, lifting her to another time and place, making her scream, the sound swallowed by his kiss.

While she was still shaking and experiencing absolute wonder, he knelt between her legs and began to fill her.

Kelly felt tears in her eyes. Tears she couldn't explain except to think that they were part of the release. He moved slowly, stretching her, making her cling to him, all the while kissing her.

His weight settled on her, surrounding her, making her feel safe and truly a part of him. He clutched her close, as if he couldn't get enough of her. Fortunately, she could relate to the feeling because despite all he'd done to her already, when he began to move inside her, it all started again.

With each thrust he carried her higher. She hadn't thought she could experience this and survive, yet she did. Again and again, going deeper and deeper. Her body tensed tighter and tighter until she knew she was going to snap. He moved faster. The world blurred, then disappeared. There was only this man and what he did to her.

She felt him collect himself. Beneath her hands, his body tensed, his hips rocked. They were both going to explode. She could feel it.

He broke the kiss and stared down at her. She looked up at his face, at his eyes, at the uncontrolled passion she saw there.

Later she could not be sure who surrendered first. One minute they were hanging on the edge of eternity, and the next they were falling together. She watched exquisite release tighten his features into a mask of passion. She felt her body being torn into millions of points of energy before being reassembled in the most perfect way possible. She heard herself calling out his name even as he spoke hers.

In the aftermath, when their breathing returned to

normal and they were once again able to talk, Tanner cupped her face in his hands. He smiled at her and spoke one word.

"Stay."

She nodded. Tonight there was nowhere else she belonged.

Chapter 13

Kelly leaned her head against Tanner's shoulder. "Before you know it, she'll be sleeping through the night," she said, nodding at the baby in Tanner's arms.

He smiled down at his already dozing child. "Is it strange that I already don't want her to grow up? She's so beautiful just as she is."

"You'll think that at every stage, that you can't possibly love her more than you do right now. And time will prove you wrong again and again."

They were both in Tanner's big bed, up against the pillows. Kelly had to fight against the urge to close her eyes and let herself believe that this was for keeps. Instead she reached out and touched one of Lia's hands.

The little baby closed her fist around Kelly's finger and held on tight. She could smell the fresh scent of baby powder and the male fragrance of Tanner's body. The combination went to her head.

Despite her best intentions, she felt her heart opening to both this man and his child. She wanted to think it was just a reaction to mind-blowing sex. Anyone would have been shaken by what she and Tanner had just experienced. Except she knew it was more than that.

He was the kind of man women dreamed about. Not just because he was handsome, but because he was strong and kind and caring. How was she supposed to resist a big, tough guy who was willing to change his life to accommodate a new baby? He'd taken Lia even knowing he was going to be a single father. He'd lacked both skills and practical knowledge. He'd been terrified, but he'd done it anyway.

He made Kelly want to lean on him, to borrow some of his amazing strength for her own. She wondered if he would mind, if it was just for a little while. Until she could figure things out for herself.

Lia finished her bottle. Tanner expertly rested the baby on his shoulder and patted her back until she burped twice; then he excused himself to put her back in bed. His quiet confidence was so different from those first few nights when he'd been afraid to do anything. He and his daughter had learned and grown together. They'd bonded. Kelly had known that would happen. But what she hadn't thought was that she might do a little bonding of her own. Somehow, when she wasn't paying attention, she had connected with both Lia and Tanner. She'd intertwined both her life and her heart with the pair, and she didn't know how to separate from them.

The timing was awful, she thought as she slid down into the bed and pulled the covers up to her chin. She was in no position to get involved with anyone right now. Her life was a mess, and she'd just started to notice. There were important issues from her past that she'd ignored. Well, it was time to stop pushing them into the closet. She had to drag them out and stare them in the face.

In the meantime, what was she supposed to do about Tanner?

"She's already asleep," he said as he walked back in the room. He hadn't bothered to pull on clothes, and she couldn't help staring at his amazing body. Even as she watched, that most male part of him began to stretch and grow. Her reaction was instinctual and immediate.

She told herself they had things to talk about. There was much she had to explain to him. Tanner slid into bed next to her and gathered her close.

"I know what you're thinking," he said as he pressed his body to hers. "You're thinking that we have to talk about how mature we're both going to be about this change in our relationship. You're thinking that it's going to take time to figure out how to balance this new intimacy with our existing friendship."

His earnest expression made her smile…almost as much as the busy hands caressing her breasts. "Actually, I wasn't thinking that at all, but you're right. We do have to discuss those things."

"I plan to be mature," he told her, reaching for a condom on the nightstand. "I plan to talk about all those things, but first I want to make love again."

As he sank into her, she knew that she'd found an incredibly special man. But she wasn't ready. If she wanted to keep him in her life, she was going to have to do something about getting ready.

His mouth claimed hers. She sighed and welcomed him. *Later*, she thought hazily as passion overwhelmed. Like Tanner, she would wrestle with this particular demon later.

* * *

"Malone," Tanner grunted into the phone. His gaze and his attention stayed focused on the schedule in front of him. They were catching up, but it was a slow process.

"Hi, it's Kelly. How are you?"

Kelly? The familiar voice took about two seconds to settle into his brain; then he was instantly back in his bed, making love with her the way they had at five that morning. The memory made him smile...and get hard.

"Well, hello yourself. This is a surprise." He glanced at his watch. It was a little after three in the afternoon. "Everything all right?"

"I'm fine. I'm here in the hospital with one of my patients."

"You could come and see me in person."

"I wish I could, but she's having twins and they can get complicated. I want to stay close."

"Twins." The thought made him shudder. Lia had been enough of a shock without him having to worry about dealing with two of them. "Good luck."

"Thanks. I'm not expecting any problems, but I want to make sure."

"You're a good doctor."

"Thank you. I appreciate the compliment."

Her voice was soft and appealing, just like her. He could listen to her for hours. He could do a lot of things with her for hours.

"About last night," he murmured. "Did I tell you how much I enjoyed being with you?"

She laughed. "You might have mentioned it a dozen or so times."

"Good. I want you to know how special our time together was. And incredible."

"I'll say. I didn't even know that my body was capable of responding that way."

She had been remarkably comfortable with him. Tanner wanted to take the credit, telling himself it was his incredible technique or skill, but the reality was he and Kelly simply clicked in bed. He never knew what made that happen. It was some kind of chemistry or emotional connection or a combination of those and other elements. Regardless, he knew that their lovemaking had been extraordinary.

"Do you want to come by after you're done birthing your babies?"

"I'd like to, but I can't."

There was an odd note in her voice. He sat straighter in his chair. "What's wrong?"

"Nothing. I just…" She drew in a breath. "I have to go out of town tomorrow. That's really why I'm calling. I wanted to let you know that I'd be gone."

Something was happening. Tanner could feel it, and he didn't like it one bit. "Usually when I don't satisfy a woman in bed she just refuses to see me again. She rarely feels the need to head out of town."

Kelly chuckled. The soft sound relieved him.

"It's not that, and you know it. This isn't even about you."

"Then what's it about?"

"I have a couple of things I have to take care of."

"Business?"

She hesitated. "More like my past. It's just the one day. I'll be back tomorrow night."

"Will you call me when you get back?"

"Would you like me to?" she asked.

"Always."

"Then I will."

He heard a voice in the background.

"I have to go, Tanner."

"All right. You take care of yourself. Have a safe trip."

"I will. Bye."

She hung up the phone.

Tanner slowly lowered the receiver to the cradle, then glanced back at his papers. But instead of seeing the work schedule, he saw Kelly's face, her smile, imagined the way she'd looked that morning when he'd entered her.

She was an amazing woman, and he was lucky to have her in his life. Even though he wondered where she was going and what she had to do there, he didn't worry that it had anything to do with another man. He wasn't jealous…yet.

However, it was just a matter of time until Kelly started wondering what she was doing, wasting her time on a guy like him. They were good friends, they were good in bed, but it would never be anything more. Even if he was the type, she wasn't for him. Eventually she would realize that she could do a whole lot better and when that time came, she would leave. Oh, she would want to stay friends for a while, but everything between them would change.

He told himself it didn't matter—that he'd survived without her before and that he could do it again. But the words were empty…as empty as his life had been before she'd entered it and showed him what he was missing.

The cab stopped in front of a pale-white house. As with most residential buildings in San Francisco, this was taller and longer than it was wide. She'd barely had time to step out onto the sidewalk before the front door opened and an older couple came out to greet her.

"Kelly," the silver-haired slender woman said, running lightly down the walkway, her arms open. "It's so good to see you." She enfolded Kelly with a warm hug. "You promised to come visit again, but I didn't think it would take this long to get you back."

"I've been busy," Kelly said.

"We're all busy," Mary Englun told her with a smile. "Life has a way of moving too fast. But you're here now, and that's all that matters."

She urged Kelly up the stairs, at the top of which Kelly received an even bigger hug from Mary's husband, Jim. He was a portly man with thinning hair and a smile that brightened a room.

"You're still beautiful as ever," he told her, ushering her inside the lovely home. "Those big eyes are just like Annie Jane's. She's a lucky girl to take after her mother."

"Thank you," Kelly said, feeling both welcomed and awkward.

Mary read her thoughts in an instant. "None of that," she said, patting Kelly's hand. "We're all family. I'll admit it's a little complicated, but that doesn't change the connection." Mary smiled at her. "And it's so good to see you again."

They took Kelly into their living room, a spacious area decorated for Christmas. A Victorian village took up nearly an entire wall. A red-and-green quilt was draped across the back of the large, comfortable sofa. As Kelly took a seat, she saw that Mary had already prepared a pot of tea and several plates of sandwiches and cookies. Mary firmly believed in feeding one's troubles, a philosophy that didn't match her girlish figure.

Mary settled next to her while Jim took a wing chair to her right. "How are things with your practice?" Mary asked as she poured three cups of tea.

"I'm very busy right now. I feel like every woman I see is pregnant. I delivered twins yesterday. A boy and a girl. The babies are healthy, and the parents are thrilled, if a little overwhelmed."

"Twins." Jim shook his head. "I'm grateful we had our three one by one."

"Me, too." Mary laughed. "It was hard enough to have all of them in diapers at the same time." She handed Kelly her tea, then passed a cup to Jim.

They chatted a little more about Kelly's practice; then Mary changed the subject. "We told Sara you'd called. She thought about meeting you this time, but the idea still makes her nervous."

"I understand." Kelly didn't tell either of them, but she was secretly grateful that her daughter's adoptive mother had stayed away. She wasn't sure she could have handled that meeting right now.

Mary placed her hand on Kelly's forearm. "Annie Jane is a wonderful child. Most of the time talks like she's twenty-five, but she's still a little girl about some things. She doesn't believe in Santa anymore, of course, but she still gets very excited about Christmas."

There was a folder next to the tea tray. Mary opened it and handed Kelly a school photo. A blonde, blue-eyed teenager stared back at her. As Jim had mentioned, Annie Jane's eyes were shaped like Kelly's although she got the color from her father. Kelly recognized her smile on the girl, and her hair. She, too, had been blonder when she was younger.

So many things were familiar and an equal number

strange. Kelly traced the photo and knew that if she and Annie Jane walked down a street together, no one would have trouble placing them as mother and daughter.

"She's doing well in school," Mary said. "Good grades and she's popular. She's not dating yet, but that day is coming. We're all terrified," she added with a laugh. "Boys and hormones. I remember what it was like when Jim and I went through that with our brood."

Kelly couldn't relate to that, but she knew what she'd been like as a teenager.

"She likes science," Jim put in. He smiled at Kelly. "She wants to be a vet. That commitment to medicine must run in the family."

"Does she know I'm a doctor?" Kelly asked.

Mary nodded. "Jim and I have told her. Sara doesn't like to talk about you very much, but we've always been available to answer Annie Jane's questions." Mary glanced at her husband. They exchanged an unspoken message.

"I think Annie Jane will want to meet you in a few years," Jim said. "Sara's not going to take it well, so that might delay things, but your daughter is open to the idea."

Kelly didn't know whether to cry or hug these two very special people. From the very beginning, Jim and Mary had included her as part of Annie Jane's family. They sent regular updates on her progress and even pictures. Sara had been unable to conceive, so she and her husband had decided to adopt. But Sara had never been able to face the birth mother of her adored only child. Instead, Jim and Mary were Kelly's connection. They even referred to Annie Jane as *her* daughter. As if she had the right to lay some claim to the child she'd given up at birth.

Mary sorted through dozens more pictures, showing

them all to Kelly, letting her pick a couple to take home. Eventually Jim excused himself, and the two women were alone.

"It's always lovely to see you," Mary said. "But I'm wondering why you came here today."

Kelly sighed. "I'm not completely sure I have an answer to that," she admitted. She looked around the beautifully furnished room. There were framed pictures crowded together above the fireplace and on small occasional tables, interspersed with Christmas decorations that had clearly been made by their children and grandchildren when they were little. Kelly could see Jim and Mary's three, along with the next generation. All the pictures and decorations were tangible proof that this family prided itself on loving one another.

"Sometimes I just need to be sure that I did the right thing," she said at last. "I've been thinking about the adoption a lot lately, and I can't help wondering if I was selfish to give up my daughter."

She looked at Mary. "Please don't think this is anything about trying to get her back. I would never do that."

"I know, my dear." Mary patted her arm again. "I just so hate to see you in pain. Why do you doubt your decision?"

"Because..." Kelly faltered. "Because I wonder if I should have tried harder. To keep her, I mean. To make it work."

Mary gestured to the pictures in the room. "Annie Jane was the most significant gift anyone has ever given this family. You brought my daughter joy. Until she held your baby in her arms, I'd begun to fear for her life. She'd been depressed for over a year. All she'd ever wanted was to be a mother, and that was the one thing her body wouldn't let her be. You and Annie Jane saved her. For that I will always be grateful. You weren't selfish, Kelly. You were wise and brave beyond your years."

Kelly wanted to believe her. "I didn't feel very brave. I was afraid."

"Answer me this. Are you a good doctor?"

Kelly nodded. "Yes. I work hard for my patients, and I care about them."

"So you gave first with your daughter, and now with your choice of career. You're a good person. We can all understand why you did what you did. I suspect you would understand these circumstances in another young woman's life. You would offer her compassion and support. Perhaps it's time to offer the same to yourself."

Mary's words hit home, but not in the way the other woman had intended. Kelly remembered her conversation with Corina, and how she'd rushed off before reassuring the young woman. Corina's situation was too much like her own for her to be comfortable. Kelly realized that was one time when she hadn't been a good doctor.

"Let go," Mary told her. "Be happy. Find some young man and fall in love. Have more babies, babies that will grow up to be as wonderful as Annie Jane." Tears filled Mary's eyes. "Every time I hold that beautiful girl I'm thankful to you. And I'm grateful to know my granddaughter has such a warm, caring person for her birth mother."

Kelly leaned into Mary's embrace. She let herself absorb the other woman's comforting words. Maybe Mary was right. Maybe it was time to forgive herself and move on.

Plans spilled over Ryan's desk until there wasn't any room for their sandwiches. Tanner pointed to a computer printout of a calendar. "Artie's ready to start coordinating with hospital personnel about the installation of equipment," he said. "This is the part of the project that's going to get tricky. Everyone thinks his or her department is the most important."

Ryan nodded thoughtfully. "You're going to have a tough time keeping egos in check."

"Agreed. That's why I want Artie in charge. He's going to trample over everyone, which will at least make it fair." Tanner grinned. "Seriously, he's good at this kind of thing. Plus if I stay out of it, he can use me as a point of arbitration when it gets really ugly."

Ryan looked at the calendar, then at the progress report. "You're only about three days behind where you'd initially projected you'd be. I'm impressed. I mean that as your customer. As your big brother, I'm proud as hell."

"Thanks," Tanner said. He'd worked damn hard on this project, and it was gratifying to see it come together. "So how was your second honeymoon?"

Ryan grinned. "Great. Patricia and the kids are the best thing that ever happened to me." He moved the plans to the side and pulled out his plate. Tanner did the same. Both men took a seat.

Ryan took a bite of his sandwich and chewed. "I tried talking her into having another, but she said she's done. I don't mind. Three is a nice number."

"She loves them."

"Yeah, she does." Ryan smiled, his love for his wife obvious. "She's a great mom." He looked back at Tanner. "We both really appreciate that you helped Kelly out with the kids."

"It was fun. We had a great weekend."

"So I heard. Drew said you two did very well for adults unused to being around children."

Tanner laughed. "That sounds just like Drew."

"He also said that you spent a lot of time making eyes at Kelly."

Tanner concentrated on eating, hoping to avoid an answer. But when Ryan continued staring at him, he knew he wasn't going to get that lucky.

"We're friends," he said at last. "Good friends. We get along."

"That's not what I heard," Ryan teased. "Rumor has it you're a little bit more than friends."

Tanner couldn't believe it. How had his brother... *Of course.* "Patricia."

"Oh yeah. They were on the phone nearly an hour. Patricia told me later she was gunning for details, but Kelly was fairly closemouthed about all but the big picture." Ryan raised his eyebrows. "So? Now that you've done the wild thing, when are you going to make an honest woman of her?"

Tanner stared at his brother. He doubted he would have been more shocked if Ryan had decked him. "What?"

"Marriage," Ryan said. "You know, long white dress, diamond ring, happily-ever-after?"

"No way." Tanner swallowed against the tightness in his chest and his throat. "I don't do commitments, at least not like that. Nothing good lasts forever. I'll admit that Kelly's very special and that I'm lucky to have had her in my life, but it's not a forever kind of thing."

Ryan's mouth tightened. "It's time to let go of the past, Tanner. We didn't get many breaks when we were growing up, and I can understand why you worry about things lasting. But you're not that scared kid anymore. You're a man. You can take care of yourself."

"It's not me I'm worried about."

"Then who? Kelly?"

He didn't have an answer, so he shrugged. "I told you I don't do permanent."

"So what about Lia? A kid is a pretty permanent fixture in a parent's life. You planning on dumping her in a couple of years?"

"Of course not." Tanner couldn't believe his brother would even suggest such a thing. "She's my daughter."

"Explain the difference."

Tanner opened his mouth, then closed it. Obviously there was a difference between a wife and a child, but that wasn't what Ryan was talking about.

Tanner leaned back in his chair and tried to figure it all out. He'd never really put it together before—the forever part. He'd known that Lia was his child and that he'd made the decision to keep her. He'd known it was going to be for a long time, but until this moment, he hadn't realized that he'd signed on for the rest of his life. That no matter what he would be there for her—because he loved her and he no longer wanted to live in a world where she wasn't a part of his life.

He waited for the terror, for the second thoughts and plans for getting away, but none of them appeared. All he felt was a deep and profound love for his daughter.

"Lia is everything to me," he said at last.

"Exactly," Ryan told him. "Loving a child uses a different part of your heart than loving a woman, but the principles are the same. Commitment, patience, time, respect. So I'm going to ask you again. What about Kelly?"

What about Kelly? Tanner didn't have an answer.

Because he'd never allowed himself to think of her that way. Not only because of who he was, but because of who she was.

"She's a doctor," he said.

"I've heard that." Ryan's voice was teasing.

"No, I mean she's a *doctor*. I'm just some contractor."

"So this is about what you do for a living?"

"Yeah."

"What about the fact that you love her? Doesn't that count?"

"I don't love her," Tanner insisted, but the words rang hollow. Love? Him? Did he love Kelly?

"You're a fool if you let her go," Ryan told him. "Women like her don't come along every day."

"You think I don't know that? But say you're right. What am I supposed to offer her?"

"Your heart."

"As simple as that?"

Ryan smiled. "It's only complicated if you make it complicated."

Ryan made it sound so easy, but Tanner knew that his brother was wrong. Even if Kelly was the right woman for him, he sure as hell wasn't the right man for her.

Chapter 14

Tanner hesitated outside his front door. Every instinct screamed at him not to go inside.

"You gotta do it, boss," Artie said. "It's not so bad."

Tanner glared at his foreman. "How do you know? Have you done this before?"

Artie shifted uncomfortably from foot to foot. "No, and if I'd kept my big mouth shut, this wouldn't be happening now. But I had to go and mention it to my wife. Gloria got all excited and said she wanted to come, too." He snorted. "As if I would have done this without her."

Tanner completely understood the other man's reluctance. Sure, Artie was with him, and Ryan had promised to drop by. *Probably just to laugh*, Tanner thought grimly. But Kelly had insisted so there was no point in putting off the inevitable.

Tanner sucked in a deep breath and pushed open his

front door. At that moment, a gale of female laughter drifted through the house. He shuddered and stepped inside.

The living room was as he'd left it that morning. Still half-finished and empty except for the Christmas tree in the corner. But the family room was a different matter. Chairs from the dining room had been pulled in beside the sofas, forming a rough circle. Kelly had told him this would be a combination Christmas party and baby shower, so he hadn't expected quite such an explosion of femininity. Come to think of it, he didn't see a single nod to Christmas in the room. This was 100 percent baby shower. Pink-and-white streamers fell from the ceiling, while matching balloons had been gathered in bunches and tied to chairs, window sashes and even the refrigerator handle. A dinner buffet covered the counter closest to the family room, and he could see the large cake waiting in the dining room. Piles of presents stood by one of the few empty chairs left. Nearly two dozen laughing, talking women sat in the remaining chairs and on the sofa.

If hell was a baby store, then purgatory was a baby shower. Why had he let himself be talked into this?

Tanner swallowed hard and thought about retreating. So far no one had seen him. He could make a clean escape and call from his car, claiming a work crisis kept him from attending. But before he could take even one step back, Kelly glanced up and saw him. Then she smiled.

He hadn't seen her much in the past week. First she'd taken her trip to San Francisco to visit her daughter's adoptive grandparents. Then she'd had a couple of emergencies. He'd had a crisis or two of his own, and while they'd spoken on the phone, they hadn't had the chance to spend any time together since the night they'd made love.

Just seeing her sitting there, her wide eyes bright with humor, her smooth skin begging to be touched, he wanted her. Not just for sex but also for conversation and even to hold. He'd missed her.

"Tanner!" she called. "You're finally here. We were beginning to wonder."

All the women turned to look at him. He recognized several of his female employees. There was Kelly, of course, and Patricia, along with the wives of some of his employees. Artie made his way to the side of a petite brunette in a business suit.

Tanner gave a general wave and walked to the waiting chair next to Kelly. He couldn't remember a time when he'd been more uncomfortable.

"Isn't this great?" Kelly asked as he sat down. "Everyone came."

"Great. Where's Lia?"

"Napping. She was up a little bit ago and was a hit with your guests."

He wanted to point out that the guests were hers, along with the idea of a baby shower. Why on earth had he agreed?

"We were about to start the games," Patricia said. "Would you like something to drink first?"

"Games? What kind of games?"

His sister-in-law grinned. "Nothing all that tough. You'll be fine. Why don't I get you some punch?"

As she stood up and started walking toward the kitchen, Tanner had his first chance to notice what the women were eating and drinking. As he did so, his mouth turned down in an involuntary grimace. Everything was pink. The punch, the salad accompanying the small sandwiches, even the cookies. Now that he thought about it, the cake had been pink, too. Or the icing had been. He didn't dare think about what it would look like when they cut it open.

He leaned toward Kelly. "If I'd had a son, would everything be blue?"

"Of course." She smiled. "Normally the baby shower occurs before the blessed event, when the sex of the child is unknown. But when the shower comes later, or the parents already know the sex, the shower theme reflects that." She patted his hand. "Don't worry. You're going to have a great time. First we'll play a few games—then you can open presents."

"I can't wait," he muttered. "What about the cake?"

"Oh, we'll do that while you're opening presents."

What he really wanted to know was when everyone would be going home. After all, this thing couldn't go on too late—could it? He wanted to spend some time alone with Kelly. He wanted to sit with her and talk; then he wanted to take her upstairs and make love with her.

The front door opened, and Ryan walked in. "Over here," Tanner called, feeling the tiniest bit rescued from the situation. "You're just in time for the games."

Ryan looked as puzzled as he had at the mention of games. Then his older brother glanced around the room and started to laugh.

Patricia handed Tanner a plastic cup filled with bright pink, foamy punch.

"It tastes better than it looks," Kelly said. She waited until Patricia had settled back on the sofa and everyone had moved over to make room for Ryan. "Let's get started." She stood up and walked into the kitchen.

"There are several pads of paper on the coffee table. Take one and pass the rest along until everyone has one.

We're going to play the first game." She returned, carrying a large tray covered by a dish towel.

Today she wore her hair up in a twist of some kind. Her long bangs hung to her eyebrows. Something shiny stained her lips, making Tanner think about licking them clean, then maybe licking her all over. A navy pantsuit emphasized her long legs and slender waist. She was tall and lovely and so much more than he'd ever known in the past. Was she all he'd ever wanted? Was Ryan right about it being time for him to let go of the past?

"The point of the game is to remember as many objects as possible. I'm going to walk around with the tray. No one can start writing until I say so. Are we ready?"

Tanner glanced at Ryan who shrugged.

Patricia grinned. "To answer that unasked question, yes, of course you two are going to play. The prize is a facial at a beauty salon near the hospital. If a man wins the game, which is so incredibly unlikely as to not even be worth mentioning, he will give the prize to his significant other." She patted Ryan's cheek. "In your case, that would be me."

"Thanks for the reminder," Ryan grumbled.

Kelly took off the towel and made a slow circuit of the room. Tanner studied the various items. He recognized most of them. A rattle, baby powder, a pair of earrings that Kelly frequently wore, Lia's baby bracelet from the hospital and a condom. The last made him raise his eyebrows, but he didn't say anything. Finally she returned to the kitchen and told them to begin.

Tanner wrote quickly but steadily. He mentally reviewed the tray, going clockwise, filling in the spaces. Had there been two cotton swabs or just one? He figured it didn't really matter. After a couple of minutes, Kelly called time. She asked everyone to count up how many items they had. The person with the most had to read his or her list aloud to verify accuracy.

"Eleven," Patricia called out, looking smug.

"Fourteen," Gloria, Artie's wife, said.

Tanner counted his list again but didn't say anything.

"How many, Ryan?" Kelly asked.

"Nine."

The women all laughed.

"Hey, I got ten," Artie called. "At least I did better than him."

"How could you remember all that?" Ryan asked.

Kelly settled her gaze on Tanner. "What about the proud father? How many do you have?"

He thought about lying, then figured Kelly would probably be able to tell. "Eighteen," he muttered.

There was a collective murmur of surprise.

"Really?" Kelly said. "Want to read them back to me?"

"Sure." He cleared his throat. "A diaper, cotton swabs, an earring, a condom—" Several women laughed.

"Yeah, well, it didn't keep *me* out of trouble," he said, then continued with his list. "Lia's hospital bracelet, baby powder, a rattle, paper clips, a fork, toothpicks, diaper ointment, a sock, lipstick, a car key, a quarter, two theater tickets, a wedding band—yours, right?" he asked, shooting his brother a look.

Ryan nodded.

"And a pager."

"Wow." Kelly picked up the tray and carried it back into the living room. "The only two things he missed are the washcloth and the battery. Very impressive, Mr. Malone. Looks like you've got yourself one facial."

Which they both knew he'd give to her. "Gee, thanks."

Somehow their gazes got locked together. Even though he told himself to look away, he couldn't. Kelly seemed to be having the same problem.

"I, um, think it's time to cut the cake," she said. "Want to help?"

"Sure."

He excused himself and followed her into the dining room. He knew that they were the center of attention, but right now he didn't care. Instead he pulled her into a corner, out of sight of the family room, and drew her close.

"I've missed you," he told her just before he kissed her.

"Me, too." Her words were muffled against his mouth.

She felt so right in his arms, he thought, needing her more than he thought possible. She wrapped her arms around him and deepened the kiss. He cupped her face and pulled back enough to talk.

"Stay with me tonight," he said. "After the baby shower. I've missed you."

"I've missed you, too." She smiled. "Actually, you'd have to throw me out. I already have an overnight bag in my car."

"I want to hear about what happened when you went out of town."

"Good, because I want to tell you."

The sound of someone clearing her throat made them step apart. Patricia stood in the doorway of the dining room.

"The crowd is getting restless," she said. "I have an idea. Why don't the two of you go back and start opening presents, while I work on cutting the cake?"

"Sounds like a plan," Kelly said and led the way.

Tanner settled down in his chair again, but now he didn't feel so very out of place. As he started to open presents, he found himself thinking about the hours that would follow, about how much he wanted to be with Kelly.

Maybe Ryan was right. Maybe it was time to let go of the past and take a chance on the future. Except he was still just a construction worker and Kelly was still a doctor. Did they have a prayer of making it work? What about his fear of losing everything he cared about? Would he survive losing her?

He opened the first box Kelly handed him. It was flat and light, so he guessed clothes. Inside was a red velvet dress with a white lace collar.

"It's for Christmas," Mattie, one of his electricians, told him. "I didn't know if Lia had a Christmas dress yet."

"Thanks. It's very nice. And, no, Lia only has one dress right now."

The next box was large and square. He shook it, then glanced at the tag. He recognized Kelly's scrawl.

"You didn't have to get anything," he told her.

"I wanted to. That's half the fun of a shower…buying a baby present."

"That and the pink punch," he said, motioning to his still-untouched cup.

He tore off the white-and-pink paper. Inside was a box with a picture of a lamp. The base was a ballerina teddy bear with a matching shade. He pointed his finger at her. "You're the reason that woman at the store kept telling me this sucker was back-ordered."

"Absolutely. Once you got serious enough to put up a border print, I knew that Lia had to have the lamp. I bought it right after you put up the wallpaper. The woman at the store knew and had been sworn to secrecy."

Ryan leaned forward and handed Tanner a slim box.

Inside was a savings bond in Lia's name. "For her college fund," Ryan explained. "It's going to be that time before you know it."

College? His daughter? Of course he wanted her to go, but it seemed so far away. Ryan's gift made him think that the future would be here quicker than he realized.

"Look at all this," Kelly said. "Dresses and lamps and money for college. You're turning into a real dad."

She was right. The baby stuff didn't scare him anymore. Nor did his daughter. No matter what happened, he now knew that he and Lia were going to make it. The question was would they make it alone, or would someone else join their little family?

"I can't get enough of you," Tanner whispered, his hands buried deep in Kelly's long hair.

She lay beneath him, her naked body all feminine curves and welcoming heat. He could feel her breasts pressing against his chest and the pressure of her legs wrapped around him, urging him deeper. He was so damn close, but he didn't want to finish…not yet. He wanted their lovemaking to last longer. As it was, they'd barely made it upstairs after the last guest had left. Their clothes lay scattered on the stairs, and it was all he'd been able to do to control himself enough to slip on a condom before plunging inside her.

"Oh, Tanner." She breathed his name with a passionate gasp. She was as responsive this time as she'd been the last.

He'd brought her to climax just by kissing her breasts. When he'd touched between her legs, she'd been so very ready. Slipping one of his fingers inside her, he'd felt the deep contractions of her muscles as she convulsed around him. Even now, with each thrust, she climaxed, shuddering and clutching, urging him on, to make her do that again.

The problem was watching her react like that was such a huge turn-on that he couldn't hold back. But he had to try. So he forced himself to think of something else. Work maybe or—

She grabbed his buttocks and pressed down, forcing him deeper. She contracted again, milking him. Pleasure built unbearably. He swore, knowing he'd just crossed the point of no return.

"I want you," he growled, then kissed her. He plunged his tongue into her mouth as he plunged his maleness deep inside her. Her movements were frantic, begging, intoxicating. She whimpered.

He moved faster and faster, lost in the moment, feeling himself collect for the ultimate release. Then it was on him. All he could do was hang on as his body collected itself, then exploded, sending his release rocketing through him. Even as he absorbed the exquisite pleasure, he felt her tightening and releasing as her own climax rippled through her.

They clung to each other until their heartbeats returned to normal. Then he opened his eyes and gazed at her. "Wow."

"My thoughts exactly," she whispered. "How do you do that to me? How do you make me react that way?"

"Just luck."

"Oh, I think it's more than that. Chemistry, maybe."

Or love. But he didn't say that because he wasn't sure. Did he love Kelly? Could he risk it all with her? He touched her face, then gently kissed her mouth. He couldn't imagine her not being a part of his world. She'd entered his life along with Lia, and in some ways the two were irrevocably linked in his mind.

"Thank you," he told her.

"Thank *you*, Tanner. It's wonderful to finally get what all the fuss is about."

He rolled onto his side, drawing her with him. "I've missed you."

"Me, too. It's been a long week." She smiled. "I have a lot to tell you. Many things have happened in the past few days."

"Good things or bad things?"

She paused to consider. "Mostly good. I've learned a lot about myself and my past. I went to see—"

An electronic beep filled the room. Kelly sat up. "That's my phone, but where on earth are my slacks?"

"The stairs," he said.

While she went to check her text message, he looked in on his daughter. Fortunately Lia had grown accustomed to the sound of Kelly's phone. The baby barely stirred.

Two minutes later he heard Kelly in the hallway. He went out to join her and found her frantically pulling on clothes. "I have to go," she said.

He frowned. "I thought you weren't on call tonight."

"I'm not. It's someone from the clinic. Corina." She looked at him. Her face had gone pale, and her eyes were huge. "It's too early. There's something wrong. Dear God, she's only seventeen. She's had enough trouble in her life already—she doesn't need this." She pulled on her shirt and headed down the stairs. "I'm sorry, Tanner. I have to be there. I don't have backup for my clinic patients."

"It's okay. I understand."

She paused at the bottom of the stairs and looked up

at him. "Are you sure? I didn't mean to end our evening this way."

"I know. It's fine. Do you want me to drive you to the hospital?"

"No. I don't know how long I'll be." She paused. "I have to go."

And then she was gone. He listened for the sound of the front door closing. After that, there was only silence. Their parting seemed so unfinished. At first Tanner wondered if he was angry with her and just didn't want to admit it. Then he realized it wasn't that at all. What bothered him was what he'd wanted to say as she'd been leaving.

I love you.

He'd wanted to speak the words to her, calling them out as both a talisman and a prayer—for her knowledge and her safekeeping.

I love you. He'd never said those words to anyone before in his life. Women had said them to him, and he'd always assumed they were lying.

He turned on his heel and returned to his daughter's room. Even though she was sleeping, he touched her face, then her tiny hand. "Hey, Lia, it's your dad. I just realized something. I've never told you I love you." His throat tightened. "Well, I do. I love you more than I can tell you. I'm going to tell you every single day for the rest of your life." He smiled. "Or at least while you're living under my roof. It'll be hard to say it every day when you're off at college. I want you to know how important you are to me. I want you to know that I'm always going to be here for you." Then he bent over and kissed her.

Finally he returned to his bedroom. Not to sleep but to wait for Kelly to return.

* * *

"She's bleeding," the nurse told Kelly as she scrubbed at the large sink. "The baby is doing all right for now."

Kelly's mind raced frantically as she considered possibilities. "Is the neonatal unit ready for us?" she asked.

"Yes, Doctor."

Kelly stepped away from the sink and headed for the labor room. She had a bad feeling they were going to have to take the baby. A C-section wasn't the end of the world, but it would probably send Corina into a panic. Still, if she was in trouble, there wasn't another choice. No way was Kelly going to lose either of her patients.

"How's it going?" she asked as she stepped into the room.

Corina looked up and tried to smile, but she was crying too hard. "Not great. Something's wrong, Dr. Kelly. I can feel it."

"Your baby wants to come a little early," Kelly said, her voice reassuring. She was frantic to start examining Corina, but experience had taught her that thirty seconds of reassurance at the beginning of a problem could literally be a lifesaver later. "It happens all the time. Some babies are impatient, and there's not much we can do about that. But you're well into your thirty-third week. It's manageable."

What was less manageable was the blood she saw staining the towels that had been tossed into a bucket below the table. Kelly glanced at the monitors attached to Corina and the baby. They didn't have a whole lot of time.

"It's my fault," Corina cried as tears poured down her cheeks. "I know I did something terrible."

"No, you didn't," Kelly told her. "It's not your fault. It just happened."

Big brown eyes bore into her soul. "My baby knows I don't want it. It's trying to die."

Kelly walked over to Corina and took her hands. "You're not doing anything wrong. You and the baby are going to be fine. Do you trust me?"

Corina stared at her, then nodded slowly.

"Good. Now try to relax. I'm going keep both of you safe."

"Doctor?"

Kelly glanced at the screen, then at the nurse monitoring the bleeding. "Let's get going," Kelly said.

She started issuing orders even as she bent to examine Corina. The rest of the world seemed to fade around her. Her mind cleared. She didn't even have to think; she just knew the next step. She was going to make sure both mother and child came out of this just fine.

Four hours later Kelly stepped into the hallway. It was well after midnight, and all she could think about was crawling into bed. The problem was it was too late to go back to Tanner's, so she was going to have to crawl into her own bed and sleep alone. Right now that seemed like an empty proposition.

Despite the late hour, there were still people in the hospital corridor. The medical institution never shut down. Which was good news. She could leave knowing that Corina and her baby would be well cared for throughout the night.

"You look exhausted," a familiar voice said.

Kelly glanced up and saw Tanner leaning against the wall. Despite how tired she felt, her heart fluttered in her chest and she couldn't help smiling.

"What are you doing here?"

He shrugged, then walked toward her. "I missed you. I was also afraid you'd get some fool idea that it was too late to come back to my place, so I wanted to be here to tell you that you were wrong. I want you in my bed. To sleep," he amended as he reached out and squeezed her hand. "As much as I'd like to do other things, we both have to get up early in the morning."

She blinked. This wasn't making sense. "You came down here in the middle of the night to see me? Where's Lia?"

"Charming the nurses," he said, jerking his head back toward the nurses' station. "I sneaked her in. So far no one has threatened to call security."

"How long have you been here?"

"About twenty minutes. I called and kept track of how things were going with your patient so I would know when you would be finished." His expression softened. "They told me it was touch and go for a while, that you saved the girl's life and her baby's."

"You're not a family member. They wouldn't have given out that information to just anyone."

"I'm not just anyone."

He wasn't. He was someone very special to her, she thought.

"I know it's not my business, or my place, but I'm proud of you, Dr. Kelly Hall. From what I heard, you pulled off a Christmas miracle tonight."

He pulled her close, and she went willingly into his arms. It hadn't been a miracle, but for a while she'd thought she might actually lose them both. Corina had started bleeding even more, and then the baby had become distressed. It could have been a disaster, but everything had turned out in the end.

"I had great training," she said. "I knew what to do to save them."

"It was more than that. I overheard a couple of nurses talking. They said that you're gifted. It's as if you know exactly how much more your patients can stand before their strength gives out."

She started to protest, but then she realized he was right. She'd always had the way of sensing the strength of both her mothers and their infants. She loved her work. Tonight wasn't the first time her skill had saved both mother and child.

Kelly pressed her lips together and tried to grasp the significance of what she'd just figured out. She'd saved lives. She was good at what she did—maybe *gifted* was too strong a term, but she was highly committed and skilled. That counted for a lot. At one time she'd chosen her specialty as a second best—not what she wanted to do but close. Yet now, after having been in practice for several years, she suddenly understood that this was where she belonged. She was a terrific gynecologist and obstetrician. She had nothing of which to be ashamed.

She wrapped her arms around Tanner's waist and hugged him tight. "Thank you for being here tonight."

He smiled at her. "I'm not even going to bother saying 'You're welcome.' Where else would I want to be?"

Chapter 15

Despite the fact that she'd only had about four hours of sleep the night before, Kelly was in her office before seven. She had a couple of things to do there before she made her way to the hospital to check on her patients, especially Corina.

Kelly set her purse on her desk, then settled in her chair. She stared at the phone for a long moment before picking it up and dialing a familiar number. With the two-hour time difference between Oregon and Kansas, she should catch her father right as he came to work.

"Pastor Hall's office, this is Betty."

"Hi, Betty, it's Kelly. Is my dad around?"

"Kelly!" The older woman's voice rose with a note of both surprise and pleasure. "How are you? Your father says you work too many hours. Is that true? You have to take care of yourself. You're not a teenager anymore. You need your sleep and lots of fruits and vegetables. Did I send you my lentil vegetable soup recipe? It's wonderful. I served it at the ladies' prayer lunch just last month, and it was a hit. I'll email it to you. Did you know we have email at the church now? Very modern. Horace and I are thinking of getting a computer of our own. The things people can do on those machines. It's just amazing. So why were you calling, dear?"

Despite her exhaustion, her worries and her questions, Kelly couldn't help smiling. Betty never changed. According to town legend, she'd been born talking.

"I'd like to speak to my father."

"Of course you would. He's right in his office. Just got here a few minutes ago, but then you'd know that. Pastor Hall is as regular as the church clock. He walks through that door every day at exactly eight fifty-eight. In the past ten years I don't know that he's been late more than once, and that was because he stopped to help old Mrs. Winston with her car. It had a flat tire, or was it out of gas? Anyway, he's quite punctual." She paused to draw breath. "I'll let him know you're on the phone."

There was a click as she was put on hold. Kelly knew that it would be a couple of minutes until her father could get Betty off the intercom so that he could pick up the phone. The older woman was a trial at times, but she was as much a part of Kelly's world as the town where she'd grown up. Betty and Horace had never had children. Despite that, and their differences—her talking constantly and him as silent as a tree—they rarely went anywhere without each other. And when they were together, they always held hands. Once when Kelly had been all of fifteen or sixteen, she'd even come across them kissing in a corner of the choir room. It had been the only time she'd known Betty to be quiet.

"This is an unexpected pleasure," her father said a few minutes later. "Good morning."

"Hi, Dad. How are you?"

"Fine, and, according to Betty, I was here right on time, which is a good thing. Otherwise I would have missed your call." He chuckled. "That woman."

"I know she makes you crazy, but you can't get rid of her. She's the only one who understands the filing system."

"Exactly. So what's on your agenda for Christmas?"

She appreciated that he asked questions rather than assuming a surprise call meant trouble. Her father had always thought the best of her, she reminded herself. He'd always been there for her. Which made the reason for her phone call more difficult.

"I have to ask you something," she said slowly, holding on to the receiver and closing her eyes. She pictured her father, in his shirtsleeves, sitting behind his large desk. "It's about when I was in high school." She cleared her throat. "More specifically, when I got pregnant."

"All right. What would you like to talk about?"

She drew in a deep breath. Her eyes began to burn, but she refused to cry. "I never wanted to disappoint you," she whispered. "I knew what you expected of me, and I wanted to do that, but things got out of hand. It was just the one time."

She heard him sigh. "I can't decide if I should tease you about it only taking one time, or if I should remind you that I love you. I always loved you. And I don't mean that with a silent 'even while you were pregnant' at the end of that sentence. I think I loved you most then because you're my daughter and you were in pain. I suffered with you. In a different way, perhaps, but no less profoundly."

"Then why did the light go out of your eyes?" she asked. "Until then, whenever you looked at me, I could see this wonderful light shining from your eyes. I knew that I was the center of your world. But when I told you, the light died. It's never come back."

"Oh, Kelly, I wish you were here instead of several thousand miles away."

She gave a soft laugh that was half a sob, as well. "So you could beat me?"

He chuckled. Daniel Hall had never once spanked her. The threat of a beating was a private joke between them. "Maybe," he teased, then grew serious. "I'll admit that I was shocked to find out about your pregnancy and a little chagrined. After all, you were the pastor's daughter. But that was more about me than you. I thought I knew where you were all the time and what you were doing. It was startling to realize you'd grown up so much. Somewhere along the way my little girl had turned into a beautiful woman, and I hadn't noticed. Probably because I didn't want to see. Once you grew up, you would go away, and I didn't think I could bear that."

Two tears escaped her tightly closed eyelids. Kelly groped for the box of tissues on her desk. She wiped her face and sniffed. "I'm sorry, Daddy."

"No. Don't you dare be sorry. I'm proud of you, Kelly. Not because you're a doctor, but because of who you are. You're the best daughter ever. Nothing changed for me. The light didn't go out of my eyes—it went out of you. And when it died inside, you couldn't see it in me anymore."

Her eyes popped open. Kelly stared unseeingly at the wall across the room. "What?"

"It's true. I've wanted to say something for years now, but it never seemed like the right time. I've watched you punish yourself over and over for something that was never your fault. You were seventeen when you got pregnant and barely eighteen when the baby was born. You had a wonderful dream of being a doctor, and the brains and opportunity to make that happen. Yes, you gave your child up for adoption. Is that so horrible?"

"I don't know."

"I've spoken with Annie Jane's grandparents just as you have, Kelly. Their daughter was desperate to have a baby. In many ways, you saved Sara. Did it ever occur to you that was the reason you got pregnant? Did you ever stop to think about the gift you gave that family? You can have more children if you choose, but Sara couldn't have any. Every life touched by that child has been blessed. Even yours."

His words swirled around in her head. She'd never thought of her circumstances this way before.

"You are a gifted healer," he continued. "You've always said that you could have made it if you'd kept the baby. And I'm sure you would have. You're smart and determined. But what would you have done with your life? Would you have gone to medical school?"

"I don't know," Kelly admitted. "It would have taken so long just to get through college, what with working full time, taking care of a child and taking classes."

"You made a choice. You weren't selfish, and you weren't bad—you just made a choice. You gave your daughter to a warm, loving family. There is no evil in that decision. Let it go, Kelly. Forgive yourself. You have been blessed. Stop turning your back on those blessings. Be grateful and move on."

Tears flowed down her cheeks, but they weren't painful or sorrowful; instead they healed her. She felt the empty spots in her heart filling with love and compassion. She felt her spirit lighten, perhaps for the first time since her baby had been born.

"You're right," she said simply. "Why didn't I see it before?"

"Because you weren't ready. You had to take the journey to get to your current destination. I love you, and I'm proud of you."

Even across half a continent, she felt the warmth of her father's love. It was as if he was with her, holding her close, just as he had when she'd been young. "I love you, too, Daddy."

He was right. The light had always been in his eyes. But she'd been too ashamed to see it shining there. She'd spent years beating herself up for something that deserved to be forgiven a long time ago. If she'd been blind to her father's love for all this time, what else was she having trouble seeing?

"Hi," Kelly said as she walked into Corina's room late that afternoon. "How are you feeling?"

The teenager smiled wanly. "Better. I slept most of the day."

"The nurses gave you high marks for cooperating," Kelly told her, then pulled up a chair. She would check vital signs in a minute; first she owed her patient an apology.

"Thank you for saving my life," Corina said before Kelly could start talking. "I know it got bad."

Kelly touched the teenager's hand. "I'm glad I was here for you this time, Corina. Because I know I wasn't the last time I saw you, and I'm sorry about that."

Corina raised her bed a few inches. Her braided dark hair spread out on her pillow. Her big eyes widened slightly. "You got called to the hospital. It was an emergency."

Kelly shook her head. "You're letting me off the hook, and it's not necessary. Yes, I was called and I had to go then, but you needed to talk. I should have made time later." She squeezed the girl's fingers, then released her hand.

"The reasons are complicated," Kelly said slowly, meeting her gaze. "Your situation reminded me too much of something that had happened in my life. Something that I was afraid to face. I got uncomfortable, and it seemed so much easier to hide. So that's what I did."

"I don't understand."

"I know. So I'm going to explain." Kelly quickly recounted the events of her own senior year in high school.

Corina stared in shock. "You gave up a baby for adoption when you were my age?"

"Yes. A little girl. Her name is Annie Jane, and she's a teenager, a little younger than you. I've kept in touch with her family through her grandparents. For a long time I thought I'd been selfish in giving up my daughter. I thought if I just tried hard enough it wouldn't have been difficult for me to make it work. But I was wrong. I had an opportunity to do something with my life. Something that would make a difference. Something that I desperately wanted. I'm not saying that giving up Annie Jane was easy. I will have to live with the consequences of that decision for the rest of my life. But I don't regret the decision. Knowing what I know now, I would do it all again."

Baby, It's Christmas

Corina's eyes widened. "You wouldn't change anything?"

"Well, I'd forgive myself a little sooner. But aside from that, I wouldn't change a thing."

Kelly drew in a deep breath and probed her heart. The sense of peace filling her told her that she spoke the absolute truth. She *wouldn't* change a thing about her life. Knowing what she knew now, she would even still have become an OB-GYN, because that was where her talent lay. Her need to be around children would be filled by having a half-dozen kids of her own.

"You have to do what's right for you," Kelly told the teenager. "The other girls in the neighborhood aren't going to live your life. They don't have your scholarship or your drive. Think long and hard before you turn your back on that opportunity. What do you really want for yourself and your child?"

Corina began to cry. Kelly rose and hugged the girl. "It's okay. You don't have to decide now."

"I feel so guilty," Corina said. "But I want to go to college. I spoke to the adoption lady a couple of days ago. She says that there are lots of really great families who want my baby. She'll help me pick the best one." Corina raised her head. Tears spilled out of her eyes. "Am I doing the right thing? Am I being selfish?"

"Not for one second. You are making a tough choice, but it's the right choice for you. I believe in you. If you want, I'll be with you when you choose the family. And I want to stay in touch while you're in college."

She brushed away the teenager's tears. "I even want to help financially. I'll cover whatever expenses the scholarship doesn't. In return, you're going to have to bust your butt to maintain your grades. The only thing I want from you is two promises. The first is that you'll always do your best, and the second is that you'll forgive yourself, and, instead of feeling guilty, that you'll spend your time counting your blessings."

Corina hugged her hard. "I promise," she whispered. "Thank you, Dr. Kelly. Thank you for everything."

"No problem."

Forty minutes later Kelly left a much-relieved Corina watching a morning talk show. The teenager would have to stay in the hospital for another night; then she would be moving into Kelly's tiny apartment. Corina never wanted to go back to her tenement neighborhood again. Life would be complicated until August, when Corina left for college, but Kelly knew they would figure it out.

She stopped in her tracks. Tomorrow was Christmas Eve, and she couldn't let Corina come home to her sterile apartment. For the first time in her adult life, Kelly was going to decorate for Christmas. And not just because of Corina, but because *she* deserved to have a home that truly felt like a home, too. She was worth it.

She felt as if the weight of the world had been lifted off her shoulders. She was filled with a sense of calm and completeness she'd never experienced before, and her first thought was to share it all with Tanner.

She paused in the hallway. Who would have thought that Tanner could have become a part of her life so very quickly? Less than two months ago she'd barely known the man existed—and what she did know she didn't like. Now she couldn't imagine her life without him. If she'd ever made a list of what she was looking for, Tanner would be everything she'd ever wanted.

She loved him.

Kelly didn't know when that had first happened, but

it was true now. She hadn't just bonded with Lia; she'd also bonded with Tanner. The time they'd spent together, the confessions they'd shared, the lovemaking had bound her to him with a connection that was strong enough to last a lifetime. She wanted to be with him always. She wanted to make a home with him, have children with him, grow old with him.

A quick glance at her watch told her that he should be getting home right about now. With his daughter. Little Lia. She loved Lia, too. Should she go to him and tell him all that she'd learned, or should she wait? Then she reminded herself that she'd waited long enough already. She'd wasted years waiting to be good enough, when the answer had been inside her all along. She was done waiting. It was time to act. Tomorrow was Christmas Eve, and she didn't want to spend one more Christmas on the outside, looking in. She wanted to belong.

Kelly threw her car into Park behind Tanner's truck in his driveway and raced toward the house. It had started snowing again, blanketing the world in white. As she breathed, the cold air felt like it was cleansing her from the inside.

Without knocking, she opened the front door. "Hello?" she called softly.

There was no response, but she heard a small sound from upstairs. She jogged up the steps and into the nursery.

Tanner didn't see her at first. He had just laid Lia into the crib, and he was leaning over to kiss the top of her head. His heart had such capacity for love, Kelly thought. Could he fit her in, too? She removed her hat and smoothed down her hair. Now that she was here, she wasn't so sure what to say.

"Hi," he said when he spotted her. "I didn't hear you come in. How are you feeling?"

"Tired." She grinned. Despite her physical and emotional exhaustion the night before, when she and Tanner had finally returned to his place and put Lia back to bed, all she'd wanted was to make love. She'd needed to feel him next to her, on top of her, filling her and making her whole. Now she recognized that she'd needed to express her love, but at the time she'd only known that she needed to fill the yawning emptiness inside.

He stretched. "Me, too. But in a good way. You can keep me awake for that any time you'd like."

She stared at him, at his familiar handsome face, at his blue eyes and his strong body. "I have to tell you something," she said. "I've been doing a lot of thinking. I spoke with my father this morning and with Corina just a few minutes ago. I finally realized I've been punishing myself for years. I've been living half a life because I didn't feel that I deserved more. I've been so worried about my past that I forgot to think about my future." She stood a little straighter.

"But all that's behind me now. I've come to understand that if I can forgive other women for the difficult choices they made, I can also forgive myself. I did the best I could at the time. I've gone on to have a successful life doing something that I love. Equally important, my daughter is a happy, healthy, well-adjusted young woman. In time she may want to meet me, or she may decide against that. Either choice is hers. I have promised myself to be as understanding of her as my father was of me."

Tanner stared at her. "You *have* been working through a lot."

She nodded. "I'm done punishing myself. I've decided to go after what I want."

He didn't move, but she sensed his withdrawal from the conversation as surely as if he'd stepped out of the room. "What's wrong?"

"Nothing. I'm happy for you." His words sounded sincere, but the bleak expression in his eyes didn't change. "It's just that I'm going to miss you. I've gotten used to having you around. I didn't think we had anything permanent, but I also hadn't figured on you leaving just yet."

Kelly told herself not to jump to conclusions. Just as she had issues from her past to come to terms with, Tanner had the same. She took a calming breath before speaking.

"I'm not going anywhere, Tanner. I'm willing to give you as much time as you need to learn to trust me."

"Oh, I do trust you. You've been a great help to Lia and me." He leaned forward and captured her hands in his. "You're an amazing woman. In time you're going to want to find the right kind of man. Maybe another doctor or a lawyer. Someone professional. Someone—"

"I love *you*," she said, interrupting. "I don't want anyone else."

He stiffened. The bleakness left his eyes, but she couldn't read what he was thinking. "You say that now, but it's because of last night. Eventually—"

She squeezed his hands, took half a step closer and met his gaze without blinking. "Eventually I'm still going to love you. Not a doctor or a lawyer or anyone else. Just you. I love you, Tanner. And Lia. I love both of you."

"Dammit, Kelly, I'm trying to be noble here."

"Why?"

"Because you deserve better."

She gathered up all her courage. Here it was—the moment of truth. Was she really going to say what she was thinking? Was she, for once in her life, going to go for it?

"Could anyone love me more or better than you do?" she asked.

She watched him wrestle with his demons. Uncertainty, longing, pain, mistrust, need—all chased across his face. She knew about his past, about the ways he'd been let down. She knew how difficult it would be for him to allow himself to believe that someone was always going to be there for him. She knew about his pride, his strength and the small dark place he kept hidden in his soul.

He reached out and stroked her cheek. "No one could love you more than I do," he said hoarsely. "Or better. You are my life, my world. I don't want anyone else in my bed or my arms. You're the one I want. For me, for Lia, for the children I want to have with you." He motioned to himself. "I'm a builder. It's what I do. Is it enough?"

He was fiercely intense, his passion and love burning hot inside of him. She loved everything about him. She took his hands in hers once more.

"You are more than enough—just as you are. You are the light shining in the darkness of my soul, and I am the same for you. I've waited all my life to find you, Tanner Malone. Don't for a moment think I'm going to let you go."

He pulled her close and kissed her. The familiar feel of his body was enough to make her melt against him. Nothing had ever been as right as being with him.

"So when do you want to get married?" he asked.

She laughed. "Not if, but when?"

He stared at her. "When," he repeated firmly. "I'm not letting you get away, Kelly. I love you too much as it is."

"I'm guilty of that, too," she said. "Yes, I'll marry you. Whenever and wherever you'd like. I don't care if we have a big wedding."

"How long do we have to wait after getting a marriage license? I want to start the new year as a family."

A family. The words brought tears to her eyes. She wanted that more than anything.

"Would you mind if I adopted Lia?"

"Mind? No. You're already her mother. We should make it legal."

And that word made the tears spill over—*mother.* In that instant, a feeling of the purest peace flowed through her. Life had come full circle. Years ago, she had given up a baby for adoption. She knew now with utter certainty that she'd made the right decision. She'd given her child to a family who loved her as much as she, Kelly, loved little Lia.

The daughter of her heart.

Tanner kissed her again, and every thought went out of her head as he worked his magic on her. After a few moments she pulled back enough to tell him, "My teenage patient is going to move in with us for a few months. I hope you don't mind."

He laughed. "Anything you want, as long as I'll have you. No matter what, I'll love you forever."

"I know." That was the best part, she thought as she hugged him close. She did know.

Epilogue

Six years later...

At the sound of the doorbell, Lia raced down the stairs with her four-year-old brother, Dane, close on her heels. The legs of her jeans were just a little too short, Kelly noted. Again. Her hair was so blond it was almost white, while Dane had his father's coloring.

"Annie's here, Mommy. She's here!"

Kelly walked—waddled—after them. Lia's feelings were wonderfully uncomplicated. Although they'd met Annie only a few months ago, Lia thought of her as "big sister," period.

Lia flung open the front door and launched herself at their guest. Dane, struck by a sudden fit of shyness, looped an arm around one of Kelly's legs.

Annie hugged Lia and turned to Kelly with a smile. "Wow, you're—"

"Huge?" Kelly supplied with a laugh. "Yes, and getting bigger every day. I'm due on January 9."

"Less than three weeks to go."

"You know it."

The baby kicked. Kelly placed Annie's hand on her baby bump so the younger woman could feel the movement. She couldn't help remembering all those years ago, when she was young and so very frightened, feeling Annie move inside her.

While Lia's feelings toward Annie were uncomplicated, Kelly's were multilayered. Although she felt maternal toward the younger woman, she wasn't her mom. Annie already had a mom. When Kelly looked at Annie, she was filled with love, wonder and maybe a hint of nostalgia for a time that never was. Mostly she felt gratitude that Annie had had such a happy childhood, and that she'd sought out her birth mother earlier that year. Annie and her parents had spent a week in Honeygrove in August. By the time they'd left, Sara seemed to have let go of the last of her reservations. She'd hugged Kelly fiercely when they said goodbye. This time, Annie had come alone, to spend the first few days of her break with them before going home for Christmas.

"I helped a cow give birth last week," Annie said. "I did my large-animal rotation this semester."

They heard a door close from the back of the house.

"Speaking of large animals…" Kelly said, then called out, "We're in here!"

Tanner rounded the corner from the kitchen. He wore his typical work clothes—jeans, a dark blue button-down and heavy boots. He looked so handsome, her heart leaped. Even after six years together, seeing her husband was an instant mood boost. Especially when his whole face lit up every time he saw her, too.

The kids ran toward him, calling, "Daddy! Daddy!"

He smiled. She knew his latest project was stressful, but he didn't bring any of that home. The moment he stepped through the door, his focus was on the family.

He and Annie greeted each other briefly; then he turned those Malone blue eyes toward Kelly. The baby kicked, but she was pretty sure that was a coincidence.

With one warm hand on her baby bump, he pressed a kiss on her lips, filled with promise for later. "Good day?"

"Very. I had two moms in labor in adjoining delivery rooms, but the babies cooperated by taking turns."

"Sounds like you overdid it," he said, guiding her toward the sofa.

She knew better than to argue. He'd been just as solicitous when she was pregnant with Dane, and just as stubborn about refusing to believe her when she said she felt fine.

"Annie, don't let her move from this spot." He lifted Kelly's feet onto the sofa and covered her legs with a knitted blanket. She had to admit, it felt wonderful to rest. "Keep her company while the kids and I go grab some takeout."

Annie met Kelly's gaze, and both women suppressed smiles.

"Yes, sir," Annie said.

As Tanner helped the kids into their winter coats, hats, and mittens, with the kids chattering all the while about the adventures they'd had today, Kelly leaned back her head. She let the sounds of her happy little family wash over her. She was blessed in every possible way.

* * * * *

Also by Maisey Yates

HQN Books

Harlequin Desire

For more books by Maisey Yates,
visit www.maiseyyates.com.

HOLD ME, COWBOY

Maisey Yates

To KatieSauce, the sister I was always waiting for.
What a joy it is to have you in my life.

Chapter 1

"Creative photography," Madison West muttered as she entered the security code on the box that contained the key to the cabin she would be staying in for the weekend.

She looked across the snowy landscape to see another home situated *far* too close to the place she would be inhabiting for the next couple of days. The photographs on the vacation-rental website hadn't mentioned that she would be sharing the property with anyone else.

And obviously, the example pictures had been taken from inventive angles.

It didn't matter. Nothing was going to change her plans. She just hoped the neighbors had earplugs. Because she was having sex this weekend. Nonstop sex.

Ten years celibate, and it was ending tonight. She had finally found *the one*. Not the one she was going to marry, obviously. *Please.* Love was for other people. People who hadn't been tricked, manipulated and humiliated when they were seventeen.

No, she had no interest in love and marriage. But she had abundant interest in orgasms. So much interest. And she had found the perfect man to deliver them.

All day, all night, for the next forty-eight hours.

She was armed with a suitcase full of lingerie and four bottles of wine. Neighbors be damned. She'd been hoping for a little more seclusion, but this was fine. It would be fine.

She unlocked the door and stepped inside, breathing a sigh of relief when she saw that the interior, at least, met with her expectations. But it was a little bit smaller than it had looked online, and she could only hope that wasn't some sort of dark portent for the rest of her evening.

She shook her head; she was not going to introduce that concern into the mix, thank you very much. There was enough to worry about when you were thinking about breaking ten years of celibacy without adding such concerns.

Christopher was going to arrive soon, so she figured she'd better get upstairs and start setting a scene. She made her way to the bedroom, then opened her suitcase and took out the preselected bit of lace she had chosen for their first time. It was red, which looked very good on her, if a bit obvious. But she was aiming for obvious.

Christopher wasn't her boyfriend. And he wasn't going to be. He was a very nice equine-vitamin-supplement salesman she'd met a few weeks ago when he'd come by the West estate. She had bought some products for her horses, and they'd struck up a conversation, which had transitioned into a flirtation.

Typically, when things began to transition into flirtation, Maddy put a stop to them. But she hadn't with him. Maybe because he was special. Maybe because ten years was just way too long. Either way, she had kept on flirting with him.

They'd gone out for drinks, and she'd allowed him to kiss her. Which had been a lot more than she'd allowed any other guy in recent years. It had reminded her how much she'd enjoyed that sort of thing once upon a time. And once she'd been reminded...well.

He'd asked for another date. She'd stopped him. Because wouldn't a no-strings physical encounter be way better?

He'd of course agreed. Because he was a man.

But she hadn't wanted to get involved with anyone in town. She didn't need anyone seeing her at a hotel or his house or with his car parked at her little home on her parents' property.

Thus, the cabin-weekend idea had been born.

She shimmied out of her clothes and wiggled into the skintight lace dress that barely covered her backside. Then she set to work fluffing her blond hair and applying some lipstick that matched the lingerie.

She was not answering the door in this outfit, however.

She put her long coat back on over the lingerie, then gave her reflection a critical look. It had been a long time since she had dressed to attract a man. Usually, she was more interested in keeping them at a distance.

"Not tonight," she said. "*Not* tonight."

She padded downstairs, peering out the window and seeing nothing beyond the truck parked at the small house across the way and a vast stretch of snow, falling harder and faster.

Typically, it didn't snow in Copper Ridge, Oregon.

You had to drive up to the mountains—as she'd done today—to get any of the white stuff. So, for her, this was a treat, albeit a chilly one. But that was perfect, since she planned to get her blood all heated and stuff.

She hummed, keeping an eye on the scene outside, waiting for Christopher to pull in. She wondered if she should have brought a condom downstairs with her. Decided that she should have.

She went back upstairs, taking them two at a time, grateful that she was by herself, since there was nothing sexy about her ascent. Then she rifled through her bag, found some protection and curled her fingers around it before heading back down the stairs as quickly as possible.

As soon as she entered the living area, the lights flickered, then died. Suddenly, everything in the house seemed unnaturally quiet, and even though it was probably her imagination, she felt the temperature drop several degrees.

"Are you kidding me?" she asked, into the darkness.

There was no answer. Nothing but a subtle creak from the house. Maybe it was all that heavy snow on the roof. Maybe it was going to collapse. That would figure.

A punishment for her thinking she could be normal and have sex.

A shiver worked its way down her spine, and she jolted.

Suddenly, she had gone from hopeful and buoyant to feeling a bit flat and tragic. That was definitely not the best sign.

No. She wasn't doing this. She wasn't sinking into self-pity and tragedy. Been there, done that for ten years, thank you.

Madison didn't believe in signs. *So there.* She believed

in fuses blowing in bad weather when overtaxed heaters had to work too hard in ancient houses. Yes, *that* she believed in. She also believed that she would have to wait for Christopher to arrive to fix the problem.

She sighed and then made her way over to the kitchen counter and grabbed hold of her purse as she deposited the two condoms on the counter. She pulled her phone out and grimaced when she saw that she had no signal.

Too late, she remembered that she had thought the lack of cell service might be an attraction to a place like this. That it would be nice if both she and Christopher could be cut off from the outside world while they indulged themselves.

That notion seemed really freaking stupid right now. Since she couldn't use the phone in the house thanks to the outage, and that left her cut off from the outside world all alone.

"Oh no," she said, "I'm the first five minutes of a crime show. I'm going to get ax-murdered. And I'm going to die a born-again virgin."

She scowled, looking back out at the resolutely blank landscape. Christopher still wasn't here. But it looked like the house across the way had power.

She pressed her lips together, not happy about the idea of interrupting her neighbor. Or of meeting her neighbor, since the whole point of going out of town was so they could remain anonymous and not see people.

She tightened the belt on her coat and made her way slowly out the front door, bracing herself against the arctic wind.

She muttered darkly about the cold as she made her way across the space between the houses. She paused for a moment in front of the larger cabin, lit up and looking all warm and toasty. Clearly, this was the premium accommodation. While hers was likely beset by rodents that had chewed through relevant cords.

She huffed, clutching her coat tightly as she knocked on the door. She waited, bouncing in place to try to keep her blood flowing. She just needed to call Christopher and find out when he would be arriving and, if he was still a ways out, possibly beg her neighbor for help getting the power going. Or at least help getting a fire started.

The front door swung open and Madison's heart stopped. The man standing there was large, so tall that she only just came up to the middle of his chest. He was broad, his shoulders well muscled, his waist trim. He had the kind of body that came not from working out but from hard physical labor.

Then she looked up. Straight nose, square jaw, short brown hair and dark eyes that were even harder than his muscles. And far too familiar.

"What are *you* doing here?"

Sam McCormack gritted his teeth against the sharp tug of irritation that assaulted him when Madison West asked the question that had been on his own lips.

"I rented the place," he responded, not inviting her in. "Though I could ask you the same question."

She continued to do a little bounce in place, her arms folded tight against her body, her hands clasped beneath her chin. "And you'd get the same answer," she said. "I'm across the driveway."

"Then you're at the wrong door." He made a move to shut said door, and she reached out, stopping him.

"Sam. Do you always have to be this unpleasant?"

It was a question that had been asked of him more than once. And he gave his standard answer. "Yes."

"Sam," she said, sounding exasperated. "The power went out, and I'm freezing to death. Can I come in?"

He let out a long-suffering sigh and stepped to the side. He didn't like Madison West. He never had. Not from the moment he had been hired on as a farrier for the West estate eight years earlier. In all the years since he'd first met Madison, since he'd first started shoeing her horses, he'd never received one polite word from her.

But then, he'd never given one either.

She was sleek, blonde and freezing cold—and he didn't mean because she had just come in from the storm. The woman carried her own little snow cloud right above her head at all times, and he wasn't a fan of ice princesses. Still, something about her had always been like a burr beneath his skin that he couldn't get at.

"Thank you," she said crisply, stepping over the threshold.

"You're rich and pretty," he said, shutting the door tight behind her. "And I'm poor. And kind of an ass. It wouldn't do for me to let you die out there in a snowdrift. I would probably end up getting hung."

Madison sniffed, making a show of brushing snowflakes from the shoulders of her jacket. "I highly doubt you're poor," she said drily.

She wasn't wrong. A lot had changed since he'd gone to work for the Wests eight years ago. Hell, a lot had changed in the past year.

The strangest thing was that his art had taken off, and along with it the metalwork and blacksmithing business he ran with his brother, Chase.

But now he was busier coming up with actual fine-art

pieces than he was doing daily grunt work. One sale on a piece like that could set them up for the entire quarter. Strange, and not where he'd seen his life going, but true.

He still had trouble defining himself as an artist. In his mind, he was just a blacksmith cowboy. Most at home on the family ranch, most proficient at pounding metal into another shape. It just so happened that for some reason people wanted to spend a lot of money on that metal.

"Well," he said, "perception is everything."

She looked up at him, those blue eyes hitting him hard, like a punch in the gut. That was the other obnoxious thing about Madison West. She was pretty. She was more than pretty. She was the kind of pretty that kept a man up all night, hard and aching, with fantasies about her swirling in his head.

She was also the kind of woman who would probably leave icicles on a man's member after a blow job.

No, thank you.

"Sure," she said, waving her hand. "Now, I *perceive* that I need to use your phone."

"There's no cell service up here."

"Landline," she said. "I have no power. And no cell service. The source of all my problems."

"In that case, be my guest," he responded, turning away from her and walking toward the kitchen, where the lone phone was plugged in.

He picked up the receiver and held it out to her. She eyed it for a moment as though it were a live snake, then snatched it out of his hand. "Are you just going to stand there?"

He shrugged, crossing his arms and leaning against the doorframe. "I thought I might."

She scoffed, then dialed the number, doing the same

impatient hop she'd been doing outside while she waited for the person on the other end to answer. "Christopher?"

The physical response Sam felt to her uttering another man's name was not something he ever could have anticipated. His stomach tightened, dropped, and a lick of flame that felt a hell of a lot like jealousy sparked inside him.

"What do you mean you can't get up here?" She looked away from him, determinedly so, her eyes fixed on the kitchen floor. "The road is closed. Okay. So that means I can't get back down either?" There was a pause. "Right. Well, hopefully I don't freeze to death." Another pause. "No, you don't need to call anybody. I'm not going to freeze to death. I'm using the neighbor's phone. Just forget it. I don't have cell service. I'll call you if the power comes back on in my cabin."

She hung up then, her expression so sharp it could have cut him clean through.

"I take it you had plans."

She looked at him, her eyes as frosty as the weather outside. "Did you figure that out all by yourself?"

"Only just barely. You know blacksmiths aren't known for their deductive reasoning skills. Mostly we're famous for hitting heavy things with other heavy things."

"Kind of like cavemen and rocks."

He took a step toward her. "Kind of."

She shrank back, a hint of color bleeding into her cheeks. "Well, now that we've established that there's basically no difference between you and a Neanderthal, I better get back to my dark, empty cabin. And hope that you aren't a secret serial killer."

Her sharp tongue left cuts behind, and he had to admit he kind of enjoyed it. There weren't very many people who sparred with him like this. Possibly because he didn't talk to very many people. "Is that a legitimate concern you have?"

"I don't know. The entire situation is just crazy enough that I might be trapped in a horror movie with a tortured artist blacksmith who is also secretly murdery."

"I guarantee you I'm not murdery. If you see me outside with an ax, it will only be because I'm cutting firewood."

She cocked her head to the side, a glint in her blue eyes that didn't look like ice making his stomach—and everything south of there—tighten. "Well, that's a relief. Anyway. I'm going. Dark cabin, no one waiting for me. It promises to be a seriously good time."

"You don't have any idea why the power is out, or how to fix it?" he asked.

"No," she said, sounding exasperated, and about thirty seconds away from stamping her foot.

Well, damn his conscience, but he wasn't letting her go back to an empty, dark, cold cabin. No matter that she had always treated him like a bit of muck she'd stepped in with her handmade riding boots.

"Let me have a look at your fuse box," he said.

"You sound like you'd rather die," she said.

"I pretty much would, but I'm not going to let *you* die either." He reached for his black jacket and the matching black cowboy hat hanging on a hook. He put both on and nodded.

"Thank you," she muttered, and he could tell the little bit of social nicety directed at him cost her dearly.

They headed toward the front door and he pushed it open, waiting for her to go out first. Since he had arrived earlier today, the temperature had dropped drastically.

He had come up to the mountain to do some planning for his next few art projects. It pained him to admit, even to himself, that solitude was somewhat necessary for him to get a clear handle on what he was going to work on next.

"So," he said, making conversation not so much for the sake of it but more to needle her and see if he could earn one of her patented death glares, "Christopher, huh? Your boyfriend?" That hot spike drove its way through his gut again and he did his best to ignore it.

"No," she said tersely. "Just a friend."

"I see. So you decided to meet a man up here for a friendly game of Twister?"

She turned slightly, arching one pale brow. "Yahtzee, actually. I'm very good at it."

"And I'm sure your...*friend* was hoping to get a full house."

She rolled her eyes and looked forward again, taking quick steps over the icy ground, and somehow managing to keep sure footing. Then she opened the door to her cabin. "Welcome," she said, extending her arm. "Please excuse the shuddering cold and oppressive darkness."

"Ladies first," he said.

She shook her head, walking into the house, and he followed behind, closing the door against the elements. It was already cold in the dark little room. "You were just going to come back here and sit in the dark if I hadn't offered to fiddle with the circuit breaker?"

"Maybe I know how to break my own circuits, Sam. Did you ever think of that?"

"Oh, but you said you didn't, Madison."

"I prefer Maddy," she said.

"Sorry, Madison," he said, tipping his hat, just to be a jerk.

"I should have just frozen to death. Then there could have been a legend about my tragic and beautiful demise in the mountains." He didn't say anything. He just looked at her until she sighed and continued talking. "I don't know where the box thingy is. You're going to have to hunt for it."

"I think I can handle that." He walked deeper into the kitchen, then stopped when he saw two purple packets sitting on the kitchen counter. That heat returned with a vengeance when he realized exactly what they were, and what they meant. He looked up, his eyes meeting her extremely guilty gaze. "Yahtzee, huh?"

"That's what the kids call it," she said, pressing her palm over the telling packets.

"Only because they're too immature to call it fucking."

Color washed up her neck, into her cheeks. "Or not crass enough."

In that moment, he had no idea what devil possessed him, and he didn't particularly care. He turned to face her, planting his hands on the countertop, just an inch away from hers. "I don't know about that. I'm betting that you could use a little crassness in your life, Madison West."

"Are you trying to suggest that I need *you*?" she asked, her voice choked.

Lightning streaked through his blood, and in that moment, he was lost. It didn't matter that he thought she was insufferable, a prissy little princess who didn't appreciate any damn thing she had. It didn't matter that he'd come up here to work.

All that mattered was he hadn't touched a woman in a long time, and Madison West was so close all he would have to do was shift his weight slightly and he'd be able to take her into his arms.

He looked down pointedly at her hand, acting as though he could see straight through to the protection beneath. "Well," he said, "you have a couple of the essential ingredients to have yourself a pretty fun evening. All you seem to be missing is the man. But I imagine the guy you invited up here is *nice*. I'm not very nice, Madison," he said, leaning in, "but I could damn sure show you a good time."

Chapter 2

The absolute worst thing was the fact that Sam's words sent a shiver down her spine. Sam McCormack. Why did it have to be Sam McCormack? He was the deadly serpent to her Indiana Jones.

She should throw him out. Throw him out and get back to her very disappointing evening where all orgasms would be self-administered. So, basically a regular Friday night.

She wanted to throw herself on the ground and wail. It was not supposed to be a regular Friday night. She was supposed to be breaking her sex fast. Maybe this was why people had flings in the spring. Inclement weather made winter flings difficult. Also, mostly you just wanted to keep your socks on the whole time. And that wasn't sexy.

Maybe her libido should hibernate for a while. Pop up again when the pear trees were blooming or something.

She looked over at Sam, and her libido made a dash to the foreground. That was the problem with Sam. He irritated her. He was exactly the kind of man she didn't like. He was cocky. He was rough and crude.

Whenever she'd given him very helpful pointers about handling the horses when he came to do farrier work at the estate, he was always telling her to go away and in general showing no deference.

And okay, if he'd come and told her how to do her job, she would have told him where he could stick his hoof nippers. But still. Her animals. So she was entitled to her opinions.

Last time she'd walked into the barn when he was doing shoes, he hadn't even looked up from his work. He'd just pointed back toward the door and shouted, *out!*

Yeah, he was a jerk.

However, there was something about the way he looked in a tight T-shirt, his muscles bulging as he did all that hard labor, that made a mockery of that very certain hatred she felt burning in her breast.

"Are you going to take off your coat and stay awhile?" The question, asked in a faintly mocking tone, sent a dart of tension straight down between her thighs.

She could *not* take off her coat. Because she was wearing nothing more than a little scrap of red lace underneath it. And now that was all she could think of. About how little stood between Sam and her naked body.

About what might happen if she just went ahead and dropped the coat now and revealed all of that to him.

"It's cold," she snapped. "Maybe if you went to work getting the electricity back on rather than standing there making terrible double entendres, I would be able to take off my coat."

He lifted a brow. "And then do you think you'll take me up on my offer to show you a good time?"

"If you can get my electricity back on, I will consider a good time shown to me. Honestly, that's all I want. The ability to microwave popcorn and not turn into a Maddycicle."

The maddening man raised his eyebrows, shooting her a look that clearly said *Suit yourself*, then set about looking for the fuse box.

She stood by alone for a while, her arms wrapped around her midsection. Then she started to feel like an idiot just kind of hanging out there while he searched for the source of all power. She let out an exasperated sigh and followed his path, stopping when she saw him leaning up against a wall, a little metal door fixed between the logs open as he examined the small black switches inside.

"It's not a fuse. That means there's something else going on." He slammed the door shut. Then he turned back to look at her. "You should come over to my cabin."

"No!" The denial was a little bit too enthusiastic. A little bit too telling. "I mean, I can start a fire here—it's going to be fine. I'm not going to freeze."

"You're going to curl up by the fire with a blanket? Like a sad little pet?"

She made a scoffing sound. "No, I'm going to curl up by the fire like the Little Match Girl."

"That makes it even worse. The Little Match Girl froze to death."

"What?"

"How did you not know that?"

"I saw it when I was a kid. It was a *cartoon*. She really died?" Maddy blinked. "What kind of story is that to present to children?"

"An early lesson, maybe? Life is bleak, and then you freeze to death alone?"

"Charming," she said.

"Life rarely is." He kept looking at her. His dark gaze was worrisome.

"I'm fine," she said, because somebody had to say something.

"You are not. Get your suitcase—come over to the cabin. We can flip the lights on, and then if we notice from across the driveway that your power's on again, you can always come back."

It was stupid to refuse him. She knew him, if not personally, at least well enough to know that he wasn't any kind of danger to her.

The alternative was trying to sleep on the couch in the living room while the outside temperatures hovered below freezing, waking up every few hours to keep the fire stoked.

Definitely, going over to his cabin made more sense. But the idea filled her with a strange tension that she couldn't quite shake. Well, she knew exactly what kind of tension it was. *Sexual tension.*

She and Sam had so much of it that hung between them like a fog whenever they interacted. Although, maybe she read it wrong. Maybe on his end it was just irritation and it wasn't at all tinged with sensual shame.

"Why do you have to be so damned reasonable?" she asked, turning away from him and stalking toward the stairs.

"Where are you going?"

She stopped, turning to face him. "To change. Also, to get my suitcase. I have snacks in there."

"Are snacks a euphemism for something interesting?" he asked, arching a dark brow.

She sputtered, genuinely speechless. Which was unusual to downright unheard of. "No," she said, her tone sounding petulant. "I have *actual snacks*."

"Come over to my place. Bring the snacks."

"I will," she said, turning on her heel, heading toward the stairs.

"Maybe bring the Yahtzee too."

Those words hit her hard, with all the impact of a stomach punch. She could feel her face turning crimson, and she refused to look back at him. Refused to react to that bait at all. He didn't want *that*. He did not want to play euphemistic board games with her. And she didn't want to play them with him.

If she felt a little bit…on edge, it was just because she had been anticipating sex and she had experienced profound sex disappointment. That was all.

She continued up the stairs, making her way to the bedroom, then changed back into a pair of jeans and a sweatshirt as quickly as possible before stuffing the little red lace thing back in the bag and zipping everything up.

She lugged it back downstairs, her heart slamming against her breastbone when Sam was in her line of sight again. Tall, broad shouldered and far too sexy for his own good, he promised to be the antidote to sexual disappointment.

But an emotionless hookup with a guy she liked well enough but wouldn't get emotionally involved with was one thing. Replacing him at the last moment with a guy she didn't even like? No, that was out of the question.

Absolutely and completely out of the question.

"Okay," she said, "let's go."

* * *

By the time she got settled in the extra room in the cabin, she was feeling antsy. She could hide, but she was hungry. And Maddy didn't believe in being hungry when food was at hand. Yes, she had some various sugar-based items in her bag, but she needed protein.

In the past, she had braved any number of her father's awkward soirees to gain access to bacon-wrapped appetizers.

She could brave Sam McCormack well enough to root around for sustenance. She would allow no man to stand between herself and her dinner.

Cautiously, she made her way downstairs, hoping that maybe Sam had put himself away for the night. The thought made her smile. That he didn't go to bed like a normal person but closed himself inside…not a coffin. But maybe a scratchy, rock-hewn box that would provide no warmth or comfort. It seemed like something he would be into.

In fairness, she didn't really know Sam McCormack that well, but everything she did know about him led her to believe that he was a supremely unpleasant person. Well, except for the whole him-not-letting-her-die-of-frostbite-in-her-powerless-cabin thing. She supposed she had to go ahead and put that in the Maybe He's Not Such a Jackass column.

Her foot hit the ground after the last stair silently, and she cautiously padded into the kitchen.

"Looking for something?"

She startled, turning around and seeing Sam standing there, leaning in the doorway, his muscular arms crossed over his broad chest. She did her best to look cool. Composed. Not interested in his muscles. "Well—"

she tucked her hair behind her ear "—I was hoping to find some food."

"You brought snacks," he said.

"Candy," she countered.

"So, that made it okay for you to come downstairs and steal my steak?"

Her stomach growled. "You have steak?"

"It's *my* steak."

She hadn't really thought of that. "Well, my…you know, *the guy*. He was supposed to bring food. And I'm sorry. I didn't exactly think about the fact that whatever food is in this fridge is food that you personally provided. I was protein blind." She did her best to look plaintive. Unsurprisingly, Sam did not seem moved by her plaintiveness.

"I mean, it seems cruel to eat steak in front of you, Madison. Especially if I'm not willing to share." He rubbed his chin, the sounds of his whiskers abrading his palm sending a little shiver down her back. God knew why.

"You *would* do that. You would… You would tease me with your steak." Suddenly, it was all starting to sound a little bit sexual. Which she had a feeling was due in part to the fact that everything felt sexual to her right about now.

Which was because of the other man she had been about to sleep with. Not Sam. Not really.

A slow smile crossed his face. "I would never tease you with my steak, Madison. If you want a taste, all you have to do is ask. Nicely."

She felt her face getting hotter. "May I please have your steak?"

"Are you going to cook it for me?"

"Did you want it to be edible?"

"That would be the goal, yes," he responded.

She lifted her hands up, palms out. "These hands don't cook."

His expression shifted. A glint of wickedness cutting through all that hardness. She'd known Sam was mean. She'd known he was rough. She had not realized he was wicked. "What do those hands do, I wonder?"

He let that innuendo linger between them and she practically hissed in response. "Do you have salad? I will fix salad. *You* cook steak. Then we can eat."

"Works for me, but I assume you're going to be sharing your candy with me?"

Seriously, everything sounded filthy. She had to get a handle on herself. "Maybe," she said, "but it depends on if your behavior merits candy." That didn't make it better.

"I see. And what, pray tell, does Madison West consider candy-deserving behavior?"

She shrugged, making her way to the fridge and opening it, bending down and opening the crisper drawer. "I don't know. Not being completely unbearable?"

"Your standards are low."

"Luckily for you."

She looked up at him and saw that that had actually elicited what looked to be a genuine grin. The man was a mystery. And she shouldn't care about that. She should not want to unlock, unravel or otherwise solve him.

The great thing about Christopher was that he was simple. He wasn't connected to her life in any way. They could come up and have an affair and it would never bleed over to her existence in Copper Ridge. It was the antithesis of everything she had experienced with David. David, who had blown up her entire life, shattered her career ambitions and damaged her good standing in the community.

This thing with Christopher was supposed to be sex. Sex that made nary a ripple in the rest of her life.

Sam would not be rippleless.

The McCormack family was too much a part of the fabric of Copper Ridge. More so in the past year. Sam and his brother, Chase, had done an amazing job of revitalizing their family ranch, and somewhere in all of that Sam had become an in-demand artist. Though he would be the last person to say it. He still showed up right on schedule to do the farrier work at her family ranch. As though he weren't raking in way more money with his ironwork.

Sam was... Well, he was kind of everywhere. His works of art appearing in restaurants and galleries around town. His person appearing on the family ranch to work on the horses. He was the exact wrong kind of man for her to be fantasizing about.

She should be more gun-shy than this. Actually, she had spent the past decade being more gun-shy than this. It was just that apparently now that she had allowed herself to remember she had sexual feelings, it was difficult for her to turn them off. Especially when she was trapped in a snowstorm with a man for whom the term *rock-hard body* would be a mere description and not hyperbole.

She produced the salad, then set about to preparing it. Thankfully, it was washed and torn already. So her responsibility literally consisted of dumping it from bag to bowl. That was the kind of cooking she could get behind. Meanwhile, Sam busied himself with preparing two steaks on the stovetop. At some point, he took the pan from the stovetop and transferred it to the oven.

"I didn't know you had actual cooking technique," she

said, not even pretending to herself that she wasn't watching the play of his muscles in his forearms as he worked.

Even at the West Ranch, where she always ended up sniping at him if they ever interacted, she tended to linger around him while he did his work with the horses because his arms put on quite a show. She was hardly going to turn away from him now that they were in an enclosed space, with said arms very, very close. And no one else around to witness her ogling.

She just didn't possess that kind of willpower.

"Well, Madison, I have a lot of eating technique. The two are compatible."

"Right," she said, "as you don't have a wife. Or a girlfriend…" She could have punched her own face for that. It sounded so leading and obvious. As if she cared if he had a woman in his life.

She didn't. Well, she kind of did. Because honestly, she didn't even like to ogle men who could be involved with another woman. Once bitten, twice shy. By which she meant once caught in a torrid extramarital affair with a man in good standing in the equestrian community, ten years emotionally scarred.

"No," he said, tilting his head, the cocky look in his eye doing strange things to her stomach, "I don't."

"I don't have a boyfriend. Not an actual boyfriend." Oh, good Lord. She was the desperate worst and she hated herself.

"So you keep saying," he returned. "You really want to make sure I know Christopher isn't your boyfriend." She couldn't ignore the implication in his tone.

"Because he isn't. Because we're not… Because we've never. This was going to be our first time." Being forthright and making people uncomfortable with said forthrightness had been a very handy shield for the past decade, but tonight it was really obnoxious.

"Oh really?" He suddenly looked extremely interested.

"Yes," she responded, keeping her tone crisp, refusing to show him just how off-kilter she felt. "I'm just making dinner conversation."

"This is the kind of dinner conversation you normally make?"

She arched her brow. "Actually, yes. Shocking people is kind of my modus operandi."

"I don't find you that shocking, Madison. I do find it a little bit amusing that you got cock-blocked by a snowbank."

She nearly choked. "Wine. Do you have wine?" She turned and started rummaging through the nearest cabinet. "Of course you do. You probably have a baguette too. That seems like something an artist would do. Set up here and drink wine and eat a baguette."

He laughed, a kind of short, dismissive sound. "Hate to disappoint you. But my artistic genius is fueled by Jack." He reached up, opening the cabinet nearest to his head, and pulled down a bottle of whiskey. "But I'm happy to share that too."

"You have diet soda?"

"Regular."

"My, this *is* a hedonistic experience. I'll have regular, then."

"Well, when a woman was expecting sex and doesn't get it, I suppose regular cola is poor consolation, but it is better than diet."

"Truer words were never spoken." She watched him while he set about to making a couple of mixed drinks for them. He handed one to her, and she lifted it in salute before taking a small sip. By then he was taking the steak out of the oven and setting it back on the stovetop.

"Perfect," he remarked when he cut one of the pieces of meat in half and gauged the color of the interior.

She frowned. "How did I never notice that you aren't horrible?"

He looked at her, his expression one of mock surprise. "Not horrible? You be careful throwing around compliments like that, missy. A man could get the wrong idea."

She rolled her eyes. "Right. I just mean, you're funny."

"How much of that whiskey have you had?"

"One sip. So it isn't even that." She eyeballed the food that he was now putting onto plates. "It might be the steak. I'm not going to lie to you."

"I'm comfortable with that."

He carried their plates to the table, and she took the lone bottle of ranch dressing out of the fridge and set it and her drink next to her plate. And then, somehow, she ended up sitting at a very nicely appointed dinner table with Sam McCormack, who was not the man she was supposed to be with tonight.

Maybe it was because of the liquored-up soda. Maybe it was neglected hormones losing their ever-loving minds in the presence of such a fine male specimen. Maybe it was just as simple as want. Maybe there was no justification for it at all. Except that Sam was actually beautiful. And she had always thought so, no matter how much he got under her skin.

That was the honest truth. It was why she found him so off-putting, why she had always found him so off-putting from the moment he had first walked onto the West Ranch property. Because he was the kind of man a woman could make a mistake with. And she had thought she was done making mistakes.

Now she was starting to wonder if a woman was entitled to one every decade.

Her safe mistake, the one who would lift out of her life, hadn't eventuated. And here in front of her was one that had the potential to be huge. But very, very good.

She wasn't so young anymore. She wasn't naive at all. When it came right down to it, she was hot for Sam. She had been for a long time.

She'd had so much caution for so long. So much hiding. So much *not doing*. Well, she was tired of that.

"I was very disappointed about Christopher not making it up here," she said, just as Sam was putting the last bite of steak into his mouth.

"Sure," he said.

"Very disappointed."

"Nobody likes blue balls, Maddy, even if they don't have testicles."

She forced a laugh through her constricted throat. "That's hilarious," she said.

He looked up at her slowly. "No," he said, "it wasn't."

She let out a long, slow breath. "Okay," she said, "it wasn't that funny. But here's the thing. The reason I was so looking forward to tonight is that I hadn't had sex with Christopher before. In fact, I haven't had sex with anyone in ten years. So. Maybe you could help me with that?"

Chapter 3

Sam was pretty sure he must be hallucinating. Because there was no way Madison West had just propositioned him. Especially not on the heels of admitting that it had been ten years since she'd had sex.

Hell, he was starting to think that *he* was the celibacy champion. But clearly, Maddy had him beat. Or she didn't, because there was no way in hell that she had actually said any of that.

"Are you drunk, Madison?" It was the first thing that came to mind, and it seemed like an important thing to figure out.

"After one Jack Daniel's and Coke? Absolutely not. I am a West, dammit. We can hold our liquor. I am… reckless, opportunistic and horny. A lot horny. I just… I need this. Sam, do you know what it's like to go *ten years* without doing something? It becomes a whole thing. Like, a whole big thing that starts to define you, even if it shouldn't. And you don't want anyone to know. Oh, my gosh, can you even imagine if my friends knew that it has been ten years since I have seen an actual...?" She took a deep breath, then forged on. "I'm rambling and I just *really* need this."

Sam felt like he had been hit over the head with a metric ton of iron. He had no idea how he was supposed to respond to this—the strangest of all propositions—from a woman who had professed to hate him only a few moments ago.

He had always thought Madison was a snob. A pain in his ass, even if she was a pretty pain in the ass. She was always looming around, looking down her nose at him while he did his work. As though only the aristocracy of Copper Ridge could possibly know how to do the lowly labor he was seeing to. Even if they hadn't the ability to do it themselves.

The kinds of people who professed to have strengths in "management." People who didn't know how to get their hands dirty.

He hated people like that. And he had never been a fan of Madison West.

He, Sam McCormack, should not be interested in taking her up on her offer. No, not in any way. However, Sam McCormack's dick was way more interested in it than he would've liked to admit.

Immediately, he was rock hard thinking about what it would be like to have her delicate, soft hands skimming over him. He had rough hands. Workman's hands. The kind of hands that a woman like Madison West had probably never felt against her rarefied flesh.

Hell, the fact that it had been ten years since she'd

gotten any made that even more likely. And damn if that didn't turn him on. It was kind of twisted, a little bit sick, but then, it was nothing short of what he expected from himself.

He was a lot of things. Good wasn't one of them.

Ready to explode after years of repressing his desires, after years of pushing said desire all down and pretending it wasn't there? He was that.

"I'm not actually sure you want this," he said, wondering what the hell he was doing. Giving her an out when he wanted to throw her down and make her his.

Maddy stood up, not about to be cowed by him. He should have known that she would take that as a challenge. Maybe he had known that. Maybe it was why he'd said it.

That sounded like him. That sounded a lot more like him than trying to do the honorable thing.

"You don't know what I want, Sam," she said, crossing the space between them, swaying her hips just a little bit more than she usually did.

He would be a damn liar if he said that he had never thought about what it might be like to grab hold of those hips and pull Maddy West up against him. To grind his hardness against her soft flesh and make her feel exactly what her snobby-rich-girl mouth did to him.

But just because he'd fantasized about it before, didn't mean he had ever anticipated doing it. It didn't mean that he should take her up on it now.

Still, the closer she got to him, the less likely it seemed that he was going to say no.

"I think that after ten years of celibacy a man could make the argument that you don't know what you want, Madison West."

Her eyes narrowed, glittering blue diamonds that looked like they could cut a man straight down to the bone. "I've always known what I wanted. I may not have always made the best decisions, but I was completely certain that I wanted them. At the time."

His lips tipped upward. "I'm just going to be another *at the time*, Maddy. Nothing else."

"That was the entire point of this weekend. For me to have something that didn't have consequences. For me to get a little bit of something for myself. Is that so wrong? Do I have to live a passionless existence because I made a mistake once? Am I going to question myself forever? I just need to... I need to rip the Band-Aid off."

"The Band-Aid?"

"The sex Band-Aid."

He nodded, pretending that he understood. "Okay."

"I want this," she said, her tone confident.

"Are you...suggesting...that I give you...sexual healing?"

She made a scoffing sound. "Don't make it sound cheesy. This is very serious. I would never joke about my sexual needs." She let out an exasperated sigh. "I'm doing this wrong. I'm just..."

Suddenly, she launched herself at him, wrapping her arms around his neck and pressing her lips against his. The moment she did it, it was like the strike of a hammer against hot iron. As rigid as he'd been before—in that moment, he bent. And easily.

Staying seated in the chair, he curved himself around Madison, wrapping his arms around her body, sliding his hands over her back, down to the sweet indent of her waist, farther still to the flare of those pretty hips.

The hips he had thought about taking hold of so many times before.

There was no hesitation now. None at all. There was only this. Only her. Only the soft, intoxicating taste of her on his tongue. Sugar, Jack Daniel's and something that was entirely Maddy.

Too rich for his blood. Far too expensive for a man like him. It didn't matter what he became. Didn't matter how much money he had in his bank account, he would always be what he was. There was no escaping it. Nobody knew. Not really. Not the various women who had graced his bed over the years, not his brother, Chase.

Nobody knew Sam McCormack.

At least, nobody alive.

Neither, he thought, would Madison West. This wasn't about knowing anybody. This was just about satisfying a need. And he was simple enough to take her up on that.

He wedged his thigh up between her legs, pressing his palm down on her lower back, encouraging her to flex her hips in time with each stroke of his tongue. Encouraging her to satisfy that ache at the apex of her thighs.

Her head fell back, her skin flushed and satisfaction grabbed him by the throat, gripping him hard and strong. It would've surprised him if he hadn't suspected he was the sort of bastard who would get off on something like this.

Watching this beautiful, classy girl coming undone in his arms.

She was right. This weekend could be out of time. It could be a moment for them to indulge in things they would never normally allow themselves to have. The kinds of things that he had closed himself off from years ago.

Softness, warmth, touch.

He had denied himself all those things for years. Why not do this now? No one would know. No one would ever have to know. Maddy would see to that. She would never, no chance in hell, admit that she had gotten down and dirty with a man who was essentially a glorified blacksmith.

No way in hell.

That made them both safe. It made this safe. Well, as safe as fire this hot could be.

She bit his lip and he growled, pushing his hands up underneath the hem of her shirt, kissing her deeper as he let his fingertips roam to the line of her elegant spine, then tracing it upward until he found her bra, releasing it with ease, then dragging it and her top up over her head, leaving her naked from the waist up.

"I…" Her face was a bright shade of red. "I… I have lingerie. I wasn't going to…"

"I don't give a damn about your lingerie. I just want this." He lowered his head, sliding his tongue around the perimeter of one of her tightened nipples. "I want your skin." He closed his lips over that tight bud, sucking it in deep.

"I had a seduction plan," she said, her voice trembling. He wasn't entirely sure it was a protest, or even a complaint.

"You don't plan passion, baby," he said.

At least, he didn't. Because if he were thinking clearly, he would be putting her top back on and telling her to go back to her ice-cold cabin, where she would be safe.

"I do," she said, her teeth chattering in spite of the fact that it was very warm in the kitchen. "I plan everything."

"Not this. You're a dirty girl now, Madison West," he said, sliding his thumb over her damp nipple, moving it in a slow circle until she arched her back and cried out. "You were going to sleep with another man this weekend, and you replaced him so damn easily. With me. Doesn't even matter to you who you have. As long as you get a little bit. Is that how it is?"

She whimpered, biting her lip, rolling her hips against him.

"Good girl," he said, his gut tightening, his arousal so hard he was sure he was going to burst through the front of his jeans. "I like that. I like you being dirty for me."

He moved his hands then, curving his fingers around her midsection, his thumbs resting just beneath the swell of her breasts. She was so soft, so smooth, so petite and fragile. Everything he should never be allowed to put his hands on. But for some reason, instead of feeling a bolt of shame, he felt aroused. Hotter and harder than he could ever remember being. "You like that? My hands are rough. Maybe a little bit too rough for you."

"No," she said, and this time the protest was clear. "Not too rough for me at all."

He slid his hands down her back, taking a moment to really revel in how soft she was and how much different he must feel to her. She squirmed against him, and he took that as evidence that she really did like it.

That only made him hotter. Harder. More impatient.

"You didn't bring your damn candy and forget the condoms, did you?"

"No," she said, the denial coming quickly. "I brought the condoms."

"You always knew we would end up like this, didn't you?"

She looked away from him, and the way she refused

to meet his eyes turned a throwaway game of a question into something deadly serious.

"Madison," he said, his voice hard. She still didn't look at him. He grabbed hold of her chin, redirecting her face so that she was forced to make eye contact with him. "You knew this would happen all along, didn't you?"

She still refused to answer him. Refused to speak.

"I think you did," he continued. "I think that's why you can never say a kind word to me. I think that's why you acted like a scalded cat every time I walked into the room. Because you knew it would end here. Because you wanted this. Because you wanted me."

Her expression turned even more mutinous.

"Madison," he said, a warning lacing through the word. "Don't play games with me. Or I'm not going to give you what you want. So you have to tell me. Tell me that you've always wanted me. You've always wanted my dirty hands on you. That's why you hate me so damn much, isn't it? Because you want me."

"I…"

"Madison," he said, his tone even more firm, "tell me—" he rubbed his hand over her nipple "—or I stop."

"I wanted you," she said, the admission rushed but clear all the same.

"More," he said, barely recognizing his own voice. "Tell me more."

It seemed essential suddenly, to know she'd wanted him. He didn't know why. He didn't care why.

"I've always wanted you. From the moment I first saw you. I knew that it would be like this. I knew that I would climb up into your lap and I would make a fool of myself rubbing all over you like a cat. I knew that from the beginning. So I argued with you instead."

He felt a satisfied smile that curved his lips upward. "Good girl." He lowered his hands, undoing the snap on her jeans and drawing the zipper down slowly. "You just made us both very happy." He moved his fingertips down beneath the waistband of her panties, his breath catching in his throat when he felt hot wetness beneath his touch. It had been way too long since he felt a silky-smooth desirable woman. Had been way too long in his self-imposed prison.

Too long since he'd wanted at all.

But Madison wasn't Elizabeth. And this wasn't the same.

He didn't need to think about her. He wasn't going to. Not for the rest of the night.

He pushed every thought out of his mind and instead exulted in the sound that Madison made when he moved his fingers over that place where she was wet and aching for him. When he delved deeper, pushing one finger inside her, feeling just how close she was to the edge, evidenced by the way her internal muscles clenched around him. He could thrust into her here. Take her hard and fast and she would still come. He knew that she would.

But she'd had ten years of celibacy, and he was pushing on five. They deserved more. They deserved better. At the very least they deserved a damn bed.

With that in mind, he wrapped his arms more tightly around her, moving his hands to cup her behind as he lifted her, wrapping her legs tightly around him as he carried them across the kitchen and toward the stairs.

Maddy let out an inelegant squeak as he began to ascend toward the bedrooms. "This is really happening," she said, sounding slightly dazed.

"I thought you said you weren't drunk."

"I'm not."

"Then try not to look so surprised. It's making me question things. And I don't want to question things. I just want you."

She shivered in his hold. "You're not like most men I know."

"Pretty boys with popped collars and pastel polo shirts? I must be a real disappointment."

"Obviously you aren't. Obviously I don't care about men in pastel polo shirts or I would've gotten laid any number of times in the past decade."

He pushed open the bedroom door, threw her down over the simply appointed bed that was far too small for the kind of acrobatics he wanted to get up to tonight. Then he stood back, admiring her, wearing nothing but those half-open jeans riding low on her hips, her stomach dipping in with each breath, her breasts thrust into greater prominence at the same time.

"Were you waiting for me?" He kept the words light, taunting, because he knew that she liked it.

She had always liked sparring with him. That was what they'd always done. Of course she would like it now. Of course he would like it now. Or maybe it had nothing to do with her. Maybe it had everything to do with the fact that he had years' worth of dirty in him that needed to be let out.

"Screw you," she said, pushing herself back farther up the mattress so that her head was resting on the pillow. Then she put her hands behind her head, her blue gaze sharp. "Come on, cowboy. Get naked for me."

"Oh no, Maddy, you're not running the show."

"Ten years," she said, her gaze level with his. "Ten years, Sam. That's how long it's been since I've seen a naked man. And let me tell you, I have never seen a naked man like you." She held up a finger. "One man. One insipid man. He wasn't even that good."

"You haven't had sex for ten years and your last lover wasn't even good? I was sort of hoping that it had been so good you were waiting for your knees to stop shaking before you bothered to go out and get some again."

"If only. My knees never once shook. In fact, they're shaking harder now and you haven't even gotten out of those pants yet."

"You give good dirty talk."

She lifted a shoulder. "I'm good at talking. That's about the thing I'm best at."

"Oh, I hope not, baby. I hope that mouth is good for a lot of other things too."

He saw her breasts hitch. Her eyes growing round. Then he smiled, grabbing hold of the hem of his shirt and stripping it off over his head. Her reaction was more satisfying than he could've possibly anticipated. It'd been a long time since he'd seen a woman looking at him that way.

Sure, women checked him out. That happened all the time. But this was different. This was raw, open hunger. She wasn't bothering to hide it. Why would she? They were both here to do this. No holds barred, no clothes, no nothing. Why bother to be coy? Why bother to pretend this was about anything other than satisfying lust. And if that was all it was, why should either of them bother to hide that lust.

"Keep looking at me like that, sweetheart, this is gonna end fast."

"Don't do that," she said, a wicked smile on her lips. "You're no good to me in that case."

"Don't worry, babe. I can get it up more than once."

At least, he could if he remembered correctly.

"Good thing I brought about three boxes of condoms."

"For two days? You did have high hopes for the weekend."

"Ten years," she reiterated.

"Point taken."

He moved his hands down, slowly working at his belt. The way that she licked her lips as her eyes followed his every movement ratcheting up his arousal another impossible notch.

Everything felt too sharp, too clear, every rasp of fabric over his skin, every downward flick of her eyes, every small, near-imperceptible gasp on her lips.

He hadn't been in a bedroom alone with a woman in a long damn time. And it was all catching up with him now.

Shutting down, being a mean bastard who didn't let anyone close? That was easy enough. It made it easy to forget. He shut the world out, stripped everything away. Reverted back to the way he had been just after his parents had died and it had been too difficult to feel anything more than his grief.

That was what he had done in the past five years. That was what he had done with his new, impossible loss that never should have happened. Wouldn't have if he'd had a shred of self-control and decency.

And now, tonight, he was proving that he probably still didn't have any at all. Oh well, just as well. Because he was going to do this.

He was going to do her.

He pushed his jeans down his lean hips, showing her the extent of his desire for her, reveling in the way her eyes widened when he revealed his body completely to her hungry gaze.

"I have never seen one that big before," she said.

He laughed. "Are you just saying that because it's what you think men need to hear?"

"No, I'm saying that because it's the biggest I've ever seen. And I want it."

"Baby," he said, "you can have it."

Maddy turned over onto her stomach and crawled across the bed on all fours in a move that damn near gave him a heart attack. Then she moved to the edge of the mattress, straightening up, raking her nails down over his torso before she leaned in, flicking her tongue over the head of his arousal.

He jerked beneath her touch, his length twitching as her tongue traced it from base to tip, just before she engulfed him completely in the warm heat of her mouth. She hummed, the vibration moving through his body, drawing his balls up tight. He really was going to lose it. Here and now like a green teenage boy if he didn't get a grip on himself. Or a grip on her.

He settled for the second option.

He reached back, grabbing hold of her hair and jerking her lips away from him. "You keep doing that and it really will end."

The color was high in her cheeks, her eyes glittering. "I've never, ever enjoyed it like that before."

She was so good for his ego. Way better than a man like him deserved. But damned if he wasn't going to take it.

"Well, you can enjoy more of that. Later. Right now? I need to be inside you."

"Technically," she said, her tone one of protest, "you were inside me."

"And as much as I like being in that pretty mouth of yours, that isn't what I want right now." He gritted his teeth, looking around the room. "The condoms."

She scrambled off the bed and shimmied out of her jeans and panties as she made her way across the room and toward her suitcase. She flipped it open, dug through it frantically and produced the two packets he had seen earlier.

All things considered, he felt a little bit triumphant to be the one getting these condoms. He didn't know Christopher, but that sad sack was sitting at home with a hard-on, and Sam was having his woman. He was going to go ahead and enjoy the hell out of that.

Madison turned to face him, the sight of that enticing, pale triangle at the apex of her thighs sending a shot straight down to his gut. She kept her eyes on his as she moved nearer, holding one of the condoms like it was a reward he was about to receive.

She tore it open and settled back onto the bed, then leaned forward and rolled it over his length. Then she took her position back up against the pillows, her thighs parting, her heavily lidded gaze averted from his now that she was in that vulnerable position.

"Okay," she said, "I'm ready."

She wasn't. Not by a long shot.

Ten years.

And he had been ready to thrust into her with absolutely no finesse. A woman who'd been celibate for ten years deserved more than that. She deserved more than one orgasm. Hell, she deserved more than two.

He had never been the biggest fan of Madison West,

but tonight they were allies. Allies in pleasure. And he was going to hold up his end of the bargain so well that if she was celibate after this, it really would be because she was waiting for her legs to work again.

"Not quite yet, Maddy," he said, kneeling down at the end of the bed, reaching forward and grabbing hold of her hips, dragging her down toward his face. He brought her up against his mouth, her legs thrown over his shoulders, that place where she was warm and wet for him right there, ready for him to taste her.

"Sam!" Maddy squeaked.

"There is no way you're a prude, Maddy," he said. "I've had too many conversations with you to believe that."

"I've never... No one has ever..."

"Then it's time somebody did."

He lowered his head, tasting her in long, slow passes, like she was an ice-cream cone that he just had to take the time to savor. Like she was a delicacy he couldn't get enough of.

Because she was.

She was all warmth and sweet female, better than he had ever remembered a woman being. Or maybe she was just better. It was hard to say. He didn't really care which. It didn't matter. All that mattered was this.

If he could lose himself in any moment, in any time, it would be this one.

It sure as hell wouldn't be pounding iron, trying to hammer the guilt out of his body. Certainly wouldn't be in his damn sculptures, trying to figure out what to make next, trying to figure out how to satisfy the customer. This deeply personal thing that had started being given to the rest of the world, when he wasn't sure he wanted the rest of the world to see what was inside him.

Hell, *he* didn't want to see what was inside him.

He made a hell of a lot of money, carving himself out, making it into a product people could buy. And he sure as hell liked the money, but that didn't make it a pleasant experience.

No, none of that mattered. Not now. Not when there was Maddy. And that sweet sugar-whiskey taste.

He tasted her until she screamed, and then he thrust his fingers inside her, fast and rough, until he felt her pulse around him, until her orgasm swept through them both.

Then he moved up, his lips almost touching hers. "Now," he said, his voice husky, "now you're ready."

Chapter 4

Maddy was shaking from head to toe, and she honestly didn't know if she could take any more. She had never—not in her entire life—had an orgasm like that. It was still echoing through her body, creating little waves of sensation that shivered through her with each and every breath she took.

And there was still more. They weren't done. She was glad about that. She didn't want to be done. But at the same time she wasn't sure if she could handle the rest. But there he was, above her, over her, so hot and hard and male that she didn't think she could deny him. She didn't want to deny him.

She looked at him, at the broad expanse of his shoulders and chest, the way it tapered down to his narrow waist, those flat washboard abs that she could probably actually wash her clothes on.

He was everything a man should be. If the perfect fantasy man had been pulled straight out of her deepest fantasies, he would look like this. It hit her then that Christopher had not even been close to being a fantasy man. And that was maybe why he had been so safe. It was why Sam had always been so threatening.

Because Christopher had the power to make a ripple. Sam McCormack possessed the power to engulf her in a tidal wave.

She had no desire to be swept out to sea by any man. But in this instance she had a life preserver. And that was her general dislike of him. The fact that their time together was going to be contained to only this weekend. So what did it matter if she allowed herself to get a little bit storm tossed. It didn't. She was free. Free to enjoy this as much as she wanted.

And she wanted. *Wanted* with an endless hunger that seemed to growl inside her like a feral beast.

He possessed the equipment to satisfy it. She let her eyes drift lower than just his abs, taking in the heart, the unequivocal evidence, of his maleness. She had not been lying when she said it was the biggest one she'd ever seen. It made her feel a little bit intimidated. Especially since she had been celibate for so very long. But she had a few days to acclimate.

The thought made her giddy.

"Now," she said, not entirely certain that she was totally prepared for him now but also unable to wait for him.

"You sure you're ready for me?" He leaned forward, bracing his hand on the headboard, poised over her like the very embodiment of carnal temptation. Just out of reach, close enough that she did easily inhale his masculine scent. Far enough away that he wasn't giving her what she needed. Not yet.

She felt hollow. Aching. And that, she realized, was how she knew she was going to take all of him whether or not it seemed possible. Because the only other option was remaining like this. Hollowed out and empty. And she couldn't stand that either. Not for one more second.

"Please," she said, not caring that she sounded plaintive. Not caring that she was begging. Begging Sam, the man she had spent the past several years harassing every time he came around her ranch.

No, she didn't care. She would make a fool out of herself if she had to, would lower herself as far down as she needed to go, if only she could get the kind of satisfaction that his body promised to deliver.

He moved his other hand up to the headboard, gripping it tight. Then he flexed his hips forward, the blunt head of his arousal teasing the slick entrance to her body. She reached up, bracing her palms flat against his chest, a shiver running through her as he teased her with near penetration.

She cursed. The sound quivering, weak in the near silence of the room. She had no idea where hard-ass Maddy had gone. That tough, flippant girl who knew how to keep everyone at a distance with her words. Who knew how to play off every situation as if it weren't a big deal.

This was a big deal. How could she pretend that it wasn't? She was breaking apart from the inside out; how could she act as though she weren't?

"Please," she repeated.

He let go of the headboard with one hand and pressed his hand down next to her face, then repeated the motion with the other as he rocked his hips forward more fully, entering her slowly, inch by tantalizing inch. She gasped when he filled her all the way, the intense stretching sensation a pleasure more than it was a pain.

She slid her hands up to his shoulders, down his back, holding on to him tightly there before locking her legs around his lean hips and urging him even deeper.

"Yes," she breathed, a wave of satisfaction rolling over her, chased on the heels by a sense that she was still incomplete. That this wasn't enough. That it would never be enough.

Then he began to move. Ratcheting up the tension between them. Taking her need, her arousal, to greater heights than she had ever imagined possible. He was measured at first, taking care to establish a rhythm that helped her move closer to completion. But she didn't need the help. She didn't want it. She just wanted to ride the storm.

She tilted her head to the side, scraping her teeth along the tendon in his neck that stood out as a testament to his hard-won self-control.

And that did it.

He growled low in his throat. Then his movements became hard, harsh. Following no particular rhythm but his own. She loved it. Gloried in it. He grabbed hold of her hips, tugging her up against him every time he thrust down, making it rougher, making it deeper. Making it hurt. She felt full with it, full with him. This was exactly what she needed, and she hadn't even realized it. To be utterly and completely overwhelmed. To have this man consume her every sensation, her every breath.

She fused her lips to his, kissing him frantically as he continued to move inside her and she held on to him tighter, her nails digging into his skin. But she knew he didn't mind the pain. She knew it just as she didn't mind it. Knew it because he began to move harder, faster, reaching the edge of his own control as he pushed her nearer to the edge of hers.

Suddenly, it gripped her fiercely, down low inside her, a force of pleasure that she couldn't deny or control. She froze, stiffening against him, the scream that lodged itself in her throat the very opposite of who she usually was. It wasn't calculated; it wasn't pretty; it wasn't designed to do anything. It simply was. An expression of what she felt. Beyond her reach, beyond her completely.

She was racked with her desire for him, with the intensity of the orgasm that swept through her. And then, just as she was beginning to find a way to breathe again, he found his own release, his hardness pulsing deep inside her as he gave himself up to it.

His release—the intensity of it—sent another shattering wave through her. And she clung to him even more tightly, needing him to anchor her to the bed, to the earth, or she would lose herself completely.

And then in the aftermath, she was left there, clinging to a stranger, having just shown the deepest, most hidden parts of herself to him. Having just lost her control with him in a way she never would have done with someone she knew better. Perhaps this was the only way she could have ever experienced this kind of freedom. The only way she could have ever let her guard down enough. What did she have to lose with Sam? His opinion of her was already low. So if he thought that she was a sex-hungry maniac after this, what did it matter?

He moved away from her and she threw her arm over her face, letting her head fall back, the sound of her fractured breathing echoing in the room.

After she had gulped in a few gasps of air, she removed her arm, opened her eyes and realized that Sam wasn't in the room anymore. Probably off to the bathroom to deal with necessities. Good. She needed some space. She needed a moment. At least a few breaths.

He returned a little bit quicker than she had hoped he might, all long lean muscle and satisfied male. It was the expression on his face that began to ease the tension in her chest. He didn't look angry. He didn't look like he was judging her. And he didn't look like he was in love with her or was about to start making promises that she didn't want him to make.

No, he just looked satisfied. A bone-deep satisfaction that she felt too.

"Holy hell," he said, coming to lie on the bed next to her, drawing her naked body up against his. She felt a smile curve her lips. "I think you about blew my head off."

"You're so romantic," she said, smiling even wider. Because this was perfect. Absolutely perfect.

"You don't want me to be romantic," he returned.

"No," she said, feeling happy, buoyant even. "I sure as hell don't."

"You want me to be bad, and dirty, and to be your every fantasy of slumming it with a man who is so very beneath you."

That, she took affront to a little bit. "I don't think you're beneath me, Sam," she said. Then he grabbed hold of her hips and lifted her up off the mattress before bringing her down over his body. A wicked smile crossed his face.

"I am now."

"You're insatiable. And terrible."

"For a weekend fling, honey, that's all you really need."

"Oh, dammit," she said, "what if the roads open up, and Christopher tries to come up?"

"I'm not really into threesomes." He tightened his grip on her. "And I'm not into sharing."

"No worries. I don't have any desire to broaden my experience by testing him out."

"Have I ruined you for him?"

The cocky bastard. She wanted to tell him no, but she had a feeling that denting the masculine ego when a man was underneath you wasn't the best idea if you wanted to have sex with said man again.

"Ruined me completely," she responded. "In fact, I should leave a message for him."

Sam snagged the phone on the nightstand and thrust it at her. "You can leave him a message now."

"Okay," she said, grimacing slightly.

She picked up the phone and dialed Christopher's number quickly. Praying that she got his voice mail and not his actual voice.

Of course, if she did, that meant he'd gone out. Which meant that maybe he was trying to find sex to replace the sex that he'd lost. Which she had done; she couldn't really be annoyed about that. But she had baggage.

"Come on," she muttered as the phone rang endlessly. Then she breathed a sigh of relief when she got his voice mail. "Hi, Christopher, it's Madison. Don't worry about coming up here if the roads clear up. If that happens, I'm probably just going to go back to Copper Ridge. The weekend is kind of ruined. And…and maybe you should just wait for me to call you?" She looked up at Sam, who was nearly vibrating with forcibly contained laughter. She rolled her eyes. "Anyway, sorry that this didn't work out. Bye."

"That was terrible," he said. "But I think you made it pretty clear that you don't want to hear from him."

"I said I would call him," she said in protestation.

"Are you going to?"

"*Hell* no."

Sam chuckled, rolling her back underneath him, kissing her deep, hard. "Good thing I only want a weekend."

"Why is that?"

"God help the man that wants more from you."

"Oh, please, that's not fair." She wiggled, luxuriating in the hard feel of him between her thighs. He wanted her again already. "I pity the woman that falls for you, Sam McCormack."

A shadow passed over his face. "So do I."

Then, as quickly as they had appeared, those clouds cleared and he was smiling again, that wicked, intense smile that let her know he was about ready to take her to heaven again.

"It's a good thing both of us only want a weekend."

Chapter 5

"How did the art retreat go?"

Sam gritted his teeth against his younger brother's questioning as Chase walked into their workshop. "Fine," he returned.

"Fine?" Chase leaned against the doorframe, crossing his arms, looking a little too much like Sam for his own comfort. Because he was a bastard, and he didn't want to see his bastard face looking back at him. "I thought you were going to get inspiration. To come up with the ideas that will keep the McCormack Ranch flush for the next several years."

"I'm not a machine," Sam said, keeping his tone hard. "You can't force art."

He said things like that, in that tone, because he knew that no one would believe that cliché phrase, even if it was true. He didn't like that it was true.

But there wasn't much he was willing to do about it either.

"Sure. And I feel a slight amount of guilt over pressuring you, but since I do a lot of managing of your career, I consider it a part of my job."

"Stick to pounding iron, Chase—that's where your talents lie."

"I don't have talent," Chase said. "I have business sense. Which you don't have. So you should be thankful for me."

"You say that. You say it a lot. I think mostly because you know that I actually shouldn't be all that thankful for your meddling."

He was being irritable, and he knew it. But he didn't want Chase asking how the weekend was. He didn't want to explain the way he had spent his time. And he really didn't want to get into why the only thing he was inspired to do was start painting nudes.

Of one woman in particular.

Because the only kind of grand inspirational moments he'd had were when he was inside Maddy. Yeah, he wasn't going to explain that to his younger brother. He was never going to tell anybody. And he had to get his shit together.

"Seriously, though, everything is going okay? Anna is worried about you."

"Your wife is meddlesome. I liked her better when she was just your friend and all she did was come by for pizza a couple times a week. And she didn't worry too much about what I was doing or whether or not I was happy."

"Yeah, sadly for you she has decided she loves me. And by extension she has decided she loves you, which means her getting up in your business. I don't think she knows another way to be."

"Tell her to go pull apart a tractor and stop digging around in my life."

"No, thanks, I like my balls where they are. Which means I will not be telling Anna what to do. Ever."

"I liked it better when you were miserable and alone."

Chase laughed. "Why, because you're miserable and alone?"

"No, that would imply that I'm uncomfortable with the state of things. I myself am quite dedicated to my solitude and my misery."

"They say misery loves company," Chase said.

"Only true if you aren't a hermit."

"I suppose that's true." His brother looked at him, his gaze far too perceptive for Sam's liking. "You didn't used to be this terrible."

"I have been for a while." But worse with Maddy. She pushed at him. At things and needs and desires that were best left in the past.

He gritted his teeth. She pushed at him because he turned her on and that made her mad. He... Well, it was complicated.

"Yes," Chase said. "For a while."

"Don't psychoanalyze me. Maybe it's a crazy artist thing. Dad always said that it would make me a pussy."

"You aren't a pussy. You're a jerk."

"Six of one, half dozen of the other. Either way, I have issues."

Chase shook his head. "Well, deal with them on your own time. You have to be over at the West Ranch in less than an hour." Chase shook his head. "Pretty soon we'll be released from the contract. But you know until then we could always hire somebody else to go. You don't have to do horseshoes if you don't want. We're kind of beyond that now."

Sam gritted his teeth. For the first time he was actually tempted to take his brother up on the offer. To replace his position with someone else. Mostly because the idea of seeing Madison again filled him with the kind of reckless tension that he knew he wouldn't be able to do anything about once he saw her again.

Oh, not because of her. Not because of anything to do with her moral code or protestations. He could demolish those easily enough. It was because he couldn't afford to waste any more time thinking about her. Because he couldn't afford to get in any deeper. What had happened over the past weekend had been good. Damn good. But he had to leave it there.

Normally, he relished the idea of getting in there and doing grunt work. There was something about it that fulfilled him. Chase might not understand that.

But Sam wasn't a paperwork man. He wasn't a business mind. He needed physical exertion to keep himself going.

His lips twitched as he thought about the kind of physical exertion he had indulged in with Maddy. Yeah, it kind of all made sense. Why he had thrown himself into the blacksmithing thing during his celibacy. He needed to pound something, one way or another. And since he had been so intent on denying himself female companionship, he had picked up a hammer instead.

He was tempted to back out. To make sure he kept his distance from Maddy. He wouldn't, because he was also far too tempted to go. Too tempted to test his control and see if there was a weak link. If he might end up with her underneath him again.

It would be the better thing to send Chase. Or to call in and say they would have to reschedule, then hire somebody else to take over that kind of work. They could more than afford it. But as much as he wanted to avoid Maddy, he wanted to see her again.

Just because.

His body began to harden just thinking about it.

"It's fine. I'm going to head over. You know that I like physical labor."

"I just don't understand why," Chase said, looking genuinely mystified.

But hell, Chase had a life. A wife. Things that Sam was never going to have. Chase had worked through his stuff and made them both a hell of a lot of money, and Sam was happy for him. As happy as he ever got.

"You don't need to understand me. You just have to keep me organized so that I don't end up out on the street."

"You would never end up out on the streets of Copper Ridge. Mostly because if you stood out there with a cardboard sign, some well-meaning elderly woman would wrap you in a blanket and take you back to her house for casserole. And you would rather die. We both know that."

That made Sam smile reluctantly. "True enough."

"So, I guess you better keep working, then."

Sam thought about Maddy again, about her sweet, supple curves. About how seeing her again was going to test him in the best way possible. Perhaps that was why he should go. Just so he could test himself. Push up against his control. Yeah, maybe that was what he needed.

Yeah, that justification worked well. And it meant he would see her again.

It wasn't feelings. It was just sex. And he was starting to think just sex might be what he needed.

"I plan on it."

Maddy took a deep breath of clean salt air and arena dirt. There was something comforting about it. Familiar. Whenever things had gone wrong in her life, this was what she could count on. The familiar sights and sounds of the ranch, her horses. Herself.

She never felt stronger than when she was on the back of a horse, working in time with the animal to move from a trot to a walk, a walk to a halt. She never felt more understood.

A funny thing. Because, while she knew she was an excellent trainer and she had full confidence in her ability to keep control over the animal, she knew that she would never have absolute control. Animals were unpredictable. Always.

One day, they could simply decide they didn't want to deal with you and buck you off. It was the risk that every person who worked with large beasts took. And they took it on gladly.

She liked that juxtaposition. The control, the danger. The fact that though she achieved a certain level of mastery with each horse she worked with, they could still decide they weren't going to behave on a given day.

She had never felt much of that in the rest of her life. Often she felt like she was fighting against so much. Having something like this, something that made her feel both small and powerful had been essential to her well-being. Especially during all that crap that had happened ten years ago. She had been thinking more about it lately. Honestly, it had all started because of Christopher, because she had been considering breaking her celibacy. And it had only gotten worse after she actually had. After Sam.

Mostly because she couldn't stop thinking about him. Mostly because she felt like one weekend could never be enough. And she needed it to be. She badly needed it to be. She needed to be able to have sex with a guy without having lingering feelings for him. David had really done a number on her, and she did not want another number done on her.

It was for the best if she never saw Sam again. She knew that was unlikely, but it would be better. She let out a deep breath, walking into the barn, her riding boots making a strident sound on the hardpacked dirt as she walked in. Then she saw movement toward the end of the barn, someone coming out of one of the stalls.

She froze. It wasn't uncommon for there to be other people around. Her family employed a full staff to keep the ranch running smoothly, but for some reason this felt different. And a couple of seconds later, as the person came into view, she realized why.

Black cowboy hat, broad shoulders, muscular forearms. That lean waist and hips. That built, muscular physique that she was intimately acquainted with.

Dear Lord. Sam McCormack was here.

She had known that there would be some compromise on the never-seeing-him-again thing; she had just hoped that it wouldn't be seeing him now.

"Sam," she said, because she would be damned if she appeared like she had been caught unawares. "I didn't expect you to be here."

"Your father wanted to make sure that all of the horses were in good shape before the holidays, since it was going to delay my next visit."

Maddy gritted her teeth. Christmas was in a couple of weeks, which meant her family would be having their annual party. The festivities had started to become a bit threadbare and brittle in recent years. Now that everybody knew Nathan West had been forced to sell off all of his properties downtown. Now that everyone knew he had a bastard son, Jack Monaghan, whose existence Nathan had tried to deny for more than thirty years. Yes, now that everybody had seen the cracks in the gleaming West family foundation, it all seemed farcical to Maddy.

But then, seeing as she had been one of the first major cracks in the foundation, she supposed that she wasn't really entitled to be too judgmental about it. However, she was starting to feel a bit exhausted.

"Right," she returned, knowing that her voice sounded dull.

"Have you seen Christopher?"

His question caught her off guard, as did his tone, which sounded a bit hard and possessive. It was funny, because this taciturn man in front of her was more what she had considered Sam to be before they had spent those days in the cabin together. Those days—where they had mostly been naked—had been a lot easier. Quieter. He had smiled more. But then, she supposed that any man receiving an endless supply of orgasms was prone to smiling more. They had barely gotten out of bed.

They had both been more than a little bit insatiable, and Maddy hadn't minded that at all. But this was a harsh slap back to reality. To a time that could almost have been before their little rendezvous but clearly wasn't, because his line of questioning was tinged with jealousy.

"No. As you guessed, I lied to him and didn't call him."

"And he call you?"

Maddy lifted her fingernail and began to chew on it, grimacing when she realized she had just ruined her manicure. "He did call," she said, her face heating slightly. "And I changed his name in my phone book to Don't Answer."

"Why did you do that?"

"Obviously you can't delete somebody from your phone book when you don't want to talk to them, Sam. You have to make sure that you know who's calling. But I like the reminder that I'm not speaking to him. Because then my phone rings and the screen says Don't Answer, and then I go, 'Okay.'"

"I really do pity the man who ends up wanting to chase after you."

"Good thing you don't. Except, oh wait, you're here."

She regretted that as soon as she said it. His gaze darkened, his eyes sweeping over her figure. Why did she want to push him?

Why did she always want to push him?

"You know why I'm here."

"Yes, because my daddy pays you to be here." She didn't know why she said that. To reinforce the difference between them? To remind him she was Lady of the Manor, and that regardless of his bank balance he was socially beneath her? To make herself look like a stupid rich girl he wouldn't want to mess around with anyway. Honestly, these days it was difficult for her to guess at her own motives.

"Is this all part of your fantasy? You want to be…taken

by the stable boy or something? I mean, it's a nice one, Maddy, and I didn't really mind acting it out with you last weekend, but we both know that I'm not exactly the stable boy and you're not exactly the breathless virgin."

Heat streaked through her face, rage pooling in her stomach. "Right. Because I'm not some pure, snow-white virgin, my fantasies are somehow wrong?" It was too close to that wound. The one she wished wasn't there. The one she couldn't ignore, no matter how much she tried.

"That wasn't the point I was making. And anyway, when your whole fantasy about a man centers around him being bad for you, I'm not exactly sure where you get off trying to take the moral-outrage route."

"I will be as morally outraged as I please," she snapped, turning to walk away from him.

He reached out, grabbing hold of her arm and turning her back to face him, taking hold of her other arm and pulling her forward. "Everything was supposed to stay back up at those cabins," he said, his voice rough.

"So why aren't you letting it?" she spat. Reckless. Shaky. She was a hypocrite. Because she wasn't letting it rest either.

"Because you walked in in those tight pants and it made it a lot harder for me to think."

"My breeches," she said, keeping the words sharp and crisp as a green apple, "are not typically the sort of garment that inspire men to fits of uncontrollable lust." Except *she* was drowning in a fit of uncontrollable lust. His gaze was hot, his hands on her arms even hotter. She wanted to arch against him, to press her breasts against his chest as she had done more times than she could count when they had been together. She wanted… She wanted the impossible. She wanted more. More of him. More of everything they had shared together, even though they had agreed that would be a bad idea.

Even though she knew it was something she shouldn't even want.

"Your pretty little ass in anything would make a man lose his mind. Don't tell me those breeches put any man off, or I'm gonna have to call you a liar."

"It isn't my breeches that put them off. That's just my personality."

"If some man can't handle you being a little bit hard, then he's no kind of man. I can take you, baby. I can take all of you. And that's good, since we both know you can take all of me."

"Are you just going to be a tease, Sam?" she asked, echoing back a phrase that had been uttered to her by many men over the years. "Or is this leading somewhere?"

"You don't want it to lead anywhere, you said so yourself." He released his hold on her, taking a step back.

"You're contrary, Sam McCormack—do you know that?"

He laughed. "That's about the only thing anyone calls me. We both know what I am. The only thing that confuses me is exactly why you seem surprised by it now."

She was kind of stumped by that question. Because really, the only answer was sex. That she had imagined that the two of them being together, that the man he had been during that time, meant something.

Which proved that she really hadn't learned anything about sexual relationships, in spite of the fact that she had been so badly wounded by one in the past. She had always known that she had a hard head, but really, this was ridiculous.

But it wasn't just her head that was hard. She had

hardened up a considerable amount in the years since her relationship with David. Because she'd had to. Because within the equestrian community, she had spent the years following that affair known as the skank who had seriously jeopardized the marriage of an upright member of the community. Never mind that she had been his student. Never mind that she had been seventeen years old, a virgin who had believed every word that had come out of the esteemed older man's mouth. Who had believed that his marriage really was over and that he wanted a life and a future with her.

It was laughable to her now. Any man nearing his forties who found himself able to relate to a seventeen-year-old on an emotional level was a little bit suspect. A married one, in a position of power, was even worse. She knew all of that. She knew it down to her bones. Believing it was another thing.

So sometimes her judgment was in doubt. Sometimes she felt like an idiot. But she was much more equipped to deal with difficult situations now. She was a lot pricklier. A lot more inured.

And that was what came to her defense now.

"Sam, if you still want me, all you have to do is say it. Don't you stand there growling because you're hard and sexually frustrated and we both agreed that it would only be that one weekend. Just be a man and admit it."

"Are you sure you should be talking to me like that here? Anyone can catch us. If I backed you up against that wall and kissed your smart mouth, then people would know. Doesn't it make you feel dirty? Doesn't it make you feel ashamed?" His words lashed at her, made her feel all of those things but also aroused her. She had no idea what was wrong with her. Except that maybe part of it was that she simply didn't know how to feel desire without feeling ashamed. Another gift from her one and only love affair.

"You're the one that's saying all of this. Not me," she said, keeping her voice steely. She lifted a shoulder. "If I didn't know better, I would say you have issues. I don't want to help you work those out." A sudden rush of heat took over, a reckless thought that she had no business having, that she really should work to get a handle on. But she didn't.

She took a deep breath. "I don't have any desire to help you with your issues, but if you're horny, I can help you with that."

"What the hell?"

"You heard me," she said, crossing her arms and giving him her toughest air. "If you want me, then have me."

Sam could hardly believe what he was hearing. Yet again, Madison West was propositioning him. And this time, he was pissed off. Because he wasn't a dog that she could bring to heel whenever she wanted to. He wasn't the kind of man who could be manipulated.

Even worse, he wanted her. He wanted to say yes. And he wasn't sure he could spite his dick to soothe his pride.

"You can't just come in here and start playing games with me," he said. "I'm not a dog that you can call whenever you want me to come."

He let the double meaning of that statement sit between them. "That isn't what I'm doing," she said, her tone waspish.

"Then what are you doing, Madison? We agreed that it would be one weekend. And then you come in here sniping at me, and suddenly you're propositioning me. I gave in to all of this when you asked the first time, because I'm a man. And I'm not going to say no in a situation like the one we were in. But I'm also not the kind of man you can manipulate."

Color rose high in her cheeks. "I'm not trying to manipulate you. Why is it that men are always accusing me of that?"

"Because no man likes to be turned on and then left waiting," he returned.

The color in her cheeks darkened, and then she turned on one boot heel and walked quickly away from him.

He moved after her, reaching out and grabbing hold of her arm, stopping her. "What? Now you're going to go?"

"I can't do this. I can't do this if you're going to wrap all of it up in accusations and shame. I've been there. I've done it, Sam, and I'm not doing it again. Trust me. I've been accused of a lot of things. I've had my fill of it. So, great, you don't want to be manipulated. I don't want to be the one that has to leave this affair feeling guilty."

Sam frowned. "That's not what I meant."

She was the one who was being unreasonable, blowing hot and cold on him. How was it that he had been the one to be made to feel guilty? He didn't like that. He didn't like feeling anything but irritation and desire for her. He certainly didn't want to feel any guilt.

He didn't want to feel any damn thing.

"Well, what did you mean? Am I a tease, Sam? Is that what I am? And men like you just can't help themselves?"

He took a step back. "No," he said. "But you do have to make a decision. Either you want this, or you don't."

"Or?"

"Or nothing," he said, his tone hard. "If you don't want

it, you don't want it. I'm not going to coerce you into any-thing. But I don't do the hot-and-cold thing."

Of course, he didn't really do any kind of thing any-more. But this, this back and forth, reminded him too much of his interaction with Elizabeth. Actually, all of it reminded him a little bit too much of Elizabeth. This seemingly soft, sweet woman with a bit of an edge. Some-one who was high-class and a little bit luxurious. Who felt like a break from his life on the ranch. His life of rough work and solitude.

But after too much back and forth, it had ended. And he didn't speak to her for months. Until he had gotten a call that he needed to go to the hospital.

He gritted his teeth, looking at Madison. He couldn't imagine anything with Madison ending quite that way, not simply because he refused to ever lose his control the way he had done with Elizabeth, but also because he couldn't imagine Maddy slinking off in silence. She might go hot and cold, but she would never do it quietly.

"Twelve days. There are twelve days until Christmas. That's what I want. Twelve days to get myself on the naughty list. So to speak." She leveled her blue gaze with his. "If you don't want to oblige me, I'm sure Christopher will. But I would much rather it be you."

"Why?" He might want this, but he would be damned if he would make it easy for her. Mostly because he wanted to make it a little harder on himself.

"Because I planned to go up to that cabin and have sex with Christopher. I had to, like, come up with a plan. A series of tactical maneuvers that would help me make the decision to get it over with after all that time. You," she said, gesturing at him, "you, I didn't plan to have anything happen with. Ever. But I couldn't stop myself.

I think at the end of the day it's much better to carry on a sex-only affair with a man that you can't control yourself with. Like right now. I was not going to proposition you today, Sam. I promise. Not today, not ever again. In fact, I'm mad at you, so it should be really easy for me to walk away. But I don't want to. I want you. I want you even if it's a terrible idea."

He looked around, then took her arm again, dragging her into one of the empty stalls, where they would be out of sight if anyone walked into the barn. Then he pressed her against the wall, gripping her chin and taking her mouth in a deep, searing kiss. She whimpered, arching against him, grabbing hold of his shoulders and widening her stance so that he could press his hardened length against where she was soft and sensitive, ready for him already.

He slid his hand down her back, not caring that the hard wall bit into his knuckles as he grabbed hold of her rear, barely covered by those riding pants, which ought to have been illegal.

She whimpered, wiggling against him, obviously trying to get some satisfaction for the ache inside her. He knew that she felt it, because he felt the same way. He wrenched his mouth away from hers. "Dammit," he said, "I have to get back to work."

"Do you really?" She looked up at him, her expression so desperate it was nearly comical. Except he felt too desperate to laugh.

"Yes," he said.

"Well, since my family owns the property, I feel like I can give you permission to—"

He held up a hand. "I'm going to stop you right there. Nobody gives me permission to do anything. If I didn't want to finish the day's work, I wouldn't. I don't need the money. That's not why I do this. It's my reputation. My pride. I'm contracted to do it, and I will do what I promised I would. But when the contract is up? I won't."

"Oh," she said. "I didn't realize that."

"Everything is going well with the art business." At least, it would if he could think of something else to do. He supposed he could always do more animals and cowboys. People never got tired of that. They had been his most popular art installations so far.

"Great. That's great. Maybe you could…not press yourself up against me? Because I'm going to do something really stupid in a minute."

He did not comply with her request; instead, he kept her there, held up against the wall. "What's that?"

She frowned. "Something I shouldn't do in a public place."

"You're not exactly enticing me to let you go." His body was so hard he was pretty sure he was going to turn to stone.

"I'll bite you."

"Still not enticed."

"Are you telling me that you want to get bitten?"

He rolled his hips forward, let her feel exactly what she was doing to him. "Biting can be all part of the fun."

"I have some things to learn," she said, her blue eyes widening.

"I'm happy to teach them to you," he said, wavering on whether or not he would finish what they'd started here. "Where should I meet you tonight?"

"Here," she said, the word rushed.

"Are you sure? I live on the same property as Chase, but in different houses. We are close, but not that close."

"No, I have my own place here too. And there's always a lot of cars. It won't look weird. I just don't want anyone to see me…" She looked away from him. "I don't want to advertise."

"That's fine." It suited him to keep everyone in the dark too. He didn't want the kind of attention that would come with being associated with Madison West. Already, the attention that he got for the various art projects he did, for the different displays around town, was a little much for him.

It was an impossible situation for him, as always. He wanted things that seemed destined to require more of himself than he wanted to give. Things that seemed to need him to reach deep, when it was better if he never did. Yet he seemed to choose them. Women like Madison. A career like art.

Someday he would examine that. Not today.

"Okay," she said, "come over after it's dark."

"This is like a covert operation."

"Is that a problem?"

It really wasn't. It was hypocritical of him to pretend otherwise. Hell, his last relationship—the one with Elizabeth—had been conducted almost entirely in secrecy because he had been going out of town to see her. That had been her choice, because she knew her association with him would be an issue for her family.

And, as he already established, he didn't really want anyone to know about this thing with Maddy either. Still, sneaking around felt contrary to his nature too. In general, he didn't really care what people thought about him. Or about his decisions.

You're a liar.

He gritted his teeth. Everything with Elizabeth was

its own exception. There was no point talking to anyone about it. No point getting into that terrible thing he had been a part of. The terrible thing he had caused.

"Not a problem," he said. "I'll see you in a few hours."

"I can cook," she said as he turned to walk out of the stall.

"You don't have to. I can grab something on my way."

"No, I would rather we had dinner."

He frowned. "Maddy," he began, "this isn't going to be a relationship. It can't be."

"I know," she said, looking up and away from him, swallowing hard. "But I need for it to be something a little more just sex too. I just... Look, obviously you know that somebody that hasn't had a sexual partner in the past ten years has some baggage. I do. Shocking, I know, because I seem like a bastion of mental health. But I just don't like the feeling. I really don't."

His chest tightened. Part of him was tempted to ask her exactly what had happened. Why she had been celibate for so long. But then, if they began to trade stories about their pasts, she might want to know something about his. And he wasn't getting into that. Not now, not ever.

"Is there anything you don't like?"

"No," he said, "I'm easy. I thought you said you didn't cook?"

She shrugged a shoulder. "Okay, if I'm being completely honest, I have a set of frozen meals in my freezer that my parents' housekeeper makes for me. But I can heat up a double portion so we can eat together."

He shook his head. "Okay."

"I have pot roast, meat loaf and roast chicken."

"I'll tell you what. The only thing I want is to have

your body for dessert. I'll let you go ahead and plan dinner."

"Pot roast it is," she said, her voice a borderline squeak.

He chuckled, turning and walking away from her, something shifting in his chest. He didn't know how she managed to do that. Make him feel heavier one moment, then lighter the next. It was dangerous. That's what it was. And if he had a brain in his head, he would walk away from her and never look back.

Sadly, his ability to think with his brain had long since ceased to function.

Even if it was a stupid idea, and he was fairly certain it was, he was going to come to Madison's house tonight, and he was going to have her in about every way he could think of.

He fixed his mouth into a grim line and set about finishing his work. But while he kept his face completely stoic, inside he felt anticipation for the first time in longer than he could remember.

Chapter 6

Maddy wondered if seductresses typically wore pearls. Probably pearls and nothing else. Maybe pearls and lace. Probably not high-waisted pencil skirts and cropped sweaters. But warming pot roast for Sam had put her in the mind-set of a 1950s housewife, and she had decided to go ahead and embrace the theme.

She caught a glimpse of her reflection in the mirror in the hall of her little house and she laughed at herself. She was wearing red lipstick, her blond hair pulled back into a bun. She rolled her eyes, then stuck out her tongue. Then continued on into the kitchen, her high heels clicking on the tile.

At least underneath the sweater, she had on a piece of pretty hot lingerie, if she said so herself. She knew Sam was big on the idea that seduction couldn't be planned, but Maddy did like to have a plan. It helped her feel more in control, and when it came to Sam, she had never felt more out of control.

She sighed, reaching up into the cupboard and taking out a bottle of wine that she had picked up at Grassroots Winery that afternoon. She might not be the best cook, or any kind of cook at all, but she knew how to pick a good wine. Everyone had their strengths.

The strange thing was she kind of enjoyed feeling out of control with Sam, but it also made her feel cautious. Protective. When she had met David, she had dived into the affair headlong. She hadn't thought at all. She had led entirely with her heart, and in the end, she had gotten her heart broken. More than that, the aftermath had shattered her entire world. She had lost friends; she had lost her standing within a community that had become dear to her… Everything.

"But you aren't seventeen. And Sam isn't a married douche bag." She spoke the words fiercely into the silence of the kitchen, buoyed by the reality of them.

She could lose a little bit of control with Sam. Even within that, there would be all of her years, her wisdom—such as it was—and her experience. She was never going to be the girl she had been. That was a good thing. She would never be able to be hurt like that, not again. She simply didn't possess the emotional capacity.

She had emerged Teflon coated. Everything slid off now.

There was a knock on her front door and she straightened, closing her eyes and taking a deep breath, trying to calm the fluttering in her stomach. That reminded her a bit too much of the past. Feeling all fluttery and breathless just because she was going to see the man she was fixated on. That felt a little too much like emotion.

No. It wasn't emotion. It was just anticipation. She was old enough now to tell the difference between the two things.

She went quickly to the door, suddenly feeling a little bit ridiculous as she pulled it open. When it was too late for her to do anything about it. Her feeling of ridiculousness only increased when she saw Sam standing there, wearing his typical black cowboy hat, tight T-shirt and well-fitted jeans. Of course, he didn't need to wear anything different to be hotter to her.

A cowboy hat would do it every time.

"Hi," she said, taking a step back and gesturing with her hand. "Come in."

He obliged, walking over the threshold and looking around the space. For some reason, she found herself looking at it through his eyes. Wondering what kinds of conclusions he would draw about the neat, spare environment.

She had lived out in the little guesthouse ever since she was nineteen. Needing a little bit of distance from her family but never exactly leaving. For the first time, that seemed a little bit weird to her. It had always just been her life. She worked on the ranch, so there didn't seem to be any point in leaving it.

Now she tried to imagine explaining it to someone else—to Sam—and she wondered if it was weird.

"My mother's interior decorator did the place," she said. "Except for the yellow and red." She had added little pops of color through throw pillows, vases and art on the wall. But otherwise the surroundings were predominantly white.

"Great," he said, clearly not interested at all.

It had felt weird, thinking about him judging her based on the space, thinking about him judging her circumstances. But it was even weirder to see that he wasn't even curious.

She supposed that was de rigueur for physical affairs. And that was what this was.

"Dinner is almost ready," she said, reminding them both of the nonphysical part of the evening. Now she felt ridiculous for suggesting that too. But the idea of meeting him in secret had reminded her way too much of David. Somehow, adding pot roast had seemed to make the whole thing aboveboard.

Pot roast was an extremely nonsalacious food.

"Great," he said, looking very much like he didn't actually care that much.

"I just have to get it out of the microwave." She treated him to an exaggerated wink.

That earned her an uneasy laugh. "Great," he said.

"Come on," she said, gesturing for him to follow her. She moved into the kitchen, grabbed the pan that contained the meat and the vegetables out of the microwave and set it on the table, where the place settings were already laid out and the salad was already waiting.

"I promise I'm not trying to Stepford-wife you," she said as they both took their seats.

"I didn't think that," he said, but his blank expression betrayed the fact that he was lying.

"You did," she said. "You thought that I was trying to become your creepy robot wife."

"No, but I did wonder exactly why dinner was so important."

She looked down. It wasn't as if David were a secret. In fact, the affair was basically open information. "Do you really want to know?"

Judging by the expression on his face, he didn't. "There isn't really a good way to answer that question."

"True. Honesty is probably not the best policy. I'll think you're uninterested in me."

"On the contrary, I'm very interested in you."

"Being interested in my boobs is not the same thing."

He laughed, taking a portion of pot roast out of the dish in the center of the table. "I'm going to eat. If you want to tell me…well, go ahead. But I don't think you're trying to ensnare me."

"You don't?"

"Honestly, Maddy, nobody would want me for that long."

Those words were spoken with a bit of humor, but they made her sad. "I'm sure that's not true," she said, even though she wasn't sure of any such thing. He was grumpy. And he wasn't the most adept emotionally. Still, it didn't seem like a very kind thing for a person to think about themselves.

"It is," he said. "Chase is only with me because he's stuck with me. He feels some kind of loyalty to our parents."

"I thought your parents…"

"They're dead," he responded, his tone flat.

"I'm sorry," she said.

"Me too."

Silence fell between them after that, and she knew the only way to break it was to go ahead and get it out. "The first guy…the one ten years ago, we were having a physical-only affair. Except I didn't know it."

"Ouch," Sam said.

"Very. I mean, trust me, there were plenty of signs. And even though he was outright lying to me about his intentions, if I had been a little bit older or more experienced, I would have known. It's a terrible thing to find out you're a cliché. I imagine you wouldn't know what that's like."

"No, not exactly. Artist-cowboy-blacksmith is not really a well-worn template."

She laughed and took a sip of her wine. "No, I guess not." Then she took another sip. She needed something to fortify her. Anything.

"But other woman that actually believes he'll leave his wife for you, that is." She swallowed hard, waiting for his face to change, waiting for him to call her a name, to get disgusted and walk out.

It occurred to her just then that that was why she was telling him all of this. Because she needed him to know. She needed him to know, and she needed to see what he would think. If he would still want her. Or if he would think that she was guilty beyond forgiving.

There were a lot of people who did.

But he didn't say anything. And his face didn't change. So they just sat in silence for a moment.

"When we got involved, he told me that he was done with her. That their marriage was a mess and they were already starting divorce proceedings. He said that he just wore his wedding ring to avoid awkward questions from their friends. The dressage community around here is pretty small, and he said that he and his wife were waiting until they could tell people themselves, personally, so that there were no rumors flying around." She laughed, almost because she was unable to help it. It was so ridiculous. She wanted to go back and shake seventeen-year-old her. For being such an idiot. For caring so much.

"Anyway," she continued, "he said he wanted to protect me. You know, because of how unkind people can be."

"He was married," Sam said.

She braced herself. "Yes," she returned, unflinching.

"How old were you?"

"Seventeen."

"How old was he?"

"Almost forty."

Sam cursed. "He should have been arrested."

"Maybe," she said, "except I did want him."

She had loved the attention he had given her. Had loved feeling special. It had been more than lust. It had been neediness. For all the approval she hadn't gotten in her life. Classic daddy issues, basically. But, as messed up as a man his age had to be for wanting to fool around with a teenager, the teenager had to be pretty screwed up too.

"How did you know him?"

"He was my… He was my trainer."

"Right, so some jackass in a position of power. Very surprising."

Warmth bloomed in her chest and spread outward, a strange, completely unfamiliar sensation. There were only a few people on earth who defended her when the subject came up. And mostly, they kept it from coming up. Sierra, her younger sister, knew about it only from the perspective of someone who had been younger at the time. Maddy had shared a little bit about it, about the breakup and how much it had messed with her, when Sierra was having difficulty in her own love life.

And then there were her brothers, Colton and Gage. Who would both have cheerfully killed David if they had ever been able to get their hands on him. But Sam was the first person she had ever told the whole story to. And he was the first person who wasn't one of her siblings who had jumped to her defense immediately.

There had been no interrogation about what kinds of clothes she'd worn to her lessons. About how she had behaved. Part of her wanted to revel in it. Another part of her wanted to push back at it.

"Well, I wore those breeches around him. I know they made you act a little bit crazy. Maybe it was my fault."

"Is this why you got mad about what I said earlier?"

She lifted a shoulder. "Well, that and it was mean."

"I didn't realize this had happened to you," he said, his voice not exactly tender but full of a whole lot more sympathy than she had ever imagined getting from him. "I'm sorry."

"The worst part was losing all my friends," she said, looking up at him. "Everybody really liked him. He was their favorite instructor. As far as dressage instructors go, he was young and cool, trust me."

"So you bore the brunt of it because he turned out to be human garbage and nobody wanted to face it?"

The way he phrased that, so matter-of-fact and real, made a bubble of humor well up inside her chest. "I guess so."

"That doesn't seem fair."

"It really doesn't."

"So that's why you had to feed me dinner, huh? So I didn't remind you of that guy?"

"Well, you're nothing like him. For starters, he was… much more diminutive."

Sam laughed. "You make it sound like you had an affair with a leprechaun."

"Jockeys aren't brawny, Sam."

He only laughed harder. "That's true. I suppose that causes trouble with wind resistance and things."

She rolled her eyes. "You are terrible. Obviously he had some appeal." Though, she had a feeling it wasn't entirely physical. Seeing as she had basically been seeking attention and approval and a thousand other things besides orgasms.

"Obviously. It was his breeches," Sam said.

"A good-looking man in breeches is a thing."

"I believe you."

"But a good-looking man in Wranglers is better." At least, that was her way of thinking right at the moment.

"Good to know."

"But you can see. Why I don't really want to advertise this. It has nothing to do with what you do or who you are or who I am. Well, I guess it is all to do with who I am. What people already think about me. I've been completely defined by a sex life I barely have. And that was… It was the smallest part of that betrayal. At least for me. I loved him. And he was just using me."

"I hope his life was hell after."

"No. His wife forgave him. He went on to compete in the Olympics. He won a silver medal."

"That's kind of a karmic letdown."

"You're telling me. Meanwhile, I've basically lived like a nun and continued giving riding lessons here on the family ranch. I didn't go on to do any of the competing that I wanted to, because I couldn't throw a rock without hitting a judge who was going to be angry with me for my involvement with David."

"In my opinion," Sam said, his expression turning dark, focused, "people are far too concerned with who women sleep with and not near enough as concerned as they should be about whether or not the man does it well. Was he good?"

She felt her face heat. "Not like you."

"I don't care who you had sex with, how many times or who he was. What I do care is that I am the best you've ever had. I'm going to aim to make sure that's the case."

He reached across the table, grabbing hold of her hand. "I'm ready for dessert," he said.

"Me too," she said, pushing her plate back and moving to her feet. "Upstairs?"

He nodded once, the slow burn in his dark eyes searing through her. "Upstairs."

Chapter 7

"Well, it looks like everything is coming together for Dad's Christmas party," Sierra said brightly, looking down at the car seat next to her that contained a sleeping newborn. "Gage will be there, kind of a triumphant return, coming-out kind of thing."

Maddy's older brother shifted in his seat, his arms crossed over his broad chest. "You make me sound like a debutante having a coming-out ball."

"That would be a surprise," his girlfriend, Rebecca Bear, said, putting her hand over his.

"I didn't mean it that way," Sierra said, smiling, her slightly rounder post-childbirth cheeks making her look even younger than she usually did.

Maddy was having a difficult time concentrating. She had met her siblings early at The Grind, the most popular coffee shop in Copper Ridge, so that they could all get on the same page about the big West family soiree that would be thrown on Christmas Eve.

Maddy was ambivalent about it. Mostly she wanted to crawl back under the covers with Sam and burrow until winter passed. But they had agreed that it would go on only until Christmas. Which meant that not only was she dreading the party, it also marked the end of their blissful affair.

By the time Sam had left last night, it had been the next morning, just very early, the sun still inky black as he'd walked out of her house and to his truck.

She had wanted him to stay the entire night, and that was dangerous. She didn't need all that. Didn't need to be held by him, didn't need to wake up in his arms.

"Madison." The sound of her full name jerked her out of her fantasy. She looked up, to see that Colton had been addressing her.

"What?" she asked. "I zoned out for a minute. I haven't had all the caffeine I need yet." Mostly because she had barely slept. She had expected to go out like a light after Sam had left her, but that had not been the case. She had just sort of lay there feeling a little bit achy and lonely and wishing that she didn't.

"Just wondering how you were feeling about Jack coming. You know, now that the whole town knows that he's our half brother, it really is for the best if he comes. I've already talked to Dad about it, and he agrees."

"Great," she said, "and what about Mom?"

"I expect she'll go along with it. She always does. Anyway, Jack is a thirty-five-year-old sin. There's not much use holding it against him now."

"There never was," Maddy said, staring fixedly at her disposable coffee cup, allowing the warm liquid inside to heat her fingertips. She felt like a hypocrite saying that. Mostly because there was something about Jack that was difficult for her.

Well, she knew what it was. The fact that he was evidence of an affair her father had had. The fact that her father was the sort of man who cheated on his wife.

That her father was the sort of man more able to identify with the man who had broken Maddy's heart than he was able to identify with Maddy herself.

But Jack had nothing to do with that. Not really. She knew that logically. He was a good man, married to a great woman, with an adorable baby she really *did* want in her life. It was just that sometimes it needled at her. Got under her skin.

"True enough," Colton said. If he noticed her unease, he certainly didn't betray that he did.

The idea of trying to survive through another West family party just about made her jump up from the coffee shop, run down Main Street and scamper under a rock. She just didn't know if she could do it. Stand there in a pretty dress trying to pretend that she was something the entire town knew she wasn't. Trying to pretend that she was anything other than a disappointment. That her whole family was anything other than tarnished.

Sam didn't feel that way. Not about her. Suddenly, she thought about standing there with him. Sam in a tux, warm and solid next to her...

She blinked, cutting off that line of thinking. There was no reason to be having those fantasies. What she and Sam had was not that. Whatever it was, it wasn't that.

"Then it's settled," Maddy said, a little bit too brightly. "Jack and his family will come to the party."

That sentence made another strange, hollow sensation

echo through her. Jack would be there with his family. Sierra and Ace would be there together with their baby. Colton would be there with his wife, Lydia, and while they hadn't made it official yet, Gage and Rebecca were rarely anywhere without each other, and it was plain to anyone who had eyes that Rebecca had changed Gage in a profound way. That she was his support and he was hers.

It was just another way in which Maddy stood alone.

Wow, what a whiny, tragic thought. It wasn't like she wanted her siblings to have nothing. It wasn't like she wanted them to spend their lives alone. Of course she wanted them to have significant others. Maybe she would get around to having one too, eventually.

But it wouldn't be Sam. So she needed to stop having fantasies about him in that role. Naked fantasies. That was all she was allowed.

"Great," Sierra said, lifting up her coffee cup. "I'm going to go order a coffee for Ace and head back home. He's probably just now getting up. He worked closing at the bar last night and then got up to feed the baby. I owe him caffeine and my eternal devotion. But he will want me to lead with the caffeine." She waved and picked up the bucket seat, heading toward the counter.

"I have to go too," Colton said, leaning forward and kissing Maddy on the cheek. "See you later."

Gage nodded slowly, his dark gaze on Rebecca. She nodded, almost imperceptibly, and stood up. "I'm going to grab a refill," she said, making her way to the counter.

As soon as she was out of earshot, Gage turned his focus to her, and Maddy knew that the refill was only a decoy.

"Are you okay?"

This question, coming from the brother she knew the

least, the brother who had been out of her life for seventeen years before coming back into town almost two months ago, was strange. And yet in some ways it wasn't. She had felt, from the moment he had returned, that there was something similar in the two of them.

Something broken and strong that maybe the rest of them couldn't understand.

Since then, she had learned more about the circumstances behind his leaving. The accident that he had been involved in that had left Rebecca Bear scarred as a child. Much to Maddy's surprise, they now seemed to be in love.

Which, while she was happy for him, was also a little annoying. Rebecca was the woman he had damaged—however accidentally—and she could love him, while Maddy seemed to be some kind of remote island no one wanted to connect with.

If she took the Gage approach, she could throw hot coffee on the nearest handsome guy, wait a decade and a half and see if his feelings changed for her over time. However, she imagined that was somewhat unrealistic.

"I'm fine," she said brightly. "Always fine."

"Right. Except I'm used to you sounding dry with notes of sarcasm and today you've been overly peppy and sparkly like a Christmas angel, and I think we both know that isn't real."

"Well, the alternative is me complaining about how this time of year gets me a little bit down, and given the general mood around the table, that didn't seem to be the best idea."

"Right. Why don't you like this time of year?"

"I don't know, Gage. Think back to all the years you

spent in solitude on the road. Then tell me how you felt about Christmas."

"At best, it didn't seem to matter much. At worst, it reminded me of when I was happy. When I was home with all of you. And when home felt like a happy place. That was the hardest part, Maddy. Being away and longing for a home I couldn't go back to. Because it didn't exist. Not really. After everything I found out about Dad, I knew it wouldn't ever feel the same."

Her throat tightened, emotion swamping her. She had always known that Gage was the one who would understand her. She had been right. Because no one had ever said quite so perfectly exactly what she felt inside, what she had felt ever since news of her dalliance with her dressage trainer had made its way back to Nathan West's ears.

"It's so strange that you put it that way," she said, "because that is exactly how it feels. I live at home. I never left. And I... I ache for something I can never have again. Even if it's just to see my parents in the way that I used to."

"You saw how it was with all of us sitting here," Gage said. "It's something that I never thought I would have. The fact that you've all been willing to forgive me, to let me back into your lives after I was gone for so long, changes the shape of things. We are the ones that can make it different. We can fix what happened with Jack— or move forward into fixing it. There's no reason you and I can't be fixed too, Maddy."

She nodded, her throat so tight she couldn't speak. She stood, holding her coffee cup against her chest. "I am looking forward to seeing you at the Christmas party." Then she forced a smile and walked out of The Grind.

She took a deep breath of the freezing air, hoping that

it might wash some of the stale feelings of sadness and grief right out of her body. Then she looked down Main Street, at all of the Christmas lights gilding the edges of the brick buildings like glimmering precious metal.

Christmas wreaths hung from every surface that would take them, velvet bows a crimson beacon against the intense green.

Copper Ridge at Christmas was beautiful, but walking around, she still felt a bit like a stranger, separate and somehow not a part of it all. Everyone here was so good. People like her and Gage had to leave when they got too bad. Except she hadn't left. She just hovered around the edges like a ghost, making inappropriate and sarcastic comments on demand so that no one would ever look at her too closely and see just what a mess she was.

She lowered her head, the wind whipping through her hair, over her cheeks, as she made her way down the street—the opposite direction of her car. She wasn't really sure what she was doing, only that she couldn't face heading back to the ranch right now. Not when she felt nostalgic for something that didn't exist anymore. When she felt raw from the conversation with Gage.

She kept going down Main, pausing at the front door of the Mercantile when she saw a display of Christmas candy sitting in the window. It made her smile to see it there, a sugary reminder of some old memory that wasn't tainted by reality.

She closed her eyes tight, and she remembered what it was. Walking down the street with her father, who was always treated like he was a king then. She had been small, and it had been before Gage had left. Before she had ever disappointed anyone.

It was Christmastime, and carolers were milling

around, and she had looked up and seen sugarplums and candy canes, little peppermint chocolates and other sweets in the window. He had taken her inside and allowed her to choose whatever she wanted.

A simple memory. A reminder of a time when things hadn't been quite so hard, or quite so real, between herself and Nathan West.

She found herself heading inside, in spite of the fact that the entire point of this walk had been to avoid memories. But then, she really wanted to avoid the memories that were at the ranch. This was different.

She opened the door, taking a deep breath of gingerbread and cloves upon entry. The narrow little store with exposed brick walls was packed with goodies. Cakes, cheeses and breads, imported and made locally.

Lane Jensen, the owner of the Mercantile, was standing toward the back of the store talking to somebody. Maddy didn't see another person right away, and then, when the broad figure came into view, her heart slammed against her breastbone.

When she realized it was Sam, she had to ask herself if she had been drawn down this way because of a sense of nostalgia or because something in her head sensed that he was around. That was silly. Of course she didn't *sense* his presence.

Though, given pheromones and all of that, maybe it wasn't too ridiculous. It certainly wasn't some kind of emotional crap. Not her heart recognizing where his was beating or some such nonsense.

For a split second she considered running the other direction. Before he saw her, before it got weird. But she hesitated, just for the space of a breath, and that was long enough for Sam to look past Lane, his eyes locking with hers.

She stood, frozen to the spot. "Hi," she said, knowing that she sounded awkward, knowing that she looked awkward.

She was unaccustomed to that. At least, these days. She had grown a tough outer shell, trained herself to never feel ashamed, to never feel embarrassed—not in a way that people would be able to see.

Because after her little scandal, she had always imagined that it was the only thing people thought about when they looked at her. Walking around, feeling like that, feeling like you had a scarlet *A* burned into your skin, it forced you to figure out a way to exist.

In her case it had meant cultivating a kind of brash persona. So, being caught like this, looking like a deer in the headlights—which was what she imagined she looked like right now, wide-eyed and trembling—it all felt a bit disorienting.

"Maddy," Sam said, "I wasn't expecting to see you here."

"That's because we didn't make any plans to meet here," she said. "I promise I didn't follow you." She looked over at Lane, who was studying them with great interest. "Not that I would. Because there's no reason for me to do that. Because you're the farrier for my horses. And that's it." She felt distinctly detached and lightheaded, as though she might drift away on a cloud of embarrassment at a moment's notice.

"Right," he said. "Thank you, Lane," he said, turning his attention back to the other woman. "I can bring the installation down tomorrow." He tipped his hat, then moved away from Lane, making his way toward her.

"Hi, Lane," she said. Sam grabbed hold of her elbow and began to propel her out of the store. "Bye, Lane."

As soon as they were back out on the street, she rounded on him. "What was that? I thought we were trying to be discreet."

"Lane Jensen isn't a gossip. Anyway, you standing there turning the color of a beet wasn't exactly subtle."

"I am not a beet," she protested, stamping.

"A tiny tomato."

"Stop comparing me to vegetables."

"A tomato isn't a vegetable."

She let out a growl and began to walk away from him, heading back up Main Street and toward her car. "Wait," he said, his voice possessing some kind of unknowable power to actually make her obey.

She stopped, rooted to the cement. "What?"

"We live in the same town. We're going to have to figure out how to interact with each other."

"Or," she said, "we continue on with this very special brand of awkwardness."

"Would it be the worst thing in the world if people knew?"

"You know my past, and you can ask me that?" She looked around the street, trying to see if anybody was watching their little play. "I'm not going to talk to you about this on the town stage."

He closed the distance between them. "Fine. We don't have to have the discussion. And it doesn't matter to me either way. But you really think you should spend the rest of your life punishing yourself for a mistake that happened when you were seventeen? He took advantage of you—it isn't your fault. And apart from any of that, you don't deserve to be labeled by a bunch of people that don't even know you."

That wasn't even it. And as she stood there, staring him down, she realized that fully. It had nothing to do with what the town thought. Nothing to do with whether or not the town thought she was a scarlet woman, or if people still thought about her indiscretion, or if people blamed her or David. None of that mattered.

She realized that in a flash of blinding brilliance that shone brighter than the Christmas lights all around her. And that realization made her knees buckle, because it made her remember the conversation that had happened in her father's office. The conversation that had occurred right after one of David's students had discovered the affair between the two of them and begun spreading rumors.

Rumors that were true, regrettably.

Rumors that had made their way all the way back to Nathan West's home office.

"I can't talk about this right now," she said, brushing past him and striding down the sidewalk.

"You don't have to talk about it with me, not ever. But what's going to happen when this is over? You're going to go another ten years between lovers? Just break down and hold your breath and do it again when you can't take the celibacy anymore?"

"Stop it," she said, walking faster.

"Like I said, it doesn't matter to me..."

She whirled around. "You keep saying it doesn't matter to you, and then you keep pushing the issue. So I would say that it does matter to you. Whatever complex you have about not being good enough, this is digging at that. But it isn't my problem. Because it isn't about you. Nobody would care if they knew that we were sleeping together.

I mean, they would talk about it, but they wouldn't care. But it makes it something more. And I just… I can't have more. Not more than this."

He shifted uncomfortably. "Well, neither can I. That was hardly an invitation for something deeper."

"Good. Because I don't have anything deeper to give."

The very idea made her feel like she was going into a free fall. The idea of trusting somebody again…

The betrayals she had dealt with back when she was seventeen had made it so that trusting another human being was almost unfathomable. When she had told Sam that the sex was the least of it, she had been telling the truth.

It had very little to do with her body, and everything to do with the battering her soul had taken.

"Neither do I."

"Then why are you… Why are you pushing me like this?"

He looked stunned by the question, his face frozen. "I just… I don't want to leave you broken."

Something inside her softened, cracked a little bit. "I'm not sure that you have a choice. It kind of is what it is, you know?"

"Maybe it doesn't have to be."

"Did you think you were going to fix me, Sam?"

"No," he said, his voice rough.

But she knew he was lying. "Don't put that on yourself. Two broken people can't fix each other."

She was certain in that moment that he was broken too, even though she wasn't quite sure how.

"We only have twelve days. Any kind of fixing was a bit ambitious anyway," he said.

"Eleven days," she reminded him. "I'll see you tonight?"

"Yeah. See you then."

And then she turned and walked away from Sam McCormack for all the town to see, as if he were just a casual acquaintance and nothing more. And she tried to ignore the ache in the center of her chest that didn't seem to go away, even after she got in the car and drove home.

Chapter 8

Seven days after beginning the affair with Maddy, she called and asked him if he could come down and check the shoes on one of the horses. It was the middle of the afternoon, so if it was her version of a booty call, he thought it was kind of an odd time. And since their entire relationship was a series of those, he didn't exactly see why she wouldn't be up front about it.

But when he showed up, she was waiting for him outside the stall.

"What are you up to?"

She lifted her shoulder. "I just wanted you to come and check on the horse."

"Something you couldn't check yourself?"

She looked slightly rueful. "Okay, maybe I could have checked it myself. But she really is walking a little bit funny, and I'm wondering if something is off."

She opened the stall door, clipped a lead rope to the horse's harness and brought her out into the main part of the barn.

He looked at her, then pushed up the sleeves on his thermal shirt and knelt down in front of the large animal, drawing his hand slowly down her leg and lifting it gently. Then he did the same to the next before moving to her hindquarters and repeating the motion again.

He stole a glance up at Maddy, who was staring at him with rapt attention.

"What?"

"I like watching you work," she said. "I've always liked watching you work. That's why I used to come down here and give orders. Okay, honestly? I wanted to give myself permission to watch you and enjoy it." She swallowed hard. "You're right. I've been punishing myself. So, I thought I might indulge myself."

"I'm going to have to charge your dad for this visit," he said.

"He won't notice," she said. "Trust me."

"I don't believe that. Your father is a pretty well-known businessman." He straightened, petting the horse on its haunches. "Everything looks fine."

Maddy looked sheepish. "Great."

"Why don't you think your dad would notice?"

"A lot of stuff has come out over the past few months. You know he had a stroke three months ago or so, and while he's recovered pretty well since then, it changed things. I mean, it didn't change *him*. It's not like he miraculously became some soft, easy man. Though, I think he's maybe a little bit more in touch with his mortality. Not happily, mind you. I think he always saw himself as something of a god."

"Well," Sam said, "what man doesn't?" At least, until he was set firmly back down to earth and reminded of just how badly he could mess things up. How badly things could hurt.

"Yet another difference between men and women," Maddy said drily. "But after he had his stroke, the control of the finances went to my brother Gage. That was why he came back to town initially. He discovered that there was a lot of debt. I mean, I know you've heard about how many properties we've had to sell downtown."

Sam stuffed his hands in his pockets, lifting his shoulders. "Not really. But then, I don't exactly keep up on that kind of stuff. That's Chase's arena. Businesses and the real estate market. That's not me. I just screw around with metal."

"You downplay what you do," she returned. "From the art to the physical labor. I've watched you do it. I don't know why you do it, only that you do. You're always acting like your brother is smarter than you, but he can't do what you do either."

"Art was never particularly useful as far as my father was concerned," Sam said. "I imagine he would be pretty damned upset to see that it's the art that keeps the ranch afloat so nicely. He would have wanted us to do it the way our ancestors did. Making leatherwork and pounding nails. Of course, it was always hard for him to understand that mass production was inevitably going to win out against more expensive handmade things. Unless we targeted our products and people who could afford what we did. Which is what we did. What we've been successful with far beyond what we even imagined."

"Dads," she said, her voice soft. "They do get in your head, don't they?"

"I mean, my father didn't have gambling debts and a secret child, but he was kind of a difficult bastard. I still wish he wasn't dead." He laughed. "It would kind of be nice to have him wandering around the place shaking his head disapprovingly as I loaded up that art installation to take down to the Mercantile."

"I don't know, having your dad hanging around disapproving is kind of overrated." Suddenly, her face contorted with horror. "I'm sorry—I had no business saying something like that. It isn't fair. I shouldn't make light of your loss."

"It was a long time ago. And anyway, I do it all the time. I think it's the way the emotionally crippled deal with things." Anger. Laughter. It was all better than hurt.

"Yeah," she said, laughing uneasily. "That sounds about right."

"What exactly does your dad disapprove of, Madison?" he asked, reverting back to her full name. He kind of liked it, because nobody else called her that. And she had gone from looking like she wanted to claw his eyes out when he used it to responding. There was something that felt deep about that. Connected. He shouldn't care. If anything, it should entice him not to do it. But it didn't.

"Isn't it obvious?"

"No," he returned. "I've done a lot of work on this ranch over the years. You're always busy. You have students scheduled all day every day—except today, apparently—and it is a major part of both the reputation and the income of this facility. You've poured everything you have into reinforcing his legacy while letting your own take a backseat."

"Well, when you put it like that," she said, the smile on her lips obviously forced, "I am kind of amazing."

"What exactly does he disapprove of?"

"What do you think?"

"Does it all come back to that? Something you did when you were seventeen?" The hypocrisy of the outrage in his tone wasn't lost on him.

"I'm not sure," she said, the words biting. "I'm really not." She grabbed hold of the horse's lead rope, taking her back into the stall before clipping the rope and coming back out, shutting the door firmly.

"What do you mean by that?"

She growled, making her way out of the barn and walking down the paved path that led toward one of the covered arenas. "I don't know. Feel free to choose your own adventure with that one."

"Come on, Maddy," he said, closing the distance between them and lowering his voice. "I've tasted parts of you that most other people have never seen. A little bit of honesty isn't going to hurt you."

She whipped around, her eyes bright. "Maybe it isn't him. Maybe it's me. Maybe I'm the one that can't look at him the same way."

Maddy felt rage simmering over her skin like heat waves. She had not intended to have this conversation—not with Sam, not with anyone.

But now she had started, she didn't know if she could stop. "The night that he found out about my affair with David was the night I found out about Jack."

"So, it isn't a recent revelation to all of you?"

"No," she said. "Colton and Sierra didn't know. I'm sure of that. But I found out that Gage did. I didn't know who it was, I should clarify. I just found out that he had another child." She looked away from Sam, trying to ignore the burning sensation in her stomach. Like there was molten lava rolling around in there. She associated that feeling with being called into her father's home office.

It had always given her anxiety, even before everything had happened with David. Even before she had ever seriously disappointed him.

Nathan West was exacting, and Maddy had wanted nothing more than to please him. That desire took up much more of her life than she had ever wanted it to. But then, she knew that was true in some way or another for all of her siblings. It was why Sierra had gone to school for business. Why Colton had taken over the construction company. It was even what had driven Gage to leave.

It was the reason Maddy had poured all of her focus into dressage. Because she had anticipated becoming great. Going to the Olympics. And she knew her father had anticipated that. Then she had ruined all of it.

But not as badly as he had ruined the relationship between the two of them.

"Like I told you, one of David's other students caught us together. Down at the barn where he gave his lessons. We were just kissing, but it was definitely enough. That girl told her father, who in turn went to mine as a courtesy."

Sam laughed, a hard, bitter sound. "A courtesy to who?"

"Not to me," Maddy said. "Or maybe it was. I don't know. It was so awful. The whole situation. I wish there had been a less painful way for it to end. But it had to end, whether it ended that way or some other way, so... so I guess that worked as well as anything."

"Except you had to deal with your father. And then rumors were spread anyway."

She looked away from Sam. "Well, the rumors I kind

of blame on David. Because once his wife knew, there was really no reason for the whole world not to know. And I think it suited him to paint me in an unflattering light. He took a gamble. A gamble that the man in the situation would come out of it all just fine. It was not a bad gamble, it turned out."

"I guess not."

"Full house. Douche bag takes the pot."

She was avoiding the point of this conversation. Avoiding the truth of it. She didn't even know why she should tell him. She didn't know why anything. Except that she had never confided any of this to anyone before. She was close to her sister, and Sierra had shared almost everything about her relationship with Ace with Maddy, and here Maddy was keeping more secrets from her.

She had kept David from her. She had kept Sam from her too. And she had kept this all to herself, as well.

She knew why. In a blinding flash she knew why. She couldn't stand being rejected, not again. She had been rejected by her first love; she had been rejected by an entire community. She had been rejected by her father with a few cold dismissive words in his beautifully appointed office in her childhood home.

But maybe, just maybe, that was why she should confide in Sam. Because at the end of their affair it wouldn't matter. Because then they would go back to sniping at each other or not talking to each other at all.

Because he hadn't rejected her yet.

"When he called me into his office, I knew I was in trouble," she said, rubbing her hand over her forehead. "He never did that for good things. Ever. If there was something good to discuss, we would talk about it around the dinner table. Only bad things were ever talked about in his office with the door firmly closed. He talked to Gage like that. Right before he left town. So, I always knew it had to be bad."

She cleared her throat, looking out across the arena, through the gap in the trees and at the distant view of the misty waves beyond. It was so very gray, the clouds hanging low in the sky, touching the top of the angry, steel-colored sea.

"Anyway, I *knew*. As soon as I walked in, I knew. He looked grim. Like I've never seen him before. And he asked me what was going on with myself and David Smithson. Well, I knew there was no point in denying it. So I told him. He didn't yell. I wish he had. He said… He said the worst thing you could ever do was get caught. That a man like David spent years building up his reputation, not to have it undone by the temptation of some young girl." She blinked furiously. "He said that if a woman was going to present more temptation than a man could handle, the least she could do was keep it discreet."

"How could he say that to you? To his daughter? Look, my dad was a difficult son of a bitch, but if he'd had a daughter and some man had hurt her, he'd have ridden out on his meanest stallion with a pair of pliers to dole out the world's least sterile castration."

Maddy choked out a laugh that was mixed with a sob. "That's what I thought. It really was. I thought… I thought he would be angry, but one of the things that scared me most, at least initially, was the idea that he would take it out on David. And I still loved David then. But no. He was angry at me."

"I don't understand how that's possible."

"That was when he told me," she choked out. "Told me that he had mistresses, that it was just something men did, but that the world didn't run if the mistress didn't know her place, and if I was intent on lowering myself to be that sort of woman when I could have easily been a wife, that was none of his business. He told me a woman had had his child and never betrayed him." Her throat tightened, almost painfully, a tear sliding down her cheek. "Even he saw me as the villain. If my own father couldn't stand up for me, if even he thought it was my fault somehow, how was I ever supposed to stand up for myself when other people accused me of being a whore?"

"Maddy…"

"That's why," she said, the words thin, barely making their way through her constricted throat. "That's why it hurts so much. And that's why I'm not over it. There were two men involved in that who said they loved me. There was David, the man I had given my heart to, the man I had given my body to, who had lied to me from the very beginning, who threw me under the bus the moment he got the opportunity. And then there was my own father. My own father, who should have been on my side simply because I was born his. I loved them both. And they both let me down." She blinked, a mist rolling over her insides, matching the setting all around them. "How do you ever trust anyone after that? If it had only been David, I think I would have been over it a long time ago."

Sam was looking at her, regarding her with dark, intense eyes. He looked like he was about to say something, his chest shifting as he took in a breath that seemed to contain purpose. But then he said nothing. He simply closed the distance between them, tugging her into his arms, holding her against his chest, his large, warm hand moving between her shoulder blades in a soothing rhythm.

She hadn't rested on anyone in longer than she could remember. Hadn't been held like this in years. Her mother was too brittle to lean on. She would break beneath the weight of somebody else's sorrow. Her father had never offered a word of comfort to anyone. And she had gotten in the habit of pretending she was tough so that Colton and Sierra wouldn't worry about her. So that they wouldn't look too deeply at how damaged she was still from the events of the past.

So she put all her weight on him and total peace washed over her. She shouldn't indulge in this. She shouldn't allow herself this. It was dangerous. But she couldn't stop. And she didn't want to.

She squeezed her eyes shut, a few more tears falling down her cheeks, soaking into his shirt. If anybody knew that Madison West had wept all over a man in the broad light of day, they wouldn't believe it. But she didn't care. This wasn't about anyone else. It was just about her. About purging her soul of some of the poison that had taken up residence there ten years ago and never quite left.

About dealing with some of the heavy longing that existed inside her for a time and a place she could never return to. For a Christmas when she had walked down Main Street with her father and seen him as a hero.

But of course, when she was through crying, she felt exposed. Horribly. Hideously, and she knew this was why she didn't make a habit out of confiding in people. Because now Sam McCormack knew too much about her. Knew more about her than maybe anybody else on earth. At least, he knew about parts of her that no one else did.

The tenderness. The insecurity. The parts that were on the verge of cracking open, crumbling the foundation of her and leaving nothing more than a dusty pile of Maddy behind.

She took a deep breath, hoping that the pressure would squeeze some of those shattering pieces of herself back together with the sheer force of it. Too bad it just made her aware of more places down deep that were compromised.

Still, she wiggled out of his grasp, needing a moment to get ahold of herself. Needing very much to not get caught being held by a strange man down at the arena by any of the staff or anyone in her family.

"Thank you," she said, her voice shaking. "I just… I didn't know how much I needed that."

"I didn't do anything."

"You listened. You didn't try to give me advice or tell me I was wrong. That's actually doing a lot. A lot more than most people are willing to do."

"So, do you want me to come back here tonight?"

"Actually," she said, grabbing hold of her hands, twisting them, trying to deal with the nervous energy that was rioting through her, "I was thinking maybe I could come out a little bit early. And I could see where you work."

She didn't know why she was doing this. She didn't know where she imagined it could possibly end or how it would be helpful to her in any way. To add more pieces of him to her heart, to her mind.

That's what it felt like she was trying to do. Like collecting shells on the seashore. Picking up all the shimmering pieces of Sam she possibly could and sticking them in her little pail, hoarding them. Making a collection.

For what? Maybe for when it was over.

Maybe that wasn't so bad.

She had pieces of David, whether she wanted them or not. And she'd entertained the idea that maybe she could sleep with someone and not do that. Not carry them forward with her.

But the reality of it was that she wasn't going to walk away from this affair and never think of Sam again. He was never going to be the farrier again. He would always be Sam. Why not leave herself with beautiful memories instead of terrible ones? Maybe this was what she needed to do.

"You want to see the forge?" he asked.

"Sure. That would be interesting. But also your studio. I'm curious about your art, and I realize that I don't really know anything about it. Seeing you in the Mercantile the other day talking to Lane..." She didn't know how to phrase what she was thinking without sounding a little bit crazy. Without sounding overly attached. So she just let the sentence trail off.

But she was curious. She was curious about him. About who he was when he wasn't here. About who he was as a whole person, without the blinders around him that she had put there. She had very purposefully gone out of her way to know nothing about him. And so he had always been Sam McCormack, grumpy guy who worked at her family ranch on occasion and who she often bantered with in the sharpest of senses.

But there was more to him. So much more. This man who had held her, this man who had listened, this man who seemed to know everyone in town and have decent relationships with them. Who created beautiful things that started in his mind and were then formed with his hands. She wanted to know him.

Yeah, she wouldn't be telling him any of that.

"Were you jealous? Because there is nothing between myself and Lane Jensen. First of all, anyone who wants anything to do with her has to go through Finn Donnelly, and I have no desire to step in the middle of *that* weird dynamic and his older-brother complex."

It struck her then that jealousy hadn't even been a component to what she had felt the other day. How strange. Considering everything she had been through with men, it seemed like maybe trust should be the issue here. But it wasn't. It never had been.

It had just been this moment of catching sight of him at a different angle. Like a different side to a prism that cast a different color on the wall and made her want to investigate further. To see how one person could contain so many different things.

A person who was so desperate to hide anything beyond that single dimension he seemed comfortable with.

Another thing she would definitely not say to him. She couldn't imagine the twenty shades of rainbow horror that would cross Sam's face if she compared him to a prism out loud.

"I was not," she said. "But it made me aware of the fact that you're kind of a big deal. And I haven't fully appreciated that."

"Of course you haven't," he said, his tone dry. "It interferes with your stable-boy fantasy."

She made a scoffing sound. "I do not have a stable-boy fantasy."

"Yes, you do. You like slumming it."

Those words called up heated memories out of the depths of her mind. Him whispering things in her ear. His rough hands skimming over her skin. She bit her lip. "I like nothing of the kind, Sam McCormack. Not with you, not with any man. Are you going to show me your pretty art or not?"

"Not if you call it pretty."

"You'll have to take your chances. I'm not putting a cap on my vocabulary for your comfort. Anyway, if you haven't noticed, unnerving people with what I may or may not say next is kind of my thing."

"I've noticed."

"You do it too," she said.

His lips tipped upward into a small smile. "Do I?"

She rolled her eyes. "Oh, don't pretend you don't know. You're way too smart for that. And you act like the word *smart* is possibly the world's most vile swear when it's applied to you. But you are. You can throw around accusations of slumming it all you want, but if we didn't connect mentally, and if I didn't respect you in some way, this wouldn't work."

"Our brains have nothing to do with this."

She lifted a finger. "A woman's largest sexual organ is her brain."

He chuckled, wrapping his arm around her waist and drawing her close. "Sure, Maddy. But we both know what the most important one is." He leaned in, whispering dirty things in her ear, and she laughed, pushing against his chest. "Okay," he said, finally. "I will let you come see my studio."

She fought against the trickle of warmth that ran through her, that rested deep in her stomach and spread out from there, making her feel a kind of languid satisfaction that she had no business feeling over something like this. "Then I guess I'll see you for the art show."

Chapter 9

Sam had no idea what in hell had possessed him to let Maddy come out to his property tonight. Chase and Anna were not going to let this go ignored. In fact, Anna was already starting to make comments about the fact that he hadn't been around for dinner recently. Which was why he was there tonight, eating as quickly as possible so he could get back out to his place on the property before Maddy arrived. He had given her directions to go on the road that would allow her to bypass the main house, which Chase and Anna inhabited.

"Sam." His sister-in-law's voice cut into his thoughts. "I thought you were going to join us for dinner tonight?"

"I'm here," he said.

"Your body is. Your brain isn't. And Chase worked very hard on this meal," Anna said.

Anna was a tractor mechanic, and formerly Chase's

best friend in a platonic sense. All of that had come to an end a few months ago when they had realized there was a lot more between them than friendship.

Still, the marriage had not transformed Anna into a domestic goddess. Instead, it had forced Chase to figure out how to share a household with somebody. They were never going to have a traditional relationship, but it seemed to suit Chase just fine.

"It's very good, Chase," Sam said, keeping his tone dry.

"Thanks," Chase said, "I opened the jar of pasta sauce myself."

"Sadly, no one in this house is ever going to win a cooking competition," Anna said.

"You keep *me* from starving," Sam pointed out.

Though, in all honesty, he was a better cook than either of them. Still, it was an excuse to get together with his brother. And sometimes it felt like he needed excuses. So that he didn't have to think deeply about a feeling that was more driving than hunger pangs.

"Not recently," Chase remarked. "You haven't been around."

Sam let out a heavy sigh. "Yes, sometimes a man assumes that newlyweds want time alone without their crabby brother around."

"We always want you around," Anna said. Then she screwed up her face. "Okay, we don't *always* want you around. But for dinner, when we invite you, it's fine."

"Just no unexpected visits to the house," Chase said. "In the evening. Or anytime. And maybe also don't walk into Anna's shop without knocking after hours."

Sam grimaced. "I get the point. Anyway, I've just been busy. And I'm about to be busy again." He stood up, anticipation shooting through him. He had gone a long time without sex, and now sex with Maddy was about all he could think about. Five years of celibacy would do that to a man.

Made a man do stupid things, like invite the woman he was currently sleeping with to come to his place and to come see his art. Whatever the hell she thought that would entail. He was inclined to figure it out. Just so she would feel happy, so he could see her smile again.

So she would be in the mood to put out. And nothing more. Certainly no emotional reasoning behind that.

He couldn't do that. Not ever again.

"Okay," Anna said, "you're always cagey, Sam, I'll give you that. But you have to give me a hint about what's going on."

"No," Sam said, turning to go. "I really don't."

"Sculpture? A woman?"

Well, sadly, Anna was mostly on point with both. "Not your business."

"That's hilarious," Chase said, "coming from the man who meddled in our relationship."

"You jackasses needed meddling," Sam said. "You were going to let her go." Of the two of them, Chase was undoubtedly the better man. And Anna was one of the best, man or woman. When Sam had realized his brother was about to let Anna get away because of baggage from his past, Sam had had no choice but to play the older-brother card and give advice that he himself would never have taken.

But it was different for Chase. Sam wanted it to be different for Chase. He didn't want his younger brother living the same stripped-down existence he did.

"Well, maybe you need meddling too, jackass," Anna said.

Sam ignored his sister-in-law and continued on out of the house, taking the steps on the porch two at a time, the frosted ground crunching beneath his boots as he walked across the field, taking the short route between the two houses.

He shoved his hands in his pockets, looking up, watching his breath float up into the dense sky, joining the mist there. It was already getting dark, the twilight hanging low around him, a deep blue ink spill that bled down over everything.

It reminded him of grief. A darkness that descended without warning, covering everything around it, changing it. Taking things that were familiar and twisting them into foreign objects and strangers.

That thought nibbled at the back of his mind. He couldn't let it go. It just hovered there as he made his way back to his place, trying to push its way to the front of his mind and form the obvious conclusion.

He resisted it. The way that he always did. Anytime he got inspiration that seemed related to these kinds of feelings. And then he would go out to his shop and start working on another Texas longhorn sculpture. Because that didn't mean anything and people would want to buy it.

Just as he approached his house, so did Maddy's car. She parked right next to his truck, and a strange feeling of domesticity overtook him. Two cars in the driveway. His and hers.

He pushed that aside too.

He watched her open the car door, her blond hair even paler in the advancing moonlight. She was wearing a hat, the shimmering curls spilling out from underneath it. She also had on a scarf and gloves. And there was something about her, looking soft and bundled up, and very much not like prickly, brittle Maddy, that made him want to pull her back into his arms like he had done earlier that day and hold her up against his chest.

Hold her until she quit shaking. Or until she started shaking for a different reason entirely.

"You made it," he said.

"You say that like you had some doubt that I would."

"Well, at the very least I thought you might change your mind."

"No such luck for you. I'm curious. And once my curiosity is piqued, I will have it satisfied."

"You're like a particularly meddlesome cat," he said.

"You're going to have to make up your mind, Sam," Maddy said, smiling broadly.

"About what?"

"Am I vegetable or mammal? You have now compared me to both."

"A tomato is a fruit."

"Whatever," she said, waving a gloved hand.

"Do you want to come out and see the sculptures or do you want to stand here arguing about whether or not you're animal, vegetable or mineral?"

Her smile only broadened. "Sculptures, please."

"Well, follow me. And it's a good thing you bundled up."

"This is how much I had to bundle to get in the car and drive over here. My heater is *not* broken. I didn't know that I was going to be wandering around out in the dark, in the cold."

He snorted. "You run cold?"

"I do."

"I hadn't noticed."

She lifted a shoulder, taking two steps to his every one, doing her best to keep up with him as he led them both across the expanse of frozen field. "Well, I'm usually very hot when you're around. Anyway, the combination of you and blankets is very warming."

"What happens when I leave?"

"I get cold," she returned.

Something about those words felt like a knife in the center of his chest. Damned if he knew why. At least, damned if he wanted to know why.

What he wanted was to figure out how to make it go away.

They continued on the rest of the walk in silence, and he increased his pace when the shop came into view. "Over here is where Chase and I work," he said, gesturing to the first building. "Anna's is on a different section of the property, one closer to the road so that it's easier for her customers to get in there, since they usually have heavy equipment being towed by heavier equipment. And this one is mine." He pointed to another outbuilding, one that had once been a separate machine shed.

"We remodeled it this past year. Expanded and made room for the new equipment. I have a feeling my dad would piss himself if he knew what this was being used for now," he continued, not quite able to keep the thought in his mind.

Maddy came up beside him, looping her arm through his. "Maybe. But I want to see it. And I promise you I won't...do *that*."

"Appreciated," he said, allowing her to keep hold of him while they walked inside.

He realized then that nobody other than Chase and Anna had ever been in here. And he had never grandly showed it to either of them. They just popped in on occasion to let him know that lunch or dinner was ready or to ask if he was ever going to resurface.

He had never invited anyone here. Though, he supposed that Maddy had invited herself here. Either way, this was strange. It was exposing in a way he hadn't anticipated it being. Mostly because that required he admit that there was something of himself in his work. And he resisted that. Resisted it hard.

It had always been an uncomfortable fit for him. That he had this ability, this compulsion to create things, that could come only from inside him. Which was a little bit like opening up his chest and showing bits of it to the world. Which was the last thing on earth he ever wanted to do. He didn't like sharing himself with other people. Not at all.

Maddy turned a slow circle, her soft, pink mouth falling open. "Wow," she said. "Is this all of them?"

"No," he said, following her line of sight, looking at the various iron sculptures all around them. Most of them were to scale with whatever they were representing. Giant two-ton metal cows and horses, one with a cowboy upon its back, took up most of the space in the room.

Pieces that came from what he saw. From a place he loved. But not from inside him.

"What are these?"

"Works in progress, mostly. Almost all of them are close to being done. Which was why I was up at the cabin, remember? I'm trying to figure out what I'm going to do next. But I can always make more things like this. They sell. I can put them in places around town and tourists will always come in and buy them. People pay obscene amounts of money for stuff like this." He let out a long, slow breath. "I'm kind of mystified by it."

"You shouldn't be. It's amazing." She moved around the space, reaching out and brushing her fingertips over the back of one of the cows. "We have to get some for the ranch. They're perfect."

Something shifted in his chest, a question hovering on the tip of his tongue. But he held it back. He had been about to ask her if he should do something different. If he should follow that compulsion that had hit him on the walk back. Those ideas about grief. About loss.

Who the hell wanted to look at something like that? Anyway, he didn't want to show anyone that part of himself. And he sure as hell didn't deserve to profit off any of his losses.

He gritted his teeth. "Great."

"You sound like you think it's great," she said, her tone deeply insincere.

"I wasn't aware my enthusiasm was going to be graded."

She looked around, the shop light making her hair look even deeper gold than it normally did. She reached up, grabbing the knit hat on her head and flinging it onto the ground. He knew what she was doing. He wanted to stop her. Because this was his shop. His studio. It was personal in a way that nothing else was. She could sleep in his bed. She could go to his house, stay there all night, and it would never be the same as her getting naked here.

He was going to stop her.

But then she grabbed the zipper tab on her jacket and shrugged it off before taking hold of the hem of her top, yanking it over her head and sending it the same way as her outerwear.

Then Maddy was standing there, wearing nothing but a flimsy lace bra, the pale curve of her breasts rising and falling with every breath she took.

"Since it's clear how talented your hands are, particularly here…" she said, looking all wide-eyed and innocent. He loved that. The way she could look like this, then spew profanities with the best of them. The way she could make her eyes all dewy, then do something that would make even the most hardened cowboy blush. "I thought I might see if I could take advantage of the inspirational quality of the place."

Immediately, his blood ran hotter, faster, desire roaring in him like a beast. He wanted her. He wanted this. There was nowhere soft to take her, not here. Not in this place full of nails and iron, in this place that was hard and jagged just like his soul, that was more evidence of what he contained than anyone would ever know.

"The rest," he said, his voice as uncompromising as the sculpture all around them. "Take off the rest, Madison."

Her lashes fluttered as she looked down, undoing the snap on her jeans, then the zipper, maddeningly slowly. And of course, she did her best to look like she had no idea what she was doing to him.

She pushed her jeans down her hips, and all that was left covering her was those few pale scraps of lace. She was so soft. And everything around her was so hard.

It should make him want to protect her. Should make him want to get her out of here. Away from this place. Away from him. But it didn't. He was that much of a bastard.

He didn't take off any of his own clothes, because

there was something about the contrast that turned him on even more. Instead, he moved toward her, slowly, not bothering to hide his open appreciation for her curves.

He closed the distance between them, wrapping his hand around the back of her head, sifting his fingers through her hair before tightening his hold on her, tugging gently. She gasped, following his lead, tilting her face upward.

He leaned in, and he could tell that she was expecting a kiss. By the way her lips softened, by the way her eyes fluttered closed. Instead, he angled his head, pressing his lips to that tender skin on her neck. She shivered, the contact clearly an unexpected surprise. But not an unwelcome one.

He kept his fingers buried firmly in her hair, holding her steady as he shifted again, brushing his mouth over the line of her collarbone, following it all the way toward the center of her chest and down to the plush curves of her breasts.

He traced that feathery line there where lace met skin with the tip of his tongue, daring to delve briefly beneath the fabric, relishing the hitch in her breathing when he came close to her sensitized nipples.

He slid his hands up her arms, grabbed hold of the delicate bra straps and tugged them down, moving slowly, ever so slowly, bringing the cups down just beneath her breasts, exposing those dusky nipples to him.

"Beautiful," he said. "Prettier than anything in here."

"I didn't think you wanted the word *pretty* uttered in here," she said, breathless.

"About my work. About you... That's an entirely different situation. You are pretty. These are pretty." He leaned in, brushing his lips lightly over one tightened bud, relishing the sweet sound of pleasure that she made.

"Now who's a tease?" she asked, her voice labored.

"I haven't even started to tease you yet."

He slid his hands around her back, pressing his palms hard between her shoulder blades, lowering his head so that he could draw the center of her breast deep into his mouth. He sucked hard until she whimpered, until she squirmed against him, clearly looking for some kind of relief for the intense arousal that he was building inside her.

He looked up, really looked at her face, a deep, primitive sense of pleasure washing through him. That he was touching such a soft, beautiful woman. That he was allowing himself such an indulgence. That he was doing this to her.

He had forgotten. He had forgotten what it was like to really relish the fact that he possessed the power to make a woman feel good. Because he had reduced his hands to something else entirely. Hands that had failed him, that had failed Elizabeth.

Hands that could form iron into impossible shapes but couldn't be allowed to handle something this fragile.

But here he was with Madison. She was soft, and he wasn't breaking her. She was beautiful, and she was his.

Not yours. Never yours.

He tightened his hold on her, battling the unwelcome thoughts that were trying to crowd in, trying to take over this experience, this moment. When Madison was gone, he would go back to the austere existence he'd been living for the past five years. But right now, he had her, and he wasn't going to let anything damage that. Not now.

Instead of thinking, which was never a good thing, not

for him, he continued his exploration of her body. Lowering himself down to his knees in front of her, kissing her just beneath her breasts, and down lower, tracing a line across her soft stomach.

She was everything a woman should be. He was confident of that. Because she was the only woman he could remember. Right now, she was everything.

He moved his hands down her thighs, then back up again, pushing his fingertips beneath the waistband of her panties as he gripped her hips and leaned in, kissing her just beneath her belly button. She shook beneath him, a sweet little trembling that betrayed just how much she wanted him.

She wouldn't, if she knew. If she knew, she wouldn't want him. But she didn't know. And she never had to. There were only five days left. They would never have to talk about it. Ever. They would only ever have this. That was important. Because if they ever tried to have more, there would be nothing. She would run so far the other direction he would never see her again.

Or maybe she wouldn't. Maybe she would stick around. But that was even worse. Because of what he would have to do.

He flexed his fingers, the blunt tips digging into that soft skin at her hips. He growled, moving them around to cup her ass beneath the thin lace fabric on her panties. He squeezed her there too and she moaned, her obvious enjoyment of his hands all over her body sending a surge of pleasure through him.

He shifted, delving between her thighs, sliding his fingers through her slick folds, moving his fingers over her clit before drawing them back, pushing one finger inside her.

She gasped, grabbing his shoulders, pitching forward. He could feel her thigh muscles shaking as he pleasured her slowly, drawing his finger in and out of her body before adding a second. Her nails dug into his skin, clinging to him harder and harder as he continued tormenting her.

He looked up at her and allowed himself to get lost in this. In the feeling of her slick arousal beneath his hands, in the completely overwhelmed, helpless expression on her beautiful face. Her eyes were shut tight, and she was biting her lip, probably to keep herself from screaming. He decided he had a new goal.

He lowered his head, pressing his lips right to the center of her body, her lace panties holding the warmth of his breath as he slowly lapped at her through the thin fabric.

She swore, a short, harsh sound that verged on being a scream. But it wasn't enough. He teased her that way, his fingers deep inside her, his mouth on her, for as long as he could stand it.

Then he took his other hand, swept the panties aside and pushed his fingers in deep while he lapped at her bare skin, dragging his tongue through her folds, over that sensitized bundle of nerves.

And then she screamed.

Her internal muscles pulsed around him, her pleasure ramping his up two impossible degrees.

"I hope like *hell* you brought a condom," he said, his voice ragged, rough.

"I think I did," she said, her tone wavering. "Yes, I did. It's in my purse. Hurry."

"You want me to dig through your purse."

"I can't breathe. I can't move. If I do anything, I'm going to fall down. So I suggest you get the condom so that I don't permanently wound myself attempting to procure it."

"Your tongue seems fine," he said, moving away from her and going to grab the purse that she had discarded along with the rest of her clothes.

"So does yours," she muttered.

And he knew that what she was referring to had nothing to do with talking.

He found the condom easily enough, since it was obviously the last thing she had thrown into her bag. Then he stood, stripping his shirt off and his pants, adding to the pile of clothing that Maddy had already left on the studio floor.

Then he tore open the packet and took care of the protection. He looked around the room, searching for some surface that he could use. That they could use.

There was no way to lay her down, which he kind of regretted. Mostly because he always felt like she deserved a little bit more than the rough stuff that he doled out to her. Except she seemed to like it. So if it was what she wanted, she was about to get the full experience tonight.

He wrapped his arm around her waist, pulling her up against him, pressing their bodies together, her bare breasts pressing hard against his chest. He was so turned on, his arousal felt like a crowbar between them.

She didn't seem to mind.

He took hold of her chin, tilting her face up so she had to look at him. And then he leaned in, kissing her lightly, gently. It would be the last gentle thing he did all night.

He slid his hands along her body, moving them to grip her hips. Then he turned her so that she was facing away from him. She gasped but followed the momentum as he propelled her forward, toward one of the iron figures—a horse—and placed his hand between her shoulder blades.

"Hold on to the horse, cowgirl," he said, his voice so rough it sounded like a stranger's.

"What?"

He pushed more firmly against her back, bending her forward slightly, and she lifted her hands, placing them over the back of the statue. "Just like that," he said.

Her back arched slightly, and he drew his fingertips down the line of her spine, all the way down to her butt. He squeezed her there, then slipped his hand to her hip.

"Spread your legs," he instructed.

She did, widening her stance, allowing him a good view and all access. He moved his hand back there, just for a second, testing her readiness. Then he positioned his arousal at the entrance to her body. He pushed into her, hard and deep, and she let out a low, slow sound of approval.

He braced himself, putting one hand on her shoulder, his thumb pressed firmly against the back of her neck, the other holding her hip as he began to move inside her.

He lost himself. In her, in the moment. In this soft, beautiful woman, all curves and round shapes in the middle of this hard, angular garden of iron.

The horse was hard in front of her; he was hard behind her. Only Maddy was soft.

Her voice was soft—the little gasps of pleasure that escaped her lips like balm for his soul. Her body was soft, her curves giving against him every time he thrust home.

When she began to rock back against him, her desperation clearly increasing along with his, he moved his hand from her hip to between her thighs. He stroked her in time with his thrusts, bringing her along with him, higher and higher until he thought they would both shatter. Until he thought they might shatter everything in this room. All of these unbreakable, unbending things.

She lowered her head, her body going stiff as her release broke over her, her body spasming around his, that evidence of her own loss of control stealing every ounce of his own.

He gave himself up to this. Up to her. And when his climax hit him, it was with the realization that it was somehow hers. That she owned this. Owned this moment. Owned his body.

That realization only made it more intense. Only made it more arousing.

His muscles shook as he poured himself into her. As he gave himself up to it totally, completely, in a way he had given himself up to nothing and no one for more than five years. Maybe ever.

In this moment, surrounded by all of these creations that had come out of him, he was exposed, undone. As though he had ripped his chest open completely and exposed his every secret to her, as though she could see everything, not just these creations, but the ugly, secret things that he kept contained inside his soul.

It was enough to make his knees buckle, and he had to reach out, pressing his palm against the rough surface of the iron horse to keep himself from falling to the ground and dragging Maddy with him.

The only sound in the room was their broken breathing, fractured and unsteady. He gathered her up against his body, one hand against her stomach, the other still on the back of the horse, keeping them upright.

He angled his head, buried his face in her neck, kissed her.

"Well," Maddy said, her voice unsteady, "that was amazing."

He couldn't respond. Because he couldn't say anything. His tongue wasn't working; his brain wasn't working. His voice had dried up like a desert. Instead, he released his grip on the horse, turned her to face him and claimed her mouth in a deep, hard kiss.

Chapter 10

Maybe it wasn't the best thing to make assumptions, but when they got back to Sam's house, that was exactly what Maddy did. She simply assumed that she would be invited inside because he wanted her to stay.

If her assumption was wrong, he didn't correct her.

She soaked in the details of his home, the simple, completely spare surroundings, and how it seemed to clash with his newfound wealth.

Except, in many ways it didn't, she supposed. Sam just didn't seem the type to go out and spend large. He was too…well, Sam.

The cabin was neat, well kept and small. Rustic and void of any kind of frills. Honestly, it was more rustic than the cabins they had stayed in up in the mountain.

It was just another piece that she could add to the Sam puzzle. He was such a strange man. So difficult to find the center of. To find the key to. He was one giant sheet of code and she was missing some essential bit that might help her make heads or tails of him.

He was rough; he was distant. He was caring and kinder in many ways than almost anyone else she had ever known. Certainly, he had listened to her in a way that no one else ever had before. Offering nothing and simply taking everything onto his shoulders, letting her feel whatever she did without telling her it was wrong.

That was valuable in a way that she hadn't realized it would be.

She wished that she could do the same for him. That she could figure out what the thing was that made Sam… Sam. That made him distant and difficult and a lot like a brick wall. But she knew there was more behind his aloofness. A potential for feeling, for emotion, that surpassed what he showed the world.

She didn't even bother to ask herself why she cared. She suspected she already knew.

Sam busied himself making a fire in the simple, old-fashioned fireplace in the living room. It was nothing like the massive, modern adorned piece that was in the West family living room. One with fake logs and a switch that turned it on. One with a mantel that boasted the various awards won by Nathan West's superior horses.

There was something about this that she liked. The lack of pretension. Though, she wondered if it reflected Sam any more honestly than her own home—decorated by her mother's interior designer—did her. She could see it, in a way. The fact that he was no-nonsense and a little bit spare.

And yet in other ways she couldn't.

His art pieces looked like they were ready to take a

breath and come to life any moment. The fact that such beautiful things came out of him made her think there had to be beautiful things in him. An appreciation for aesthetics. And yet none of that was in evidence here. Of course, it would be an appreciation for a hard aesthetic, since there was nothing soft about what he did.

Still, he wasn't quite this cold and empty either.

Neither of them spoke while he stoked the fire, and pretty soon the small space began to warm. Her whole body was still buzzing with the aftereffects of what had happened in his studio. But still, she wanted more.

She hadn't intended to seduce him in his studio; it had just happened. But she didn't regret it. She had brought a condom, just in case, so she supposed she couldn't claim total innocence. But still.

It had been a little bit reckless. The kind of thing a person could get caught doing. It was definitely not as discreet as she should have been. The thought made her smile. Made her feel like Sam was washing away some of the wounds of her past. That he was healing her in a way she hadn't imagined she could be.

She walked over to where he was, still kneeling down in front of the fireplace, and she placed her hands on his shoulders. She felt his muscles tighten beneath her touch. All of the tension that he carried in his shoulders. Why? Because he wanted her again and that bothered him? It wasn't because he didn't want her, she was convinced of that. There was no faking what was between them.

She let her fingertips drift down lower. Then she leaned in, pressing a kiss to his neck, as he was so fond of doing to her. As she was so fond of him doing.

"What are you doing?" he asked, his voice rumbling inside him.

"Honestly, if you have to ask, I'm not doing a very good job of it."

"Aren't you exhausted?"

"The way I see it, I have five days left with you. I could go five days without sleep if I needed to."

He reached up, grabbing hold of her wrist and turning, then pulling her down onto the floor, onto his lap. "Is that a challenge? Because I'm more than up to meeting that."

"If you want to take it as one, I suppose that's up to you."

She put her hands on his face, sliding her thumbs alongside the grooves next to his mouth. He wasn't that old. In his early to midthirties, she guessed. But he wore some serious cares on that handsome face of his, etched into his skin. She wondered what they were. It was easy to assume it was the death of his parents, and perhaps that was part of it. But there was more.

She'd had the impression earlier today that she'd only ever glimpsed a small part of him. That there were deep pieces of himself that he kept concealed from the world. And she had a feeling this was one of them. That he was a man who presented himself as simple, who lived in these simple surroundings, hard and spare, while he contained multitudes of feeling and complexity.

She also had a feeling he would rather die than admit that.

"All right," he said, "if you insist."

He leaned in, kissing her. It was slower and more luxurious than any of the kisses they had shared back in the studio. A little bit less frantic. A little bit less desperate. Less driven toward its ultimate conclusion, much more about the journey.

She found herself being disrobed again, for the second time that day, and she really couldn't complain. Especially not when Sam joined her in a state of undress.

She pressed her hand against his chest, tracing the strongly delineated muscles, her eyes following the movement.

"I'm going to miss this," she said, not quite sure what possessed her to speak the words out loud. Because they went so much deeper than just appreciation for his body. So much deeper than just missing his beautiful chest or his perfect abs.

She wished that they didn't, but they did. She wished she were a little more confused by the things she did and said with him, like she had been earlier today. But somehow, between her pouring her heart out to him at the ranch today and making love with him in the studio, a few things had become a lot clearer.

His lips twitched, like he was considering making light of the statement. Saying something to defuse the tension between them. Instead, he wrapped his fingers around her wrist, holding her tight, pressing her palms flat against him so that she could feel his heart beating. Then he kissed her. Long, powerful. A claiming, a complete and total invasion of her soul.

She didn't even care.

Or maybe, more accurately, she did care. She cared all the way down, and what she couldn't bother with anymore was all the pretending that she didn't. That she cared about nothing and no one, that she existed on the Isle of Maddy. Where she was wholly self-sufficient.

She was pretty sure, in this moment, that she might need him. That she might need him in ways she hadn't needed another person in a very long time, if ever. When she had met David, she had been a teenager. She hadn't had any baggage; she hadn't run into any kind of resistance in the world. She was young, and she didn't know what giving her heart away might cost.

She knew now. She knew so much more. She had been hurt; she had been broken. And when she allowed herself to see that she needed someone, she could see too just how badly it could go.

When they parted, they were both breathing hard, and his dark eyes were watchful on hers. She felt like she could see further than she normally could. Past all of that strength that he wore with ease, down to the parts of him that were scarred, that had been wounded.

That were vulnerable.

Even Sam McCormack was vulnerable. What a revelation. Perhaps if he was, everyone was.

He lifted his hand, brushing up against her cheek, down to her chin, and then he pushed her hair back off her face, slowly letting his fingers sift through the strands. And he watched them slide through his fingers, just as she had watched her own hand as she'd touched his chest. She wondered what he was thinking. If he was thinking what she'd been. If he was attached to her in spite of himself.

Part of her hoped so. Part of her hoped not.

He leaned down, kissing her on the shoulder, the seemingly nonsexual contact affecting her intensely. Making her skin feel like it was on fire, making her heart feel like it might burst right out of her chest.

She found herself being propelled backward, but it felt like slow motion, as he lowered her down onto the floor. Onto the carpet there in front of the fireplace.

She had the thought that this was definitely a perfect component for a winter affair. But then the thought made her sad. Because she wanted so much more than a winter affair with him. So much more than this desperate grab in front of the fire, knowing that they had only five days left with each other.

But then he was kissing her and she couldn't think anymore. She couldn't regret. She could only kiss him back.

His hands skimmed over her curves, her breasts, her waist, her hips, all the way down to her thighs, where he squeezed her tight, held on to her as though she were his lifeline. As though he were trying to memorize every curve, every dip and swell.

She closed her eyes, gave herself over to it, to the sensation of being known by Sam. The thought filled her, made her chest feel like it was expanding. He knew her. He really knew her. And he was still here. Still with her. He didn't judge her; he didn't find her disgusting.

He didn't treat her like she was breakable. He could still bend her over a horse statue in his studio, then be like this with her in front of the fire. Tender. Sweet.

Because she was a woman who wanted both things. And he seemed to know it.

He also seemed to be a man who might need both too.

Or maybe everybody did. But you didn't see it until you were with the person you wanted to be both of those things with.

"Hang on just a second," he said, suddenly, breaking into her sensual reverie. She had lost track of time. Lost track of everything except the feel of his hands on her skin.

He moved away from her, the loss of his body leaving her cold. But he returned a moment later, settling himself in between her thighs. "Condom," he said by way of explanation.

At least one of them had been thinking. She certainly hadn't been.

He joined their bodies together, entering her slowly, the sensation of fullness, of being joined to him, suddenly so profound that she wanted to weep with it. It always felt good. From the first time with him it had felt good. But this was different.

It was like whatever veil had been between them, whatever stack of issues had existed, had been driving them, was suddenly dropped. And there was nothing between them. When he looked at her, poised over her, deep inside her, she felt like he could see all the way down.

When he moved, she moved with him, meeting him thrust for thrust, pushing them both to the brink. And when she came, he came along with her, his rough gasp of pleasure in her ears ramping up her own release.

In the aftermath, skin to skin, she couldn't deny anymore what all these feelings were. She couldn't pretend that she didn't know.

She'd signed herself up for a twelve-day fling with a man she didn't even like, and only one week in she had gone and fallen in love with Sam McCormack.

"Sam." Maddy's voice broke into his sensual haze. He was lying on his back in front of the fireplace, feeling drained and like he had just had some kind of out-of-body experience. Except he had been firmly in his body and feeling everything, everything and then some.

"What?" he asked, his voice rusty.

"Why do you make farm animals?"

"What the hell kind of question is that?" he asked.

"A valid one," she said, moving nearer to him, putting her hand on his chest, tracing shapes there. "I mean, not that they aren't good."

"The horse seemed good enough for you a couple hours ago."

"It's good," she said, her tone irritated, because she obviously thought he was misunderstanding her on purpose.

Which she wasn't wrong about.

"Okay, but you don't think I should be making farm animals."

"No, I think it's fine that you make farm animals. I just think it's not actually you."

He shifted underneath her, trying to decide whether or not he should say anything. Or if he should sidestep the question. If it were anyone else, he would laugh. Play it off. Pretend like there was no answer. That there was nothing deeper in him than simply re-creating what he literally saw out in the fields in front of him.

And a lot of people would have bought that. His own brother probably would have, or at the very least, he wouldn't have pushed. But this was Maddy. Maddy, who had come apart in his arms in more than one way over the past week. Maddy, who perhaps saw deeper inside him than anyone else ever had.

Why not tell her? Why not? Because he could sense her getting closer to him. Could sense it like an invisible cord winding itself around the two of them, no matter that he was going to have to cut it in the end. Maybe it would be best to do it now.

"If I don't make what I see, I'll have to make what I feel," he said. "Nobody wants that."

"Why not?"

"Because the art has to sell," he said, his voice flat.

Although, that was somewhat disingenuous. It wasn't that he didn't think he could sell darker pieces. In fact, he was sure that he could. "I don't do it for myself. I do it for Chase. I was perfectly content to keep it some kind of weird hobby that I messed around with after hours. Chase was the one who thought that I needed to pursue it full-time. Chase was the one who thought it was the way to save our business. And it started out doing kind of custom artistry for big houses. Gates and the detail work on stairs and decks and things. But then I started making bigger pieces and we started selling them. I say *we* because without Chase they would just sit in the shop."

"So you're just making what sells. That's the beginning and end of the story." Her blue eyes were too sharp, too insightful and far too close to the firelight for him to try to play at any games.

"I make what I want to let people see."

"What happened, Sam? And don't tell me nothing. You're talking to somebody who clung to one event in the past for as long as humanly possible. Who let it dictate her entire life. You're talking to the queen of residual issues here. Don't try to pretend that you don't have any. I know what it looks like." She took a deep breath. "I know what it looks like when somebody uses anger, spite and a whole bunch of unfriendliness to keep the world at a safe distance. I know, because I've spent the past ten years doing it. Nobody gets too close to the girl who says unpredictable things. The one who might come out and tell you that your dress does make you look fat and then turn around and say something crude about male anatomy. It's how you give yourself power in social situations. Act like you don't care about the rules that everyone else is a slave to." She laughed. "And why not? I already broke the rules.

That's me. It's been me for a long time. And it isn't because I didn't know better. It's because I absolutely knew better. You're smart, Sam. The way that you walk around, the way you present yourself, even here, it's calculated."

Sam didn't think anyone had ever accused him of being calculated before. But it was true. Truer than most things that had been leveled at him. That he was grumpy, that he was antisocial. He was those things. But for a very specific reason.

And of course Madison would know. Of course she would see.

"I've never been comfortable sharing my life," Sam said. "I suppose that comes from having a father who was less than thrilled to have a son who was interested in art. In fact, I think my father considered it a moral failing of his. To have a son who wanted to use materials to create frivolous things. Things that had no use. To have a son who was more interested in that than honest labor. I learned to keep things to myself a long time ago. Which all sounds a whole lot like a sad, cliché story. Except it's not. It worked. I would have made a relationship with my dad work. But he died. So then it didn't matter anymore. But still, I just never... I never wanted to keep people up on what was happening with my life. I was kind of trained that way."

Hell, a lot of guys were that way, anyway. A lot of men didn't want to talk about what was happening in their day-to-day existence. Though most of them wouldn't have gone to the lengths that Sam did to keep everything separate.

"Most especially when Chase and I were neck-deep in trying to keep the business afloat, I didn't like him seeing that I was working on anything else. Anything at all." Sam took a deep breath. "That included any kind of relationships I might have. I didn't have a lot. But you know Chase never had a problem with people in town knowing that he was spreading it around. He never had a problem sleeping with the women here."

"No, he did not," Maddy said. "Never with me, to be clear."

"Considering I'm your first in a decade, I wasn't exactly that worried about it."

"Just making sure."

"I didn't like that. I didn't want my life to be part of this real-time small-town TV program. I preferred to find women out of town. When I was making deliveries, going to bigger ranches down the coast, that was when I would..."

"When you would find yourself a buckle bunny for the evening?"

"Yes," he said. "Except I met a woman I liked a lot. She was the daughter of one of the big ranchers down near Coos County. And I tried to keep things business oriented. We were actually doing business with her family. But I... I saw her out at a bar one night, and even though I knew she was too young, too nice of a girl for a guy like me... I slept with her. And a few times after. I was pretty obsessed with her, actually."

He was downplaying it. But what was the point of doing anything else? Of admitting that for just a little while he'd thought he'd found something. Someone who wanted him. All of him. Someone who knew him.

The possibility of a future. Like the first hint of spring in the air after a long winter.

Maddy moved closer to him, looking up at him, and he decided to take a moment to enjoy that for a second.

Because after this, she would probably never want to touch him again.

"Without warning, she cut me off. Completely. Didn't want to see me anymore. And since she was a few hours down the highway, that really meant not seeing her. I'd had to make an effort to work her into my life. Cutting her out of it was actually a lot easier."

"Sure," Maddy said, obviously not convinced.

"I got a phone call one night. Late. From the hospital. They told me to come down because Elizabeth was asking for me. They said it wasn't good."

"Oh, Sam," Maddy said, her tone tinged with sympathy.

He brush right past that. Continued on. "I white-knuckled it down there. Went as fast as I could. I didn't tell anyone I was going. When I got there, they wouldn't let me in. Because I wasn't family."

"But she wanted them to call you."

"It didn't matter." It was difficult for him to talk about that day. In fact, he never had. He could see it all playing out in his mind as he spoke the words. Could see the image of her father walking out of the double doors, looking harried, older than Sam had ever seen him look during any of their business dealings.

"I never got to see her," Sam said. "She died a few minutes after I got there."

"Sam, I'm so sorry…"

"No, don't misunderstand me. This isn't a story about me being angry because I lost a woman that I loved. I *didn't* love her. That's the worst part." He swallowed hard, trying to diffuse the pressure in his throat crushing down, making it hard to breathe. "I mean, maybe I could have. But that's not the same. You know who loved her? Her family. Her family loved her. I have never seen a man look so destroyed as I did that day. Looking at her father, who clearly wondered why in hell I was sitting down there in the emergency room. Why I had been called to come down. He didn't have to wonder long. Not when they told him exactly how his daughter died." Sam took a deep breath. "Elizabeth died of internal bleeding. Complications from an ectopic pregnancy."

Maddy's face paled, her lips looking waxen. "Did you…? You didn't know she was pregnant."

"No. Neither did anyone in her family. But I know it was mine. I know it was mine, and she didn't want me to know. And that was probably why she didn't tell me, why she broke things off with me. Nobody knew because she was ashamed. Because it was my baby. Because it was a man that she knew she couldn't have a future with. Nobody knew, so when she felt tired and lay down for a nap because she was bleeding and feeling discomfort, no one was there."

Silence settled around them, the house creaking beneath the weight of it.

"Did you ever find out why…why she called you then?"

"I don't know. Maybe she wanted me there to blame me. Maybe she just needed me. I'll never know. She was gone before I ever got to see her."

"That must have been…" Maddy let that sentence trail off. "That's horrible."

"It's nothing but horrible. It's everything horrible. I know why she got pregnant, Maddy. It's because… I was so careless with her. I had sex with her once without a condom. And I thought that it would be fine. Hell, I figured if something did happen, I'd be willing to marry her. All of that happened because I didn't think. Because I lost control. I don't deserve…"

"You can't blame yourself for a death that was some kind of freak medical event."

"Tell me you wouldn't blame yourself, Maddy. Tell me you wouldn't." He sat up, and Maddy sat up too. Then he gripped her shoulders, holding her steady, forcing her to meet his gaze. "You, who blame yourself for the affair with your dressage teacher even though you were an underage girl. You could tell me you don't. You could tell me that you were just hurt by the way everybody treated you, but I know it's more than that. You blame yourself. So don't you dare look at me with those wide blue eyes and tell me that I have no business blaming myself."

She blinked. "I… I don't blame myself. I don't. I mean, I'm not proud of what I did, but I'm not going to take all of the blame. Not for something I couldn't control. He lied to me. I was dumb, yes. I was naive. But dammit, Sam, my father should have had my back. My friends should have had my back. And my teacher should never have taken advantage of me."

He moved away from her then, pushing himself into a standing position and forking his fingers through his hair. She wasn't blaming him. It was supposed to push her away. She certainly wasn't supposed to look at him with sympathy. She was supposed to be appalled. Appalled that he had taken the chances he had with Elizabeth's body. Appalled at his lack of control.

It was the object lesson. The one that proved that he wasn't good enough for a woman like her. That he wasn't good enough for anyone.

"You don't blame yourself at all?"

"I don't know," she said. "It's kind of a loaded question. I could have made another decision. And because of that, I guess I share blame. But I'm not going to sit around feeling endless guilt. I'm hurt. I'm wounded. But that's not the same thing. Like I told you, the sex was the least of it. If it was all guilt, I would have found somebody a long time ago. I would have dealt with it. But it's more than that. I think it's more than that with you. Because you're not an idiot. You know full well that it isn't like you're the first man to have unprotected sex with a woman. You know full well you weren't in control of where an embryo implanted inside a woman. You couldn't have taken her to the hospital, because you didn't know she was pregnant. You didn't know she needed you. She sent you away. She made some choices here, and I don't really think it's her fault either, because how could she have known? But still. It isn't your fault."

He drew back, anger roaring through him. "I'm the one…"

"You're very dedicated to this. But that doesn't make it true."

"Her father thought it was my fault," he said. "That matters. I had to look at a man who was going to have to bury his daughter because of me."

"Maybe he felt that way," Maddy said. "I can understand that. People want to blame. I know. Because I've been put in that position. Where I was the one that people wanted to blame. Because I wasn't as well liked. Because I wasn't as important. I know that David's wife certainly wanted to blame me, because she wanted to make her marriage work, and if she blamed David, how would she do that? And without blame, your anger is aimless."

Those words hit hard, settled somewhere down deep

inside him. And he knew that no matter what, no matter that he didn't want to think about them, no matter that he didn't want to believe them, they were going to stay with him. Truth had a funny way of doing that.

"I'm not looking for absolution, Maddy." He shook his head. "I was never looking for it."

"What are you looking for, then?"

He shrugged. "Nothing. I'm not looking for anything. I'm not looking for you to forgive me. I'm not looking to forgive myself."

"No," she said, "you're just looking to keep punishing yourself. To hold everything inside and keep it buried down deep. I don't think it's the rest of the world you're hiding yourself from. I think you're hiding from yourself."

"You think that you are qualified to talk about my issues? You. The woman who didn't have a lover for ten years because she's so mired in the past?"

"Do you think that's going to hurt my feelings? I know I'm messed up. I'm well aware. In fact, I would argue that it takes somebody as profoundly screwed up as I am to look at another person and see it. Maybe other people would look at you and see a man who is strong. A man who has it all laid out. A man who has iron control. But I see you for what you are. You're completely and totally bound up inside. And you're ready to crack apart. You can't go on like this."

"Watch me," he said.

"How long has it been?" she asked, her tone soft.

"Five years," he ground out.

"Well, it's only half the time I've been punishing myself, but it's pretty good. Where do you see it ending, Sam?"

"Well, you were part of it for me too."

He gritted his teeth, regretting introducing that revelation into the conversation.

"What do you mean?"

"I haven't been with a woman in five years. So I guess you could say you are part of me dealing with some of my issues."

Maddy looked like she'd been slapped. She did not, in any way, look complimented. "What does that mean? What does that mean?" She repeated the phrase twice, sounding more horrified, more frantic each time.

"It had to end at some point. The celibacy, I mean. And when you offered yourself, I wasn't in a position to say no."

"After all of your righteous indignation—the accusation that I was using you for sexual healing—it turns out you were using me for the same thing?" she asked.

"Why does that upset you so much?"

"Because…because you're still so completely wrapped up in it. Because you obviously don't have any intention to really be healed."

Unease settled in his chest. "What's me being healed to you, Maddy? What does that mean? I changed something, didn't I? Same as you."

"But…" Her tone became frantic. "I just… You aren't planning on letting it change you."

"What change are you talking about?" he pressed.

"I don't know," she said, her throat sounding constricted.

"Like hell, Madison. Don't give me that. If you've changed the rules in your head, that's hardly my fault."

She whirled around, lowering her head, burying her face in her hands. "You're so infuriating." She turned back to him, her cheeks crimson. "I don't know what either of us was thinking. That we were going to go into this and come out the other side without changing anything? We are idiots. We are idiots who didn't let another human being touch us for years. And somehow we thought we could come together and nothing would change? I mean, it was one thing when it was just me. I assumed that you went around having sex with women you didn't like all the time."

"Why would you think that?"

"Because you don't like anyone. So, that stands to reason. That you would sleep with women you don't like. I certainly didn't figure you didn't sleep with women at all. That's ridiculous. You're... *Look* at you. Of course you have sex. Who would assume that you didn't? Not me. That's who."

He gritted his teeth, wanting desperately to redirect the conversation. Because it was going into territory that would end badly for both of them. He wanted to leave the core of the energy arcing between them unspoken. He wanted to make sure that neither of them acknowledged it. He wanted to pretend he had no idea what she was thinking. No idea what she was about to say.

The problem was, he knew her. Better than he knew anyone else, maybe. And it had all happened in a week. A week of talking, of being skin to skin. Of being real.

No wonder he had spent so many years avoiding exactly this. No wonder he had spent so long hiding everything that he was, everything that he wanted. Because the alternative was letting it hang out there, exposed and acting as some kind of all-access pass to anyone who bothered to take a look.

"Well, you assumed wrong. But it doesn't have to

change anything. We have five more days, Maddy. Why does it have to be like this?"

"Honest?"

"Why do we have to fight with each other? We shouldn't. We don't have to. We don't have to continue this discussion. We are not going to come to any kind of understanding, whatever you might think. Whatever you think you're pushing for here...just don't."

"Are you going to walk away from this and just not change? Are you going to find another woman? Is that all this was? A chance for you to get your sexual mojo back? To prove that you could use a condom every time? Did you want me to sew you a little sexual merit badge for your new Boy Scout vest?" She let out a frustrated growl. "I don't want you to be a Boy Scout, Sam. I want you to be you."

Sam growled, advancing on her. She backed away from him until her shoulder blades hit the wall. Then he pressed his palms to the flat surface on either side of her face. "You don't want me to be me. Trust me. I don't know how to give the kinds of things you want."

"You don't want to," she said, the words soft, penetrating deeper than a shout ever could have.

"No, you don't want me to."

"Why is that so desperately important for you to make yourself believe?"

"Because it's true."

She let silence hang between them for a moment. "Why won't you let yourself feel this?"

"What?"

"*This* is why you do farm animals. That's what you said. And you said it was because nobody would want to see this. But that isn't true. Everybody feels grief,

Sam. Everybody has lost. Plenty of people would want to see what you would make from this. Why is it that you can't do it?"

"You want me to go ahead and make a profit off my sins? Out of the way I hurt other people? You want me to make some kind of artistic homage to a father who never wanted me to do art in the first place? You want me to do a tribute to a woman whose death I contributed to."

"Yes. Because it's not about how anyone else feels. It's about how you feel."

He didn't know why this reached in and cut him so deeply. He didn't know why it bothered him so much. Mostly he didn't know why he was having this conversation with her at all. It didn't change anything. It didn't change him.

"No," she said, "that isn't what I think you should do. It's not about profiting off sins—real or perceived. It's about you dealing with all of these things. It's about you acknowledging that you have feelings."

He snorted. "I'm entitled to more grief than Elizabeth's parents? To any?"

"You lost somebody that you cared about. That matters. Of course it matters. You lost… I don't know. She was pregnant. It was your baby. Of course that matters. Of course you think about it."

"No," he said, the words as flat as everything inside him. "I don't. I don't think about that. Ever. I don't talk about it. I don't do anything with it."

"Except make sure you never make a piece of art that means anything to you. Except not sleep with anyone. Except punish yourself. Which you had such a clear vision of when you felt like I was doing it to myself but you seem to be completely blind to when it comes to you."

"All right. Let's examine your mistake, then, Maddy. Since you're so determined to draw a comparison between the two of us. Who's dead? Come on. Who died as a result of your youthful mistakes? No one. Until you make a mistake like that, something that's that irreversible, don't pretend you have any idea what I've been through. Don't pretend you have any idea of what I should feel."

He despised himself for even saying that. For saying he had been through something. He didn't deserve to walk around claiming that baggage. It was why he didn't like talking about it. It was why he didn't like thinking about it. Because Elizabeth's family members were the ones who had been left with a giant hole in their lives. Not him. Because they were the ones who had to deal with her loss around the dinner table, with thinking about her on her birthday and all of the holidays they didn't have her.

He didn't even know when her birthday was.

"Well, I care about you," Maddy said, her voice small. "Doesn't that count for anything?"

"No," he said, his voice rough. "Five more days, Maddy. That's it. That's all it can ever be."

He should end it now. He knew that. Beyond anything else, he knew that he should end it now. But if Maddy West had taught him anything, it was that he wasn't nearly as controlled as he wanted to be. At least, not where she was concerned. He could stand around and shout about it, self-flagellate all he wanted, but when push came to shove, he was going to make the selfish decision.

"Either you come to bed with me and we spend the rest of the night not talking, or you go home and we can forget the rest of this."

Maddy nodded mutely. He expected her to turn and

walk out the door. Maybe not even pausing to collect her clothes, in spite of the cold weather. Instead, she surprised him. Instead, she took his hand, even knowing the kind of devastation it had caused, and she turned and led him up the stairs.

Chapter 11

Maddy hadn't slept at all. It wasn't typical for her and Sam to share a bed the entire night. But they had last night. After all that shouting and screaming and love-making, it hadn't seemed right to leave. And he hadn't asked her to.

She knew more about him now than she had before. In fact, she had a suspicion that she knew everything about him. Even if it wasn't all put together into a complete picture. It was there. And now, with the pale morning light filtering through the window, she was staring at him as though she could make it all form a cohesive image.

As if she could will herself to somehow understand what all of those little pieces meant. As if she could make herself see the big picture.

Sam couldn't even see it, of that she was certain. So she had no idea how she could expect herself to see it.

Except that she wanted to. Except that she needed to. She didn't want to leave him alone with all of that. It was too much. It was too much for any one man. He felt responsible for the death of that woman. Or at least, he was letting himself think he did.

Protecting himself. Protecting himself with pain.

It made a strange kind of sense to her, only because she was a professional at protecting herself. At insulating herself from whatever else might come her way. Yes, it was a solitary existence. Yes, it was lonely. But there was control within that. She had a feeling that Sam operated in much the same way.

She shifted, brushing his hair out of his face. He had meant to frighten her off. He had given her an out. And she knew that somehow he had imagined she would take it. She knew that he believed he was some kind of monster. At least, part of him believed it.

Because she could also tell that he had been genuinely surprised that she hadn't turned tail and run.

But she hadn't. And she wouldn't. Mostly because she was just too stubborn. She had spent the past ten years being stubborn. Burying who she was underneath a whole bunch of bad attitude and sharp words. Not letting anyone get close, even though she had a bunch of people around her who cared. She had chosen to focus on the people who didn't. The people who didn't care enough. While simultaneously deciding that the people who did care enough, who cared more than enough, somehow weren't as important.

Well, she was done with that. There were people in her life who loved her. Who loved her no matter what. And she had a feeling that Sam had the ability to be one of those people. She didn't want to abandon him to this.

Not when he had—whether he would admit it or not—been instrumental in digging her out of her self-imposed emotional prison.

"Good morning," she whispered, pressing her lips to his cheek.

As soon as she did that, a strange sense of foreboding stole over her. As though she knew that the next few moments were going to go badly. But maybe that was just her natural pessimism. The little beast she had built up to be the strongest and best-developed piece of her. Another defense.

Sam's eyes opened, and the shock that she glimpsed there absolutely did not bode well for the next few moments. She knew that. "I stayed the night," she said, in response to the unasked question she could see lurking on his face.

"I guess I fell asleep," he said, his voice husky.

"Clearly." She took a deep breath. Oh well. If it was all going to hell, it might as well go in style. "I want you to come to the family Christmas party with me."

It took only a few moments for her to decide that she was going to say those words. And that she was going to follow them up with everything that was brimming inside her. Feelings that she didn't feel like keeping hidden. Not anymore. Maybe it was selfish. But she didn't really care. She knew his stuff. He knew hers. The only excuse she had for not telling him how she felt was self-protection.

She knew where self-protection got her. Absolutely nowhere. Treading water in a stagnant pool of her own failings, never advancing any further on in her life. In her existence. It left her lonely. It left her without any real, true friends. She didn't want that. Not anymore. And if she had to allow herself to be wounded in the name of authenticity, in the name of trying again, then she would.

An easy decision to make before the injury occurred. But it was made nonetheless.

"Why?" Sam asked, rolling away from her, getting up out of bed.

She took that opportunity to drink in every detail of his perfect body. His powerful chest, his muscular thighs. Memorizing every little piece of him. More Sam for her collection. She had a feeling that eventually she would walk away from him with nothing but that collection. A little pail full of the shadows of what she used to have.

"Because I would like to have a date." She was stalling now.

"You want to make your dad mad? Is that what we're doing? A little bit of revenge for everything he put you through?"

"I would never use you that way, Sam. I hope you know me better than that."

"We don't know each other, Maddy. We don't. We've had a few conversations, and we've had some sex. But that doesn't mean knowing somebody. Not really."

"That just isn't true. Nobody else knows how I feel about what happened to me. Nobody. Nobody else knows about the conversation I had with my dad. And I would imagine that nobody knows about Elizabeth. Not the way that I do."

"We used each other as a confessional. That isn't the same."

"The funny thing is it did start that way. At least for me. Because what did it matter what you knew. We weren't going to have a relationship after. So I didn't have to worry about you judging me. I didn't have to worry about anything."

"And?"

"That was just what I told myself. It was what made it feel okay to do what I wanted to do. We lie to ourselves. We get really deep in it when we feel like we need protection. That was what I was doing. But the simple truth is I felt a connection with you from the beginning. It was why I was so terrible to you. Because it scared me."

"You should have kept on letting it scare you, baby girl."

Those words acted like a shot of rage that went straight to her stomach, then fired onto her head. "Why? Because it's the thing that allows you to maintain your cranky-loner mystique? That isn't you. I thought maybe you didn't feel anything. But now I think you feel everything. And it scares you. I'm the same way."

"I see where this is going, Maddy. Don't do it. Don't. I can tell you right now it isn't going to go the way you think it will."

"Oh, go ahead, Sam. Tell me what I think. Please. I'm dying to hear it."

"You think that because you've had some kind of transformation, some kind of deep realization, that I'm headed for the same. But it's bullshit. I'm sorry to be the one to tell you. Wishful thinking on a level I never wanted you to start thinking on. You knew the rules. You knew them from the beginning."

"Don't," she said, her throat tightening, her chest constricting. "Don't do this to us. Don't pretend it can stay the same thing it started out as. Because it isn't. And you know it."

"You're composing a really compelling story, Madison." The reversion back to her full name felt significant. "And we both know that's something you do. Make more out of sex than it was supposed to be."

She gritted her teeth, battling through. Because he wanted her to stop. He wanted this to intimidate, to hurt. He wanted it to stop her. But she wasn't going to let him win. Not at this. Not at his own self-destruction. "Jackass 101. Using somebody's deep pain against them. I thought you were above that, Sam."

"It turns out I'm not. You might want to pay attention to that."

"I'm paying attention. I want you to come with me to the Christmas party, Sam. Because I want it to be the beginning. I don't want it to be the end."

"Don't do this."

He bent down, beginning to collect his clothes, his focus on anything in the room but her. She took a deep breath, knowing that what happened next was going to shatter all of this.

"I need more. I need more than twelve days of Christmas. I want it every day. I want to wake up with you every morning and go to bed with you every night. I want to fight with you. I want to make love with you. I want to tell you my secrets. To show you every dark, hidden thing in me. The serious things and the silly things. Because I love you. It's that complicated and that simple. I love you and that means I'm willing to do this, no matter how it ends."

Sam tugged his pants on, did them up, then pulled his shirt over his head. "I told you not to do this, Maddy. But you're doing it anyway. And you know what that makes it? A suicide mission. You stand there, thinking you're being brave because you're telling the truth. But you know how it's going to end. You know that after you make this confession, you're not actually going to have to deal with the relationship with me, because I already told you it isn't happening. I wonder if you would have been so brave if you knew I might turn around and offer you forever."

His words hit her with the force of bullets. But for some reason, they didn't hurt. Not really. She could remember distinctly when David had broken things off with her. Saying that she had never been anything serious. That she had been only a little bit of tail on the side and he was of course going to have to stay with his wife. Because she was the center of his life. Of his career. Because she mattered, and Maddy didn't. That had hurt. It had hurt because it had been true.

Because David hadn't loved her. And it had been easy for him to break up with her because he had never intended on having more with her, and not a single part of him wanted more.

This was different. It was different because Sam was trying to hurt her out of desperation. Because Sam was lying. Or at the very least, was sidestepping. Because he didn't want to have the conversation.

Because he would have to lie to protect himself. Because he couldn't look her in the eye and tell her that he didn't love her, that she didn't matter.

But she wasn't certain he would let himself feel it. That was the gamble. She knew he felt it. She knew it. That deep down, Sam cared. She wasn't sure if he knew it. If he had allowed himself access to those feelings. Feelings that Sam seemed to think were a luxury, or a danger. Grief. Desire. Love.

"Go ahead and offer it. You won't. You won't, because you know I would actually say yes. You can try to make this about how damaged I am, but all of this is because of you."

"You have to be damaged to want somebody like me. You know what's in my past."

"Grief. Grief that you won't let yourself feel. Sadness you don't feel like you're allowed to have. That's what's in your past. Along with lost hope. Let's not pretend you blame yourself. You felt so comfortable calling me out, telling me that I was playing games. Well, guess what. That's what you're doing. You think if you don't want anything, if you don't need anything, you won't be hurt again. But you're just living in hurt and that isn't better."

"You have all this clarity about your own emotional situation, and you think that gives you a right to talk about mine?"

She threw the blankets off her and got out of bed. "Why not?" she asked, throwing her arms wide. She didn't care that she was naked. In fact, in many ways it seemed appropriate. That Sam had put clothes on, that he had felt the need to cover himself, and that she didn't even care anymore. She had no pride left. But this wasn't about pride.

"You think you have the right to talk about mine," she continued. "You think you're going to twist everything that I'm saying and eventually you'll find some little doubt inside me that will make me believe you're telling the truth. I've had enough of that. I've had enough of men telling me what I feel. Of them telling me what I should do. I'm not going to let you do it. You're better than that. At least, I thought you were."

"Maybe I'm not."

"Right now? I think you don't want to be. But I would

love you through this too, Sam. You need to know that. You need to know that whatever you say right now, in this room, it's not going to change the way that I feel about you. You don't have that kind of power."

"That's pathetic. There's nothing I can say to make you not love me? Why don't you love yourself a little bit more than that, Madison," he said, his tone hard.

And regardless of what she had just said, that did hit something in her. Something vulnerable and scared. Something that was afraid she really hadn't learned how to be anything more than a pathetic creature, desperate for a man to show her affection.

"I love myself just enough to put myself out there and demand this," she said finally, her voice vibrating with conviction. "I love myself too much to slink off silently. I love myself too much not to fight for what I know we could have. If I didn't do this, if I didn't say this, it would only be for my pride. It would be so I could score points and feel like maybe I won. But in the end, if I walk away without having fought for you with everything I have in me, we will have both lost. I think you're worth that. I know you are. Why don't you think so?"

"Why do you?" he asked, his voice thin, brittle. "I don't think I've shown you any particular kindness or tenderness."

"Don't. Don't erase everything that's happened between us. Everything I told you. Everything you gave me."

"Keeping my mouth shut while I held a beautiful woman and let her talk? That's easy."

"I love you, Sam. That's all. I'm not going to stand here and have an argument. I'm not going to let you get in endless barbs while you try to make those words something less than true. I love you. I would really like it if you could tell me you loved me too."

"I don't." His words were flat in the room. And she knew they were all she would get from him. Right now, it was all he could say. And he believed it. He believed it down to his bones. That he didn't love her. That everything that had taken place between them over the past week meant nothing. Because he had to. Because behind that certainty, that flat, horrifying expression in his eyes, was fear.

Strong, beautiful Sam, who could bend iron to his will, couldn't overpower the fear that lived inside him. And she would never be able to do it for him.

"Okay," she said softly, beginning to gather her clothes. She didn't know how to do this. She didn't know what to do now. How to make a triumphant exit. So she decided she wouldn't. She decided to let the tears fall down her cheeks; she decided not to make a joke. She decided not to say anything flippant or amusing.

Because that was what the old Maddy would have done. She would have played it off. She would have tried to laugh. She wouldn't have let herself feel this, not all the way down. She wouldn't have let her heart feel bruised or tender. Wouldn't have let a wave of pain roll over her. Wouldn't have let herself feel it, not really.

And when she walked out of his house, sniffling, her shoulders shaking, and could no longer hold back the sob that was building in her chest by the time she reached her car, she didn't care. She didn't feel ashamed.

There was no shame in loving someone.

She opened the driver-side door and sat down. And then the dam burst. She had loved so many people who had never loved her in return. Not the way she loved them. She had made herself hard because of it. She had put the shame on her own shoulders.

That somehow a seventeen-year-old girl should have known that her teacher was lying to her. That somehow a daughter whose father had walked her down Main Street and bought her sweets in a little shop should have known that her father's affection had its limits.

That a woman who had met a man who had finally reached deep inside her and moved all those defenses she had erected around her heart should have known that in the end he would break it.

No. It wasn't her. It wasn't the love that was bad. It was the pride. The shame. The fear. Those were the things that needed to be gotten rid of.

She took a deep, shaking breath. She blinked hard, forcing the rest of her tears to fall, and then she started the car.

She would be okay. Because she had found herself again. Had learned how to love again. Had found a deep certainty and confidence in herself that had been missing for so long.

But as she drove away, she still felt torn in two. Because while she had been made whole, she knew that she was leaving Sam behind, still as broken as she had found him.

Chapter 12

Sam thought he might be dying. But then, that could easily be alcohol poisoning. He had been drinking and going from his house into his studio for the past two days. And that was it. He hadn't talked to anyone. He had nothing to say. He had sent Maddy away, and while he was firmly convinced it was the only thing he could have done, it hurt like a son of a bitch.

It shouldn't. It had been necessary. He couldn't love her the way that she wanted him to. He couldn't. There was no way in hell. Not a man like him.

Her words started to crowd in on him unbidden, the exact opposite thing that he wanted to remember right now. About how there was no point blaming himself. About how that wasn't the real issue. He growled, grabbing hold of the hammer he'd been using and flinging it across the room. It landed in a pile of scrap metal, the sound satisfying, the lack of damage unsatisfying.

He had a fire burning hot, and the room was stifling. He stripped his shirt off, feeling like he couldn't catch his breath. He felt like he was losing his mind. But then, he wasn't a stranger to it. He had felt this way after his parents had died. Again after Elizabeth. There was so much inside him, and there was nowhere for it to go.

And just like those other times, he didn't deserve this pain. Not at all. He was the one who had hurt her. He was the one who couldn't stand up to that declaration of love. He didn't deserve this pain.

But no matter how deep he tried to push it down, no matter how he tried to pound it out with a hammer, it still remained. And his brain was blank. He couldn't even figure out how the hell he might fashion some of this material into another cow.

It was like the thing inside him that told him how to create things had left along with Maddy.

He looked over at the bottle of Jack Daniel's that was sitting on his workbench. And cursed when he saw that it was empty. He was going to have to get more. But he wasn't sure he had more in the house. Which meant leaving the house. Maybe going to Chase's place and seeing if there was anything to take. Between that and sobriety it was a difficult choice.

He looked around, looked at the horse that he had bent Maddy over just three days ago. Everything seemed dead now. Cold. Dark. Usually he felt the life in the things that he made. Something he would never tell anyone, because it sounded stupid. Because it exposed him.

But it was like Maddy had come in here and changed things. Taken everything with her when she left.

He walked over to the horse, braced his hands on the

back of it and leaned forward, giving into the wave of pain that crashed over him suddenly, uncontrollably.

"I thought I might find you in here."

Sam lifted his head at the sound of his brother's voice. "I'm busy."

"Right. Which is why there is nothing new in here, but it smells flammable."

"I had a drink."

"Or twelve," Chase said, sounding surprisingly sympathetic. "If you get too close to that forge, you're going to burst into flame."

"That might not be so bad."

"What's going on? You're always a grumpy bastard, but this is different. You don't usually disappear for days at a time. Actually, I can pick up a couple of times that you've done that in the past. You usually reemerge worse and even more impossible than you were before. So if that is what's happening here, I would appreciate a heads-up."

"It's nothing. Artistic temper tantrum."

"I don't believe that." Chase crossed his arms and leaned against the back wall of the studio, making it very clear that he intended to stay until Sam told him something.

Fine. The bastard could hang out all day for all he cared. It didn't mean he had to talk.

"Believe whatever you want," Sam said. "But it's not going to make hanging out here any more interesting. I can't figure out what to make next. Are you happy? I have no idea. I have no inspiration." Suddenly, everything in him boiled over. "And I hate that. I hate that it matters. I should just be able to think of something to do. Or not care if I don't want to do it. But somehow, I can't make it work if I don't care at least a little bit. I hate caring, Chase. I *hate* it."

He hated it for every damn thing. Every damn, fragile thing.

"I know," Chase said. "And I blame Dad for that. He didn't understand. That isn't your fault. And it's not your flaw that you care. Think about the way he was about ranching. It was ridiculous. Weather that didn't go his way would send him into some kind of emotional tailspin for weeks. And he felt the same way about iron that you do. It's just that he felt compelled to shape it into things that had a function. But he took pride in his work. And he was an artist with it—you know he was. If anything, I think he was shocked by what you could do. Maybe even a little bit jealous. And he didn't know what to do with it."

Sam resisted those words. And the truth in them. "It doesn't matter."

"It does. Because it's why you can't talk about what you do. It's why you don't take pride in it the way that you should. It's why you're sitting here downplaying the fact you're having some kind of art block when it's been pretty clear for a few months that you have been."

"It shouldn't be a thing."

Chase shrugged. "Maybe not. But the very thing that makes your work valuable is also what makes it difficult. You're not a machine."

Sam wished he was. More than anything, he wished that he was. So that he wouldn't care about a damn thing. So that he wouldn't care about Maddy.

Softness, curves, floated to the forefront of his mind. Darkness and grief. All the inspiration he could ever want. Except that he couldn't take it. It wasn't his. He didn't own it. None of it.

He was still trying to pull things out of his own soul, and all he got was dry, hard work that looked downright ugly to him.

"I should be," he said, stubborn.

"This isn't about Dad, though. I don't even think it's about the art, though I think it's related. There was a woman, wasn't there?"

Sam snorted. "When?"

"Recently. Like the past week. Mostly I think so because I recognize that all-consuming obsession. Because I recognize this. Because you came and kicked my ass when I was in a very similar position just a year ago. And you know what you told me? With great authority, you told me that iron had to get hot to get shaped into something. You told me that I was in my fire, and I had to let it shape me into the man Anna needed me to be."

"Yeah, I guess I did tell you that," Sam said.

"Obviously I'm not privy to all the details of your personal life, Sam, which is your prerogative. But you're in here actively attempting to drink yourself to death. You say that you can't find any inspiration for your art. I would say that you're in a pretty damn bad situation. And maybe you need to pull yourself out of it. If that means grabbing hold of her—whoever she is—then do it."

Sam felt like the frustration inside him was about to overflow. "I can't. There's too much… There's too much. If you knew, Chase. If you knew everything about me, you wouldn't think I deserved it."

"Who deserves it?" Chase asked. "Does anybody? Do you honestly think I deserve Anna? I don't. But I love her. And I work every day to deserve her. It's a work in progress, let me tell you. But that's love. You just kind of keep working for it."

"There are too many other things in the way," Sam said, because he didn't know how else to articulate it. Without having a confessional, here in his studio, he didn't know how else to have this conversation.

"What things? What are you afraid of, Sam? Having a feeling? Is that what all this is about? The fact you want to protect yourself? The fact that it matters more to you that you get to keep your stoic expression and your who-gives-a-damn attitude intact?"

"It isn't that. It's never been that. But how—" He started again. "How was I supposed to grieve for Dad when you lost your mentor? How was I supposed to grieve for Mom when you were so young? It wasn't fair." And how the hell was he supposed to grieve for Elizabeth, for the child he didn't even know she had been carrying, when her own family was left with nothing.

"Of course you could grieve for them. They were your parents."

"Somebody has to be strong, Chase."

"And you thought I was weak? You think somehow grieving for my parents was weak?"

"Of course not. But… I was never the man that Dad wanted me to be. Now when he was alive. I didn't do what he wanted me to do. I didn't want the things that he wanted."

"Neither did I. And we both just about killed ourselves working this place the way that he wanted us to while it slowly sank into the ground. Then we had to do things on our terms. Because actually, we did know what we were talking about. And who we are, the gifts that we have, those mattered. If it wasn't for the fact that I have a business mind, if it wasn't for the fact that you could do the artwork, the ranch wouldn't be here. McCormack

Ironworks wouldn't exist. And if Dad had lived, he would be proud of us. Because in the end we saved this place."

"I just don't... I had a girlfriend who died." He didn't know why he had spoken the words. He hadn't intended to. "She wasn't my girlfriend when she died. But she bled to death. At the hospital. She had been pregnant. And it was mine."

Chase cursed and fell back against the wall, bracing himself. "Seriously?"

"Yes. And I want... I want to do something with that feeling. But her family is devastated, Chase. They lost so much more than I did. And I don't know how... I don't know what to do with all of this. I don't know what to do with all of these feelings. I don't feel like I deserve them. I don't feel like I deserve the pain. Not in the way that I deserve to walk away from it unscathed. But I feel like it isn't mine. Like I'm taking something from them, or making something about me that just shouldn't be. But it's there all the same. And it follows me around. And Maddy loves me. She said she loves me. And I don't know how to take that either."

"Bullshit," Chase said, his voice rough. "That's not it."

"Don't tell me how it is, Chase, not when you don't know."

"Of course I know, Sam. Loss is hell. And I didn't lose half of what you did."

"It was just the possibility of something. Elizabeth. It wasn't... It was just..."

"Sam. You lost your parents. And a woman you were involved with who was carrying your baby. Of course you're screwed up. But walking around pretending you're just grumpy, pretending you don't want anything, that you don't care about anything, doesn't protect you from pain. It's just letting fear poison you from the inside."

Sam felt like he was staring down into an abyss that had no end. A yawning, bottomless cavern that was just full of need. All the need he had ever felt his entire life. The words ricocheted back at him, hit him like shrapnel, damaging, wounding. They were the truth. That it was what drove him, that it was what stopped him.

Fear.

That it was why he had spent so many years hiding.

And as blindingly clear as it was, it was also clear that Maddy was right about him. More right about him than he'd ever been about himself.

That confession made him think of Maddy too. Of the situation she was in with her father. Of those broken words she had spoken to him about how if her own father didn't think she was worth defending, who would? And he had sent her away, like he didn't think she was worth it either. Like he didn't think she was worth the pain or the risk.

Except he did. He thought she was worth defending. That she was worth loving. That she was worth everything.

Sam felt… Well, nothing on this earth had ever made him feel small before. But this did it. He felt scared. He felt weak. Mostly he felt a kind of overwhelming sadness for everything he'd lost. For all the words that were left unsaid. The years of grief that had built up.

It had never been about control. It had never been based in reality. Or about whether or not he deserved something. Not really. He was afraid of feeling. Of loss. More loss after years and years of it.

But his father had died without knowing. Without

knowing that even though things weren't always the best between them, Sam had loved him. Elizabeth had died without knowing Sam had cared.

Protecting himself meant hurting other people. And it damn well hurt him.

Maddy had been brave enough to show him. And he had rejected it. Utterly. Completely. She had been so brave, and he had remained shut down as he'd been for years.

She had removed any risk of rejection and still he had been afraid. He had been willing to lose her this time.

"Do you know why the art is hard?" he asked.

"Why?"

"Because. If I make what I really want to, then I actually have to feel it."

He hated saying it. Hated admitting it. But he knew, somehow, that this was essential to his soul. That if he was ever going to move on from this place, from this dry, drunken place that produced nothing but anguish, he had to start saying these things. He had to start committing to these things.

"I had a lot behind this idea that I wasn't good enough. That I didn't deserve to feel. Because…the alternative is feeling it. It's caring when it's easier to be mad at everything. Hoping for things when so much is already dead."

"What's the alternative?" Chase asked.

He looked around his studio. At all the lifeless things. Hard and sharp. Just like he was. The alternative was living without hope. The alternative was acting like he was dead too.

"This," he said finally. "And life without Maddy. I'd rather risk everything than live without her."

Chapter 13

Madison looked around the beautifully appointed room. The grand party facility at the ranch was decorated in evergreen boughs and white Christmas lights, the trays of glittering champagne moving by somehow adding to the motif. Sparkling. Pristine.

Maddy herself was dressed in a gown that could be described in much the same manner. A pale yellow that caught the lights and glimmered like sun on new-fallen snow.

However, it was a prime example of how appearances can be deceiving. She felt horrible. Much more like snow that had been mixed up with gravel. Gritty. Gray.

Hopefully no one was any the wiser. She was good at putting on a brave face. Good at pretending everything was fine. Something she had perfected over the years. Not just at these kinds of public events but at family events too.

Self-protection was her favorite accessory. It went with everything.

She looked outside, at the terrace, which was lit by a thatch of Christmas lights, heated by a few freestanding heaters. However, no one was out there. She took a deep breath, seeing her opportunity for escape. And she took it. She just needed a few minutes. A few minutes to feel a little bit less like her face would crack beneath the weight of her fake smile.

A few minutes to take a deep breath and not worry so much that it would turn into a sob.

She grabbed hold of a glass of champagne, then moved quickly to the door, slipping out into the chilly night air. She went over near one of the heaters, wrapping her arms around herself and simply standing for a moment, looking out into the inky blackness, looking at nothing. It felt good. It was a relief to her burning eyes. A relief to her scorched soul.

All of this feelings business was rough. She wasn't entirely certain she could recommend it.

"What's going on, Maddy?"

She turned around, trying to force a smile when she saw her brother Gage standing there.

"I just needed a little bit of quiet," she said, lifting her glass of champagne.

"Sure." He stuffed his hands in his pockets. "I'm not used to this kind of thing. I spent a lot of time on the road. In crappy hotels. Not a lot of time at these sorts of get-togethers."

"Regretting the whole return-of-the-prodigal-son thing? Because it's too late to unkill that fatted calf, young man. You're stuck."

He laughed. "No. I'm glad that I'm back. Because of you. Because of Colton, Sierra. Even Jack."

"Rebecca?"

"Of course." He took a deep breath, closing the distance between them. "So what's going on with you?"

"Nothing," she said, smiling.

"I have a feeling that everybody else usually buys that. Which is why you do it. But I don't. Is it Jack? Is it having him here?"

She thought about that. Seriously thought about it. "No," she said, truthful. "I'm glad. I'm so glad that we're starting to fix some of this. I spent a long time holding on to my anger. My anger at Dad. At the past. All of my pain. And Jack got caught up in that. Because of the circumstances. We are all very different people. And getting to this point... I feel like we took five different paths. But here we are. And it isn't for Dad. It's for us. I think that's good. I spent a lot of time doing things in response to him. In response to the pain that he caused me. I don't want to do that anymore. I don't want to act from a place of pain and fear anymore."

"That's quite a different stance. I mean, since last we talked at The Grind."

She tried to smile again, wandering over to one of the wooden pillars. "I guess some things happened." She pressed her palm against the cold surface, then her forehead. She took a deep breath. In and out, slowly, evenly.

"Are you okay?"

She shook her head. "Not really. But I will be."

"I know I missed your first big heartbreak. And I feel like I would have done that bastard some bodily harm. I have quite a bit of internalized rage built up. If you need me to hurt anyone... I will. Gladly."

She laughed. "I appreciate that. Really, I do. It's just that…it's a good thing this is happening. It's making me realize a lot of things. It's making me change a lot of things. I just wish it didn't hurt."

"You know…when Rebecca told me that she loved me, it scared the hell out of me. And I said some things that I shouldn't have said. That no one should ever say to anyone. I regretted it. But I was running scared, and I wanted to make sure she didn't come after me. I'm so glad that she forgave me when I realized what an idiot I was."

She lifted her head, turning to face him. "That sounds a lot like brotherly advice."

"It is. And maybe it's not relevant to your situation. I don't know. But what I do know is that we both have a tendency to hold on to pain. On to anger. If you get a chance to fix this, I hope you forgive the bastard. As long as he's worthy."

"How will I know he's worthy?" she asked, a bit of humor lacing her voice.

"Well, I'll have to vet him. At some point."

"Assuming he ever speaks to me again, I would be happy to arrange that."

Gage nodded. "If he's half as miserable as you are, trust me, he'll be coming after you pretty quick."

"And you think I should forgive him?"

"I think that men are a bunch of hardheaded dumbasses. And some of us need more chances than others. And I thank God every day I got mine. With this family. With Rebecca. So it would be mean-spirited of me not to advocate for the same for another of my species."

"I'll keep that under advisement."

Gage turned to go. "Do that. But if he keeps being a

dumbass, let me know. Because I'll get together a posse or something."

"Thank you," she said. "Hopefully the posse won't be necessary."

He shrugged, then walked back into the party. She felt fortified then. Because she knew she had people on her side. No matter what. She wasn't alone. And that felt good. Even when most everything felt bad.

She let out a long, slow breath and rested her forearms on the railing, leaning forward, staring out across the darkened field. If she closed her eyes, she could almost imagine that she could see straight out to the ocean in spite of the fact that it was dark.

She was starting to get cold, even with the artificial heat. But it was entirely possible the chill was coming from inside her. Side effects of heartbreak and all of that.

"Merry Christmas Eve."

She straightened, blinking, looking out into the darkness. Afraid to turn around. That voice was familiar. And it didn't belong to anyone in her family.

She turned slowly, her heart stalling when she saw Sam standing there. He was wearing a white shirt unbuttoned at the collar, a black jacket and a pair of black slacks. His hair was disheveled, and she was pretty sure she could see a bit of soot on his chest where the open shirt exposed his skin.

"What are you doing here?"

"I had to see you." He took a step closer to her. "Bad enough that I put this on."

"Where did you get it?"

"The secondhand store on Main."

"Wow." No matter what he had to say, the fact that

Sam McCormack had shown up in a suit said a whole lot without him ever opening his mouth.

"It doesn't really fit. And I couldn't figure out how to tie the tie." And of course, he hadn't asked anyone for help. Sam never would. It just wasn't him.

"Well, then going without was definitely the right method."

"I have my moments of brilliance." He shook his head. "But the other day wasn't one of them."

Her heart felt as if it were in a free fall, her stomach clenching tight. "Really?"

"Yeah."

"I agree. I mean, unreservedly. But I am open to hearing about your version of why you didn't think you were brilliant. Just in case we have differing opinions on the event."

He cursed. "I'm not good at this." He took two steps toward her, then reached out, gripping her chin between his thumb and forefinger. "I hate this, in fact. I'm not good at talking about feelings. And I've spent a lot of years trying to bury them down deep. I would like to do it now. But I know there's no good ending to that. I know that I owe you more."

"Go on," she said, keeping her eyes on his, her voice trembling, betraying the depth of emotion she felt.

She had never seen Sam quite like this, on edge, like he might shatter completely at any moment. "I told you I thought I didn't deserve these feelings. And I believed it."

"I know you did," she said, the words broken. "I know that you never lied on purpose, Sam. I know."

"I don't deserve that. That certainty. I didn't do anything to earn it."

She shook her head. "Stop. We're not going to talk

like that. About what we deserve. I don't know what I deserve. But I know what I want. I want you. And I don't care if I'm jumping the gun. I don't care if I didn't make you grovel enough. It's true. I do."

"Maddy…"

"This all comes because we tried to protect ourselves for too long. Because we buried everything down deep. I don't have any defenses anymore. I can't do it anymore. I couldn't even if I wanted to. Which you can see, because I'm basically throwing myself at you again."

"I've always been afraid there was something wrong with me." His dark eyes were intense, and she could tell that he was wishing he could turn to stone rather than finish what he was saying. But that he was determined. That he had put his foot on the path and he wasn't going to deviate from it. "Something wrong with what I felt. And I pushed it all down. I always have. I've been through stuff that would make a lot of people crazy. But if you keep shoving it on down, it never gets any better." He shook his head. "I've been holding on to grief. Holding on to anger. I didn't know what else to do with it. My feelings about my parents, my feelings about Elizabeth, the baby. It's complicated. It's a lot. And I think more than anything I just didn't want to deal with it. I had a lot of excuses, and they felt real. They even felt maybe a little bit noble?"

"I can see that. I can see it being preferable to grief."

"Just like you said, Maddy. You put all those defenses in front of it, and then nothing can hurt you, right?"

She nodded. "At least, that's been the way I've handled it for a long time."

"You run out. Of whatever it is you need to be a person. Whatever it is you need to contribute, to create. That's why I haven't been able to do anything new with my artwork." He rolled his eyes, shaking his head slightly. "It's hard for me to…"

"I know. You would rather die than talk about feelings. And talk about this. But I think you need to."

"I told myself it was wrong to make something for my dad. My mom. Because they didn't support my work. I told myself I didn't deserve to profit off Elizabeth's death in any way. But that was never the real issue. The real issue was not wanting to feel those things at all. I was walking across the field the other night, and I thought about grief. The way that it covers things, twists the world around you into something unrecognizable." He shook his head. "When you're in the thick of it, it's like walking in the dark. Even if you're in a place you've seen a thousand times by day, it all changes. And suddenly what seemed safe is now full of danger."

He took a sharp breath and continued. "You can't trust anymore. You can't trust everything will be okay, because you've seen that sometimes it isn't. That's what it's like to have lost people like I have. And I can think about a thousand pieces that I could create that would express that. But it would mean that I had to feel it. And it would mean I would have to show other people what I felt. I wanted… From the moment I laid my hands on you, Maddy, I wanted to turn you into something. A sculpture. A painting. But that would mean looking at how I felt about you too. And I didn't want to do that either."

Maddy lifted her hand, cupping Sam's cheek. "I understand why you work with iron, Sam. Because it's just like you. You're so strong. And you really don't want to bend. But if you would just bend…just a little bit, I think you could be something even more beautiful than you already are."

"I'll do more than bend. If I have to, to have you, I'll break first. But I've decided... I don't care about protecting myself. From loss, from pain...doesn't matter. I just care about you. And I know that I have to fix myself if I'm going to become the kind of man you deserve. I know I have to reach inside and figure all that emotional crap out. I can't just decide that I love you and never look at the rest of it. I have to do all of it. To love you the way that you deserve, I know I have to deal with all of it."

"Do you love me?"

He nodded slowly. "I do." He reached into his jacket pocket and took out a notebook. "I've been working on a new collection. Just sketches right now. Just plans." He handed her the notebook. "I want you to see it. I know you'll understand."

She took it from him, opening it with shaking hands, her heart thundering hard in her throat. She looked at the first page, at the dark twisted mass he had sketched there. Maybe it was a beast, or maybe it was just menacing angles—it was hard to tell. She imagined that was the point.

There was more. Broken figures, twisted metal. Until the very last page. Where the lines smoothed out into rounded curves, until the mood shifted dramatically and everything looked a whole lot more like hope.

"It's hard to get a sense of scale and everything in the drawings. This is just me kind of blocking it out."

"I understand," she whispered. "I understand perfectly." It started with grief, and it ended with love. Unimaginable pain that was transformed.

"I lost a lot of things, Maddy. I would hate for you to be one of them. Especially because you're the one thing I chose to lose. And I have regretted it every moment since. But this is me." He put his fingertip on the notebook.

"That's me. I'm not the nicest guy. I'm not what anybody would call cheerful. Frankly, I'm a grumpy son of a bitch. It's hard for me to talk about what I'm feeling. Harder for me to show it, and I'm in the world's worst line of work for that. But if you'll let me, I'll be your grumpy son of a bitch. And I'll try. I'll try for you."

"Sam," she said, "I love you. I love you, and I don't need you to be anything more than you. I'm willing to accept the fact that getting to your feelings may always be a little bit of an excavation. But if you promise to work on it, I'll promise not to be too sensitive about it. And maybe we can meet somewhere in the middle. One person doesn't have to do all the changing. And I don't want you to anyway." She smiled, and this time it wasn't forced. "You had me at 'You're at the wrong door.'"

He chuckled. "I think you had me a lot sooner than that. I just didn't know it."

"So," she said, looking up at him, feeling like the sun was shining inside her, in spite of the chill outside, "you want to go play Yahtzee?"

"Only if you mean it euphemistically."

"Absolutely not. I expect you to take the time to woo me, Sam McCormack. And if that includes board games, that's just a burden you'll have to bear."

Sam smiled. A real smile. One that showed his heart, his soul, and held nothing back. "I would gladly spend the rest of my life bearing your burdens, Madison West."

"On second thought," she said, "board games not required."

"Oh yeah? What do you need, then?"

"Nothing much at all. Just hold me, cowboy. That's enough for me."

* * * * *

We hope you enjoyed reading

BABY, IT'S CHRISTMAS

by *New York Times* bestselling author
SUSAN MALLERY

and

HOLD ME, COWBOY

by *New York Times* bestselling author
MAISEY YATES

Both were originally
Harlequin® Special Edition
and HQN stories!

"Why me—and why won't you take a hint that I'm just not interested?"

He stared into his single malt, neat, as if the answer to her question waited in the smoky amber depths. "I don't believe you're not interested. You just don't trust me."

"Duh." She poured on the sarcasm and made a big show of tapping a finger against her chin. "Let me think. I wonder why?"

"How many times do I need to say that I messed up? I messed up twice. I'm so damn sorry and I need you to forgive me. You're the best thing that ever happened to me. And..." He shook his head. "Fine. I get it. I smashed your heart to tiny, bloody bits. How many ways can I say I was wrong?"

Okay. He was kind of getting to her. For a second there, she'd almost reached across the table and touched his clenched fist. She so had to watch herself. Gently she suggested, "How about this? I accept your apology. It was years ago and we need to move on."

He slanted her a sideways look, dark brows showing

glints of auburn in the light from above. "Yeah?"

"Yeah."

"So then we can try again?"

Should she have known that would be his next question? Yeah, probably. "I didn't say that."

"I want another chance."

"Well, that's not happening."

"Yes, it is. And when it does, I'm not letting you go. This time it's going to be forever."

She almost grinned. Because that was another thing about Deck. Not only did he have big arms, broad shoulders and a giant brain.

He was cocky. Very, very cocky.

And she was enjoying herself far too much. It really was a whole lot of fun to argue with him. It always had been. And the most fun of all was finally being the one in the position of power.

Back when they'd been together, he was the poor kid and she was a Bravo—one of the Bastard Bravos, as everybody had called her mother's children behind their backs. But a Bravo, nonetheless. Nell always had the right clothes and a certain bold confidence that made her popular. She hadn't been happy at home by any stretch, but guys had wanted to go out with her and girls had kind of envied her.

And all she'd ever wanted was Deck. So, really, he'd had all the power then.

Now, for some reason she didn't really understand, he'd decided he just had to get another chance with her. Now she was the one saying no. Payback was a bitch, all right. Not to mention downright delicious.

Don't miss
MARRIED TILL CHRISTMAS by Christine Rimmer,
available December 2017 wherever
Harlequin® Special Edition books and ebooks are sold.

www.Harlequin.com

H HARLEQUIN®

SPECIAL EDITION

Life, Love and Family

Save **$1.00**

on the purchase of ANY
Harlequin® Special Edition book.

Available wherever books are sold, including
most bookstores, supermarkets, drugstores
and discount stores.

Save **$1.00**

on the purchase of any Harlequin Special Edition book.

Coupon valid until January 31, 2018.
Redeemable at participating outlets in the U.S. and Canada only.
Not redeemable at Barnes & Noble stores. Limit one coupon per customer.

52615261

5 65373 00076 2   (8100)0 12320

® and ™ are trademarks owned and used by the trademark owner and/or its licensee.

© 2017 Harlequin Enterprises Limited

NYTCOUP1117

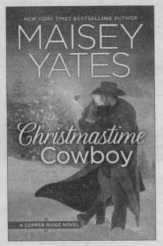